A MU MOST VEGAN

Katie Jay

A Murder Most Vegan
© Katie Jay 2022

ISBN: 978-1-922461-70-4 (Paperback)
       978-1-922461-71-1 (eBook)

 A catalogue record for this book is available from the National Library of Australia

Editors: Kristy Martin and Jason Martin
Cover Design: Ocean Reeve Publishing
Design and Typeset: Ocean Reeve Publishing
Printed in Australia by Ocean Reeve Publishing and Clark & Mackay Printers

Published by Katie Jay and Ocean Reeve Publishing
www.oceanreevepublishing.com

The Great Eternal Silence

Missing in the darkness
Vanished without a trace
With only memories and photographs to
Fill an empty space

—By Aquinas T. Duffy
Irish Missing Persons Register
June 2000

Contents

1

Cecilia stood still, her eyes narrowed into slits as she assessed the scene in the kitchen of The Vegan Café. A slim, youngish man was sprawled face-down on the polished concrete floor. His white chef's hat, stained in dark red, lay crumpled near his head, one long arm stretched out towards the half-open freezer door, and his hand rested in a puddle of water. Cecilia presumed he was the café's cook.

Her gaze swept up and around the room, which was sizeable for a commercial kitchen. A giant frying pan and two small glasses were drying on a double-sized sink top. A battered red plastic crate full of fruit and vegetables sat on a long metal bench, and tucked behind the crate was a bottle of vodka. That, Cecilia figured, was the culprit—he'd passed out from drinking too much alcohol.

She folded her arms, annoyed her inspection of The Vegan Café was now derailed. In her line of work as an environmental health officer for Glenelg Council, a historic beach community and tourist hotspot in South Australia, she had come across a few drunken cooks, but at least they had been upright.

'Wake up!' She prodded his denim leg with the pointy end of her pink high-heeled shoes.

There was no response. She poked the man again. Still no response. Cecilia looked closer. He was lying in an uncomfortable position, with one leg askew and his nose squashed against the concrete floor. She bent down and placed two fingers on his neck, shifting them around to check for a pulse; there was no answering throb. Still, knowing pulses could be hard to find, she reached into her handbag to fish out her powder compact.

Just as she was about to press the mirror against the man's nose to see if it misted up with his breath, she saw it: an eye open, the white tinged with grey, lifeless and spongy like a boiled egg, and it was staring motionlessly at the freezer.

Cecilia reared back. *Goddamn it!* The man was dead, not drunk. His lips were stained with a blue hue, and his face was white and blank, devoid of any regular human expression. No wonder he had felt so stiff when she touched him.

Her heart started thundering in her chest, and her stomach roiled. She rushed over to the small handwashing basin and threw up her breakfast muesli, the nuts and seeds scraping her throat.

Cecilia braced herself against the basin for a few moments with her eyes closed, until the bitter taste in her mouth forced her to open her eyes and pull herself together. She rummaged around her handbag and pulled out her water bottle, gargling some water.

All she wanted was to get the hell out of the kitchen and away from that confronting dead man, but the mirror above the sink was telling her something more important. Her bright pink lipstick was smudged, and her forehead was glistening with sweat. She knew The Vegan Café would soon be swarming with ambulance officers and police, and she did not want to face them looking like a clown.

Cecilia attended to her make-up and smoothed her thick, black, shiny hair in the style of a Mary Poppins bun. Straightening her knee-length, flamingo-patterned frock, which fitted tightly around her short and round figure, she noticed the man's reflection in the mirror. He wore his hair in a high, loose man-knot. Underneath, his hair was matted with gunk. She flinched and turned away from the mirror.

Meanwhile, Astra Nardhamuni, who owned the café with her husband, materialised in the kitchen doorway, which was tucked in behind the counter, separate to the cafe. Astra had been playing with her phone in the main café area, leaving Cecilia to inspect the kitchen alone.

'I heard weird noises coming from the kitchen,' Astra told Cecilia. 'Like someone was being sick. How gross. I don't do germs. Were you throwing up in our kitchen?'

'I'm sorry,' said Cecilia, feeling spaced out. She hadn't paid Astra much attention when they met at the front door of The Vegan Café. Cecilia had been intent on her inspection. But now, her brain was racing trying to take it all in. Astra was pretty; the type of pretty you couldn't help but stare at. She had long, strawberry-blonde hair, streaming in waves down her back. She wore a white broderie anglaise cardigan over a long, flowing dress, finished with heavy-looking brown work boots, combining the yin and yang trend in boho-chic fashion in a spectacular way. The soulful look was not Cecilia's style, however—she liked to be bold, colourful, and up-front.

This was too bizarre. From dead bodies to an astonishingly pretty woman with fabulous hair. Cecilia found a cloth under the sink and a disinfectant spray bottle marked in handwriting and began cleaning the bowl.

Astra leant against the door frame. 'Why is Phil lying on the floor?' she asked.

'I'm sorry to say that your cook is dead,' said Cecilia, trying to keep her tone light and matter of fact.

'No, I don't think so.' Astra gave her employee a passing glance. 'Phil's far too young to die. And he's a vegan. The universe looks after vegans.'

'Huh?' said Cecilia, surprised. 'Well, maybe not always.'

'Have you looked properly?'

'Yes.'

'He's probably in a state of *sahaj samadhi*. That's the deepest state of meditation.' Astra gestured at the corpse. 'You have to bring him back. Give him the kiss of life.'

Cecilia shuddered at the thought of blowing air into those cold, blue lips. 'I know it's awful, but he's been dead for a few hours. I think you need to call an ambulance.'

'Me?' Astra's wide green eyes fluttered in shock. 'Why me?'

'It's your café!' Cecilia was astonished at Astra's lack of responsibility. 'I'm just the council's health inspector.'

'Oh, my stars! I can't be making phone calls at a time like this. I need to go through my essential oils. I'm sure I can wake Phil up in an organic way.'

In an organic way? Cecilia put her water bottle back in her handbag. What the hell did that mean? How was death anything *but* organic?

For a split second, Cecilia felt a rare moment of uncertainty. Surely, she was not mistaken about the young man's demise. It was the first time she had seen a dead person; coffins had been closed in the funerals Cecilia had attended. She made herself look at the cook's face again. There was no-one home there.

'I think I'm going to need two boxes,' said Astra, pulling wooden trays out of a kitchen drawer. 'I keep them in the kitchen in case Phil needs to use them in the purifier if customers have been difficult.' She piled them up on top of each other on the bench and turned to Cecilia. 'You could at least try and help me!'

'Sorry,' said Cecilia automatically. But how could she help? She knew nothing about aromatherapy. Her practical self kicked in. 'Would you like me to call the ambulance? This must be dreadful for you.'

'It *is* terrible for me,' Astra agreed, fiddling with the jars, picking up one and then putting it back. 'But he can't have passed on. I would have felt it. These are my aromatherapy oils.' She fluttered her hands over the wooden boxes filled with tiny brown bottles neatly labelled in small curly writing. 'I'm an aromatherapist,' she announced. 'And I know your type,' she added, frowning at Cecilia who must have been looking sceptical. 'You don't believe in natural and holistic medicine, do you? But let me tell you that essential oils have been used in medicine since the eleventh century! I'm sure I can bring Phil back to life with the right combination of oils. I have a good reputation in the science of aromatherapy.'

Cecilia's jaw dropped open. How could Phil be resuscitated with aromas when he couldn't even breathe?

'We'll go into the café,' said Astra. 'I need to concentrate on what I'm doing without distractions.'

Such as a dead body, thought Cecilia. Nevertheless, she was keen to leave the kitchen too and held the kitchen door open for Astra and her box of oils to pass through, then Cecilia carefully closed the door. She walked into the main area of the café, placing her bag on a table and retrieving her mobile phone, which had a bright pink cover to match her dress. She pressed the numbers and reached an operator, although it was hard to communicate because Astra was thrusting and shaking a small brown bottle at her.

'This is Bush Flower Remedy Essence,' said Astra, her voice squeaking. 'You put four drops on his tongue and one on his third eye.'

'Shush,' Cecilia told her. 'I can't hear the operator.'

Astra was undeterred. 'You're not helping!' she cried. 'You have to give him the drops because I can't. It upsets me to see Phil lying on the floor.'

With a clatter of high-heeled shoes, Cecilia speedily found herself a corner in the café far away from Astra. Cecilia told the emergency services operator her name was Cecilia Archer, she was Glenelg Council's environmental health officer, and there was a dead body in the kitchen of The Vegan Café.

'I'm going to tell the police on you!' Astra trapped Cecilia in the corner of the café, shaking her bottle in Cecilia's face. 'You're supposed to help people when they've had an accident, and you're not even trying to revive Phil.'

'I am a health inspector, not an aromatherapist!'

Astra squinted at Cecilia. 'What's wrong with you? I've told you where to put the drops on Phil. You're an old person, so you should know how to do all these sorts of things.'

Cecilia rolled her eyes. Old person? She was fifty-three. Did that qualify her to bring the dead back to life, even with Astra's 'elixir of life'?

And how the hell was she supposed to open the dead man's mouth and give him four drops of the Remedy Essence? That was crazy. Although, it must be shocking to find your cook dead on the kitchen floor—no wonder Astra was flipping out, even if it was at Cecilia's expense. 'Can I make you a cup of tea?' she offered, trying to calm things down.

'Tea? How can you think of tea at a time like this?' Astra clutched a handful of her floaty dress and scrunched it in agitation.

Cecilia thought of something else and hurried to the front door.

'Are you leaving me?' Astra's voice wobbled.

'No, I am putting the *closed* sign up in case a customer wanders in. Are you sure you don't want a cup of tea? It might settle your nerves.'

'I am a very sensitive person,' conceded Astra. 'That's one of the special things about me. I'm connected to the universe, so I feel things more. Do you know that when the earthquakes happened in New Zealand, I felt something was wrong? I dropped my kiwi pendant, and it broke!'

Cecilia blinked. Was this woman for real? No-one could be *that* new age. Behind the front counter, she found a kettle and an extensive range of herbal teas. She might as well have one herself and get the taste of vomit out of her mouth.

While she waited for the tea leaves to brew, she wandered around the cafe. It was brightly lit, and the walls were lined with illuminated orange cube boxes that held expensive-looking vegan produce. They seemed to sell everything from fat white blocks of tofu to cruelty-free beauty products, including a nice shade of bright-red lipstick. There were also ankle boots made from recycled plastic bottles, the same ones Astra was wearing. They were expensive, which was a shame considering the good environmental intentions. Scattered throughout the café were white round tables with orange chairs. The room ticked all the requirements for a sunny, sanitary café—except for the dead man in the kitchen.

Cecilia gave Astra some chamomile tea but took her own cup to the magazine rack. She was starting to feel nauseous again and needed a distraction. Choosing a magazine called *Vegan Harmony,* she sat down at a table, flipping through it to find some recipes while waiting for emergency services. Hannah, her twenty-one-year-old daughter, had become a vegan recently, and Cecilia liked to cook. The magazine even had menus for vegan dogs. Cecilia thought of her daughter's dogs—two highly emotional dachshund puppies. The recipe involved blending cooked lentils, sweet potatoes, and rice. Would the puppies be less hyperactive if they were vegans? Not if Astra was any example of veganism, who was alternately sobbing and complaining that Cecilia was unfeeling and shouldn't be loafing around reading magazines. There was a strong floral perfume wafting through the café as Astra liberally applied herself with Emergency Remedy Essence.

Cecilia sighed and got up from her chair. Duty called. Someone had to take charge and that unlucky one was Cecilia. She carried her cup over to Astra and sat down next to her. 'I think you need support. Could you phone your husband? This is a terrible thing to have happened.'

'It is, especially for someone like me. But he's meditating now and can't be interrupted.'

'Surely he would want to be here for you.'

'Not while he's meditating. He does important work for the world when he meditates.'

'Huh?' Cecilia contemplated her green tea, wishing it was a strong latte.

'Prayer can have a powerful effect by releasing peace and harmony into the world during troubled times,' Astra explained.

'Oh?' Cecilia tried to keep her voice pleasant and neutral, but obviously was unsuccessful.

'Duh,' said Astra, tossing her mane of rose-gold hair and glaring at Cecilia. 'Don't you know? There have been studies to prove it!'

The doorbell tinkled, and two uniformed police entered the café, followed by paramedics dressed in green. All were young. Introductions were made, and Cecilia pointed them in the direction of the kitchen. The paramedics disappeared through the swinging door while the policemen stayed in the main café area, clustered around the café's counter.

Cecilia returned to her seat, but Astra, revived, latched onto a fit-looking young policeman with floppy brown hair and kind eyes. She managed to snuggle under his arm.

'It's Phil, our cook. He's lying on the kitchen floor. You have to resuscitate him,' she told the young policeman, looking up at him with big, innocent eyes. 'That health inspector wouldn't do it. She just walked out of the kitchen.'

Cecilia raised an eyebrow but said nothing. She was watching the kitchen door to see who came out.

The young policeman was courteous and caring. He introduced himself as Lyall and said, 'This must be a traumatic experience for you,' he told Astra. 'You're coping really well.'

As if he was a goddamned counsellor, thought Cecilia. Not like that fat old policeman, Investigator Longbottom, who she had met years ago when her Grandma Snow went missing. He'd treated everybody with cold, surly suspicion and had grease spots on his shirt.

Then, Lyall, Astra's young policeman, had to pry himself out of her embrace as the paramedics emerged from the kitchen without the cook.

So, Phil was dead.

Cecilia began to wonder what he'd been like when he was alive. Her mind hovered tentatively over the image of his back. His T-shirt was nothing out of the ordinary: a plain grey colour, and it looked clean. His long legs were encased in blue jeans, and he was wearing mandatory non-slip shoes. Black crocs. But the puddle next to the freezer was big enough to cause the most slip-resistant shoes to falter.

The news of his death would be a big shock to his family and friends. He was far too young to die. Tears pricked at Cecilia's eyes, and she took a couple of deep, calming breaths.

There was a brief conversation among the police and ambulance officers as they leant on the counter. Lyall pulled a phone out of his pants pocket and made a call. When he'd finished, Cecilia got up from her chair and walked over to him, her high heels clicking on the polished concrete floor.

'Do you want me to make a statement? I found the deceased man when I was inspecting the café. I work for Glenelg City Council.'

'I've called Criminal Investigations from Sturt Street Station,' he replied. 'They'll be here soon and will want to talk to you.'

'Do I have to stay? Couldn't I pop into the police station this afternoon?'

'Please wait.'

Cecilia returned to her seat and drummed her clear, polished fingernails on the table. It was going to be a long morning. She picked up her magazine again.

Astra was now in top form, bustling around the counter making cups of herbal tea and handing out butter-free biscuits while explaining to the puzzled police and paramedics, as they peered dubiously at their iridescent yellow tea, that veganism was the way of the future.

Eventually, the bell dinged again. Lyall moved quickly to the front door and opened it. Two men sauntered in. By the way they took stock of the situation, Cecilia assumed they were plainclothes detectives. One was large and middle-aged with slicked-back hair, the other was youngish and had a square superhero jaw. Astra darted out from behind the counter and zeroed in on the investigator with the superhero jaw.

'A terrible thing has happened. Our cook has passed on. I can feel it now. There is an empty space in my heart. My chakras are all jumbled, and I am going to need a lot of reiki to get myself together.' And bingo! She was nestled under his armpit. *Astra has a talent for getting attractive young men to hug her,* Cecilia thought. Being so pretty and innocent-looking, it was not surprising she had that effect on men—but she sure was a fruitcake.

Cecilia checked out the older detective whose dark eyes were sweeping the café.

'Where's the body?' he demanded, taking off his jacket and neatly folding up his shirt sleeves below his elbows.

Cecilia heard one of the uniformed policemen muttering to the other, 'Bloody hell, the Italian is on the case.'

'Come on, Hugh,' said the middle-aged cop to the younger one. 'First, the body, and then we talk to the people.'

They all trooped into the kitchen.

For a moment, Astra stood marooned in the middle of the café, bereft of her policemen and paramedics, but then she fished out a phone from a pocket in her dress, checked the time, and gave a big sigh of relief. She began dialling. In a little girl's voice, she told the person on the other end of the phone—presumably her husband, Mr Nardhamuni, the other owner of the café—that he must come straight away to the café because his 'baby girl' was 'most upset.'

Cecilia also breathed a sigh of relief. Astra was no longer her problem. Browsing through the bookshelf while she waited, Cecilia found books on animal cruelty with ghastly photos, some spectacular landscapes photography books with wise captions, and there were quite a few copies of *Inner Stillness* and *The Enlightened Vegan*. The latter were written by Swami Nardhamuni. Cecilia had never considered her inner spiritual life—she wasn't even sure if she had one—and horror stories of animal abuse made her feel queasy, so she returned to her seat and the vegan recipes.

The kitchen door opened, and the middle-aged detective strode out. He looked at Astra, then at Cecilia.

Gosh! What a snappy dresser, thought Cecilia. His trousers were made from dark wool, possibly cashmere. He wore a crisp, white, ironed shirt with faint red lines. His tie looked like it was made of silk, and the slanting red stripes matched his shirt. Exquisite! Certainly not what she expected an Australian plainclothes cop to wear.

The older detective sat down at a table, crossing his trousered legs and revealing polished black brogues. He patted the tabletop. 'Come, come,' he ordered. 'Tell me all about this man in the kitchen. I am Investigator Giovanni. Who are you?'

Cecilia tilted her chin and pushed her shoulders back, walking over to him while casually holding her magazine and her handbag slung over her shoulder. 'I'm Cecilia Archer from Glenelg Council. I'm the health and safety officer. I was doing an inspection when I found the man dead on the floor.'

'That must have been shocking,' he said, his brown eyes concerned. 'Are you okay?'

'You need to speak to me,' Astra announced, plonking herself down at the table. 'I'm the owner of the café; she's just a health inspector.'

Inspector Giovanni was looking intently at Cecilia. 'Have we met before?' He gave her a half-smile.

The smile triggered something deep in Cecilia's subconscious. She felt a sudden jolt of recognition and memories came flooding back. She looked away from him. Oh my god! Why did it have to be him?

'Look, she's still reading a magazine. How could she at a time like this?' Astra pursed her lips. 'She's all bottled up with her feelings. She didn't seem at all upset finding Phil dead. I think there's something wrong with her *anahata* chakra. That's the green one, and it's all about the heart.'

'Excuse me!' Cecilia's cheeks flamed.

'I'm psychic,' said Astra, limpid-eyed. 'I know about things.'

'Nonsense! I think you're just rude!' Cecilia dumped the magazine, pushed back her chair, and plucked a business card and pen out of her bag. She wrote her mobile number on the back and handed it to Investigator Giovanni. 'I don't have much to say, except this is a newish café and my first inspection here. The freezer was leaking, so I assume that he slipped and fell. There is not much to say, except it seems a tragedy.'

'I don't need you now,' he said, looking at her curiously, 'but I will call you later for a formal statement.'

Cecilia stalked out of The Vegan Café.

***

Nursing an extra-large cup of milky, sweet coffee she had bought from a local café, Cecilia sat in her work car and absentmindedly watched the inhabitants of a small local playground in Glenelg South. It was a restful spot, compared to the clamour and bustle of Jetty Road—the main tourist route for Glenelg.

'Higher! Higher, Mummy!' sang out a small boy wrapped in a lime-green puffer jacket, which made him look like some weird upside-down beetle, as his mum pushed him on the swing. An older couple, also dressed in layers of warm clothes and wearing matching yellow-and-black Glenelg Tigers football scarves, were seated on the park bench and smiling at the small boy. It was a cold day to be in the park. Perhaps they were locals who needed to get out of the house for a bit, despite the inclement weather.

Now what was she going to do? Investigator Giovanni had let her go until he needed her to make a written statement. She could call in sick to work and wait for the police to call while cleaning her saucepan cupboards, or she could carry on with her working day.

It was a no-brainer. She was fired up with adrenaline from the events at The Vegan Café. She was like the kid on the swing, busy, and she had to do something to take her mind off the dead man. It certainly wasn't going to be cupboard cleaning.

Cecilia looked at her watch, the pearl-faced one with a silver wrist band she usually wore with her pastel-coloured frocks. She had planned to go to Sun-Kissed Motel for an inspection after The Vegan Café, and she still had time to do it before lunch.

It didn't take long to arrive at the motel, a shabby and cheap conglomeration of units located on Moseley Street. Everywhere in Glenelg was within a ten- or fifteen-minute car ride. Glenelg Council had staved off attempts by other local governments to swallow it up and make mega local governments. Glenelg claimed successfully that the historical importance of the suburb was unique and paramount to South Australia's tourist trade.

She parked her car behind an old white kombi van at the front of the motel. There was a new parking sign limiting cars to fifteen-minute parking.

I'd better be quick, Cecilia thought. Council officers had to abide by parking rules or pay the fine. The new parking inspector, Ian, was such a jerk that even Anne from reception waited until he was out on his rounds to quickly dump his correspondence on his desk. Ian loved pinging his fellow officers.

She retrieved her coat from the passenger seat and stepped out of the car. Fetching her bag of pool-testing equipment from the boot, she briskly walked into the motel office and rang the bell on the counter.

A middle-aged man, wearing a faded polo shirt which was too small for his paunch, came out from the back office. He curled his lip. 'You're that woman from the council. What do you want?'

'That's right,' she said brightly. 'Cecilia Archer from Glenelg Council. I'm here to test your pool.'

'In this weather? Are you nuts? The forecast said it was going to be ten degrees, and it looks like it's going to rain.'

Cecilia shrugged. She had her thick red coat on, so she didn't care.

She turned, walking out of the office and over to the pool. It was an old cement affair, enclosed by spiked black fencing and squatting amid a yellow brick arc of two-storey motel units. Small pebbles were cemented into the concrete around the pool, which would be painful to walk on with bare feet—hardly inviting.

Speedily, she set about testing the pool's chemicals. They were insufficient.

'You still have to keep the swimming pool's chemicals at the correct levels, even in winter,' she explained to the motel owner. A gust of wind had lifted his comb-over, giving his head a cobwebby look.

'No-one swims in this weather.' He crossed his arms across his chest and shivered. 'It's so cold out here.' He looked back at his heated office longingly.

'Drunks might.'

'That's not my fault.'

'Yes, it is! If the water chemistry is not up to speed, your drunk could get meningitis. Remember that little girl, Alice, from Rising Waves Motel? She died from swimming in a dirty pool.'

'It's not worth running the pool in winter, or even in summer. No-one uses it. I wish it weren't there. It soaks up money.'

That was not her problem. 'I will be back in a week to test your pool chemistry.' She carefully picked her way out of the pool enclosure, making sure her high heels did not catch on the lumpy pebbles.

Cecilia closed the pool gate and looked back. It was a cheap and dreary motel, even if it was in a good location. It had the reputation of being a place where you could go for an illicit hour, or to have a party. Only a few weeks before, a drunken youth had fallen off a balcony and sustained severe injuries. The council's building inspector had done an inspection, but the balcony wall was the correct height.

The motel was a source of continuous irritation to the council. The childcare centre next door complained about sleazy men, noisy drunks, and women in short skirts, but nothing changed because Sun-Kissed was legal and a good source of rates revenue for the council.

Cecilia opened her boot to pack her equipment away. She noticed the kombi van still parked in front of her—it was way beyond its time limit. Her eyes narrowed. She remembered that kombi, now, and it meant trouble for the council.

She drove down Moseley Street and turned left onto Jetty Road, following the tram tracks towards Mosely Square and Colley Terrace. Tall palm trees, clustered in the square at the end of the tram tracks, fluttered as the wind whistled through their fronds. Only a few hardy backpackers and local senior citizens sat rugged up in the outdoor cafés. Even the seagulls had retreated from the wind.

Cecilia turned left on the roundabout at the end of Jetty Road and onto Adelphi Terrace. She then made another turn and swung into the council's car park, which was situated behind the town hall—a grand

and imposing Victorian building with a tall clock tower, decorated with ornate blue stone. Council's car park was right next to the beach and had uninterrupted views of the ocean foreshore. Now and then, a property developer would unsuccessfully try to hustle the council to sell the land for a high-rise building. However, parking was more important to elected members, who enjoyed popping into the town hall or doing some shopping on Jetty Road whenever they liked, with free car parking.

She entered the town hall through the back door and walked down a corridor of thick, heritage-green carpet, which muffled the sound of her high heels. At the front desk, she returned the car keys to Anne, the receptionist, whose eyes were glued to her computer screen. From a quick look, Cecilia saw that Anne was entranced by a podcast on exercising abdominal muscles. As Cecilia had no intention of being skinny, or super fit, she chose not to engage Anne in conversation and walked speedily past Anne's desk, twinkling her fingers in a friendly way, leaving the receptionist with an unanswered, 'Hey! Look at these cool exercises.'

Cecilia put her bag back in the bottom drawer of her filing cabinet and checked her emails. There was nothing there that couldn't wait. Her tummy growled, empty from its purging earlier that morning.

Walking into the lunchroom—an airy room facing the beach—she saw that Garth, the animal control officer, and Ian, who was in traffic management, were already seated. She retrieved her Tupperware box from the staff fridge and sat down at the table.

Cecilia opened her box and jerked back in horror. There was a boiled egg nestling in green leaves. It reminded her of the cook's lifeless eye. She retrieved the biscuits and salad, closing the lid firmly. It would be a long time before she could face a boiled egg.

'How's your morning been, Cecilia?' Garth asked, taking a big bite of his chicken burger; there was a lot of him that needed feeding.

Cecilia hesitated and looked at Ian. She didn't want to talk about the events at The Vegan Café in front of him. He was annoying, always looking for people's weaknesses, and then rubbing it in. There was no way she was going to share with him her emotions, which were disordered after finding a man's body lying sprawled on the café's kitchen floor. She picked a safer option, one that would make her feel composed.

'I visited Sun-Kissed Motel,' she replied. 'The pool was dirty, and the owner is such a creep.'

'Who would swim in this weather?' asked Ian, stirring his protein drink in a disposable plastic bottle. 'It's still too cold.'

'Drunks,' she said.

Garth shook his long white beard and looked out the lunchroom's window to a vista of drizzling rain hovering over a grey ocean. Cecilia and Garth had been colleagues and friends for more than a decade, and she had never known him to cut his beard. The current CEO, Tristan, had once hinted it would lift the image of the council in the community by not having a hairy animal control officer. Garth flipped back a comment about the cultural rights of First Nations people, which had left Tristan red-faced with embarrassment about a possible racial slur, and so the beard stayed.

'Sun-Kissed gets some cheeky customers,' said Garth.

'I know,' said Cecilia. 'Sex workers, philanderers, and drunks.'

'I think I've managed to solve that problem,' boasted Ian. 'I've put up signs limiting parking to fifteen minutes. I told the works department to install them last week.'

Cecilia's eyes narrowed into slits as she looked suspiciously at Ian. 'Have you got permission for those signs?'

'Not yet, but I will. It's on the council's agenda for next month.' He slurped some of his murky protein drink. Ian did weights, was a short, square man, and was constantly ready for an argument on his beat, or even to provoke one.

She stared at him in disbelief. 'Have you put up parking signs without permission?'

'That won't matter.' Ian smirked. 'Council will be so pleased with the idea.'

'You're in big trouble, Mister Parking Inspector,' said Garth, a smile hiding in his shaggy beard.

'Why?' Ian crushed his plastic bottle.

Cecilia explained, 'When I was there late this morning, there was an old white kombi van parked in front of Sun-Kissed. I bet it's still there.'

Ian sniggered. 'I know that, and I've given him a ticket. I saw you there, too. You stayed for fourteen minutes and fifty seconds. I nearly got you as well.'

She looked at him with disgust. 'Where were you hiding? Behind a tree?'

Garth rolled back his chair, laughing. 'An old kombi, hey? I remember that van.'

'Yes!' she said, lashing out at Ian. 'You've made a big mistake putting up signs without permission. The previous aged care officer, the first one who started the community bus scheme? Well, she got the works department to put up a reserved parking sign for the bus, forgetting to get it approved by the council. So, that ancient kombi sat in the bus car park for a fortnight enjoying a five-star view of the ocean before the new parking regulations were passed by the council. There was a lot of entertaining publicity in the local newspaper. Our council was most miffed.' Cecilia smiled at Ian. Gotcha!

'Old Man Jones is at it again,' Garth reflected. 'Ferreting out illegal parking signs. Why doesn't he get himself a life, hey? Like, playing lawn bowls.'

'But Mr Jones does have a life,' she pointed out. 'He travels around Australia in his van, and he gets to see the sights. For free! I heard he visited Uluru last year and had unrestricted gold-star parking for a week because the car park owners had illegal disabled parking signage.'

'I don't know what you're talking about,' muttered Ian.

Cecilia spelt it out for him. 'Mr Jones travels Australia looking for parking signs that have restrictions, and then he checks out their validity. Has the parking sign passed the proper process? If not, then he parks his kombi there.'

'Whatever. The sign is on the council's agenda for next month.'

'Don't hand out any parking tickets until it's been approved.'

Ian's face flushed with anger.

She looked at him more closely. 'Have you got another black eye?'

Ian shifted in his seat.

'Another unhappy car parker?' Garth enquired. 'You're one crazy whitefella, Ian.'

Cecilia pursed her lips. The former parking inspector, Jim, a nice old bloke who retired after thirty years of service, had never got into fistfights. How Ian had managed to pass the traffic management course was a mystery to Cecilia.

Ian tossed his container in the bin, patted his shirt pocket to check his smokes, and stormed out of the lunchroom.

She nibbled on a biscuit. 'Something terrible happened at The Vegan Café,' she confessed to Garth. She might as well get used to talking about it.

'What was that?' Garth asked.

'I opened the kitchen door, ready to do my inspection, and there was a dead man on the floor.'

'Who was he?' Garth jolted back in his seat.

'The Vegan Café's cook.'

'How did he die?' Garth leaned in closer, in a protective sort of way, and she felt herself relax a little.

'I'm not sure what happened. Maybe he fell, slipping on water from the leaking freezer, and landed head-first onto the floor.'

'A kitchen accident?' wondered Garth. 'What was his name?'

'I think his name was Phil. He was only young. I hope the police sort it out soon.'

'I know a Phil who's a cook,' said Garth slowly. 'He comes to the pub on Saturdays to watch the footy. What's he look like?'

'Slim, young, and he wore his hair in a man bun.'

'Bugger me!' spluttered Garth. 'That's my Phil. He's a mate. I can't imagine him slipping over. He wasn't a boozer—a falling-over drunk. A couple of vodka-and-tonics and that was it. He was part of the Saturday footy crowd at the Broadway. I don't get it.'

'I know, and he was wearing chef's slip-resistant shoes,' said Cecilia, going over to the sink to rinse her coffee mug out.

'Something's not right,' grumbled Garth.

'But what?' Cecilia placed her cup back in the cupboard. 'Maybe it was only because his shoes couldn't cope with the puddle.'

***

Cecilia lived in an old brick bungalow on Partridge Street which was built in the early 1920s. She bought it from her parents, who had been successful real estate agents until they retired. Most of the houses on the south end of Partridge Street in Glenelg South were variations on the bungalow theme circled with little bricked-in porches.

The house was located in an upper-middle-income community a few streets back from the beach, but not part of the tourist scene. The area prided itself on being the 'original' Glenelg, a coastal town, and the oldest European settlement in South Australia. Cecilia ignored the snob factor but enjoyed the historical one. She was a fourth-generation Glenelg resident and proud of it.

Her daughter lived with her, and her son was nearby, staying with his girlfriend in a small flat on Holdfast Shores. As a long-time divorcee, Cecilia was content with her single status. She considered herself far too busy to have a relationship with a man. Her mantra was, 'A woman needs a man like an octopus needs a mobile phone.'

As soon as she opened the front door, there was a cacophony of high-pitched barking. Her daughter, Hannah, must have forgotten to close the passageway door at the end of the corridor that confined the puppies to the back of the house.

Reaching into her handbag, she fished out her water spray bottle. Her handbags were always large and ready to cope with any emergency. Opening the door, two excited dachshund puppies—Ziggy and Stardust—greeted her with leaping and yapping, their claws catching on her stockings—the second pair they had ruined this week.

'Ziggy! Stardust! Down!' Cecilia sprayed the puppies with water, and they stopped mid-bark. She walked down the long Baltic pine passageway, stepping on the honey-coloured original floorboards marking the old part of the house, built over a hundred years ago. She stopped briefly to put her keys on the hall table and then carried on down the passageway, which ended with a stained-glass door decorated with winding red roses and green leaves. Through the door, she then stepped out into a modern extension at the back, which had wall-to-wall glass and a large open-plan space serving as the family room and kitchen.

Putting her bag on the kitchen bench, she sat down on the sofa and caressed the dogs. Her stockings were ruined anyway, and she would change in a few minutes.

Then one dachshund thought the other was getting too much attention. Teeth were flashed, and a fight broke out. Out came the water spray again. The dachshunds slunk off in different directions, occasionally turning to give each other a malevolent look.

She got up, poured herself a glass of sauvignon blanc, and read the note from her daughter: *Mum, can you feed the babies? I am going to a dance class. Love you! Hannah.*

She was pleased Hannah was getting out. Her broken heart should be mended by now. Hannah's long-time boyfriend, Kim, had dumped her several months before, and since then she had been attached to the sofa.

It was cold in the family room, so Cecilia turned on the gas heater: a cosy, faux log fire surrounded by a pine mantelpiece. She sipped her wine and considered changing out of her dress and into her home wear— black leggings and a loose top. However, Investigator Aldo might call, and she did not want to meet him underdressed. Mostly, Cecilia aimed to look like someone you didn't want to mess with, despite her small and round shape. It helped her working life, too, which was predominantly with men. She achieved this look with her collection of colourful vintage sheath dresses, bright lipstick, a sharp wit, and lethal high-heeled shoes.

At home, however, Cecilia liked her open-plan family and kitchen area to be neutral. She showcased a subdued coastal style, utilising creamy neutral tones and weathered wood. The L-shaped living area consisted of a medium-sized lounge room filled with two taupe fabric sofas covered with soft throws, a leather recliner, and a Tasmanian blackwood dining table with six matching chairs. There were seaside prints on some of the walls and the back of the family room was floor-to-ceiling glass, achieving maximum light. It looked out onto an expanse of lush green grass, a row of small hedges along the back fence, a shed tucked away in the corner, and three gnarled, flourishing citrus trees with sturdy branches. Cecilia was not a gardener, but she liked a glossy green lawn.

The dachshunds, recovered from their sulks, planted themselves back-to-back in front of the heater, tranquilised by the warmth.

Cecilia lay on the sofa with her legs up and her high heels discarded on the floor. *What a shocker of a day, and it's still not finished,* she thought, twirling her wine and gazing at the pale gold liquid in motion. Now she had to think about what to make for dinner. A carrot covered with tomato sauce in a slice of nutty bread, posing as a vegan hot dog? That was what Hannah had made the night before. She shuddered. Carrot and tomato sauce did not go together.

No, it was going to be burritos with refried beans and veggies bought from the local grocer on Jetty Road. Although she wasn't a vegan like Hannah, Cecilia was a vegetarian; she also bought vegan shoes and handbags. She did not want her feet to be covered by the skin of a slaughtered animal. Besides, there were lots of smart high-heeled shoes available in shops and online that were not made from animals.

Her day's events kept replaying in her mind. On a minor note, she was still annoyed with Ian for putting up restricted parking signs outside Sun-Kissed Motel without permission. She and the building inspector had come up with the idea in the council's lunchroom after that unfortunate youth had fallen from the balcony and broke his back. It was a good idea—because it would partially inhibit the motel's sex and party trade—but nothing was more certain to annoy the elected members, who were precious about their power to give out parking decrees, than a cowboy parking inspector. Maybe she could pop into the mayor's menswear shop for a quick chat, to see if she could mend some of the damage the parking inspector had wrought. Fifteen minutes' parking was still a good way to curtail some of the motel's activities.

Then, there was no avoiding it.

Cecilia's mind turned to the young man who had died. As a motherly woman, she wondered about the man's mum and what she must be feeling. It would be shocking to bury a child; an unnatural, gut-wrenching pain that would never go away. Tears welled up in her eyes and she had a quiet cry.

Wiping her eyes, Cecilia rose to her feet and opened the kitchen drawer where she stored scented candles. She lit a cedarwood-scented candle for Phil and his mother. She took out a book she had been reading, a Liane Moriarty one, but she couldn't concentrate. She kept wondering what had caused Phil's death. Kitchens could be slippery places. If he'd been drinking, he might not have been careful and had taken a terrible fall. But as a careful bloke, why was he drinking on the job? That seemed to contradict his character. Garth had said he was only a social drinker.

Then another thought popped up. Why had Astra been so insistent that Phil was not dead?

Her mobile phone rang. It was Investigator Giovanni, asking her to come to Glenelg police station and give a statement. He was brief but polite. There would be no burritos tonight.

Cecilia blew out the candle, fed the puppies, and changed her stockings. She left a fifty-dollar note for Hannah, and a message saying she had a late meeting and suggesting she order a vegan biryani from the local Indian takeaway.

***

The police station had large shopfront windows shuttered in dusty off-white venetian blinds; some of the slats were broken. It looked like a dilapidated ice-cream shack, which it was until the late 1960s when the South Australian Police Department (SAPOL) bought it and tacked on some rooms and cells out the back. The station was in a good location, situated in the heart of Mosely Square where tourists congregated; however, it was an eyesore and out of kilter with the stately Victorian buildings that surrounded it. Over the years, the council had written to SAPOL proposing they build something in keeping with Glenelg's historical profile, but to no avail. A lack of funds was cited as a reason for inaction.

Cecilia turned the handle of the front door, and a bell rang. At the front counter, she announced her presence to a young policeman and took a seat in a row of chairs. She avoided one that had a rip in its black padded seat.

Cecilia looked around the room. Did it have to be so awful? Not everyone who visited the police station was a criminal.

And it hadn't changed since she was a girl. On the floor was still the same black-and-white linoleum patterned in diamond shapes—dizzying to the eye if stared at for too long—and the same dismal corkboards were hung on the wall with their flapping posters of missing people.

She winced. Grandma Snow had been up there once.

Missing. Eva Snow. Aged seventy-five years. Last seen 25 June 1978, Glenelg.

The poster had shown a black-and-white photo of Grandma Snow with her white hair in a thick side plait. That was more than forty years ago.

Cecilia resolved not to depress herself by looking at lost faces. She fished out her mobile phone and started playing Bridge Baron. She was a keen bridge player and played at her local club and online.

Investigator Giovanni emerged. 'Come, come!' he insisted. He led her into an interview room and closed the door. There was a laptop on the desk.

Cecilia sat down on a plastic chair that, once upon a time, had been white.

He leaned back in his chair and studied her. 'I remember you now. I was a rookie cop, and you were a teenager. How about that! A lifetime has passed. You were dressed in black all the time and had big panda eyes. I hardly recognised you today in your pink dress and lipstick!'

'Well, you haven't changed,' retorted Cecilia. Her punk period had been her angry teenage stage. Since then, her fashions had gone through many incarnations. 'You still look like an Italian gangster with your hair slicked back, but you talk a lot more and wear nice suits.'

Investigator Giovanni roared with laughter. 'You're just the same—sassy!'

She couldn't help but smile back.

His expression changed to a frown. 'I am sorry about the investigation into your grandma's disappearance. I was very upset.' Investigator Giovanni put a hand to his heart. 'It was not at all well-handled.'

'It was shocking. You trashed Grandpa's vegetable garden looking for my grandma. All the neighbours thought he had buried her in the pumpkin patch! Grandpa was mortified.'

'My superior officer was … how can I say it? Old fashioned?'

Cecilia rolled her eyes. His senior officer, Investigator Longbottom, had been a bully, was irritating and inept.

'We do things differently these days,' Investigator Giovanni said encouragingly. 'We make community connections with local people who can help us with our investigations.'

'What? Do you mean as a police informant?'

'No, no!' Aldo sounded shocked. 'Now, we aim to build trust with the family and communities we work with. Detective work is very different these days.'

Raising an eyebrow, she thought she would wait and see whether there had been any changes in their detective work. Change was not reflected in the decor of the Glenelg police station. Nothing had changed for at least thirty years. The police station still had the same old frightful linoleum and crappy chairs.

'But you solved your grandma's disappearance, didn't you?' Aldo smiled at her. 'Spotting her missing surfboard was the major clue.'

Cecilia smoothed her dress around her knees. Many people thought Grandma Snow had got up early one Sunday morning, made a cinnamon tea cake, went surfing, and never came back. 'I am not so sure,' she said slowly. 'I always thought there were holes in that theory. I can't imagine Grandma Snow carrying that surfboard. It was an antique, intricately carved and made of redwood and very heavy. She was seventy-five years old and hadn't been surfing in years. It was a good ten minutes' walk to the beach, and then she would have had to paddle it out to sea. She wasn't strong enough.'

'Yes, but it's amazing what people can do if they are determined enough, especially if they have a mental condition.'

'Mental?' She glared at him. Grandma Snow had not been crazy, just forgetful.

'I am sorry. I didn't mean to be rude. It was tough on you and your younger sister. It's chaos when someone you love goes missing.'

Avoiding his sympathetic look, she stared into space, trying not to cry. She had loved Grandma and Grandpa Snow. They had lived next to the Patawalonga River in Glenelg North. Their house was an old Tudor with an expansive garden. It was sold after Grandma Snow's disappearance and Grandpa's sudden heart attack a year later, knocking him dead in the pumpkin patch. The house was sold and then survived several generations of families with children—but several years ago, the magnificent house with the black-and-white gables had been squashed to make way for an onslaught of cheaply made townhouses with a hefty price tag, which characterised Glenelg North these days.

Cecilia's childhood, along with that of her younger sister, Angel, was spent in Grandma Snow's kitchen after school, and on weekends while their parents were at work selling residential real estate, Grandma Snow liked to bake cakes, and she was a big fan of treasure hunts. She once hid a packet of Smarties, secured with sticky tape, under the hand basin in the bathroom. As Cecilia and Angel had grown older, the hunts were taken further afield, and the clues became more intricate. Grandma Snow had taught her grandchildren to be observant and to have a passion for puzzles.

'I was really impressed by you,' Investigator Giovanni told Cecilia. 'You had a good eye for detail. I thought you would make an excellent policewoman.'

'Well, I'm like a policewoman,' she said. 'I investigate violations of health and environmental safety regulations.'

'I don't think I have met a health inspector before,' he said, giving her a lazy smile.

'There's a first time for everything,' she said smartly. She was proud of her work.

Investigator Giovanni winked, and she blushed, confused. He pushed a photo across to her, and she examined it. A clean-shaven young man looked back at her. He had fine features, a sensitive look about him, and his lips were slightly parted in a gentle half-smile.

'Is that him? The cook?'

'Yes,' he said, opening another document on his laptop. 'I should say we are treating Phil Dyson's death as a homicide.'

'What? Why?' Cecilia spluttered. She jerked back in her seat. *Homicide? God almighty! It wasn't an accident.* She felt nauseated and looked around for a bin.

'Take a breath, slowly,' Investigator Giovanni told her gently. 'We are waiting results from the autopsy. Did you know Phil?'

'No. It's a newish café, so I hadn't visited it before.'

'What happened when you arrived?'

'I met Astra at nine. We arrived at the same time. She stayed in the main café area while I went into the kitchen and found the cook lying on the floor. At first, I thought he was drunk, but then he seemed unnaturally still, so I checked for a pulse. There was none … and then I saw his face.' Cecilia bit her lip. 'There was no doubt that he was dead.'

'How did you feel?'

She hesitated, not expecting the question. 'I was scared, and I wanted to run and get the hell out of the kitchen. I don't know why. He couldn't hurt me.'

'Unexpected dead bodies can be confronting.' Investigator Giovanni leaned forward in his chair, his brown eyes studying her face. 'Some people do strange things when they see a corpse. Often, they run away, even if they have nothing to do with it. They find somewhere to try to calm down, process what's happened, then they ring the police, or else they become difficult and uncooperative. The psychologists call it the fight-or-flight reaction.'

'Except I didn't run. I threw up and then did my make-up.'

'What? You put on lipstick?' He looked puzzled.

Cecilia waved his question aside. Looking smart was her armour for dealing with the world.

'Then I walked out of the kitchen, but I did make sure the door was closed—twice. I didn't want to see him lying there, dead on the floor. I called an ambulance and sat in the café with Astra to wait for the paramedics.' Cecilia wondered about Astra. She had vacillated between being rude to Cecilia and latching onto policemen. Maybe Astra had been in both 'flight' and 'fight' mode.

'Did Astra touch the body?'

Cecilia shook her head.

'Do you mind if we take your fingerprints and DNA?'

Her eyes widened. Investigator Giovanni didn't think she had anything to do with Phil's death, did he?

'It's because you touched the body and were in the kitchen,' he reassured her. 'We need to rule out extraneous DNA data.'

'When is he going to stop being a body and become "Phil"?'

'You're good at this,' he told her. 'He will be Phil again after the autopsy.'

Cecilia bit her lip. She didn't want to think about that process.

He reached into his pocket and took out a coin. He rolled it up and down his long, tapered fingers for a few moments and then pocketed it. He stared thoughtfully at Cecilia.

'You investigate kitchens, don't you? Was there anything out of the ordinary at The Vegan Café?'

'Hmmm. I didn't properly inspect the kitchen, but it looked clean. Nothing was lying around except for the frying pan and glasses on the sink. Oh, and the vodka bottle. Plus, there was a plastic box of fruit and vegetables that somehow looked out of place. It should have been in the fridge.' She thought some more. 'The freezer was much bigger than one would expect for a small café, and it was leaking. But …' Cecilia brooded. 'It was an interesting kitchen.'

'Interesting? What do you mean?'

'Not because of the cook,' Cecilia hastened to say. 'But because the kitchen was spacious and light, and also … I'm not sure.' After visiting so many commercial kitchens over the years, The Vegan Café stood out. But why? She had focused more on the young man than his surroundings.

'Can you meet me there tomorrow morning? Is eight o'clock too early?'

'That's fine. Anything I can do to help.'

He looked at his watch. 'It's going to be a long night, tracking down his *famiglia*—his family.'

'What's with the Italian expressions? Were you born there?'

'My family migrated from Italy when I was eight years old. I am proud to be an Aussie Italian and it helps people talk to me. They feel like I'm human, and not a dreary robot cop.' He made his face go blank, and said in a monotone, 'Where were you last Wednesday night?'

'Playing bridge at my club,' she said promptly.

'Well, maybe now you feel okay with talking to the police.' He beamed at her as if she was a student who had made a clever remark.

'It depends who,' she said, thinking of Inspector Longbottom.

'See! I make you feel comfortable.' He closed his laptop, stood up, and tweaked his expensive trousers into shape. He was all business now. 'Let's do the thumbprints and mouth swabs for the DNA now.'

Cecilia's thoughts tumbled as he pressed her thumbs into the ink. Homicide? On her patch? That was so creepy. Could she trust the police? They had caused bedlam when Grandma Snow had disappeared and had discovered nothing.

***

I run into the kitchen in a panic. She must be here. There's the familiar red laminate table and four chairs with spongy seats which fill the middle of the room. A small jam jar with white daisies is placed at the centre of the table, and the oven is working overtime producing delicious baking smells. But Grandma Snow is not there. She should be, but she's not. Where is she? My heart revs up. I have to find Grandma Snow before it's too late.

Bills, recipes, newspapers, and photographs clutter the counter tops. I rifle through the muddle of things, looking for her note, a clue, explaining where she has gone. I know it's in the kitchen somewhere. Grandma Snow must have hidden it. She loves playing hide-and-seek. Once she hid a message folded into an origami bird for me and Angel, my younger sister, to find. I just have to find her note.

I search every cupboard, drawer, shelf, and even the fridge. Suddenly, I hear a crashing sound hitting the back door. It is loud and insistent. The door holds back something dangerous, something unnatural, and it's swelling in strength, wanting to come in and swallow me up.

Fear paralyses me. I want to run, but I can't. My legs don't work, and the back door is buckling from an unknown force.

***

Cecilia felt something wet on her face. She woke up in her kitchen, curled up in a ball on the floor, with the puppies are vigorously licking her face. She was shocked to see all her household paperwork scattered over the floor. *Oh my god! I've been sleepwalking. For the first time in years. Why was this happening?* She stumbled back to bed, desperately hoping this was a one-off event.

2

The following morning, for her meeting at the café with Inspector Giovanni, Cecilia chose her aqua and silver starfish dress and, for extra fun, added her new green heels with little silver tassels. If he could dress smart, so could she.

She was hyped up about going back to the crime scene at The Vegan Café. She had many questions. Glenelg was *her* community, and it was her job to keep people safe. Who on earth would want to kill the cook of The Vegan Café?

Inspector Giovanni was parked in a red sporty two-door Alfa Romeo out the front of the café and talking on his phone. Cecilia stepped out of her own car, a white 2010 Subaru Forester, and walked to the front door of the café, waiting for him to finish his phone call.

He strolled over. 'Sorry about that.'

Cecilia studied him. He was a big man, well over six feet tall, and he carried some extra weight around his middle. He was wearing his dark navy-blue wool suit, and today's shirt was dusky pink. 'That's okay, Inspector Giovanni.'

'Call me Aldo. Have you seen the news?'

'No.'

Watching the news was not how Cecilia liked to start the day. There were too many atrocious stories for her taste. She would, however, occasionally listen to the weather report. Cecilia spent a lot of time on Jetty Road and didn't like to get wet from the rain. Besides, dining in the council's lunchroom and its mostly male presence kept her up-to-date with terrorist attacks, solar panels, and the benefits of unhomogenised milk.

'It's all over the news about the body found in The Vegan Café,' said Aldo.

'Who told the media?'

'Astra. She was interviewed on TV.'

'What did she say? Nothing about my unaligned chakras, I hope.'

'No. When she spoke to the reporter, it was all about how Phil was now a bright star in the cosmos because he was an enlightened vegan.'

'You're kidding!'

'No,' said Aldo cheerfully. 'She's *pazzo*—a fruitcake. Let's go in. Quick, quick! I can see some journalists coming our way.'

Cecilia turned to see a gaggle of men and women armed with cameras and mobile phones hurrying down the street towards them.

Aldo retrieved a key from his pocket and opened the front door of The Vegan Café. A shade was over the door, but the journalists could still see in through the big picture window. They gathered there, gesticulating and waving like a swarm of flapping seagulls zeroing in on chips.

'Ignore them,' Aldo told Cecilia. 'They will eventually get tired of knocking.'

'Do you want me to do a thorough investigation?' she asked. 'Like I would do normally, such as check the cutlery drawers for food scraps that have fallen in, or do you want me to look for something unusual?'

'My team is finished here,' he replied. 'It's all yours.'

She popped her bag on a table and produced a tablet from its depths. Her high heels clicked on the concrete floor as she stepped into the kitchen.

It was filled with light, empty of clutter, and was accommodated by generously sized windows, unusual for a commercial kitchen. Typically, café and restaurant kitchens were dark and cramped places. In the far corner of the bench was a flourishing peace lily—its shiny green leaves presumably oxygenating the kitchen—and next to it was a miniature drying rack where silicone wraps were hanging, secured by wooden pegs.

The stainless-steel benches were gleaming. Cecilia looked underneath and trailed a finger for dust. It came up clean. She opened the top drawer next to the sink, looking for onion peel and crumbs. Instead, she found generic spray bottles, neatly lined up with their contents labelled. There were rows of eucalyptus oil, vinegar, baking soda, and hydrogen peroxide.

She was impressed. Avoiding petrochemicals was laborious, but Phil was obviously committed to green cleaning. Boiling water was also an essential ingredient for green cleaning, and she searched for rubber gloves. Under the sink were sponges, brushes, and rags—but no gloves. Perhaps the police had taken them for forensic reasons. She would ask Aldo.

The vodka bottle, the glasses, and the frying pan were gone, also presumably for evidence, but the old red crate of fruit and vegetables, such a battered article and so at odds with the pristine kitchen, was still there. Cecilia searched for an invoice. She found a piece of paper with no letterhead tucked behind an avocado. A sum of money was scrawled on it, as well as a list of fruit and vegetables. The writing was cramped and vaguely familiar.

It was strange there was no invoice, merely that scrap of paper. Was the produce home-grown? She picked up a carrot. It had no dirt or green stalks; clean, like the rest of the produce, which looked as if it had come from a shop rather than a backyard. All of it should have been in the fridge, not on the counter.

In the top drawer of the enormous freezer, Cecilia found two beige-coloured sandwich-sized blocks, tightly covered in silicone wrap and placed in sealed tubs. Cecilia lifted one out and sniffed the contents. She blinked in surprise and took another sniff. It smelled like marijuana and coconut oil. *Interesting,* she thought as she placed them on the kitchen bench.

The rest of the freezer was full of pies and frozen vegan produce. Everything would have to be thrown out, as the door had been left open during Phil's passing. Again, she noticed a small pool of water drip-fed by the freezer. It was a safety hazard. The freezer needed to be fixed.

At the bottom of the freezer was a drawer. She opened it and plumes of icy, white air floated out. She wondered if this was a liquid nitrogen drawer, but that would be unusual to find in a café's kitchen. Inside were tubs of vegan vanilla ice cream, and pushed behind them was a tray of pillbox-sized containers with labels dated and marked *CS*. This made no sense to her.

She moved on to the pantry, sniffing for marijuana cookies, but there was no tell-tale smell. She ran her fingers across the spice rack, then the canned products, picking up a tin of coconut milk. It was a popular brand. She typed its name into her tablet, planning to check it out later. Cecilia had heard rumours about some brands of coconut milk not being up to scratch with vegan principles.

On the ceiling near the back door of the kitchen was a spider web and a delicate spider with long, fine legs was busy making repairs to its web. She paused. Was it deliberately permitted to be there? Was a spider's web a natural way to control flies—a green alternative to electric fly killers?

Cecilia left the kitchen for the counter in the main café and looked in the drawers for the paperwork on deliveries. She found nothing except for bundles of pamphlets extolling the virtues of meditation and providing information on classes, upcoming workshops, and retreats led by Swami Nardhamuni. The owner of the café must be some kind of guru.

She was now ready to talk to Aldo, who was on his mobile phone again. While she waited, she scrolled through her phone, searching vegan recipes for marijuana cookies. She was right; to avoid the dairy problem, they used coconut oil instead of butter.

When Aldo had finished, Cecilia led him back to the kitchen and showed him the container of fruit and vegetables and the scrappy invoice.

'It's not an authenticated supplier, and everything here should have been in the fridge.'

'It could have been delivered the previous night,' said Aldo.

'Even so, why didn't he put the produce away? He seemed a fastidious cook. And then there's this.' She lifted one of the frozen blocks of marijuana cooking oil. 'It's cannabutter, used for making vegan marijuana cookies.'

'Did you find any cookies?'

She shook her head.

'Two blocks of cannabutter,' mused Aldo. 'Not much. Maybe it was for his personal use.'

She did the maths. 'He could have made at least thirty cookies with one block of cannabutter. That's a lot for one person to consume.'

'Do you think he sold cookies?' Aldo asked.

'I don't know, but this also has me perplexed.' She bent to open the lowest drawer of the freezer, accidentally giving Aldo an eyeful of her plump bottom. *Whoops.* She felt embarrassed and straightened up, diverting his attention to the medical containers. He took a couple and slid them into an evidence bag.

'Why did my team miss all this evidence?' Aldo scowled.

'That's why you got me in,' said Cecilia, pleased with herself. 'Are you sure it was a homicide? The leaking freezer could be a death trap. It's so easy to slip and fall on a wet floor.'

'The initial autopsy showed that he had multiple injuries to his head,' said Aldo thoughtfully. 'You don't get that from a fall.'

Cecilia winced. 'It was the frying pan, wasn't it? Do you know who did it?'

Aldo shook his head.

Cecilia took a deep breath and carried on. 'There were no rubber gloves in the kitchen. Did you take them?'

Aldo frowned. 'No.'

'Check this out.' She showed him the small drying rack with the silicone wraps. 'Phil was awesome.' She shook her head in wonder. 'He was a proper green vegan—a devotee. He didn't even use beeswax wraps because that would be stealing from bees.'

'Huh? Sounds complicated. What does being a vegan mean?'

'Vegan means you don't consume any foods made from animals. No dairy, no eggs, no honey. Vegans regard these as stolen from animals and other living creatures, whereas dairy is okay for vegetarians.'

'I can't imagine dinner without meat,' grumbled Aldo.

She didn't persuade him otherwise, keeping her focus on her job. She gestured to the counter. 'What I can't find is bookkeeping.'

Aldo rifled through the drawers but also came up empty.

'It should be somewhere,' said Cecilia. 'It's mandatory for a food outlet.'

There was a knock on the window, and a wrinkled face peered in.

'I might let this one in,' mused Aldo. 'She doesn't look like a vegan or a journalist.' He opened the door.

A woman, her hair a cluster of greys curls, stood on the doorstep clutching a worn red-and-white-striped shopping bag. She looked at him in surprise.

'Sorry, *bella,* the shop is closed,' he told her.

'Closed? Where's Phil?'

Aldo hesitated. 'He passed away on Wednesday night.'

'Passed away? You mean, he's dead?' The woman's hands tightened on the bag. 'But he was so young!'

Cecilia moved to comfort her but came to a stop. There was a distinctive smell. It was coming from the woman's shopping bag.

'Did you know Phil?' Aldo asked.

'Are you from the police?' the woman asked.

Aldo smiled in agreement. 'What's your name, please?'

'Mavis.' She frowned. 'Mavis Aldicott.' She searched Aldo's face. 'How did he die?'

'Blunt force trauma,' he answered quietly.

'What's in your bag?' asked Cecilia gently. 'Do you think you could show us?'

'Oh no, I can't! I must be going. I'm Phil's Auntie Mavis. Oh, dearie me. This is terrible. Poor Phil!' Mavis seemed genuinely upset. 'I have to see Phil's parents. They will be devastated.' Then she paused, as if having second thoughts. 'At least, they should be upset. I best leave you to your work.'

Cecilia caught Aldo's eye, tapped her nose, then gestured to the woman's bag.

Aldo's eyes widened with astonishment. 'Bella, show us what you have in your bag.'

The woman tottered away from the front doorstep at a surprising speed, zipping past the journalists who tried to block her way. From the window, they watched her climb into a battered older hatchback.

Aldo typed her registration number into his tablet. 'She had marijuana in that big striped shopping bag.'

Cecilia raised an eyebrow. 'It looks like you are never too old to be a drug dealer.'

Aldo shrugged. 'I've heard of a ninety-two-year-old man being busted for selling meth. It helped pay for a carer.'

'Are you going to tell the drug squad?'

'I'll be visiting her soon about her nephew. I can examine the extent of her horticultural activities then.'

Cecilia sat down at an orange table near the counter, and Aldo joined her. He was so easy to be with. She no longer felt squeamish about being in a café where a young man had died, or that she had met Aldo a long time ago under dreadful circumstances—when Grandma Snow had gone missing.

'Auntie must have a good reason to be growing and selling marijuana, because she's certainly not spending the money on herself.' Cecilia gestured to the window where she could see the old hatchback stopped at the pedestrian crossing on Jetty Road. 'I'm surprised her car even works.'

'But perhaps we know where Phil's marijuana came from,' said Aldo. 'How old was he?'

'Twenty-nine.'

'Did he have a girlfriend? Or was he having an affair with someone? Could this be a crime of passion?'

'Hey!' Aldo raised his hand, softening it with a half-smile. 'I'm the one who should be leading this investigation.'

'Of course, you are!' She couldn't help herself. 'Was he an only child?'

'No, he had a sister. I am going to drive up to Clare Valley tomorrow to see her.'

'There are some fabulous restaurants in Clare Valley,' she said without thinking.

Aldo brightened up. 'Why don't you come with me? I can interview the sister while you look at the shops, and we can have lunch afterwards.'

Cecilia was astonished. He was asking her out to lunch. But why? Sure, they had been talking easily, but this was a homicide investigation. Perhaps she had morphed into a community connection, the latest method of police investigation, to help Aldo. She decided that it must be a working lunch.

'So?' He looked at her.

'That sounds lovely.'

It was hard to resist an invitation from such an attractive man.

***

Cecilia stood with a towel around her and surveyed her wardrobe. All her dresses, silk pants, and floating long tops, size 14 or 16, were organised by colour and lined up on hangers. She flicked through the garments. What colour should she wear for lunch with a homicide detective? She had a wide choice. Bright and pastel colours, but not white or beige; they made her look washed out. It would be a dress, of course, as she didn't wear jeans—although, she did have leggings for wearing at home.

She fingered a sunset dress but eventually picked an A-line frock patterned in marigold flowers, pulled on nude stockings, and slid her feet into shiny black pumps, which had a moderate heel. It was cold in the Valley, so she laid her red coat over her cream upholstered armchair, ready to grab on her way out.

She spent ten minutes doing her hair and make-up. This included eyeliner and eyeshadow on her forest-green eyes and orange-hued lipstick on her plump lips. She parted her black hair in the middle with a comb, pulling it back in a low bun. Her appearance was a statement: here was a woman who knew her own mind and was unafraid to show it. She brushed a light dusting of powder over her skin. Foundation was not needed because she was blessed with milky-white skin.

Cecilia still wondered if it was appropriate for Aldo to take her out to lunch while he was working. She decided it was his problem, not hers. He was more than old enough to know the rules. She still had a quarter of an hour to go before he picked her up. Closing her bedroom door, ensuring it was shut and secure from marauding puppies, she headed for the family room.

Peaking around the passageway door, she looked for Ziggy and Stardust. They were asleep, lying on either side of her daughter, who was lounging on the couch playing with her phone. Hannah was delicately built, and the tops of her ears were slightly pointed, like an elf's. She had wide green eyes, like Cecilia's, and wore an old tracksuit, her long brown hair tied in a plait. Cecilia suspected she hadn't showered for a couple of days.

In case there was a sudden attack of love from the puppies, Cecilia perched on a kitchen stool so she could swing her stockinged legs out of the way.

'Look at Ziggy and Stardust,' said Hannah. 'Aren't they adorable?'

'When they're asleep.'

'I gave them sweet potatoes this morning and they attacked them and shook them about like they had to kill those potatoes before eating them.'

Cecilia remembered finding a dead blue-tongue a few weeks ago; its neck had been broken. She had removed it and not told Hannah in case it upset her. Since then, the lizards had vanished, hopefully to a dachshund-free garden.

'Well, they are a hunting breed,' Cecilia observed.

Hannah stroked her dogs. 'My babies are sleeping the sleep of the innocent.'

Cecilia laughed. There was nothing innocent about the babies. However, it was good to hear her daughter making jokes.

Even though Hannah was attached to the sofa and not the shower, Cecilia was glad not to have her ex-boyfriend, Kim, around anymore. He was a narcissist and took advantage of Hannah's loving nature. If it took a while for her to accept the relationship was over, that was okay. Eventually, she would realise Kim was not worth loving.

Nevertheless, Cecilia felt she had to try to do something to break through Hannah's depression. She thought Hannah needed something to love and perhaps two sweet little puppies would help her through the grieving process.

Hannah was excited. 'They can sit on my lap, keep me company, and I can cuddle them.' She chose dachshunds. 'I don't want a fluffy toy dog, but I don't want a big dog, either. I want to be able to snuggle up with them.' An alarming thought crossed her face. 'If I have two dogs, would they still love me? Perhaps I should just have one.'

Cecilia persuaded her to have two dogs—an argument cinched by the council's animal control officer, Garth, who said it was lonely for a dog to be on its own. Most of the complaints about barking dogs were from solitary dogs stuck in a backyard with nothing to do but yap.

Ziggy and Stardust were nothing like Cecilia had expected. They were supercharged and chewed everything, especially Hannah's bras, because they liked to gnaw the underwires.

And they fought. Both wanted to be the alpha dog. Once, when Hannah had been on the floor, patting them, a terrible fight broke out. Luckily, Cecilia had been there, and she'd emptied a saucepan of cold water over the snarling puppies.

Hannah had been upset. She loved the puppies, but she wanted cute, cuddly dogs—not warring ferals. Cecilia took more advice from Garth.

'They gotta know who the alpha dog is among themselves and in your mob,' he said. 'Try using a spray bottle and pick who you think should be the alpha dog. You need to organise your pack.'

Cecilia tried to encourage Hannah to be the alpha dog, which didn't always work because she was soft-hearted. 'They're just puppies. They don't mean any harm.'

Cecilia had no qualms about quelling the dachshunds into submission. 'You need to find your inner warrior,' she told Hannah. *And in more ways than one, too,* thought Cecilia. Kim had taken advantage of Hannah's loving soul.

Hannah looked at her mum sitting on a stool, immaculately dressed, and waiting for Aldo to come. 'You look nice, and your dress is so flamboyantly vintage. Are you playing bridge?'

'No, I am off to Clare Valley for lunch.'

'Who are you going with?'

'A policeman.'

'Someone new?'

'Yes and no. I met him a hundred years ago.'

'Mum, you're amazing. You have a more active social life than me at the moment.'

The doorbell rang. The puppies woke, keen for some action, but Cecilia leapt off her stool and blew her daughter a kiss. She closed all the doors before disappearing outside.

***

Aldo stood, a large presence on her doorstep. He wore a navy linen jacket with comfortable-looking chino pants and brown Oxford shoes.

Good heavens, thought Cecilia. *What a snappy dresser, even on weekends.*

He ushered her to his red, sporty Alfa Romeo and opened the door for her.

'This is not a police car,' she said.

'I like to drive my own car, even for work. It's a special car. I've had it for ten years.'

It was an hour-and-a-half trip to Clare, so she adjusted the back of her seat to be more comfortable.

He turned to her before he took off. 'What music do you like?'

'From the eighties.'

'Not punk music,' he groaned. 'What about Elvis? Everyone likes Elvis. I'll find you his hit single "Blue Suede Shoes". It's happy music. Forever songs.' Vigorously, he pressed buttons on his phone and put it on the dash.

'Was Elvis Italian?' Cecilia wondered.

'No, he was Irish, Scottish, and Cherokee. But us Italians, we love Elvis. He's kind of an honorary Italian.' Suddenly, Aldo began wagging and jabbing his finger at the car in front of him. 'Did you see that car just pull out in front of me without indicating? Unbelievable!'

A finger poised at her lips, Cecilia hoped he wasn't going to get out of his car, flag the driver, and make a scene. She opted for distracting him. The offending car belonged to a neighbour, a widow in her sixties with whom Cecilia was friendly.

'When I was working as a chef in London at a restaurant, one of the waiters was an Elvis impersonator.'

'I'm not an impersonator.' Aldo pressed a fist to his heart. 'What you see is what you get.'

'But don't you step on my blue suede shoes,' Cecilia sang.

Aldo had other matters on his mind. 'Don't tell me you can cook as well.' He gave her a wink. 'My favourite type of woman.'

Cecilia snorted. 'That's what my ex-husband, Steve, said.'

'Sorry.'

'Don't be. Steve's long gone. We've been divorced for more than fifteen years. He used to be a talking purple grape,' Cecilia teased Aldo.

'Huh?'

'There was an ABC children's TV program called *Fruit Play,* and Steve was the purple grape.'

'Are you serious?'

'Yes, and when the ABC changed the program and turned it into a cartoon, his pay was cut because they only used his voice. He did some successful commercials because he looks like a handsome, friendly dad, but he's not. He's promiscuous and doesn't have much time for our kids. He stayed in Sydney, and I moved back home to Adelaide.' She wondered why she was giving Aldo so much personal information. Maybe because he was a good listener. She looked out the window at heritage houses and rows of vines, which stretched for kilometres.

'Why did you become a health inspector?'

'The hours were more child-friendly for a single mum. Chefs have to work nights.'

'That must have been tough.' His brown eyes filled with sympathy.

'No, you mustn't feel sorry for me. That really won't do. I'm not a victim, and I love my work. It makes me feel useful.'

'That's true,' said Aldo. 'I find you useful.'

Cecilia rolled her eyes, cynical. 'So, tell me. What's the cook's story?' she asked.

'It's emerging.'

'I think he was a true-blue vegan. All his cleaning products were homemade with vinegar, bi-carb soda, and eucalyptus oil. He didn't even use butter in his marijuana cookies—he used coconut oil, which would have made the extracting process even more laborious. Is he on Facebook? I might find some more information there.'

Aldo kept his eyes on the road.

Cecilia picked up her bag from the floor of his car and began rummaging through it for her phone. 'His name is Phil Dyson, right?'

'Yes.'

It took several minutes to find his page. His Facebook picture was the same one Aldo had shown her in the interview room. She studied it again. He was attractive, but not in a muscular way; more of a sensitive one. Perhaps girls or guys felt he understood them. An appealing attribute.

His photos were also informative. They showed him standing at a table, arranged with green cleaning products, sporting a palm tree motif. Another photo showed him mixing up a batter, presumably marijuana dough, and there were a few photos of him looking soulfully out to the ocean. One was captioned with *Enlightenment means waking up to who you truly are and then being that.*

'He looks inoffensive,' Cecilia mused. 'Although, I think he was more complex than he appears. He wasn't your ordinary marijuana dealer either. Selling gourmet marijuana cookies is classy.'

'People don't generally kill for cannabis biscuits.'

'Okay, then why did someone get so cross with him that they killed him? Who did it? Should I be worried if there is a serial cook-killer in my community? Or a crazy cookie customer?'

'Murder isn't usually elaborate. Sometimes the reasons can be mundane, such as the victim never did the dishes.' Aldo tapped a finger on the steering wheel.

'My ex-husband was slack around the house. He was slack, full stop. But I got a divorce. I didn't have to knock him off to get rid of him.' Cecilia sighed. 'I'm guessing Phil was killed with the frying pan, and there are no fingerprints.'

Aldo said nothing and kept his eyes on the road. He slowed down and put his indicator on to turn into the main street of Clare, a historic country town boasting many wineries, and boutique restaurants for tourists. 'I'll meet you in front of the post office in an hour,' he said, as he pulled up in front of a sixties building with a large mural of rolling hills painted on the side wall.

Cecilia looked at it. 'I was expecting something *quaint* for the post office of a historic town.'

'I can't find a park here,' grumbled Aldo. 'Where can I find one? I will have to double park and let you off there. Will you look at that! People are unbelievable. That four-wheel-drive has just taken up two spaces!'

Cecilia looked at the woman from the offending car struggle to get her baby out from the back seat. 'Are you able to hand out traffic offences?'

'I could, but why would I?'

'Because you get annoyed with other drivers.'

'No, I'm not. It's the way I drive. I give commentary about other people on the road. It's not like when I am really annoyed.' He smoothed back his slightly long hair. 'I will drop you here and find somewhere else to park.'

Cecilia eyed him for a moment. 'You look like someone from the Mafia with your hair slicked back. Scary!'

'You're not afraid to say what you think! Anyway, it's part of my Italian heritage.'

'Was Grandpa a Mafia gangster?' Cecilia held the door half-open.

'No, the opposite. My family left Sicily and came to Australia to get away from the Mafia.' Aldo jerked his head at her. 'Out!'

She twinkled her fingers at him, closed the car door, and spent a relaxing hour browsing in the shops. She bought her son, Luke, some locally made craft beer; Hannah, a big stripey lollipop; and the puppies some organically grown carrots.

She considered buying herself a pink cardigan that felt soft and would go with her floral dresses; however, on closer inspection, she discovered it was partially made from possum hair, and she put it back on the rack.

Aldo was waiting for her outside the post office.

'Any ideas for lunch?' she asked.

'There's a place called the Pantry,' he replied. 'I have checked out their menu. It looks nice.'

'Okay,' she said, hoping there were vegetarian options.

The Pantry was an old stone building with windows of small, rectangular panes set in wood. Its dining tables were decked out with red-and-white checked tablecloths. Dried grasses and old-fashioned brass pots hung on the walls, and someone had an enthusiasm for old typewriters, which were dotted around the place. The historic look was in full force. Cecilia inspected the cutlery—it gleamed, meeting her approval.

They were given menus attached to wooden clipboards. Cecilia chose a mushroom risotto while Aldo tucked into an Angus beef sirloin steak. They drank a glass of red wine with their meals.

While they waited for the bill, Aldo took out a coin and began rolling it up and down the back of his fingers.

'What's with the coin rolling?' she asked.

'I do tricks.' The coin slid up and down his fingers, then he clapped his hands. He spread his empty fingers. 'Where's the coin?'

'Huh?'

Aldo reached out and plucked a coin from her ear.

'Are you a magician as well as a policeman?'

He smiled.

A waitress wearing a flouncy white apron presented the bill, which Aldo grabbed. After a heated discussion, because Cecilia wanted to pay for her own meal, she relented and said she would pay next time.

Aldo gave her a big smile. 'Next time?'

She blushed and got up from her chair.

In the car on the way home, she asked about Phil's sister.

'What am I going to do with all your questions?' Aldo asked. 'I have to keep confidentiality.'

'I'm persistent, aren't I? Give me her Facebook name.'

'Kylie Dyson.'

She looked her up on her phone. 'Wow! She is gigantic. Well over six feet tall, and a bodybuilder. You should see her biceps—they're huge mounds of flesh. It looks like she lives alone and works at the local service station.' Cecilia scrolled through the photos again. 'She sure has a lot of televisions. There's even one bolted to the ceiling over her weights area.'

'I have never seen so many TVs in one house,' said Aldo. 'It was like a TV shop, and all the screens were playing *Salacious,* that cooking show. There were so many close-ups of tomato soup.'

'It's a good cooking show. It has a sexy chef.'

'Too much red soup,' Aldo complained. 'She had screens in the kitchen, in the living room, and as I passed the toilet, you could hear the TV going on in there. The back porch was filled with dozens of old TVs. You know, the ones that were deep and wide and weighed a ton.'

'Wow! A TV hoarder. What did she say about her brother?'

'She said they didn't see much of each other.'

'Was she sad?'

'No, not really. Kylie said Phil was always banging on about green cleaning.'

'She's certainly strong enough to wield a giant-sized frying pan,' said Cecilia, looking at Kylie's photos. 'Does she have an alibi? Did she say was working at the service station on the night of Phil's murder?'

Aldo was silent, avoiding her eyes, which usually meant she was right. Kylie had been working when Phil had been dispatched.

Cecilia abandoned the bodybuilding sister as a suspect, for the moment. 'I'm still puzzled by the lack of bookkeeping at The Vegan Café. The cash economy is rife in some food outlets. Maybe someone was rorting the cash flow in The Vegan Café. The leaking freezer is a safety hazard, too. I have also missed something else there, but I can't pinpoint it. I'm going to make an appointment to see the owner.'

'And deal with Astra again?'

'Hopefully with her husband, when he's not meditating.'

He looked across the seat to Cecilia; her skirt had shifted, exposing a pale thigh. She noticed his glance and tugged it down. Maybe the dress was a little too tight.

Aldo turned on the smile.

'Enough of that,' she scolded him. 'Do you have kids?'

'I have a son, Leon. He is nineteen.' Aldo's face tightened and then relaxed. 'Leon is autistic. He's on the lower end of the spectrum. But he has anxiety problems and lives with my parents and me.'

Cecilia had a cousin whose four-year-old grandchild had autism. He was an angel one moment, then threw tantrums the next.

She also registered there was no Mrs Aldo included in the equation, and it seemed Aldo lived with his parents, which she thought odd; a middle-aged man living at home with his parents. But maybe it suited caring for Aldo's son.

'My son works at a workshop for people with disabilities. He catches a train to and from work. He loves trains. His bedroom walls are covered with maps of famous train routes around the world, like the Ghan and the Orient Express.'

'That sounds like a nice hobby.'

'What are your hobbies?' Aldo asked her.

'Bridge, spending time with my sister, and judo.'

'Say what?'

'Say judo!' Cecilia was used to the disbelief when she told people she did judo.

'I can't imagine you doing judo. Those high heels and dresses you wear are so un-judo.'

'Oh yeah? I can do a lot of things in high heels.'

Aldo bit his lip. He looked like he was holding back a laugh. She sniffed. He was crossing the line into sexism, or maybe even into sexy talk. Come to think of it, she had accidentally phrased her words so they could have a double meaning. But did she really mind?

'I have to be able to protect myself in my job,' she explained. 'I don't have the luxury of being able to carry a Taser, a gun, or a baton—unlike most of you law enforcement officers!'

'What?' Aldo sounded confused.

'I mostly deal with non-compliance regulations; that has its hazards, too. I've had deranged chefs point knives at me. Once a crazy beautician threw hot wax at me!'

'*Mama mia!*'

Cecilia smoothed her hair. 'Now you know how the other half of law enforcement lives—the less-sexy half.'

'Sexy?' He winked at her.

'Hunting down cockroaches in a restaurant is not glamorous.'

'Nor is hunting human cockroaches.'

'Or psychopaths,' said Cecilia, sighing. She thought about how protective she was of her community and how important it was that people were kept safe from accidents, from food poisoning, and now from killers wielding frying pans.

The vegan cook's death felt personal now.

***

Nothing much had changed on the home-front when Cecilia returned from Clare Valley. Her daughter was still lying on the couch, Ziggy and Stardust were sleeping in front of the heater, but her son was now sitting in the recliner and filling it with his long, muscular body. He was wearing a stained black-and-yellow footy guernsey.

'Hi, Luke. Have you come home to do your washing?'

He slumped back in his chair. 'I'll do a load later.'

'How was your hot date with the policeman, Mum?' Hannah asked.

Cecilia put her bag down on the bench and climbed onto the kitchen stool, keeping a wary eye out for the puppies.

'I don't have hot dates; I go out to lunch with my favourites.'

'Favourites?' Luke peered at his mum.

'That's right,' chimed in Hannah. 'Mum has her favourite neurosurgeon, her favourite dog catcher, and now her favourite policeman. Let's hope she doesn't end up having lunch with her favourite criminal.'

'Really, Hannah? You exaggerate things.' She turned to Luke. 'What's happening with you?'

Luke's face reddened. He'd tried for years to get rid of the blush before he learnt to ignore it. There was no remedy for blushing. Luke discovered that, being such a big, handsome, and football-hardened bloke, he could get away with it.

'I'd like to move back here for a bit, if it's okay with you, Mum?'

'Of course!'

Then the puppies woke up, and Cecilia beat a hasty retreat to her bedroom, changing out of her stockings and into her dog-proof leggings and an oversized sweater.

'What happened?' she asked Luke on her return.

Luke looked away, unable to answer.

'Amy cheated on Luke!' said Hannah. 'With that long-haired guy from the Save the Orangutans organisation. I don't get it. I didn't think she was a tart.'

'Be careful about judging,' Cecilia warned her. Amy and Luke had split up before, then got back together. They'd been an item since high school and had gradually grown apart. Luke worked at the Broadway, the local pub, played Australian rules footy for the Tigers, the Glenelg team, and he watched a lot of sports on television. In contrast, Amy was studying environmental studies at TAFE and busy lying down on the streets during peak hour traffic, demanding the government do something about climate change.

'Are you having a timeout?' Cecilia asked.

Luke shook his head miserably. 'No, it's over. We decided not to renew the lease on the flat.'

'I'm sorry,' she said.

There was nothing more coming from Luke. Now she had two broken-hearted kids. Coffee was required, and she made it extra-strong.

The puppies were getting restless despite Hannah's gentle hands, and Cecilia knew there would be a fight soon about who was getting the most attention. She reached into her pink handbag and produced the organically grown carrots. She was unconcerned with the possibility of a mess; the puppies vacuumed up all traces of their food. They split to separate corners of the living room with their goodies and munched away, each keeping a beady eye out in case one dashed over to steal a carrot from the other.

'I've got a murder on my patch,' Cecilia said, hoping to distract Luke from his misery.

'A murder!' Luke and Hannah both exclaimed. 'Who?'

'The cook at The Vegan Café, Phil Dyson. Someone hit him over the head with a frying pan. Repeatedly.'

'What? Huh?" Luke exploded in shock.

'You have to be kidding me,' said Hannah, sitting up on the sofa, giving her mum full attention. 'Not at The Vegan Café. I love going there. They have fantastic products, but they're expensive.' Hannah was on a tight budget, living off unemployment benefits since quitting art school.

Cecilia bit back a comment that it would be nice if Hannah got a job instead of being supported by her mum, the government, and the sofa.

Luke was on the case, too. 'I knew Phil. He was part of the Saturday footy crowd at the Broadway,' Luke said, referring to Glenelg South's pub that was popular among the locals. 'Occasionally Phil would drop in mid-week as well. Why would someone want to knock him off? He was a nice bloke.'

'I don't know,' said Cecilia. She frowned in frustration.

'He never caused any trouble, and his spicy legume pies were fantastic,' continued Luke, swinging a muddy leg, capped with the Tigers' black-and-yellow striped socks. His boots were at the front door. Usually, people didn't take their shoes off when they came to Cecilia's house; however, she drew the line at muddy boots.

'Sometimes Phil would bring in samples for the pub regulars to try,' Luke added. 'He was building up his repertoire at the café. I liked the pie with ancient grains the best.'

'And his sweets were yummy.' Hannah smacked her lips. 'He made chocolate mousses out of avocado. Why would someone want to murder a harmless vegan cook? That's crazy. We're peace-loving people.'

'This is confidential,' Cecilia warned. 'The cook made marijuana biscuits, too. Did you know that?'

Luke nodded. 'I've heard about The Vegan Café being a source of weed cookies from working at the pub. People said they were nice, not stinky like other marijuana cookies. It's hard to make marijuana cookies edible because weed gives off a terrible pong.'

'Was the café a well-known cannabis outlet?'

Hannah was also informative. 'Not really. He only dealt on Tuesday nights. I tried one, once. It was like surfing the high. It came in waves, coming and going, as the cookie was digested.'

Cecilia had also experimented with marijuana when young, but she hadn't liked it because her thoughts became scattered. She preferred to be in charge of her mind.

'The cookies were expensive, too,' Hannah added.

'How much?'

'Thirty dollars each.'

'Was Phil a stoner?'

Luke frowned. 'I don't think so. It was more of a business arrangement.'

'Who were Phil's clients?' Cecilia pressed.

'Well, I'm guessing they're mostly recreational users,' said Hannah. 'But I know among them are the diet-obsessed vegans—like Vee, Amy's sister. She's always buying cookies.'

'Vee?' Cecilia pondered. 'Have I met her?'

'You must remember her, Mum,' said Hannah. 'She has pink hair and came to Luke's birthday party wearing that sick picture of a caged chicken pasted on her T-shirt. She said she had it specially made.'

Cecilia shuddered. She did remember the T-shirt. It was truly dreadful. A scrawny-looking chicken with mad eyes, behind bars.

'Vee's not a true vegan,' announced Hannah. 'She puts on the T-shirt, but does she walk the talk? Not in those leather boots! Even if they are second-hand, she is still wearing animal skins. And she's always half-stoned.'

'I don't think cannabis was the reason the cook was killed,' Cecilia mused.

Hannah agreed. 'People do crazy things to get ice and other hardcore drugs, but not for a handful of marijuana cookies.'

'What was he like as a person?'

'I don't know much about him,' said Hannah. 'I noticed him at the café a few times—he was a nice guy—and we talked about veganism.'

'He was not someone you would notice,' said Luke. 'Not like your animal control officer, Mum. When *he* walks into the Broadway with his long white beard and big voice, everyone notices him.'

Cecilia made a mental note to talk more with Garth.

'Phil would sit quietly at the bar and people would come up and talk to him. Often, they were girls,' said Luke.

Hannah frowned. 'I thought Glenelg is supposed to be a safe community. No-one normally gets murdered here. Not even backpackers!'

'Why backpackers, Hannah?' Cecilia asked.

'Because they come to Australia and meet psychopaths. But it's usually in the outback.'

'Glenelg has always had more than its fair share of crime and mysteries,' said Cecilia. 'We've had to fight to keep our town safe. Usually, it's the yobbos who come and cause trouble. Glenelg has always attracted them. Ever since HMS *Buffalo* arrived at Glenelg in 1836 and laid the founding stone for South Australia, there's been trouble. The sailors who came with the ship got drunk on rum and ran riot. They were tied to a tree to sober up. Policing the drunks was a big issue for the early settlers.' Grandma Snow had collected newspaper clippings about Glenelg, and Cecilia kept them in one of the boxes in her wardrobe.

'They didn't teach us that at school when they were banging on about local history,' said Luke. 'And I wouldn't mind tying some idiots to a tree when they're tanked and causing trouble.'

Cecilia smiled. 'And then in 1927, in the next famous brawl at Glenelg, your great-great grandad, Reginal Archer—he was a local copper—was called to the beach on a hot Boxing Day night. A group of cricketers fought with a bunch of hooligans who were drinking beer and using bad language in front of women and children. The cricketers told them off for swearing, and a big fight broke out. One of the cricketers got half his ear bitten off. Your great-great-granddad broke up the fight and made an arrest.'

'Well, bugger me,' said Luke, impressed.

'I remember great-grandfather Reginald,' said Hannah. 'There's a photo of him in our family albums. He's looking serious, dressed up in his thick woollen police uniform. He must have got so hot wearing all that gear—and he wore that amazing peaked helmet. You could see he was proud of wearing his uniform.'

'So, people have been boozing and carrying on here for over two hundred years?' asked Luke.

'Yes,' said Cecilia. 'Glenelg is not just a heritage beach resort with a fun park. Even I got caught up in a local riot when I was young.'

'Mum was in a riot!' Hannah was shocked. 'Unbelievable. You're so law-abiding. You wouldn't even let me get kids' prices at the movies after I turned twelve. You could have, because I was so small, people thought I was younger than I was.'

'Yeah, you've always been a squirt.' Luke nudged her with his foot.

'And you're a lout with all that football you play. In fact, football seems to me an excuse to have a riot!' Hannah shot back.

'It wasn't intentional,' said Cecilia, a smile twitching at the corner of her mouth. 'I was a teenager, and I had snuck out with a girlfriend to go to a heavy metal concert at Colley Reserve.'

'What were you wearing, Mum?' Hannah asked.

Cecilia paused. 'Black jeans and a punk T-shirt. It was a Dead Milkmen one.'

'Really?' Hannah stared round-eyed at her. 'Were you a goth? I don't believe it.'

'Well, yes ... it was the fashion. Anyway, it was one of those sweltering nights that make people cranky. Someone started throwing ice cubes, more joined in, and then it got completely out of control with beer bottles and fists flying. The local cops tried to break it up, but they couldn't because the brawl was too big. My girlfriend and I fled the scene; we were so scared.

'The next day, the riot was on the front page of the newspapers. Police cars had been torched, and the local coppers had to barricade themselves into the police station until backup arrived. Sixty-three people were arrested. It was crazy.

'And then some bright spark, an entrepreneur, made up a T-shirt saying, Visit Glenelg—*it's a riot.* The council was livid because, of course, riots are bad for the tourist trade. They mostly fixed the problem by declaring Colley Reserve, Moseley Square, and South Esplanade as dry zones.'

'Making public places alcohol-free has helped,' said Luke, 'but you still get the odd scuffle.'

'I know … yet … this murder has got me worried.'

'Do you think a meth-head did it?' Luke scratched his head. 'Or a psycho?'

Moodily, Cecilia swirled her coffee, looking into its depths. 'If he'd been found dead on the beach, or in a park, then maybe it was a random bashing. But in his kitchen at work? And on a Wednesday night, too. That wasn't cookie-dealing night. They were Tuesday nights, as Hannah has said. I think his death might have been personal.'

There was a thumping sound, and Ziggy and Stardust hurtled into the living room, each one holding one of Luke's football boots in its jaw.

'Give them back!' Luke ordered.

The puppies bolted for the dog door in the laundry with Luke in hot pursuit. He emerged with his boots and turned to the disappointed puppies. 'Grrr!'

'Leave the boots in the laundry sink,' Cecilia told Luke. 'You can clean them there.'

The puppies gave Luke a look with half-lidded eyes before they retreated to Hannah and safety on the sofa.

Cecilia thought of something else. 'There was no paperwork at the café.' She turned to Luke, who had recently completed his training to be a chef. 'Can you do it all on a laptop?'

'Yes, but there are invoices. You have to keep a paper trail with them, especially with deliveries.'

'That's what I thought,' said Cecilia. Had Phil been creative with the bookkeeping at the café?

'Mum's a super sleuth!' Hannah said, smiling. 'With her favourite policeman!'

Luke peered at his mum. 'A policeman?'

'I know,' said Hannah with a gleam in her eye. 'Mum gets around.'

Cecilia frowned at her children. The puppies were now play-fighting and making loud growling noises. 'I think you should take the puppies for a walk.'

Hannah persuaded Luke to help her, and they left with the puppies, who were beside themselves with excitement at the prospect of a walk.

Cecilia decided to make pasta with sweet corn, pine nuts, and mushrooms in a white sauce for dinner. As she stirred in the almond milk, she wondered if she had gone beyond her jurisdiction in wanting to revisit The Vegan Café. Homicide was not part of her brief, but when it came to safety requirements of food outlets, those were her territory. Falls from slippery floors were common, and you could get awful burns in a commercial kitchen. Maybe homicide was an extreme violation of occupational health and safety regulations? Moreover, she was in an excellent position to help the police solve the murder. She knew her community and had networks that stretched far and wide.

Something was driving her to clear up the mystery of Phil's death—and anyway, it was up to Aldo to draw the line about her involvement.

Meanwhile, she would do her own research.

***

I stand at my white marble bench. Neatly lined up in front of me is a colourful display of bright yellow butter cut into slabs, a small brown jar of cinnamon, containers of white sugar, flour, and a carton of free-range eggs. I'm going to make a cinnamon tea cake. It's one of Grandma Snow's recipes. I am convinced Grandma Snow will recognise the sweet aromas of the cake and will find her way home.

Suddenly, a cacophony of loud, muddled sounds surges into the kitchen. Church bells are ringing, sirens blaring, and there is the roar of the ocean on a wild and windy day. I clap my hands over my ears. The onslaught of noise is razor-sharp painful, and it's getting louder—unbearably so. I know my eardrums are going to burst from this onslaught.

***

Like ripping off a wide band-aid, Cecilia was torn away from her dreaming self and found herself crouched down on her kitchen floor with her hands protecting her ears. She looked around and saw the line-up of cake ingredients on the bench and the oven light on. There was a beeping sound, indicating the oven had reached the correct temperature.

It was the middle of the night, and she was making a cake.

What the hell? The enormity of what was happening felt like a slap in her face. She was cooking in her sleep. What if she had forgotten to use oven mitts? What if she went back to bed and the cake burned in the oven, setting the house on fire?

She sat on the floor, hugging her knees while shivering with fear. Her dreaming self was way out of control. She struggled for breath and her ears buzzed. Memories of panic attacks as a teenager floated to the surface. She had to pull herself together. She reached for a long-dusty psychological tool and started breathing exercises to relieve her panic. She sat cross-legged, straightened her back, and began breathing slowly, in and out, focusing on her breath and nothing more.

Eventually, she stood up, made herself a cup of coffee, and invited the puppies to sit with her on the sofa. They snuggled in on either side of her, and she soaked up their warmth. Their tails thumped, enjoying an ecstasy of unexpected nocturnal love.

Going back to sleep was not an option. She could watch TV, but she had to deal with the cake ingredients on the bench first. She thought some more. *Maybe making a cake is not a bad idea.*

She closed the passageway door to avoid waking the kids and put the gas fire on for the dachshunds who were curious about her night-time activities.

As she carefully placed the cake in the oven and closed the door, she remembered something. Opening the door quietly, she walked up the hallway and into her bedroom. Fetching a basket from the bottom of her walk-in wardrobe, she took out her blue memory box. She kept it so she could remember Grandma Snow as a person and not just someone who went missing.

She took out birthday cards, unfolded riddles written in purple ink hidden in paper birds, shook a snow globe, and fingered photos. The photo she liked the best was of Grandma Snow as a young girl in her early twenties. Wet strands of hair, like seaweed, were plastered down the sides of her face, and she was smiling her gap-toothed smile. She was holding a surfboard. It was the 1950s, and it was unusual for girls to surf, but Grandma Snow did. She was radical.

Grandma Snow had always been way ahead of her time. Was that why she disappeared? She wanted to be one step ahead of her Alzheimer's.

Or was it something else? Something dreadful?

3

At lunchtime, Hannah emerged glassy-eyed and wearing her daggiest tracksuit—the bitumen-grey one that sagged at the backside area.

Cecilia eyed her thoughtfully. Mechanically, Hannah reached into the cupboard for the container of muesli, found a big bowl, and poured almond milk into it. She took it over to the kitchen table and slurped.

Something must have happened to Hannah the night before. Cecilia let her finish her muesli. It was better to talk to her kids when they had a full tummy.

When Hannah finished, she spent some time staring into space, then with a big sigh, she brought her bowl over to the kitchen sink.

'You had a big sleep-in,' said Cecilia.

'Kim came around last night and tapped on my window. I let him in. We're going to be friends.'

Cecilia grimaced. Not Kim again. Just when Hannah was starting to get better.

'I think it's a good idea,' said Hannah. 'I've been isolating myself. I need friends in my life.'

Cecilia pressed her lips together. This friendship looked like it was going to be a tap on the window whenever Kim wanted sex. Why couldn't he go away? He was terrible for Hannah's self-esteem. She longed to say something but knew she would hit a brick wall. Hannah was stubborn.

'It'll work out, Mum. Kim's not a bad bloke.'

At afternoon tea time, Angel, Cecilia's younger sister, arrived in her six-seater Toyota. Cecilia stood at the front door and watched Angel's four primary-school-aged children and a chocolate brown labrador emerge from the van, pushing and shoving. Angel materialised next, smiling, oblivious to the kerfuffle her kids and dog were creating. Her blonde hair was tied up in a high, bouncy ponytail. She was dressed in white jeans and a white tailored silk shirt. How she remained clean and serene with all those kids was a mystery to Cecilia.

Currently, Angel was between husbands. She and the kids came most Sundays to visit for an hour or two.

Angel's tribe surged down the passageway to the backyard to play in the fruit trees, which had good climbing branches, while the sisters sat in the front sitting room. The room was filled with fat green and pink sofas, which attracted dust and little nests of mahogany side tables. The furnishings had been their parents' wedding furniture from the 1960s, and the room faced south and did not get much sunlight, so the light had to be turned on. However, on the plus side, it was as far away from Angel's kids as possible.

'I'll fetch our tea,' Cecilia told Angel, who had kicked off her white-and-gold sandals and was curled up on a sofa.

'Watch out for your shoes. The puppies will steal them,' Cecilia warned Angel before she left the room. She cut a quarter of the tea cake for her and Angel and left the rest for her young niece and nephews. While she waited for the kettle to boil, she watched them. They were shooting each other with toy guns, showcasing their fighting techniques, and jumping out of the trees.

Their exuberant activities were even too extreme for the dachshunds, who knew when they were beaten as far as the ability to cause mayhem was concerned. They retreated to the front sitting room with the labrador, Angel, and Cecilia. Angel put her shoes on the mantelpiece.

'Nice cake, Cee-Cee,' said Angel, using the family nickname for Cecilia. 'Is it one of Grandma Snow's recipes?'

Cecilia nodded. 'I thought I would surprise you and the kids with a treat.'

'Grandma Snow's cakes were the best,' said Angel, neatly forking a piece of cake.

Cecilia sipped her tea and took the conversation in a new direction. 'A really strange thing has happened in Glenelg. Someone killed the cook at The Vegan Café the other day. I discovered his body during an early morning inspection.'

'What? You found him? How awful! It must have been a shock for you,' Angel commiserated. 'I did hear something about a suspicious death at a local café on the news.'

'Uh-huh.' Cecilia brooded for a moment. 'When I opened the kitchen door, I saw him lying face-down on the floor. At first, I thought he was drunk, but when I checked him out it was clear that he was dead. I could tell by his lifeless eyes.' Cecilia shuddered. 'He was only a young man, which is such a shame. He had a whole life ahead of him.'

'It's sad when young people die.'

'It was chaos, too. I had the owner's wife, Astra, with me, and she went into hysterics while I was trying to talk to the emergency operator on the phone. I couldn't hear the operator with all the racket she was making. She wanted me to bring the cook back to life with essential oils.'

'Huh?'

'She's that kind of person—new age and drippy-hippy.'

'Do the police know who killed the cook?'

'It's all a bit confusing at the moment. Guess who's in charge of the investigation?'

'Who?'

'Aldo Giovanni! Remember him? He was the policeman who helped investigate Grandma Snow's disappearance.'

'Was he the one with the awesome smile?'

'The same, but thirty years older.'

'Has it been that long?' Angel sighed. The two sisters were silent.

Angel roused herself. 'What's the story with the vegan cook? Did he have bikie connections? I've heard a biker gang has taken over part of Glenelg North, mainly the new housing development at the Patawalonga

River. The bikies lend people money at exorbitant interest rates, and when they can't pay them back, the bikers take over their townhouses.'

'I didn't know that,' said Cecilia. 'No wonder the North looks like a dead zone these days.'

'It's a shame, what they have done to the real estate along Patawalonga River,' complained Angel. 'All those new townhouses look crappy. I am so glad I ended up in Glenelg East. It may be on the other side of Brighton Road, but it's a family community.'

'Glenelg's social mix has a little bit of everything,' ruminated Cecilia. 'You have the tourists, old people in units, families in heritage houses, arty types in cute art-deco homes, and mansions for invisible mega-rich people on South Esplanade. It is like a trifle with layers of cake, jelly, and custard.' Cecilia frowned. 'And one with nuts. They're the bikers, and I don't like nuts in trifles.' Angel agreed about the nuts. 'Would bikies be bothered by Phil?' Cecilia pondered. 'He was a small-time boutique dealer in vegan marijuana cookies. Hardly a threat to the bikie's drug trade. His auntie, who must be pushing eighty, grew the marijuana, and he combined it with coconut oil and then made cookies with it, but only in small quantities.'

'We have an eighty-year-old boutique drug dealer? In our town?'

'She's probably just a good gardener.'

'Not like me,' said Angel. 'I just have trees and grass. The kids would squash plants with the way they play.' She cut herself another piece of cake. 'Mmm,' she said. 'I still reckon it's the bikies. They own the local drug trade, the tattoo shops, and brothels. They're protective of their territory. Maybe they decided Phil was encroaching on it.'

'Maybe.'

'How is Hannah?' Angel switched subjects.

Cecilia slumped in her chair. 'She is now "friends with benefits" with Kim.'

'He came back?'

'Yes, and Hannah is a mess.'

'She needs to meet someone else.' Angel tapped her phone which was covered in silver bling. 'There're dating apps for young people.'

'Hannah needs to find her inner warrior and tell him to bugger off. Then she can move on.'

'Oh, Cee-Cee,' Angel laughed. 'You never swear.'

'I do when I'm annoyed.' Cecilia shrugged. 'How's the dating scene going for you? What happened on the date with the heart surgeon?'

'He had this weird hobby.'

'What was it?'

'Beetle fighting.'

'You're kidding!'

'I know,' said Angel, wide-eyed and leaning forward in her seat. 'It's crazy, huh? Beetle fighting is big in Japan. The beetles are put on a log, and then they try to push each other off. Beetles are territorial. The one who stays on the log is the winner.'

'Does a beetle get hurt falling off a log? Is it beetle cruelty?'

'I don't think so, they have hard shells. But I don't like beetles. They remind me of cockroaches, so I didn't go on a second date with him,' said Angel. 'However, I'm still dating. It's fun meeting different people. Brad didn't like to socialise. He wanted to keep me all to himself—and he was such a control freak. Remember how he went off his face when I brought Chloe home?' Brad was Angel's most recent partner. Chloe, the Labrador, was currently lying in front of Angel and trying to ignore the dachshunds who were licking her face.

'Brad was a jerk,' said Cecilia, feeling the fabric on her chair, thinking she must find time to brush off the dust.

'At least he was a wealthy one and didn't wipe me out financially when he left.'

Angel was part-owner of Love That Bump, a successful online shop that sold clothes for pregnant women and babies.

'I love the crunchy sugar and cinnamon butter topping,' said Angel, taking her last mouthful of cake. 'The other thing about online dating I like is that I go to restaurants. I love eating out.'

There wasn't even a crumb of cake on Angel's lips. 'Aren't you scared about online dating?' Cecilia asked. 'You could meet a psychopath.'

'Everyone does online dating now.' Astra waved her hand at her phone, which was encased in white glitter. 'Besides, anyone can be a psychopath—even a vegan!'

'No, not a true vegan,' said Cecilia. 'Hannah can't even kill a spider. She traps them in a glass and releases them in the park.'

'You can't let fear stop you from getting on with life.' Angel looked fierce, then her features relaxed into her naturally sweet expression. 'What about you and your favourites?'

Cecilia laughed and shook her head. 'You know me. No time for a bloke.'

'Oh yeah,' said Angel disbelieving. 'You just haven't met the right one. What about that cute cop with the amazing smile? Is there a Mrs Aldo?'

Cecilia flipped her sister a finger.

'I remember him now,' said Angel, putting down her cake plate. 'I thought he was the most handsome man in the whole world. I would giggle whenever he spoke to me. He must have thought I was a dippy blonde in the making. How old was I? Thirteen? A crush was such a relief from those terrible times.'

Cecilia didn't remember Angel's crush on Aldo. She had been too busy trying to find Grandma Snow. She refilled Angel's teacup.

Frowning in thought, Angel sipped her tea. 'I saw Inspector Giovanni— Aldo—a couple of years back on TV for solving a murder. I think it was the one about the missing child from the Royal Show. The stepfather did it, but they had to get him to confess because the police never found the body. The child had some rare cancer and the new medicine needed to halt the progress of the disease was going to cost over a hundred thousand dollars. The step-father didn't want to pay for it, even though he was wealthy.'

'I would hate to be a homicide detective,' said Cecilia. 'Having to find a killer as part of your working day would be so stressful.' She placed her cup and saucer back on the tea tray, thinking. Aldo did not seem to be a stressed-out person. He was the opposite—he seemed to stroll through crime scenes, wearing his elegant suits, and absorbing information like a giant human sponge.

Chloe, tired of the dachshunds licking her face, walked up to Angel and planted herself in front of her with reproachful eyes.

'I think it's time for us to go,' said Angel, picking up her handbag and retrieving her shoes from the mantelpiece, safe from the puppies' oral intentions. The sisters and all the dogs walked to the back of the house, where Angel gathered up her offspring and made them take their debris into the kitchen. The cake was completely gone.

Before she left, Angel looked at Cecilia. 'Hey, Cee-Cee, take it easy with this homicide. It's police business, and it sounds very worrying.'

'Do I look like someone who is easily upset?'

'No, but you took Grandma Snow's disappearance hard.'

Cecilia sighed. 'We both did.'

***

On Monday, Cecilia's choice of outfit was her 'tropical trees' frock with a little white lace collar, and her phone was encased in a cover that had a green palm tree on it. She was going for the demure and rainforest-friendly look, mainly because she planned to inspect The Vegan Café mid-morning and wanted to make a good impression. Maybe she would learn something new about Phil.

She rang the café. Swami Nardhamuni answered, speaking in a quiet, pleasant voice. Cecilia explained she needed to inspect the place because there were health hazards and queries about the produce, and she needed to see the bookwork.

'Is an inspection really necessary?' he asked in a gentle tone. 'We're still recovering from Phil's passing.'

Cecilia put on her bright and cheerful voice—the one she reserved for small children and non-compliant restaurant owners. She said it wouldn't take long, that she needed to point out some urgent safety issues and would be there at ten o'clock.

There was a sign reading *closed* on the door of the Vegan Café. Cecilia knocked vigorously. A tall, willowy man wearing a loose cream-coloured tunic and drawstring pants emerged and opened the door. He had wavy, brown, shoulder-length hair and astonishing sky-blue eyes.

'Hello,' he said quietly. 'I am Swami Nardhamuni, but you can call me Swami N.'

'And I am Cecilia Archer from Glenelg City Council, here to do a health and safety inspection on your café.'

'Welcome,' he said, ushering her in. 'May your time here be peaceful and harmonious.'

'Huh?' Cecilia blinked at him in astonishment. She had never been welcomed by a café owner in such a fashion—usually, they couldn't wait to get rid of her. Swami Nardhamuni kept his blue eyes fixed on her. She felt like he could see into the depths of her soul, and she waited, transfixed by his presence.

He gave a small wistful smile and his blue eyes glistened, filling with compassion. For what? Her character defects or for being a health inspector? Cecilia jerked into action, opening her laptop. No-one, not even a guru, was going to make her an object of pity.

She did feel embarrassed, though—perhaps she *was* being nosy. But there was no going back now. She took a deep breath, picked up her things, and began walking towards the kitchen.

In a deep, warm voice, Swami N said, 'There is no need to hurry. Take your time to explore. To hurry is to deny yourself inner peace.'

Cecilia was wide-eyed. This sure was a different inspection, and from Cecilia's limited knowledge, Swami N was definitely some kind of guru. He radiated peace.

Entering the kitchen, which was bathed in natural light, Cecilia noticed that nothing had changed; the fruit and vegetable crate was still on the bench, the freezer full of produce, the puddle of water drip-fed by the freezer, and the medical containers tucked behind the ice cream in the liquid nitrogen drawer. Cecilia wondered what they were. She couldn't think of any additive to vegan cooking which required that kind of freezing.

She opened a drawer to admire the homemade green-cleaning products again. The little rack with the clothes pegs holding silicone wraps was cute, and the flourishing green peace lily in the corner gave its finishing touch to a healthy workplace. What had gone wrong in this divine workplace? The question bugged her as it did when she made the first inspection with Aldo.

She returned to the restaurant area, where the guru was sipping herbal tea at the counter.

She passed him her laptop with the report she had typed. 'I will send you a paper copy when I get back to the office.'

He passed the laptop back. 'It would be easier if you tell me what this report is about.' He sat down on a table, folded his legs under him, and smiled gently.

Cecilia considered the hygiene implications of sitting on a table that café guests would be eating from.

'You need to empty your freezer and dump all the produce. The door was left open for at least twenty-four hours. Plus, it's leaking. You have to get that fixed before someone slips and falls.'

'Yes, the new cook can do that.'

'Are you going to stay closed until you get a new cook?'

'The café requires some healing from this dark event.'

Cecilia told him his pantry was pristine.

'That is how it should be. Purity is the essence of life.'

'I'm not sure about you sitting on a table,' she said. 'It's not hygienic.'

Swami N put his hands together. 'It's a meditative pose, and the table can easily be washed.'

Cecilia decided not to push the point. It had been made. She moved on to the next issue.

'I know it's not my jurisdiction, but I thought you would want to know that you've got coconut milk from a non-vegan brand.' She showed him the can. She'd done her research after Hannah had informed her you have to be careful about what brand of coconut milk you buy.

'Coconut milk is vegan,' objected the guru.

'This brand uses monkeys to collect coconuts.'

'Monkeys!' The guru's eyes widened in horror. 'Please! No!'

He jumped off the table, picked up the can like he was handling a dead rodent, and dropped the can in the bin—then he washed his hands in the sink behind the counter.

'I will not have any animal-related products in my café. There is so much animal abuse and cruelty hidden away in factory farms, slaughterhouses, and animal export.'

'I agree,' said Cecilia. 'It's shocking the way they cram pigs and chickens into cages so they can't move, and then they get slaughtered. What kind of life is that?'

Swami N sighed. He walked over to the big picture window near the front door and stood in a reflective stance, looking at the grey skies.

'Who did the ordering for the café?'

'Phil took care of the cooking and cleaning, and *The Aussie Vegan* recommends products. I take care of the spiritual side of things.' He turned around and waved his long, slender hand at the bookshelf. 'You must read one of my books sometime.'

'I've looked at *The Enlightened Vegan*. I like the cover you chose. It's a lovely picture of a sunrise.'

'We do everything vegan.' Swami N put his palms together in a prayer sign. 'In our own modest way, we are part of a movement that is sweeping the country.'

Cecilia nodded. 'Many people are going vegan these days.' She bit her lip. For some reason, she did not want to upset him. She felt a sense of harmony being in his presence. His voice was soothing, and the café was a charming place. Nevertheless, she had a job to do, and she ploughed ahead. The café was an unsafe work environment.

'You also have a problem with the lack of accreditation of your fruit and vegetable suppliers.'

'What do you mean?'

'In order to make sure no-one gets sick from eating your food, you need to be sure the suppliers of your fruit and vegetables conform to the food and safety regulations. For example, you can get food poisoning from bad bean sprouts.'

'Bean sprouts?' Swami N looked bewildered. 'I thought people only got sick from eating meat.'

'Fruit and vegetables can cause infections. When I made my inspection, there was a box of produce on the kitchen counter with no tax invoice and no name of the supplier. Where did it come from?'

'I don't know anything about that. As I said, Phil did all the ordering—and of course, we only have organic produce.'

'And you just paid the bills?'

'My job is to keep the ethos of the place going. I am providing the first vegan café in Glenelg. I am educating people about veganism and holding meditation classes. You need to realise that veganism is not just a diet; it is a way of life. It's about living in harmony with the world and not butchering it.'

Cecilia agreed with him. However, she wasn't planning to become a vegan because she felt dairy was okay if it came from farms where cows could wander around and eat grass. Free-range eggs were on her list, too. She had a local supplier, an old Polish man, who had a stall at the markets.

'What do you think happened to Phil?'

'Who knows what the universe has planned for us?'

'What?' Cecilia was confused. The poor guy had been murdered. Was that part of some divine plan?

'To be a true vegan, you have to check everything. He brought animal products into my café!'

'I am sure it was an honest mistake.'

'Perhaps,' Swami N sighed. 'None of us are infallible.'

'And the marijuana butter in the fridge?'

'I know nothing about that.' He folded his arms and gave Cecilia a piercing stare.

The front door opened and in walked Astra. She took one look at Cecilia and squeaked. 'What are you doing here?'

'Making sure your café is a safe place.'

'How can you be so cruel as to bother us at a time like this?'

'I am sorry, but I was concerned you could have an accident with your leaking freezer.'

'I can't go into that kitchen, not until we have purified it with herbs and prayers.'

'My wife is a sensitive and spiritual soul.' Swami N put his arm around her.

From under the cover of her husband's arm, Astra played with a lock of her strawberry-blonde hair and gave Cecilia a quick, darting look. 'Why is she really here?'

Cecilia felt a wave of heat rush to her cheeks. She took a few deep, slow breaths while packing up her bag and then resuming her work role, she said. 'I hope my inspection has been useful to you. I am sorry for your loss.'

She turned, picked up her bag, and left. She wasn't going to hang around and be insulted by Astra.

Swami N walked her out. 'Thank you so much for coming,' he said, opening the door for her. 'It was lovely to meet you. I think the work you do is so important, keeping people safe. We will make our café balanced and harmonious again.'

Cecilia gaped, blushed, and then sighed with contentment. It was nice to be appreciated for her work—and then she looked down at her hands, and found she was holding a pamphlet about meditation classes.

***

Cecilia lightly pushed her office door open. A big box was squatting on her desk, invading her workspace. She glared at it. She knew who had sent it to her.

She squeezed her handbag into the bottom drawer of her filing cabinet and sat down at her desk, looking out the window and ignoring the box. She had one of the best office views. It looked directly out onto the jetty and ocean, but because it was so small and close to the reception desk, senior staff did not fight her for it. The furniture in her room was expensive, too. She had a mahogany desk, a leather executive's chair, and a heritage-green tub chair for visitors. The council liked its town hall to look posh because it wanted to create a powerful and historic impression for tourists and real estate values. Glenelg traded on its heritage image, hence its palavers about landmark mansions and icons like the Old Gum Tree and the HMS *Buffalo*.

Most people who came knocking on the receptionist's counter were not wishing to admire the elegance of the town hall, though. If they weren't coming in to pay dog registrations or rates, they were looking for a fight with someone—usually the town planner. His office was hidden deep in the bowels of the town hall. The town planner was not good with altercations—they made him nervous—unlike Cecilia, who was always ready to sail in and do battle.

She opened the box reluctantly, slicing the tape with a pair of scissors. It was filled with posters on how to wash your hands in five easy steps. She was supposed to hand these out to all her food outlets. As well as the five easy steps, this year's poster included a cartoon of a jolly chef with a big handlebar moustache putting his hands under a tap. Cecilia was unimpressed. There had been so many 'washing your hands' posters over the years, she was sure a café could cover an entire wall with them. She dumped the box in the space between her desk and filing cabinet.

It was also time for her monthly report to the council. Should she include finding The Vegan Café's cook lying dead on the kitchen floor in her report? Usually, she told the council little as possible to save herself time and irritation and to protect her food outlets who usually screwed up from ignorance or personal problems. But finding a dead cook in a café she was inspecting was something elected members would want to know. If she didn't tell them, they would make a fuss.

At lunchtime, Cecilia enjoyed a pasta salad in the blissfully empty lunchroom. She replayed her meeting with Swami N. He had made a good impression on her. Here was someone living in her town who was devoting his life to stopping animal cruelty in the food production business, rather than just making money—and he had been nice to her! He'd told her not to hurry. How good was that? She felt calm after the inspection, even with Astra's snide little comments. Maybe having an inner spirituality and being connected to the universe could be a good thing?

She began to wonder about Phil. What would it be like having Swami N as a boss? It would be a dream for a cook not to be told to hurry up all the time. To be able to take your time to bake pies and make sweets would be a welcome change from the frenetic pace of most kitchens, and to have a view was unheard of in a commercial kitchen. While washing the dishes with baking soda, Phil could have looked out a big clean window to a gum tree that stood at the back of the car park.

And yet something had gone wrong in that delightful kitchen. Someone had killed Phil with a frying pan.

She decided to take a couple of posters and walk down Jetty Road, delivering them to restaurants to get a feel for what was happening on the main street.

Halfway down on the other side of the street, she spotted the squat figure of Ian, the parking inspector. He was standing next to a woman who was leaning on a walking stick, pointing with swollen knuckles to a small white car that had a parking ticket on the wiper. The woman tapped her watch.

'One minute over,' she cried. 'I can't walk fast.'

Ian crossed his arms.

'Please,' begged the woman. 'I'm a pensioner. I can't afford a fine.'

Ian smirked and walked off.

Cecilia was disgusted. The previous parking inspector would never have done that.

Back at the town hall, she met Garth in the corridor. He was leading a small white fluffy dog sporting an expensive pink leather collar liberally adorned with rhinestones. It also had a muzzle on its snout.

Cecilia stepped aside. 'Who have we got here?'

'A crazy, rotten dog. He belongs to Councillor Johnson.'

'Is that why he's got the muzzle?'

'He bites.'

'Councillor Johnson's not going to be happy that you've nabbed his dog.'

'This thing escaped and bit a three-year-old.'

'Badly?'

'On the face! The kiddie is in hospital having stitches.'

'Oh, no!' Cecilia hitched her hefty handbag more comfortably on her hip. 'That's terrible. The poor child could be scarred for life.'

'I know!' fumed Garth. 'A few weeks ago, I told Councillor Johnson to fix his fencing because I'd picked up his dog wandering the streets. I gave him a warning because this is not the first time I've found his dog on the loose, but Councillor Johnson—"Mister Important"—thinks he's above the law since he's an elected member.'

'What's going on?' Tristan, the CEO, emerged from the lunchroom. He leaned against the doorway; his brown brogue shoes stuck out from his tight-fitting trouser pants. Tristan was about forty years old and prided himself on being a modern dresser and thinker. 'Why is there a dog in the office?'

Garth scowled and the small white fluffy dog began growling through its muzzle. 'I was coming to see you.'

'With that?' Tristan smirked.

'This is Councillor Johnson's dog. It escaped and—'

'Dogs escape all the time,' interrupted Tristan airily. 'Just return the damn thing to its house. We have an important building vote happening at the council's meeting tonight, and Councillor Johnson is the swinging voter. We need to keep him sweet.'

'What building is that?' Cecilia asked.

'We are going to knock down that awful, sixties apartment building on the corner of South Esplanade The Broadway and build luxury apartments. A new apartment block on the foreshore is going to lift Glenelg's image. We need more prestigious buildings.'

'Unlike Sun-Kissed Motel?'

'That's good for backpackers.'

'And who else?' Cecilia asked innocently.

Tristan glared at her.

'Why is Councillor Johnson the swinging voter?' Cecilia was never shy about asking questions at work. As a council worker and ratepayer, she considered that she had the right to know about developments in her community.

'Councillor Johnson's community platform is to maintain affordable housing and preserve the historic nature of Glenelg.'

'Really?' asked Cecilia. Like Garth, she thought Councillor Johnson served on the council because of his ego.

'I know,' agreed Tristan, misunderstanding her. 'There's nothing historic about that ugly apartment block.' He frowned at Garth and Cecilia. 'Not that it's any of your business.'

'I don't care about any apartment blocks,' snapped Garth. 'This dog bit a three-year-old girl on her face!'

'That tiny thing? It could hardly bite a fly.'

'The little girl is in hospital getting stitches! I'm going to impound the dog and press charges to have the dog put down. It's a danger to the community. Several times I've asked Councillor Johnson to fix his fencing, but no; he just makes up excuses and says that his scumbag dog is his wife's pride and joy.'

'Can't you wait until tomorrow?'

'Are you serious? This is a killer dog.'

There was a standoff moment where Garth and Tristan locked eyes, then Tristan stormed back to his office.

Garth kicked the skirting board on the corridor wall with a few short jabs, and the dog sat down and began licking its bum. 'That little kid could be traumatised!' Garth's beard shook with rage. 'Dog bites are dangerous. I had to show the boss what is going on.'

'Is that why you brought the dog into the offices?'

'Yep.'

'Tristan still might weasel out of it and blame it on the kid and mother. He could say the mother did not supervise her child properly, allowing her child to approach a strange dog.'

'He's a bloody nuisance. We gotta get rid of him,' said Garth.

'Like how?'

Garth had a faraway look in his eyes. He turned and hauled the dog to the back door and out to the car park.

Cecilia followed him out to his van. 'What do you think happened to Phil? Did you know about his marijuana cookie business?'

Garth nodded. 'It was no big deal.' His phone rang. 'Hang on for a moment and hold this.' He passed the dog lead to her. 'No, I don't do bees,' he said to the person on the other end of the phone. 'You gotta get a beekeeper. What? I don't know who pays for removing the swarm. You have to read your lease agreement and talk to someone at the council, maybe someone in Community Services. Do you want the name of a beekeeper? I can send you one.' Garth scrolled through his list of contacts, found what he was looking for, and pressed send.

'Who's having a problem with bees?' Cecilia asked.

'Glenelg Tennis Club has a swarm in one of their nets. They lease the courts from the council, so they thought we could fix the problem, and then, of course, it gets passed onto me. I get calls about anything that can fly, walk, or buzz.'

The dog lifted its leg and peed. Cecilia jumped to one side and held the lead at arms-length. She was sure it was aiming at her leg.

'The little bugger,' said Garth. 'Did he get you?'

Cecilia shook her head. Garth opened the doors to the back of the van and put a water bowl in one of the cages. He retrieved the lead from Cecilia and placed the dog into the cage. 'I'm going to take this one to the depot and impound it. I'm not handing it back to Councillor Johnson.'

Cecilia waited until the dog was safely stashed away. 'Do you think Phil was stepping on the bikies' turf with his cookie business?'

Garth chewed on his bottom lip. 'Phil deliberately kept his operation small. He didn't want to get in trouble with the cops or the bikers.'

'I've heard the bikies have taken over Glenelg North.'

Garth shrugged. 'They look after their dogs better than most and pay the registrations. Usually, they hang out at their clubhouse which is way down south. Bikers are a reclusive mob. They only hang out with their own. Occasionally, you might see a biker family having a counter meal at St Leonard's Hotel on the highway in Glenelg North, but generally, they keep a low profile.'

'What was Phil like?' she asked.

'Phil was harmless.' Garth twisted a strand of his beard as he thought. 'He'd come to the Broadway with his cousin, John. They were true-blue mates—but different, if you know what I mean.'

'What? Opposites?'

'That's right. Phil never got into arguments. He would go into a Zen-like state when people got aggro from too much boozing, unlike his cousin, who's not afraid to show his fists. John is nuts about football. Oh, and did I tell you he can't speak?'

'Do you mean he's hearing impaired?'

'And mute. He uses sign language. When the Crows aren't playing well, he goes bananas; stamps his feet, waves his arms, and his hands and fingers go wild. Although, he does have a sense of humour. He's a good mimic, too. He does a skit of me, stroking my beard and looking like a wise Aboriginal elder.' Garth paused and gave Cecilia a sly smile.

Cecilia raised an eyebrow and said nothing. Very few people would have gotten away with that. Garth took his First Nation's heritage seriously.

'I bet John is sad,' said Garth. 'I haven't seen him at the pub since Phil died.'

'What about Phil? You said he wasn't a drinker.' Cecilia steered the conversation. 'But a bottle of vodka was found in the kitchen.'

'Maybe he had it for visitors.'

'Huh?'

'He had a few cottage businesses going on. The marijuana cookies, green cleaning products, and some other stuff. Maybe he wanted to be hospitable to his clients.'

'Really?' Cecilia was disbelieving.

'He was the kind of guy who wanted to be liked,' said Garth. 'A people pleaser, which makes it even crazier that someone bumped him off.'

The little dog started barking, upset with its new quarters. By unspoken mutual consent, Garth and Cecilia moved away from the van and stepped up to the esplanade and stood on the lush green glass in front of the information and souvenir shop.

'I've talked to the blokes at the pub and no-one knows anything, except he left at seven o'clock the night he died. Said he had to clean the café because that nosy parker from the council was coming in the morning.'

'Thanks for sharing that!' Cecilia flipped him a finger.

Garth winked at her. 'Girls liked him because he was easy on the eye, and pleasant, but he wasn't cocky. I think he was surprised by his popularity.'

'Where did he live?' Cecilia asked. Her lips felt dry. She reached into her handbag and felt around for her make-up pouch. She unzipped it and pulled out a lipstick.

'You know that yellow-brick apartment block Tristan was talking about? Phil lived there.'

Cecilia paused while unscrewing the lid of her lipstick. 'The one the council wants to squash?'

'Phil said that a big developer was trying to buy him out of his apartment.'

'Was he interested in selling?'

'No.'

'How could he afford to buy it?' Even old and tired real estate on the esplanade was expensive.

'Through the government's first-home-buyer scheme. He worked and saved hard to buy the flat. He had a big mortgage, which is why he had all these sideline businesses.'

Cecilia ran the lipstick around her mouth and then smacked her lips. 'Phil would have been under pressure to sell.'

Garth stared beyond the thirty-odd cars parked in the council's car park and out to the azure blue sea. 'It was getting him down. He said he had visits from the developers, men in suits and ties offering him a good sale price for his unit.'

The dog's barking in the van was reaching a crescendo, causing passers-by to stop and look at the van.

'I gotta go,' said Garth. 'That little bugger is going psycho. But don't worry Cecilia; I'm going to look into this. These developers, they're mongrels. Always trying to take over our town and bulldoze it for big quick money.'

Cecilia made a mental note to give Aldo a call. There was a hell of a lot of money tied up on South Esplanade's real estate. Millions of dollars. The developers needed to be checked out. As a daughter of real estate agents, she knew that some of them existed on dubious money.

***

Cecilia sat in Dr Davidson's office, pressing her forest-green handbag against her tummy. His office was in the eastern suburbs of Adelaide, about twenty minutes' drive from Glenelg. Cecilia wanted to be discreet. She was embarrassed about seeing a psychiatrist, and it had taken a lot of inner arguments before she was able to make the appointment.

She looked around his office. It was cluttered with amateur drawings and paintings—presumably from patients—a bust of a famous Greek philosopher, and big, heavy medical books lined the shelves.

'How can I help you?' Dr Davidson asked quietly.

'I'm sleepwalking again and doing dodgy things. I haven't done that for years—not since I was a girl.'

'What sort of dodgy things?'

'Cooking,' Cecilia paused, feeling giddy from the memories. 'I was halfway through making a cake, and I had the oven turned on when I woke up.'

Dr Davidson nodded. 'That is a serious problem and unsafe behaviour.'

'I know,' said Cecilia, a little irritated at having her behaviour spelt out. She was an environmental safety officer, for goodness sake. She knew kitchens could be dangerous places. 'That's why I'm here.'

'When you were a girl, what happened?'

'My sleepwalking started when my grandma officially became a missing person. I would wake up curled in a ball next to the rocks on the beach. It was scary. I felt so vulnerable, and I never want to feel like that again. My parents had to deadlock the house at night to keep me in and they hung bells over my bedroom door.'

'What happened the day your grandmother disappeared?' Dr Davidson asked.

Cecilia winced. These memories were painful.

'The back door slammed, and Grandpa came bursting into our house, shouting that Grandma Snow had vanished and she had left a cinnamon cake in the oven. He was gasping for breath and crying big, soggy tears. I'd never seen an adult lose it like that before. My sister and I scoured Glenelg; walked up and down the beach, questioned people, and asked at the corner shop. Mum and Dad phoned all the relatives, Grandma Snow's friends, and eventually the police. We kept hoping she would suddenly appear in the kitchen as if nothing had happened—but she didn't. She never came back.'

Dr Davidson was silent.

Cecilia soaked up a tear with a tissue from the box stationed next to her chair. 'It took me a long time to accept she had gone. I must have pasted every pole in Glenelg with her missing posters.'

'Did you have medical treatment for the sleepwalking?'

'Anti-depressants and sleeping pills, which I binned when I was in my mid-twenties and living in London.'

'Has something recently happened to you that is out of the ordinary?'

She smoothed the straps on her green bag. Did she really need to be here?

'The other day, I found a young man lying dead on the kitchen floor of a café. I had gone there for an inspection., At first, I thought he was drunk, but then it turned out to be homicide. Someone bashed him with a frying pan, and the police don't know who did it.'

'It must have been a terrible shock.'

'Yes.' Cecilia looked away from him to a watercolour painting of a child. Half of her face was washed out in hues of blue and fading away as if part of her was missing.

'And?' Dr Davidson was watching her.

She felt like she was under a microscope. 'It does bother me that the café's cook's death is unexplained, which is why I am helping with the investigation. I don't want another goddamned mystery in my life. There's got to be an explanation and justice for the poor man.'

'You could have post-traumatic stress disorder,' says Dr Davidson. 'This unexplained homicide could be a trigger for your PSTD, and that's why you sleepwalk.'

'Why? I feel sorry for Phil, the cook, but I didn't know him. He is a stranger, whereas I loved my grandma. I spent a big chunk of my childhood in her kitchen.'

Dr Davidson was silent.

Cecilia felt the need to explain herself and show him she was competent. 'I understand that Grandma Snow's disappearance was the initial cause of my anxiety and sleepwalking, but I thought I had done my grieving. I'm not someone who hangs onto stuff.'

'It's not grief; it's trauma,' Dr Davidson said. 'It's the ambiguity of not knowing what happened that plays havoc with your mind. No-one can tell you what really occurred. How can you grieve without knowing?'

'Are you saying that until there is a resolution to the cook's killing, I'm going to do crazy things in my sleep? It's like a trigger for my PTSD?'

'I can prescribe anti-anxiety medication and refer you to a psychologist who is very good with PSTD sufferers. We've come a long way in treating this since the 1980s. Do you think sleeping pills would help?'

Cecilia pulled a face. She was wary of drugs. They made her feel hazy and as if she was sleepwalking through life, although that was exactly why she was here: to stop sleepwalking!

Dr Davidson signed the scripts. 'You also need things to wake you up when you are sleepwalking,' he said. 'Hanging a bell over your door is good. There are also sensor pads you can put beside your bed. They give your feet a buzzing sensation when you step on them.'

Cecilia walked out of his office, clutching her scripts. She was neither happy nor sad. Instead, she was seized with a grim determination; she was not going to let her subconscious screw up her life again.

Crap happened, that was all.

4

Today's phone cover was decorated in yellow and black stripes, the Tigers' football colours, which Luke had given to her last Christmas. The case was not her style but she didn't want to offend him, so she used it from time to time. It was 8.40 am, and Cecilia sat in her office. She yawned and stretched, thinking about the high-rise housing development in Glenelg.

She wondered if she could get information from her parents. After making a comfortable living from selling real estate now, in their retirement, they lived on the South Esplanade in a penthouse apartment at the Stamford Grand Hotel. They were, however, currently cruising Scandinavia, and knowing her parents' enthusiasm for prestigious high-rise developments and their pride in living in the iconic Grand hotel, they would not give a toss about the old sixties apartment being squashed for something new.

She fired up her computer, searching through building agendas from the council's meetings and finding the drawings of the proposed high rise. They promised an impressive building with historical overtones. It was a sandy colour and had ample balconies, surrounded by a black laced balustrade—nothing like the black-glassed affairs that were the trend in cities.

She rang Aldo with the news about Phil causing difficulties for developers and the council.

'That's interesting,' said Aldo. 'Do you know the name of the developer?'

'Neptune.'

'Thanks. I will give this lead to Hugh—Inspector Davidson—to research. He's my partner.'

The one with the superhero jaw, thought Cecilia.

'Anyway, how are you?' Aldo asked. 'I'm sorry I haven't had time to take you out to lunch. Work is busy-busy.'

'That's okay, Aldo, you don't have to worry about me. I just want to help you with the investigation.'

'*Grazie,* but we must meet soon.'

Cecilia looked over the top of her computer and out to sea. The waves were choppy, making café latte swirls, triggering her need for a decent coffee. Aldo had thrown her off course. Apologising for not taking her out to lunch? That came out of the blue. She did not know what to think. She thought she was simply giving him information about the case.

Cecilia popped out to the bakery across the road and got a large-sized takeaway coffee and took it back to her office. She needed to focus. She fired up Google and checked out local bikie gangs, coming up with a sizeable list of criminal behaviour, but it seemed more like bikie-on-bikie violence.

She then changed her focus to Neptune, the would-be developers of Phil's apartment block. They were big players and had built high rises in most of the capital cities of Australia. Would they have exerted pressure on Phil to agree to sell? Was he offered money or physical threats?

Developers or bikies? Did they kill Phil?

Cecilia pushed her chair back from her desk and swivelled it in frustration.

***

After a regional meeting with health and environmental officers from the southern councils, where nothing much new was said, Cecilia pulled up in the council car park as Ian was getting off his motorbike. She pretended not to see him, hoping he would leave her alone. She switched on her phone and began playing a game of bridge.

Ian tapped on her window. Grudgingly, she got out of her car. He stood at eye level with her, and Cecilia screwed up her nose; he smelled of sour sweat.

'Guess how much money I made today for the council?' His upper lip was quivering with glee. 'I made two thousand and ninety dollars!'

She shook her head dismissively. 'Traffic control is not about making money. It's about having safe road traffic and supporting local businesses.'

'The CEO will be delighted to have the extra income. That old parking inspector was piss-weak.'

Cecilia shook her head again, this time in disgust. 'Bugger off, Ian!' she snapped and stalked off.

As she passed the lunchroom, Tristan called out to her. He was sitting at the table with his laptop on show, surrounded by a small group of bored staff. 'Come and have a look at my holiday pictures!'

Reluctantly, she had a quick peek of Tristan and his family standing in the foyer of an expensive-looking hotel in Noosa. 'Must dash, I've phone calls to make,' she told Tristan, hurrying away.

She walked down the corridor, and Garth called out to her from his cubicle. She walked in and sat down on a chair without arms, squeezed into a corner. Space was at a premium in Garth's office, which was fine by him because it was out of the public eye.

'I have some news for you,' said Garth. 'Last night, I spoke to one of the guys at the pub, Old Ron. He's a cameleer and has been around Glenelg forever. He knew Phil quite well because they were both fanatical Crows supporters. I only had a quick chat with Ron, because he was leaving early the next day for a road trip to the Northern Territory to see a man about a camel. Anyway, what was really interesting is that Ron said that he had visited Phil on the night of Phil's murder. He said that Phil was in a very good mood and had told Old Ron that he was making a tree change and leaving Glenelg to go work in the Clare Valley with his new girlfriend.'

Clare Valley? That's where she and Aldo went. *And what a nice day that had been,* she thought dreamily.

She wrenched herself back to the present. 'But did the council and the developers know Phil had changed his mind? Would developers resort to murder? It seems like a corny motive. They have a high profile in the business world. They look posh, not shonky.'

'Corny is real,' said Garth. 'Remember the ruckus over the green bins?'

Cecilia did. Council had approved a more expensive green bin service, but then it turned out the business was owned by the son-in-law of an elected member. The elected member was forced to retire, and the contract went to another organic collection service.

She sighed. That meant she would have to troll through the minutes from the council's last meeting again and maybe have a word with the town planner. She looked at her watch. 'It's knock-off time. I'm going home. I'll do some research after dinner.'

***

The next day brought an urgent email from the state health department; some packaged alfalfa sprouts had listeria found in them. She made numerous phone calls to her food outlets.

By the time Cecilia had finished her calls, it was lunchtime. Only Garth was in the lunchroom.

'I've been meaning to catch up with you,' Garth told Cecilia, unwrapping a burger on the lunchroom table. 'You know the house in Florence Street? Number seven? The run-down house neighbours keep complaining about, with all the weeds and the broken-down cars out front?'

'Mmm.' Cecilia had a mouthful of a salad sandwich.

'It belongs to Phil's parents.'

'Really? That's weird. I can't imagine him in that place. It's so squalid, and he was super neat, super green, and labelled everything. I don't think I have ever seen such an organised kitchen.'

'Yeah,' said Garth. 'It's one extreme to another.'

Cecilia and Garth paused for a moment in thought.

'Oh, what I wanted to tell you is that Florence Street got raided last night,' said Garth.

'By the bikies?'

'No, by the STAR squad—the special tasks and rescue group—and two ambulances.' Garth peeled back half the paper of his burger. 'The old lady had a stroke and needed an ambulance but, because she was upstairs, the paramedics couldn't put her on a stretcher and carry her down the stairs, so they called the STAR squad to winch her out from the balcony. They came in with sirens blazing and a big mob of journalists.'

'Why bring journalists?'

'It must have been payback time for the police. They owe the media a good story sometimes. Cameras filmed the STAR squad levering a hugely obese woman out from the second story of the house, then the husband had a heart attack, and another ambulance was called to take him to hospital. The camera crews managed to get into the house and film it. They're calling it the *House of Horrors.*'

Cecilia squeezed her eyes shut, dreading what Garth would say next. 'Why were you called in? I hope it wasn't for animal hoarding.'

'No, my mate, who is a paramedic, called me in to pick up the old people's dog. He felt sorry for it.'

'Did the old lady have her bedroom upstairs? How could she possibly manage to climb the stairs if she was morbidly obese?'

'The husband said she wanted to visit her son's bedroom. My paramedic mate said she was found lying on his bed, draped in Thomas the Tank Engine sheets, and holding a shoebox full of old photos.'

'That sounds sad.'

'The house is uninhabitable,' said Garth. 'That's where you come in. The bathroom was clogged up with magazines and plastic bottles, making the toilet and shower a no-go area. Some rooms were blocked off with piles of clothes and bags. It looked like they never threw anything away.'

She massaged her temple. 'Don't I get all the treats?'

'Yeah, and there are pictures of the choked-up rooms all over the news channels and on the internet. There will be a lot of stickybeaks coming to look at the house.'

'How's the dog?' she asked, playing for time. There was a whole lot of trouble coming her way and no getting out of it.

'He's a corgi—fat and very friendly. The paramedics had difficulty getting Mr Dyson into the ambulance. He did *not* want to leave his dog. I promised him I would arrange to board the dog until he and his wife came out of the hospital.'

'That's nice of you.'

'He's a sweet old dog.'

'But living in squalor?'

Garth frowned. 'I walked through the house and out the back to fetch the dog. There was no shit lying around the house. They must have had some system to get rid of it in the outside laundry. I think the blue bin was operational. There were bags of what looked like poo in it.'

'For both dog and human?'

'Possibly.'

Tristan popped his head around the lunchroom door. 'I would like a word with you, Cecilia, when you've finished.'

Garth smirked. 'Lucky you.'

She rolled her eyes, rinsed out her Tupperware container, and sallied forth to Tristan's office.

He was tapping his silver pen on his green leather desk pad. 'I saw the news on TV this morning and I was shocked to see that filthy house and those old people living in it. Here in historic Glenelg! It's unthinkable.' He stabbed the pen into the pad. 'I can just imagine the headlines: *Seniors living in squalor in Glenelg!* It will be so bad for our public image.'

'Get the public relations officer to handle it. It's her job.' Cecilia was unmoved.

Tristan attempted to stern-gaze her. 'You will have to do an environmental health inspection on the property.'

'Obviously.'

'Make this your priority. Find out if they had any home-care services so we can switch the blame.'

'Is blame necessary? Surely, it's just human tragedy.'

'The media is always looking for someone to blame and shame, particularly government.'

She looked away, wishing the green velvet curtains were open so she could see the sea. Tristan had an enormous office with fabulous views of the ocean, but he didn't like tourists walking past his window and peeping in at him, hence the closed curtains.

'And what's this?' He shoved the local newspaper across his desk to her.

Council puts up illegal parking signs! the headline shouted. There was a picture of Old Mr Jones standing in front of his kombi van, and next to him, the owner of Sun-Kissed Motel with his hands in his pockets and a turned-down mouth.

She skimmed the paragraphs. Mr Jones was doing his civic duty, finding illegalities, and the Sun-Kissed Motel owner was being harassed.

'Ian said you had suggested the idea.'

'It's not my fault Ian was stupid and put signs up without permission.'

'You're the senior officer here.'

'Traffic control is not my jurisdiction. We were only floating the notion in the lunchroom.'

Tristan swivelled in his over-large leather chair. 'Make sure you fix up that mess in Florence Street as soon as possible.'

Cecilia was deep in thought as she walked down the passageway and past the toilets. There were so many connections. But how did they explain the cook's death?

'Help! Help!'

Startled, Cecilia stopped. The cries were coming from the men's toilets. She opened the door and there was Garth. He had Ian up against a wall, holding him there by the scruff of his shirt. Ian's shoes were dangling in the air.

'This is workplace harassment,' Ian spluttered. 'You're a witness, Cecilia!'

'Am I?' She was calm. 'Here I was thinking you and Garth were having a friendly man-to-man chat.'

'Lay off Percy the parrot! And leave your ex-wife alone. No more threats!' Garth roared, shaking Ian. 'If anything happens to that bird, like poisoning or disappearing, you'll be charged—and there'll be a lot of publicity about you and cruelty to pets. I'll make sure of that, you little arse-wipe!'

'I was only kidding. My wife knows I wouldn't do anything like that.'

'Your ex-wife, you mean.'

'You don't understand,' he whined. 'We love each other.'

Cecilia closed the door and walked away. It was none of her business, and she did not want to be a witness to Garth's unorthodox methods of solving Percy the parrot's problems.

Not long after, Garth poked his head around Cecilia's office door.

'You've had a busy morning,' she said. 'Dealing with the dog from Florence Street, and now the parking inspector.'

'Do you mind if we shut the door? I want to talk to you about what happened.'

'I'm not sure what I saw. I don't normally go into the men's bathroom.'

'Ian is a real scumbag. His ex-wife, Jessie, ran away from him. She works with my missus, Daphne, at Marigolds Nursing Home. Daphne told me all about Jessie and Ian. He's an abuser.'

Cecilia grimaced. 'Why am I not surprised?'

'Jessie has tried to leave him several times, but he makes her come back. Then she met someone at a meditation workshop. They took a shine to each other, and it gave her the confidence to leave Ian. Ian's a vicious drunk, though, so Jessie decided to move across town to a cheap holiday rental. Unfortunately, Ian tracked her down through the nursing home network, and he threatened to kill her pet parrot if she did not come back to him.'

'How revolting.'

'Daphne's asked me to sort Ian out.'

Cecilia nodded, having confidence in Garth despite—or perhaps because of—his unorthodox methods of shirt-fronting someone as a problem solver. 'Let's hope Percy the parrot and Jessie are now safe.'

'And there's more interesting info to come!' Garth leaned forward in his chair, his eyes glittering. 'Guess who she met at the workshop?'

'I have no idea.'

'Phil! I only found that out from Daphne last night. We got talking about Jessie, and Daphne mentioned she'd met a guy called Phil, and so we started joining the dots. Daphne said Jessie met Phil a couple of months ago and it was love at first sight. Everything seemed to be going sweet, except Ian began harassing Jessie, threatening her parrot and all that. I figure that's why Phil and Jessie were going to move to Clare Valley: Jessie wanted to move far away from Ian.'

Cecilia's eyes widened.

'So, my Daphne gives Jessie a call to see if she's okay and finds out Jessie has fallen apart and is hiding in a caravan park. Jessie is terrified Ian has somehow discovered she was dating Phil and is wondering if Ian bashed Phil. Daphne and I want her to come stay with us until things settle down.'

'You have to tell the police. Detective Aldo Giovanni is in charge of the case. I can give you his mobile number. Maybe Ian killed Phil in a jealous rage?'

'I don't like to dob, but—'

'No buts! Ian is violent. Not only does he abuse Jessie, but he also gets into punch-ups and brawls over parking disputes.'

Garth nodded, heaved himself out of the chair, and left.

Cecilia reapplied her lipstick without the aid of a mirror; she was an expert. How creepy to have shared a lunchroom with Ian. She had always thought he was revolting—and now it looked like he was a killer.

Her phone buzzed. It was the CEO demanding to see her. Not again. She sailed into Tristan's office.

'I believe you were a witness to workplace harassment. Ian has reported Garth for assault.'

Cecilia said nothing.

'Haven't you got anything to say? Where's Garth? He is not answering his phone.'

'Maybe he is talking to the RSPCA about Ian. Or the police? There have been some issues involving Ian and a parrot.'

'What?' Tristan spluttered, his eyes popping in shock. 'Not the RSPCA. Oh my god! Think of the publicity. Cruelty to animals is worse than hoarding. It's going to look so bad for Glenelg's image as a nice holiday spot. What has Ian done?'

Cecilia shrugged.

Tristan shook himself. 'I've always thought there was something dubious about Ian, but it has nothing to do with the council. We'll distance ourselves from whatever it is.'

***

For several days, Cecilia enjoyed some unexpected tranquillity at the office. The police were hanging on to the Florence Street keys, and the receptionist told her Ian had phoned in saying he had the flu. Garth was out of action, too, and the CEO. It seemed as if half of the town hall had come down with the flu, and so issues of harassment, squalid houses, and threats to birdlife were temporarily abandoned. Quietly, Cecilia hoped Ian was being nailed for Phil's murder.

She did her job, trying hard not to think what Aldo meant about having lunch, and thrusting away unwelcome visions of Ian bashing Phil with a saucepan. Hopefully, Aldo had arrested him, and he was safely locked away.

One morning, towards the end of the week, the sky was blue, and the sun had come out for a look. Cecilia felt like she needed to get out of the office and take in some fresh air. She retrieved her black handbag with the brass buckles from the bottom drawer of her filing cabinet and set out for a stroll down Jetty Road. She planned to check if any cafés were opening or closing; Jetty Road shops had a moderate change-over rate. She also wanted to drop into Vince's fruit and veg shop to make sure Vince had received the message she had left on his phone about listeria being found in alfalfa sprouts.

Halfway down Jetty Road, she saw Ian in uniform standing on the driver's side of a car. What the hell? Why was he out on the streets? And in uniform, too. She thought he would be locked up by now.

She watched him open the car door and pull a woman out by the arm. He shook her violently and hissed something into her ear.

Cecilia's temper flared, and she was onto Ian in a moment. 'What are you doing? Physically harassing a woman is a criminal offence.'

'Piss off, Cecilia,' Ian sneered. 'It's none of your business.'

She took out her mobile phone. 'I'm calling the police.' It was a sure bet the woman from the car was Jessie, his ex-wife.

'Don't bother,' he sneered. 'I'm just telling her that I'm talking to a divorce lawyer.' He stabbed a finger in Jessie's direction. 'I don't know why I bothered with her in the first place. She's nothing to write home about. She and her bird never stop talking and squawking.'

'You're such a creep,' Cecilia told him, keeping her phone aloft until he skulked off.

The young woman was crying and pulling at her long, mousey brown ponytail. She wore a nurse's shirt.

'Are you okay? Can I help you?'

'I … don't know what to do.'

'Come off the road.'

They stood on the pavement, backed against a shop wall to avoid the surge of a group of Japanese tourists passing by.

'Are you Jessie?' Cecilia asked. 'Garth's told me Ian has been hassling you.'

She gave a small nod.

'My name is Cecilia. I work at Glenelg Council, too, and I know Garth well. I know Ian, too, unfortunately. What about a nice cup of tea or coffee? We can go to Industrial Coffee; they're nearby.'

Jessie wrung her hands. 'I don't know what to do. He stalks me, despite saying the marriage is over!'

'Ian shouldn't get away with abusing you. It's a criminal offence.'

'I know, but I'm scared.'

'Come on,' Cecilia insisted. 'Why don't you relax a bit? Have some cake.'

Nervously, Jessie looked down Jetty Road for Ian, but he had disappeared.

'Industrial Coffee makes vegan cakes too,' said Cecilia wondering if Jessie was a vegan like Phil. She offered Jessie a tissue, which she peeled off from a pocket-sized pack.

'I'm not vegan,' said Jessie, wiping her eyes. 'And I do like cakes.'

Cecilia steered her into the coffee shop, which in a previous incarnation was a mechanic's garage. The new owners scraped half the paint off the top of the walls, exposing red bricks, and painted the lower part of the walls in a wave of white. The counter was covered in grey galvanised iron, and the floors—being on-trend, of course—were polished concrete. Cecilia was a supporter of the polished-concrete fashion because it was much more hygienic than carpet.

Avoiding the bench and the black metal stools, which were too uncomfortable and positioned in the centre of the café where it was noisy, Cecilia found a table in a dark corner of the room. There was a menu lying on the table. Cecilia handed it to Jessie.

Jessie's tears had dried, and she turned her focus to the menu. She took her time choosing a drink and cake from the menu, eventually picking a hot chocolate with a marshmallow and a strawberry iced doughnut. Cecilia had her usual café latte and a small lemon friand.

Cecilia waited for their drinks and cakes to arrive, giving Jessie time to get her sugar hit.

'I heard you had met Phil and were leaving Ian for him,' said Cecilia softly. 'I'm sorry for your loss.'

'When I saw Phil, I knew he was the one,' Jessie whispered, scooping out the marshmallow from her hot chocolate. 'We spent hours talking, and we had so much in common … but now he's dead … I don't know what to do.'

'What did you and Phil have in common?'

Jessie gave a small smile. 'We liked bushwalking, getting in touch with nature, and we're both followers of Swami N. Have you heard of him? He runs *Pathways to Enlightenment* classes here in Glenelg.'

'I've met him,' said Cecilia, 'and his wife.'

'What am I going to do?' Jessie subsided into tears. 'Should I still move to Clare Valley? I don't know if I can do it by myself. All my friends are here.'

'Ian is going to be a bad memory soon. You're going to shove him into a compartment of your mind and lock the door.'

'Do you think he killed Phil? Was it my fault Phil got killed? If I hadn't been in a relationship with him, he could still be alive.'

'It's not your fault. The police will take care of Ian.' Cecilia snapped her fingers in dismissal. 'In the meantime, put a restraining order on him. Then there'll be no more hassles from him.'

'I don't feel safe. Daphne has asked me to stay with her and Garth.'

'That's a good idea. Ian is afraid of Garth.'

'I'll stay until after the funeral.'

Cecilia put her arm around Jessie, who snuggled into her shoulder like a child. After more encouragement and reassurances from Cecilia that she would be safe, Jessie looked at her watch and decided it was time she left for work.

Waiting at the pedestrian crossing, Cecilia spotted Vince in his greengrocer apron across the street. The traffic stopped to let her cross, and she approached Vince, greeting him warmly as he restocked the apples. She asked him if he got her message about the dodgy alfalfa sprouts.

Vince nodded and said, 'You got to be-a very careful. Contamination can happen when you don't use local suppliers. Vegetables go bad because they go through too many hands. They are seeded somewhere, grown somewhere else, packaged in another place, and then shipped by someone else.'

'Too many players,' Cecilia agreed, admiring a small mountain of bright red apples. 'Although if alfalfa sprouts are cooked, it seems to be okay.'

'Too risky,' disagreed Vince. 'No sprouts in my shop.'

'The same thing happened with rocket lettuce a few years ago,' mused Cecilia. 'That had listeria in it, too.'

Vince had other things on his mind. 'Come and have a look at this!' He led her to behind the counter, rummaged through a drawer, and produced the most recent local paper. It was the one with the front page, featuring Mr Jones and the illegal parking sign.

'Parking inspector. He is in big trouble, no?' asked Vince hopefully.

'He's certainly made a mistake.'

'Parking inspector makes trouble for me,' Vince said, gesturing to the 'No Parking' sign out the front of his shop. 'I have big problems with my delivery trucks. They come at six am in the morning, but nowhere can they park. Why does the parking inspector not say, 'No parking between 6 and 8 am?'

'You could take it up with your elected member. Who is it? The mayor? He should be sympathetic. He has a menswear shop up the road.' Cecilia thought about the parking sign in front of the mayor's shop. It was the only place on Jetty Road you could park for two hours. Everywhere else, it was for one hour; except for the fruit and veg shop, where parking was not permitted. Parking was an ad hoc affair in Glenelg. Whoever had the most influence on the council won the most advantageous parking restrictions in front of their business.

'Parking inspector is a bad man.'

Cecilia's eyes narrowed.

'Every week, the parking inspector takes from poor old Vince a big box of fruit and vegetables in exchange for no parking tickets.'

'How much fruit and veg?'

'A big box. Maybe seventy dollars' worth.'

'What?' She wondered what Ian did with seventy dollars' worth of fruit and vegetables. He seemed to live on packaged protein drinks.

'He brings his plastic box and a list on a piece of paper then goes around and raids my shop. Mostly avocados. Very expensive.'

'What kind of box? Is it a battered red one?'

Vince nodded.

Could it be the mysterious container of fruit and veg found at the Vegan Café? She remembered the scrappy invoice in the box; the writing had been somehow familiar. And then she twigged. She'd seen it on the goodbye card to the previous town planner who had retired recently. She had been the last one to sign and had amused herself by looking at her colleagues' messages and writing styles. Some of them suited the character of the author. Garth's writing had big flourishing strokes, the aged care officer had sprinkled her message with smiley faces, and the parking inspector's script had been tiny and cramped.

'Let me look into this,' she reassured Vince. 'I think we can come up with a solution. He's blackmailing you, which should not be tolerated. And let me tell you, as usual, your shop is tickety-boo!'

'That's me: tickety-boo Vince. Maybe it will be tickety-splat for bad parking inspector.'

Cecilia smiled and walked back out to Jetty Road, thrusting her hands in her coat pockets.

Maybe Aldo had to release Ian because of a lack of evidence. There was now proof Ian had been at the Vegan Café before Phil was murdered. The box of veggies was evidence. Ian must have bashed Phil in a jealous rage.

She rang Aldo immediately, but he was not available, so she left a message.

***

'How's your murder going?' Angel asked Cecilia. They were curled up on Angel's four-poster bed, nestled among clouds of white embroidered cushions and pillows. Cecilia and Angel each had a glass of sauvignon blanc on either side of the bed.

'My murder?' Cecilia questioned, sipping her wine. 'That sounds indelicate.'

'Don't be a prude.' Angel elbowed Cecilia in the ribs. 'I can't imagine you allowing one of your cooks to be killed, and for the murderer to go unpunished. You're far too bossy.'

'Careful!' Cecilia held her glass aloft. 'I don't want to spill my wine on your spotless white bed.'

'Have the police caught the murderer yet?'

Cecilia smiled, put her glass down on the French-styled bedside table —the one with the curved legs and tipped with a small floral engraving. She settled herself more comfortably in the pillows. 'I'm hoping it's the parking inspector.'

'Hoping?' Angel asked.

'He's a horrible short man and a wife slapper. I saw him grab Jessie, his ex-wife, on Jetty Road. It wasn't a pretty sight. I had to step in.'

'For a small-sized woman, you sure know how to fight.'

'Like your Bazza,' said Cecilia, referring to her sister's youngest child and the reason Cecilia was sitting on Angel's bed on a weeknight. It was Bazza's seventh birthday, and Angel had produced a mountain of little pies and pasties, a litre of tomato sauce, chocolate brownies, and a Mexican chickpea salad for Cecilia and herself.

'Tell me more about the parking inspector,' Angel urged.

'His wife, Jessie, had left him for Phil, the cook at The Vegan Café.'

'What a coincidence! And now Phil, his wife's lover, is dead.'

'Yep.'

'How did Phil and Jessie meet?' Angel asked. 'On a dating site?'

'No, at a meditation workshop.'

Angel pulled a face. 'I can't meditate. My mind is too busy with work and the kids.'

'And dating.'

'That too,' said Angel, her eyes lighting up.

Cecilia tweaked a cushion into a more comfortable position. 'Things were going nicely for Jessie and Phil, but Ian was harassing Jessie and threatening to poison Percy, her pet parrot.'

'What? You can't go around killing people's pets,' said Angel outraged. 'It's a criminal offence.'

'That's right,' Cecilia pulled a disgusted face. 'Anyway, the two love birds decided to make a tree change and live far away from Ian. They were planning to move to Clare Valley.'

'Ooh, I love going to the wineries in the valley. They have some amazing restaurants,' said Angel, momentarily sidetracked. 'Do you think Ian killed Phil in a jealous rage?'

'Possibly. The other interesting thing was Phil and Ian knew each other. They had a business arrangement. Once or twice a week, Ian would sell Phil a box of fruit and vegetables—high-quality produce. And where did Ian get his fruit and vegetables? He was certainly not the type to get up early and browse the Adelaide markets.'

'Okay. So where?'

'From Vince's Fruit and Veg on Jetty Road. The one with a bunch of carrots painted on the canopy.'

'I know that place. Vince has fabulous fruit and vegetables, but his produce can be expensive, and the kids only like strawberries. I have to hide the veggies in casseroles.'

'Ian found a way to get old Vince to give him a box for free.'

'How?'

'There's a "no parking any time" sign out the front of Vince's shop. When Vince gets his deliveries, usually about six in the morning, Ian would arrive at work two hours earlier in order to issue fines to Vince's delivery truck drivers. I guess that's when Ian came up with the idea Vince could give him free produce in exchange for unrestricted parking.'

'Isn't that illegal?'

'Yes, it's blackmail. Vince is most unhappy about it.'

'Did Phil know where the box came from?'

Cecilia shrugged. 'I think it was a pub deal. There is a lot of wheeling and dealing at the Broadway.'

'What are you going to do?'

'Tell the police. It's more evidence against Ian.'

Angel gave her sister a sidelong look. 'Which cop are you going to talk to? Let me guess! The one with the most amazing smile?'

'Yes,' said Cecilia, ignoring the tease. 'That one.'

***

The lunchroom had run out of fresh milk. Cecilia loathed the long-life milk that remained, so she volunteered to nip over to the bakery to pick up a fresh carton.

On her way back, past the Pioneer Memorial monument on Moseley Square, someone grabbed her by the shoulder. She spun around. It was Ian with a big smirk on his face.

She smacked his hand away with a quick side-chop. 'Get off me!'

'Ouch,' said Ian, nursing his hand. Cecilia had struck him hard, judo-style. 'There's no need to be tetchy. You'd better watch out, Cecilia. I'm still around, and I could make life very difficult for you. Oh, yes, I can. Your fat policeman friend thought he could pin Phil's murder on me, but he couldn't!'

Cecilia narrowed her eyes and said nothing.

'I've seen you and that cop talking all cosy-like in The Vegan Café while I was doing my rounds.'

'Haven't you got better things to do than spy on people?'

'Our CEO likes to know what is going on.'

'Why hasn't someone locked you up and thrown away the key?'

'Your fat detective had me in the station for hours, just because that sneaky Phil had made off with my missus.'

Cecilia gritted her teeth. 'What's your alibi, Ian?'

'I've got nothing to hide. I did see Phil on the night he got himself killed because I had a delivery for him. He was disrespectful, and I felt like decking him one, but I've got self-control. The police tried to pin his death on me, but they couldn't, because Phil died between 10 pm and 2 am at the café, and I was on night duty, handing out parking tickets around St Leonard's Hotel at that exact time! How about that? It's justice, really. I was the one who was shafted by Phil. He nicked off with my wife.'

Cecilia was seething. 'What a shame you were working the drunks' shift.'

St Leonard's Hotel had a late-night license that infuriated nearby residents. They complained of drunks urinating on trees and shouting at all hours of the night. The council had put up 'No Parking' signs from 10 pm to 2 am around the hotel to curtail the street traffic and noise. It was a lucrative business for parking tickets, but they had had to employ two traffic officers for safety reasons, which Cecilia thought gave Ian carte blanche to beat up drunks.

Cecilia walked off and left him by the monument. She wished it would fall on him and squash him like the cockroach he was. She dropped the milk back at the lunchroom and then headed out again to sit on a bench on the esplanade and calm down. She detested the idea of still having to work with Ian. There had to be another way to get rid of him.

Spring now had a foot firmly in the door, and visitors to Glenelg were returning. Small children were running around or eating ice cream, unemployed youths were hanging out in clumps, lovers of all ages were holding hands, and the usual plethora of seagulls were pecking at takeaway scraps.

A large figure appeared in front of her.

'Cecilia,' said Aldo. 'I got your message, but I didn't have time to call you back because I was busy interviewing lots of people.' He sat down on the bench and looked her over. 'What's wrong? You seem flat.'

She turned to him. 'I've just spoken to Ian, and he was boasting about his alibi for Phil's murder. I'm so depressed! For his ex-wife Jessie, too. She needs to get a restraining order against him. He's an abuser.'

'Isn't Garth looking after her?' He stretched out his arm so it lay behind her on the bench.

She leaned back into the comfort of his arm. 'Did Garth come and see you?'

Aldo nodded. 'He also spoke to the sergeant about Ian and filing domestic violence charges.'

'Oh, good. Garth could be the perfect community informant for you. He's worked all his life in Glenelg, except for a couple of years when he did a stint at Tennant Creek. Not much happens here that escapes his attention.'

'He's useful,' agreed Aldo, '… but he's not as interesting as you, Cecilia.'

She shot him a side-long look, but he had his smile on; the one which looked like he was pleased with her.

'Has anyone ever told you you're a flirt?'

'Never,' said Aldo promptly.

Cecilia scooted away from him to the far end of the bench. She had serious matters to discuss, and Aldo's physical presence was a distraction. 'Did Ian tell you about his business dealings with Phil?'

'Just that he would drop off a box of fruit and veg once a week to The Vegan Café.'

'Do you know where he got it?'

'From the markets, I suppose. I didn't ask. Why?'

'He pinched it from Vince's Fruit and Veg on Jetty Road. Vince told me Ian would stroll in once a week and help himself to about seventy dollars' worth of produce in exchange for not fining the delivery vans; there's a *no parking* sign in front of Vince's. Ian then sold the fruit and veg on to The Vegan Café. Remember the crate on the bench?'

'I do,' said Aldo.

'It's Ian's crate. If you can't nail him for murder, can he at least go down for blackmail? Surely, it's a criminal and sackable offence.' Cecilia let loose her alpha-dog glare on Aldo. 'You must do something about Ian!'

Aldo put his hands up in surrender. 'Leave it up to me,' he assured her. 'Old Vince is a relative of mine.'

'You need to speak to the mayor, Rob Manning. He'll get rid of Ian. The council's CEO is useless and would probably let Ian off with a warning.' She frowned. 'I think Tristan has some kind of deal with Ian. He is always hovering around Tristan's office.'

'I'll take care of it. Relax a little.'

Cecilia watched a family group with a pram, in which a toddler, his face smeared with chocolate ice cream, was fast asleep. His mum was watching her other child climb on the rust-coloured snake, a public sculpture from the 1980s, erected during a time when the federal government funded local councils for public art projects. Now and then an elected member would suggest dumping it because it was ugly, but the rusty snake sculpture had become a Glenelg icon and kids loved it. So, it stayed.

'I don't suppose there is anything in the bikie link. Did anyone hear the sound of a motorbike that night?'

Aldo shook his head. 'It doesn't feel like a bikers' hit, although I am checking with the vice squad. Usually, the bikies just demand a cut of the takings. I can't imagine Phil standing up to heavy-duty thugs. Normally, bikers firebomb people's houses or shoot them. They don't come into a café, share a glass of vodka, and then bash their target over the head with a frying pan.'

'How did you go with the developers?' It was her last shot. She pointed to the row of high rises and stately homes that lined South Esplanade, and in the distance, the pee-yellow brick apartment block, the building in question, glowed. 'Phil was blocking the development until the last minute when he decided to leave Glenelg with Jessie to get away from Ian.'

'The developers knew Phil had agreed to sign,' said Aldo. 'They had the paperwork to prove it.'

'That wipes them out,' said Cecilia, frustrated. 'Who else would have a motive? His family, the people he worked with …'

'It's a complicated case,' Aldo said, as he adjusted a pale-blue handkerchief in his breast suit pocket.

They were quiet for a few moments, listening to the gentle wash of the waves lapping on the beach.

'I not only have a murder, but I also have a filthy hoarder house to fix,' she said moodily. 'The house was on the news. Did you know the occupants were Phil's parents?'

Aldo took out a twenty-cent coin and began rolling it up and down his fingers. 'Yes, I knew it was Phil's parents' house.'

'Maybe that's why Phil was so clean. He must have grown up in a pigsty. My CEO is jumping up and down about the bad publicity and wanting someone to blame. Meanwhile, the occupants, Mr and Mrs Dyson, are still in hospital. I am not sure how I am going to get the place cleaned up.'

'I wouldn't like to have to clean it up,' said Aldo, pocketing his coin. 'It will take weeks and a dozen big skip bins.'

Cecilia sighed. 'The hardest part is getting the resident to agree to get help to clean up, but I am going to bring the council's aged care officer along for the ride because this seems to be an elder care problem as well.'

'My partner, Hugh, says Mr Dyson is going to be discharged in a few days. Mr Dyson is furious about the TV coverage. He says it's an invasion of his privacy.'

'How is the wife?'

'She is still in intensive care.'

'Maybe Mr Dyson will be more amenable to cleaning up without his wife around.' From her position on the bench, Cecilia looked over the little wall that divided South Esplanade from the beach and stared at the ocean, which had taken on early springtime blue hues. 'I need the keys to the hoarders' house. It's an environmental health disaster. I don't know why the police station have delayed handing them over.'

'I had them. I wanted to have a look around Phil's family home to see if I could make any sense of his murder. I will get them for you. Sorry for the hold-up.'

'Oh? You've been to 7 Florence Street?'

'Yes, it was revolting and eerily surreal.' He stood up. 'Come with me. We will get the keys. The sergeant has them. I'm sorry we kept you waiting.'

She followed him into the police station and signed a book for the requisition of the keys. As Aldo walked her back out the door, a gentle sea breeze blew some of her hair loose, and softly Aldo smoothed it. Startled, Cecilia said a hurried goodbye and kept walking back to the office as if the gesture never happened—although, underneath, she was shocked.

Aldo was getting intimate.

***

Cecilia knocked on the office door of the aged care officer, Wendy, who was talking on the phone. Cecilia gathered from the conversation she was arranging a river cruise for one of her clients. She waited until Wendy was finished.

'I've come about 7 Florence Street,' Cecilia said. 'We need to do an inspection. I've heard it doesn't meet residential health and safety requirements.'

'We?' Wendy asked. She was young, fresh out of university, and had a perpetually worried face peeking out from under a fringe of brown hair.

'It's an elder care issue as well. Do you know the residents? Mr and Mrs Dyson?'

'Yes,' Wendy said, chewing a fingernail. 'I did try to see Mr and Mrs Dyson. The social worker from Meals on Wheels told me the deliverers were concerned about their living conditions. I knocked and knocked on their front door, and they eventually answered, but they wouldn't let me in. I stood on the front porch, and they told me they were fine—that the neighbours should get a life and stop complaining. I said I wasn't there because of the neighbours, I was there to assist them, and I offered the council's handyman service to help clean up the front yard. The weeds were knee-high and there were junked cars lying around.'

'What did they say?'

'Mrs Dyson told me to bugger off! It was scary. She was so huge, and she shook her walking frame at me.'

Cecilia squashed her laughter. 'Let's go.'

Reluctantly, Wendy followed Cecilia to the council car park.

They pulled up outside 7 Florence Street. It was situated in a quiet, tree-lined street in South Glenelg, close to Brighton Road, one of the major thoroughfares for Glenelg. The house backed onto a butcher's shop and was a corner block, limiting the house to just one neighbour on the side, thus increasing the privacy of the house.

No media or stickybeaks were hanging around, so it was handy that Cecilia's inspection had been delayed.

From her bag, she pulled out paper face masks and disposable gloves, offering them to Wendy.

'A facemask?' Wendy wondered. 'Did the Dysons have a virus?'

'It's to reduce the smell.'

'OMG! Is this going to be creepy?'

Cecilia squared her shoulders, slung her handbag more securely on her shoulder and, after a little fiddling with the high tin gate, managed to push it open. The front yard was littered with broken-down cars. Cecilia cast an eye over them. All of them had dents or were missing body panels. *Someone was a lousy driver*, she thought and headed for the house.

The key to the front door also required some wriggling, but eventually, it swung open, revealing a long, dark hallway that had a curious smell to it, like someone had gone crazy with cheap air freshener. The lights did not seem to be working. Next to the front door was a small hall table, surprisingly free from dust.

'I think that's where the Meals on Wheels people delivered the food,' whispered Wendy, as if they were in church.

There is nothing godly about a hoarder's house, thought Cecilia. 'Mrs Dyson couldn't have got so obese from Meals on Wheels,' she observed in her usual tone of voice, and she pushed on the door to the right. It stuck halfway. She looked in and saw the room was filled with grey slag-like piles that, on closer inspection, were waist-high stacks of newspapers, magazines, aerosol cans, and abandoned clothes.

'What has happened here?' Wendy looked horrified.

'Well, nothing. That's the point of a hoarder's house. They isolate and do nothing.'

The next room she investigated was presumably the couple's bedroom. There were no sheets on the double bed, just a stained mattress and a crumpled, grungy-looking quilt. At the foot of the bed was a new-looking, clean dog bed.

Halfway down the hallway was a large staircase—possibly made from jarrah wood, judging by the footprints in the dust exposing a rust-red wood. Cecilia climbed the stairs with Wendy trailing miserably behind her.

There were two rooms upstairs, untouched by time. One was a girl's room, and the other a boy's room, presumably belonging to Phil and his sister, Kylie. Old posters of superheroes, lined up neatly in a row, framed Phil's walls, and his bed linen sported Thomas the Tank Engine with the red and blue motif. When did Phil leave home? Or did he have to put up with Thomas the Tank Engine through his teens? The bedsheets were crumpled from where his mother had lain, looking at old photos from a shoebox before she was taken to hospital. Cecilia rifled through the box of photos and picked out one of Phil posing in his school uniform, perhaps on his first day at school. He was an average-looking boy, a bit dorky, and his smile was tentative.

There was also a photo of him and Kylie when they were about seven and nine years old. Kylie had big bunches of blonde plaits which hung stiffly down her cheekbones, and her look was hostile—she was glaring at the camera.

Not much joy there, Cecilia decided, and she stuck her head around Kylie's bedroom door for a quick look. Barbie sheets adorned the bed, and a big, old television hunkered down in the corner. Pink love hearts were pasted to her walls. Cecilia paused, considering them. There was something odd about some of the love hearts; they had been stuck upside down.

Cecilia trotted down the stairs, paused out the front of the bathroom, and adjusted her mask.

'You don't have to come in with me to the bathroom,' she said to Wendy. 'This is probably going to be revolting.'

'What? Oh.' Wendy backed away.

Cecilia folded her arms and surveyed the scene. The toilet seat was rusted out, and the pan was filled with used toilet paper. It was surrounded by toilet paper rolls, unspooling and covering the floor. It was an apocalypse of dried-out brown shit and paper. Cecilia walked out. There was no way that dunny was functioning. She didn't need to test it.

'Am I being remiss in my duties?' Wendy fretted. 'Should I have a look?'

'No, honey, you are not. We just have to do the kitchen and then we are done.'

A tap in the kitchen was still working, but they had to navigate a path through because a proliferation of cake boxes was jamming up the kitchen. Nothing seemed to have been thrown away, especially food packaging.

At the back door was a large recycle bin with a yellow lid. Cecilia opened it and discovered that it was filled with scratch-and-win cards. Cecilia picked up a handful and noticed some of them hadn't been scratched. That was weird. Why would you buy a lottery ticket and not see if you had won anything?

Cecilia tossed them back in. She believed in certainty, not luck.

Next to the yellow bin were a couple of camp chairs and several buckets with razors and shaving cream. In the outside laundry, there was a commode and a blue bin. Cecilia eyed the blue bin with misgivings. It smelled. Cautiously, she opened the lid and then slammed it down quickly. It was full of plastic bags of poo—maybe not just dog poo, but human poo, too. The maggots were in paradise.

Finally, Cecilia scanned the backyard. She could see the top of a big shed, partially hidden by weeds.

She wrinkled her nose with disgust. It was unnecessary to live like this in suburban Australia. It was typical of the hoarders' homes she had visited over the years, with the cat lady's house being the most tragic one. Dozens of dead and diseased cats lay all over the sofas and tables; the old lady had the misguided idea that she was doing them a service and saving them from being euthanised at the animal shelter. However, at least she'd had an operational bathroom and kitchen.

Cecilia would notify the council and say the house would be unfit for human habitation until the bathroom and kitchen were made functional. People could pile up stuff in rooms, but sanitation was a must.

She beckoned to Wendy, who was speechless with horror, and they walked back down the hallway. Cecilia noted that dotted along the architraves were a festoon of brightly coloured caps of air freshener cans, lending colour and even an eerie air of festivity to an otherwise grey and gloomy environment.

They stepped out into the sunshine. Cecilia looked back at the house, then she rushed to the front corner of the yard, ripped off her face mask and threw up next to a broken-down Corolla.

'Are you alright?' Wendy put her hand tentatively on her back.

Cecilia pulled out some tissues from her bag, wiping her mouth. She was thankful for the small water bottle she always carried in her bag. She gargled and kicked some leaves over her vomit.

'Sorry about that,' she said to Wendy. 'When I see something unpleasant, I almost always throw up. It's inconvenient, but I can't help it.'

Wendy's eyes were round with surprise. 'I always thought you were the most put-together person.'

'And now you don't?'

'Oh, I didn't mean to be rude.'

Cecilia smiled. 'You weren't.'

In the car, they stripped off their gloves and masks and deposited them in a plastic bag Cecilia had brought along.

She looked back at the house. It could be a lovely house. It was a building from the 1920s, and the upstairs was nicely bricked with an arched balcony, presumably where Mrs Dyson was winched down in a crane.

No doubt some keen young things would buy the house and do it up, unless the daughter returned to live here. Cecilia didn't think the old couple would be back, despite the husband's imminent discharge from the hospital. A nursing home was a likely destination.

What was it like growing up with parents who were hoarders? Phil must have been lonely, not being able to have friends over to play because of the shame of living in such awful filth. With the secrecy and isolation that accompanies squalor and hoarding, it would have been hard to cope. Perhaps that's why he'd been passionate about cleaning.

Cecilia was no further along with solving Phil's death. Could have he got into a quarrel with his dad? Maybe Phil had told his dad he was a lunatic because he lived in a hovel, and that he was going to report them to the council. Was Mr Dyson strong enough to wield a frying pan?

Not having met him yet, Cecilia could only speculate.

***

I am looking for Grandma Snow's surfboard in the shed. Granddad keeps it there and polishes the wood regularly. It's an exquisite piece, especially carved and made of redwood pine. When I was little, I would lick a finger and trace the patterns in the wood.

But the surfboard is not in the shed. There is an empty spot where it usually stands.

And then I know something is coming for me. Something huge, dark, and spectral. Through the open door of the shed surges a wave of junk. It pours in, burying me under old clothes, tin cans, and lottery tickets. I try to make it to the surface, and I get a hand free, but it's getting harder to breathe.

I am slowly suffocating.

Suddenly, someone catches hold of my hand and pulls me out. It's a young man wearing jeans. I can't see his face. He has turned his back, yet, somehow, I know it's Phil who has saved me from the tsunami of junk.

Panting, grateful, I thank him, but he has disappeared.

***

Cecilia coughed from the dust and woke up, gasping. Her heart raced. *Where am I?*

In a dark place.

Blindly, she felt around with her hands stretched out in front so she could feel for any obstacles. Her feet caught on something square, and she fell, banging her knee painfully. Cecilia's hands scrambled over the thing she had fallen over, trying to make sense of where she was.

Slowly, it dawned on her what her fingers were feeling; the broken vacuum cleaner she'd placed in the shed a few days ago.

She has sleepwalked out of her house and into the shed.

Cecilia burst into tears. She had no control over her sleeping self. It was crazy scary stuff, and her knee hurt; she could feel blood trickling down her left leg.

Why hadn't she prevented this sleepwalking crap? She hadn't bought a bell, because she didn't want to disturb the kids; she hadn't purchased a sensor pad, because that meant driving for twenty minutes to where they sold dementia aids, and she hadn't taken her pills, because they made her feel groggy during the day.

Cecilia thought the sleepwalking was a temporary thing, and that somehow the visit to Dr Davidson had miraculously cured her.

Limping back inside the house, Cecilia took the first aid kit into the bathroom. It was a minor scrape, and she washed and cleaned it, then returned to the loungeroom and threw herself onto the sofa. The puppies jumped up and cuddled in.

Cecilia planned and made promises to herself that it was time to get real, take her medications, and barricade herself in her bedroom at night. Because what else would she do while sleepwalking?

5

'It's not sucking,' Cecilia told the salesman, whose name was Ken, according to his badge. 'And the motor makes a funny clicking sound.'

She stood at the counter of Godfrey's electrical store with her vacuum cleaner on the floor beside her, the one she had retrieved from the shed that morning. She was having second thoughts about buying a new one, not wishing to add to landfill. Australia was running out of space to dump its junk. She was hoping her vacuum cleaner could be fixed.

The salesman looked up from the newspaper he was reading, and Cecilia thought it dated him; anyone under fifty would be looking at their phone.

'Maybe the hose is disintegrating,' said Ken. 'I haven't seen that brand in years. How old is it?'

Cecilia looked down at her yellow vacuum cleaner. When did she buy it? When Hannah started high school. 'About nine years ago.'

'That's pretty old. We could probably replace the motor, but you might find it more economical to buy a new one.' Ken's eyes drifted back down to the paper he was reading.

Cecilia leaned over the counter and had a look, too. What was so interesting that Ken couldn't be bothered to give her his full attention? It was a photo of Phil and an article.

'Are you reading about the poor guy who was killed in The Vegan Café?' she asked.

'Yeah, he came into the shop the day before he died,' said Ken. 'He was a customer I'm not going to forget.'

'Why?'

'He brought his own dirt in! He had it in a Tupperware container.'

'Huh?'

'When I do demonstrations, I sprinkle some baking soda on the carpet and then vacuum it up. He said baking soda was dead-easy to suck up and it was the real dirt that counted.' Cecilia laughed, but Ken was not amused. 'He must have tried every vacuum cleaner in the shop. He was here for at least an hour. I lost two customers who couldn't be bothered waiting. He was comparing eco-friendliness and energy usage and kept banging on about reducing carbon emissions with household appliances. One of the vacuum cleaners couldn't cope with the gravel. It took me half an hour after to get it out of the hose.'

'I sort of knew him, too,' said Cecilia, encouraging the conversation.

'And guess what?' Ken slapped his hand on the counter. 'After all that, he ended up buying a $39.95 natural carpet and floor sweeper. What a cheapskate.'

'You mean the one that's like a broom with a square box with two rollers at the end? You push it around and it doesn't use electricity.'

'That's the one.'

'Did it extract Phil's dirt?'

'Well, yes.'

'I'll have a look around.'

The shop had bright-red carpet that made the white vacuum cleaners stand out, and there was a wide variety to choose from. She was tempted by the cordless ones. She picked one up. They would be easier to use because they were light and you wouldn't have to drag an electrical cord around, but she wondered how long they would last.

Cecilia returned to the counter.

'Can you give me a quote to repair my machine?'

The salesman pulled a sour face but nodded.

'In the meantime, I'll buy a natural carpet sweeper,' Cecilia said, thinking that using it might entail some exercise, which was a good thing, considering her mostly sedentary lifestyle.

Ken pointed to the picture of Phil in the paper. 'He was a pain in the neck as a customer with his finicky ways, but that's no excuse for killing him. He must have really annoyed someone for that to have happened.'

'It shouldn't have happened. Not in Glenelg. We're not homicide-friendly.' Cecilia was feeling flippant after enduring being shown at least a dozen vacuum cleaners.

'What a terrible thing to say!' Ken disapproved. 'Now that Moseley Square is a dry zone, the teenage brawls have stopped. It was a good thing what the council did. Glenelg should be a peaceful place for tourists and residents.'

'Are you a local too?'

'I have had this shop for twenty years.'

And the red carpet, too, Cecilia thought, as she handed over her credit card. She stashed her natural floor and carpet sweeper in the boot of her car.

It seemed like Phil was many things. Fussy and pedantic to some, and gentle and likeable to others.

But, as Ken said, Phil must have irritated somebody badly enough for him to be killed.

***

Cecilia sat at her desk and stared moodily at her computer screen. Her internet search on somnambulism was not making her feel any better. In fact, worse. She'd been horrified to read the homicide statistics of people who killed while sleepwalking. She closed that window quickly and found a video by comedian Mike Birbiglia, whose stand-up routine was about the chaos he created while sleepwalking, when she was interrupted by a text on her phone.

Do you want to get an ice cream and meet on the bench?

She did.

Cecilia looked out the window. The sun was shining with springtime brightness and had enough ultraviolet for her to think about her porcelain white skin. She picked up her straw hat, which had a couple of white daisies adorning the band, and shook it for any dust; it had been on top of the filing cabinet all winter.

Inside the Danish ice-cream shop, Aldo stood in front of the long glass cabinet intently studying the expansive and colourful range of flavours that were on display.

'There is so much to choose from,' he told her, swinging his black fedora hat.

Cecilia selected one scoop of lemon gelati in a cup, and Aldo picked out three flavours—chocolate, lemon, and passionfruit—which were jammed into a cone.

As they walked down Jetty Road, Cecilia said, 'You look like a proper detective in your black fedora hat.'

'And you look very feminine in yours,' he replied cordially.

'My daughter bought and decorated it,' said Cecilia. 'She calls it my *Mary Poppins hat.*'

He elbowed her in the ribs. 'We look like a smart couple, yes?'

They found an empty bench on South Esplanade. Cecilia sat down first. Aldo parked himself next to her, leaving some space between their shoulders.

Aldo hoed into his ice cream, taking one large mouthful at a time. Cecilia was fascinated; he had such a big tongue. When he was down to the last bit of cone, he snapped his jaws shut and crunched, as the puppies did with sweet potatoes.

When her cup of ice cream was finished, she walked over to the bin and threw her cup away. This time, as she sat down, her shoulders were almost touching his. She was still uncertain, unsure if she wanted to walk through the possibly romantic door he was opening. Or maybe it was simply flirtatious. She was cautious.

'Do you want to hear a joke?' Aldo asked.

'What?' Cecilia was jolted from her thoughts of his proximity. 'Huh?'

'What would you do if I stole a kiss?'

Cecilia's mouth dropped open.

'Call the police!' Aldo looked at her face and bellowed with laughter.

Cecilia did an eye roll.

He reached out, stroked her hair, then with a flourish waved a red rose. 'Look what I found in your hair.'

'Honestly?' The rose was plastic.

Aldo folded the rose into a tiny ball and put it in his pocket.

She didn't know what to say. A homicide detective with a penchant for corny jokes. Would she have to be careful getting into his car in case he planted a fart cushion? Or if she got in his bed, would he have short-sheeted it? Good heavens! Why was she thinking of going to bed with him?

Aldo gave her a big smile. 'I'm a magician, yes?'

'It's just unexpected,' she replied. 'Especially from a homicide detective.'

'Even though my job is sad, I like to be happy.'

'Why did you become a homicide detective?'

'I have always wanted to be a detective. I want justice for the victims. My favourite uncle in Sicily was killed by the Mafia, and nothing was done about it.'

'Oh,' said Cecilia. 'I'm sorry.'

He searched her face. 'You seem flat. I thought I would cheer you up. How are things with you?'

'Good, fine …'

'You can talk to me if you like. Not as a policeman, but as a friend.'

Cecilia settled more comfortably on the bench. She felt nurtured. That was the thing about Aldo, he seemed to care about her. However, she was not going to share with him her night-time terrors. He'd think she was neurotic.

'Who are you interviewing now?' she asked.

Aldo sighed. 'That's confidential.'

'Fair enough,' she said. 'This situation has got me beat. Slapping a food and safety condemnation sign is a lot easier than trying to figure out who bashed the cook. Are you sure it's not Ian?'

'Not unless the ticket machine was faulty, which it wasn't.'

'Hey!' She nudged him on the shoulder. 'Look who's out for a stroll.'

Walking along South Esplanade were Swami N and Astra. They were holding hands. Astra was looking lovely with her curly golden hair streaming behind her and her flowing dress swishing at her sturdy ankle boots. Swami N appeared dignified in his white kaftan and loose pants.

Not far from Aldo and Cecilia's bench, Astra pulled Swami N over to the small wall that divided the beach from South Esplanade. They sat down. He got out his phone and fiddled with it while Astra sat on the wall. After fussing about finding the right pose, she chose one with her face turned, looking wistfully out to the ocean. Swami N took several photos, but before it was his turn to be photographed, Astra had jumped off the wall and was approaching the lifesavers' look-out chair. A young man sat there, wearing a yellow shirt and red swim briefs.

Cecilia watched and laughed. 'Astra is priceless! She loves a man in uniform, even one wearing budgie smugglers.'

Swami N remained on the wall, looking at his phone. A young woman with her head down and wearing tattered blue-and-white canvas shoes wandered by and stopped. She looked up at Swami N and, after a few moments of hesitation, approached him. Cecilia recognised her with a start. It was Amy, Luke's ex-girlfriend. Was she now part of Swami N's following?

Amy held her hands together and made a small bow to Swami N—a namaste greeting. He gracefully inclined his head and sat up straight. She dabbed at her eyes and seemed to be talking fast. He pointed to the sky and spoke. Amy put her hands on her ribs, perhaps feeling her breath, and looked upwards at the sky too. Cecilia was impressed. Amy was a highly-strung little thing and would go into hysterics about the smallest of things, like the time Cecilia offered her paracetamol for a headache. Amy had burst into tears. 'Don't you know the drug companies are trying to poison us?'

There was a flurry of golden hair and Astra leapt over the wall, tucking her hand into her husband's. She stared at Amy with her big, innocent eyes. Making another gesture of reverence to Swami N, Amy turned and walked towards Mosely Square with her head higher and looking less dejected.

'Wow,' said Cecilia to Aldo from their bird's eye view on the bench. 'Do you think that's why Astra comes on to young men? Her husband is a magnet for lost girls.'

Aldo scratched his ear thoughtfully.

'I don't do flirting,' said Cecilia. This was a good time to set things straight with Aldo. 'My ex-husband was promiscuous, and it made me feel awful to see him making eyes at other women. I felt as if I was not attractive enough.'

'I'm loyal to my women,' murmured Aldo, watching Swami N and Astra leave the wall and head towards one of the side streets which led off South Esplanade.

'Are you married?'

He swivelled back to Cecilia. 'Not for a long time. My wife left me years ago.'

'You must have had girlfriends since your wife left.'

Aldo nodded. 'There have been a couple, but my working hours put an end to any real chance of a relationship. I would let them down and not be available. They complained they were way down my list of priorities, which is true. What with work and Leon, I don't have much time. But I'm going to make more time. I'm not getting any younger, and I would like to have a woman in my life, instead of dead people. I'm getting out of active police work and am going to be on a task force soon which means I'll be working normal hours.'

'I am not sure if I could squeeze a relationship into my life,' said Cecilia. 'My life is jam-packed with playing bridge, and I love playing cards, and then there is judo, spending time with my sister—we're very close—and of course, my kids, family, and friends take up a lot of time too. And now this murder!'

'I like an independent woman,' said Aldo, giving her a wink.

Cecilia paused and looked at her watch. She should go back to the office. She stood up, and so did he.

'That was a nice ice-cream break from the humdrum life of a health inspector,' she said.

He touched her on the shoulder briefly. 'Is this okay? I don't want to annoy you.'

'I hardly know you,' she said softly.

'Give me a chance and you'll see. I will look after you.'

She flushed from pleasure or embarrassment. There was a voice clamouring deep in her subconscious: *He may not be promiscuous but maybe he flatters women, and you should step back.*

*** *

Cecilia drove down her street, looking forward to a judo workout and then a relaxed evening with Jodi Picoult's new book. She liked Jodi's books because they were interesting, and were mostly family stories about people struggling with diseases and ensuing courtroom scenes. Her novels were like a skipping stone, flying across the sea, the ripples and splashes bringing up unexpected twists—and, most importantly, there was no sex or violence towards women and children.

She was about to pull into her carport when she slammed the brakes on. Someone was dancing in the driveway. She had long rainbow-coloured hair that flew around as she swooped and circled.

It was Hannah.

Cecilia looked around and saw the man from across the road, standing on his front porch, leaning on his walking frame, and watching with a smile. The woman from the townhouse next door, whose driving Aldo had criticised, was peeping over the brush fence, too. The puppies stood attentively at the gate, their ears cocked, looking approvingly at Hannah's antics. Perhaps they thought Hannah was play-fighting.

Cecilia parked her car on the street and got out. She walked to the driveway and waved to Hannah, who stopped dancing and took an earbud out of her ear.

'Mum! I wasn't expecting you home this early.'

'I took an early minute. I've heaps of overtime owing. Why are you pirouetting in our driveway?'

'I'm practising being happy. Driveway dancing brings me joy and it gives other people a smile.' She pointed to the man across the road, who was clapping.

'And the rainbow hair? That's pretty spectacular.'

'I know!' Hannah was gleeful. 'I posted my new look on Facebook, and Kim sent a dislike emoji.'

If rainbow hair could keep Kim away, that was fine by Cecilia. She hadn't seen her daughter so happy in months.

Hannah helped her carry in the shopping.

'I am going to eat late tonight,' said Cecilia. 'I need to start a regular routine with judo again.'

'What's happening, Mum? You seem tired.'

'Work is stressful at the moment, and I need to get fit.'

'Are you going to throw people about, then let them throw you as stress therapy?'

'Well, yes. I'm going to try to go at least once a week. I lost motivation during winter when it was too cold to go out.'

'I'll cook tonight,' said Hannah. 'How about a lentil curry with a pickled cucumber salad?' She was still bobbing around with an earphone in her ear.

'Are you high?' Cecilia asked.

'No, dancing gives you feel-good endorphins. Guess what else has happened? I am going to be a fairy!'

Cecilia blinked. 'What?'

'I got a job working as a fairy for children's parties. It's going to be so much fun. I love little kids.'

'You're good with Angel's kids, and they're a handful.'

'With them, I need combat gear, not a pink tutu and a silver wand.'

Cecilia walked back to her room to get changed into her judo clothes. Was Phil afraid of physical fights? A lot of men and women had no experience with them.

There had been no sign of a scuffle at the café. Had Phil not fought back against his frying pan-wielding assailant? Did he freeze?

Cecilia exhaled deeply. She was looking forward to her judo workout.

***

Another invitation from Aldo arrived on Cecilia's phone. This time it was for fish and chips on their bench on the esplanade.

Cecilia felt a small thrill at the prospect of seeing Aldo again. She spent a little time in the staff bathroom patting powder on her face and reapplying her bright red lipstick.

He was sitting on the bench with a white paper parcel beside him when she arrived. Today's shirt was black with a silky black tie.

'Your suits are amazing,' she said. 'I have always thought of detectives wearing cheap white shirts and old ties.'

'I like to look nice for the victim's families and the community. It shows respect for the loss of a loved one. I will never forget that homicide is terrible and traumatic. Besides, one of my uncles is a tailor.' Aldo tweaked his trouser leg into place. 'So, it's not too expensive for me.'

He spread his haul from the fish and chip shop between them. There was silence while they concentrated on eating.

'How are you?' asked Aldo, emerging from wolfing down half a butterfish.

'Good,' she said promptly. 'And you?'

He lifted his shoulders. 'I had a disrupted night's sleep.'

'Work?'

'No, Leon. He had a nightmare and woke me up last night. He was distressed.'

'Nightmares are awful. Leon is lucky he has got someone to wake him up.'

'Do you have to handle nightmares on your own?'

She closed her eyes briefly, feeling the sickening terror of the drowning dream, and then dumped the memory. 'When the kids were little, I would sneak into bed with them if I had a nightmare.' She smiled, taking the heat out of her memories. 'I can't now. They would think it weird. Although recently, when Hannah—my twenty-one-year-old daughter—was depressed and anxious, I woke up several times and found her lying next to me.'

'Has Hannah not been well?' Aldo asked sympathetically.

'A broken heart.'

'The stakes are high in young love. One feels things more.'

'I guess so,' said Cecilia. 'It feels like a lifetime ago when I was in love.'

He smiled at her. 'Perhaps you haven't met the right man?'

'I did. His name was Ivan, but he suddenly dropped dead in the dairy aisle of our local supermarket. He was a violin-maker and a true craftsman. Musicians from all over the world bought his instruments. He was only forty-five when he died from an aneurysm. He was a sweet, gentle man.'

'How long ago was that?'

'About five years.'

'He was not like me.'

'Well, no. You have wildly different occupations.'

'Which makes it hard for me to compete.' Aldo sought out her eyes.

Well, maybe not. She could feel the heat of a blush coming on. She concentrated on the chips, savouring each salty, crunchy mouthful. She hadn't had chips for years.

'I've slapped an order on 7 Florence Street,' she said, returning to business. 'There was no working plumbing, so the house has been shut down until it's cleaned up and the amenities restored.'

'The hospital wants to discharge Mr Dyson. I interviewed him.'

'Is Mr Dyson strong enough to wield a heavy frying pan?'

Aldo stared at the choppy grey, blue waves of the ocean. 'Maybe, but unlikely.'

'Is he sane? I'm going to have to work with someone to clean up the house.'

'He's just grumpy. He's sane enough.'

'When is he going to be discharged?'

'At the end of the week.'

'He can't go home until the place is fixed up,' Cecilia said firmly. 'Do I and social services have to work through their daughter to clean up the house?'

'I don't think so. The daughter is also estranged from her parents. You might get assistance from Mavis. Remember her? She was the old lady who came to The Vegan Café with a bag of marijuana. She's Mr Dyson's sister.'

'Really?' Cecilia brooded. 'It doesn't seem fair she should be dumped with fixing up that hellhole. She's a bit too old for such a strenuous task.'

Aldo looked down at the parcel between them. 'Do you want any more chips?'

Cecilia thought he looked like the puppies, eyes gleaming and hopeful when waiting for their dinner. 'Go ahead. Was Phil estranged from his parents, too?'

'Mmm.' Aldo had his mouth full of chips.

Sighing, Cecilia said, 'It looks like I'll have to work with Mr Dyson. I don't think I can avoid it.'

'I don't envy you that job.'

'What about Phil's funeral? When are you going to release the body?'

'Don't wear yourself out over this case.' His hand hovered over the remaining chips. 'Why don't you think about me instead?'

'Excuse me?'

'I want you to like me.' Aldo glanced sideways at her. 'You are exotic; a bird of paradise, and beautiful!'

Cecilia shook her head. Beautiful? Aldo must have a vivid imagination. Anyway, he was distracting her from the case. 'What is the story of those strange medical-type containers I gave you? The ones found in that liquid nitrogen drawer in the café's freezer?'

Aldo was silent.

'Am I crossing the line asking questions about the case? People say I am incurably inquisitive.'

'Not at this stage. I will let you know. Currently, I am gathering information any way I can. It's a difficult case.'

'What is in the containers in the freezer?'

'Forensics says it's camel semen.'

Her mouth dropped open. 'What! Camel semen? Why on earth would a vegan cook have camel semen in his freezer?'

'I know. It's crazy.'

'Did he cook with it? Surely not!' She took out her phone and typed quickly. 'Listen to this. There is a cookbook containing semen recipes.'

Aldo screwed up his face, but Cecilia was enthralled. 'There is a cookbook called *Natural Harvest*. It's a collection of semen-based recipes. It says semen is not only nutritious, but that it also has an interesting texture. Good heavens! Oh, and you can find it in most homes.' Cecilia looked up from her phone. 'Can you imagine semen soup?'

'Stop!' he exclaimed. 'Yuck!'

'I don't think he used camel semen in his lentil pies and sweet cakes. I think our cook was a vegan, at least in terms of his cooking. Was he a vegan at home?'

'I got my team to check after you inspected the café. I wanted to see if there were any contradictions, seeing as being vegan requires a lot of rules and pitfalls.' Aldo took out his tablet and scrolled through. He turned to her, shaking his head. 'There was no meat or cheese in his fridge.'

'Who would want camel semen? Why put it in a vegan freezer?'

'The most interesting thing about the camel semen was the date marked on the collection bottles.'

She waited.

'It was the same day the cook was killed.'

Cecilia's eyes widened, wanting to consider possible implications. There were none. It was too bizarre.

Aldo smoothed his hair back with his fingers. 'Garth suggested I pay a visit to Old Ron, a local, and also a cameleer.'

'I know him! He gives kids camel rides on the foreshore. I had to sort him out a couple of years ago. Council was furious that the front lawn on South Esplanade was littered with camel droppings. I told him he couldn't leave the cleaning up of camel droppings until the end of the day, so he brought in a lad to clean up after every dropping.'

'That lad was John, Phil's cousin, the one who is deaf and mute.'

'Really? There are so many community connections in this case.'

'I still can't get my head around the camel semen,' complained Aldo, scrunching the empty fish and chip paper into a ball.

'Have you met the café owner, Swami N? He would have a fit if he knew camel semen was being stored in his freezer. He went off his face when I showed him the coconut milk.'

'Coconut milk? Have I missed something? How are animals involved?'

'Some brands exploit monkeys in the collection of coconuts.'

'Mama mia!' said Aldo. 'You have to check everything if you are a vegan. And yes, I did interview Swami N. It was weird. I've never had to deal with a guru before. I had to interview him twice. He wouldn't answer questions normally and he kept trying to stare me down.'

'You got the soul-searching stare,' Cecilia teased.

'And a quote!' Aldo was indignant. 'He told me if external things pained me, it is not they that disturb me, but my judgement of them.'

She burst out laughing. 'That's good advice to give to a homicide investigator. Don't judge!'

Aldo stood up and took the fish and chips papers over to the bin.

'Thanks for lunch,' she said.

He stood in front of her with his hands in his pockets. They stared at each other for a moment. 'I have to go,' he said.

'Why don't you nip back and confiscate a couple of pies, see if the cook used camel semen as an ingredient?'

'You're not funny.'

She twinkled her fingers at him as he walked off. 'Happy investigating!'

***

Mid-afternoon, Garth wandered into Cecilia's office and plopped himself down on her visitor's chair.

'I'm extremely annoyed,' Cecilia told him. 'Did you hear Ian has been let out of the police station—free?'

Garth nodded. 'He came to the pub boasting about being interviewed by the police and that he had a watertight alibi. I told him he was not welcome to come to the pub. We don't talk to wife-bashers. Daphne and I now have Jessie and her parrot staying with us.'

'I met Jessie on Jetty Road. Did she tell you? Ian was harassing her, although he said the marriage was over. How's she going?'

'She talks a lot to Daphne and cries. It's a sorry business. She's still scared of Ian.'

'He's disgusting,' grumbled Cecilia. 'Anyway, at least I think there is enough evidence to sack him. He was helping himself to fruit and veg at Vince's for free, then selling it on to The Vegan Café.'

'I didn't know that,' said Garth. 'And I don't think the boss knows, either.'

Cecilia put her finger to her mouth to shush Garth. The mayor was at the front counter, looking for Tristan.

The receptionist said he was in a meeting.

'Ring him and tell him to get rid of his meeting. I need to speak to him now!'

'I hope that means Ian's being fired,' said Cecilia, looking at the mayor's rigid back. 'Perhaps Aldo told the mayor about our parking inspector's blackmail activities,' she continued. 'But he's not a murderer. We're still back to the question of who killed Phil. Maybe the answer lies in Phil's character?'

'Phil was harmless,' said Garth. 'Everyone liked him.'

Cecilia asked the question which had been vexing her. 'What do you know about camel semen?'

Garth crinkled his eyes at her in laughter. 'Why do you want to know about camel semen, Cecilia?'

'Is there money in it?' She couldn't imagine it. The semen cookbook had been written as a gag. However, the bottles of semen in The Vegan Café were stored in serious-looking medical containers.

'We have many wild camels in central Australia, the finest ones in the world, but they're pests. They rampage through the country towns and cause a lot of damage. My colleagues out bush have a bothersome time with camels.'

'Who would want their semen?'

'Arabs are keen on our camels. Their herds are so inbred they're looking for new breeds.'

Cecilia picked up a pen and twiddled it between her fingers. Garth was making her work for his information.

'Why would a vegan cook have camel semen in his freezer?' she asked. 'Normally vegans don't have anything to do with animal products.'

Garth smiled knowingly. 'You found the camel semen?'

Her eyes narrowed. 'You know about it. Come on, tell me.'

'You need a special type of freezer to store it. Some commercial freezers have liquid nitrogen drawers, which are the best place to store semen. The Vegan Café is the only place known in Glenelg to have a liquid nitrogen drawer, apart from medical facilities. Phil was very proud of his new freezer, which he had persuaded the owners to buy.'

'But Phil was a vegan. He would be horrified by having animal products in his kitchen.'

'Maybe he didn't have a choice.' Garth gave her a wink.

'Why?'

'Coercion,' said Garth. 'Old Ron tried to pay Phil to store the semen, but Phil, being a true-blue vegan, refused. So, Ron had to resort to exerting a little pressure on him.'

'How was Phil coerced into keeping camel semen in his freezer?'

'I am guessing Ron must have threatened Phil with going to the media about his parents living in filth. The media loves a hoarder story.'

'How did Ron know about 7 Florence Street?'

'The pub grapevine. Most of the locals know about it. Phil was frightened of the publicity. He was a clean freak and guarded that reputation. Ron said Phil eventually accepted a little cash for storage.'

'What's so special about the camel semen?'

'Old Ron harvests it.' Garth lounged back in his chair, looking pleased with himself. 'There's money to be made from camel semen.'

Cecilia leant forward, giving him a menacing look. He was being provocative.

'Ron may be eccentric, but he knows everything about camels. He keeps them clean, fit, and healthy. They live better than he does. And Ron's proud of his dummy female camel,' Garth said slyly.

'What's that?'

'A dummy camel is made for collecting semen. Old Ron made it himself. He's an inventor, too. He showed it to me; it's got fur, a head, and a back. Old Ron even managed to get the neck and head to move, because that's what male camels like. Kneeling and a bit of head-waving. It gets male camels excited. He uses the dummy to harvest semen, which he sells to the Arabs.'

'Oh, no!' Cecilia was regretting this conversation.

'Oh, yes,' said Garth. 'Male camels have a low reproductive rate. They only come into season for about three months a year. Usually getting their sperm takes about eight people with a high chance of being bitten. It's much easier to use a dummy female camel with a foam vagina. That way, you can catch the sperm without being bitten.'

'Well!' said Cecilia. 'I've learnt more about camels than I ever thought possible.'

'Uh-huh.'

'What time did Old Ron visit Phil?'

'I'm not sure. I left the pub before Ron did. Maybe at nine o'clock.'

'Could Ron have bashed Phil with a frying pan?'

'Why would he? Now he doesn't have access to the liquid nitrogen drawer.'

Cecilia turned away from him and looked out her window to the fat creamy white clouds hovering over the blue ocean. 'It gives me the creeps to think we have a murderer on the loose in our hometown. It should have been Ian.'

'It's a big stretch to go from dodgy dealing to killing. I think it was a random bashing.'

Cecilia turned back to Garth. 'Maybe, but it still makes his death awful. Phil had a lot more living to do, and someone took that away from him.'

***

There were voices in the background as Cecilia waited for Mr Dyson to answer the phone from his hospital bed. Finally, the nurse's apologetic voice came through, saying Mr Dyson refused to take phone calls.

Perhaps he thought she was a journalist, or, more likely, he was isolating himself. Hoarders were not social creatures. Nevertheless, she had to inform him about the sanitation order on his house.

She knocked on the door of Wendy's office. Wendy was wearing earbuds, and on her screen was a picture of Swami N standing by a waterfall. Wendy removed her earbuds and turned an innocent face to Cecilia.

'Is that one of Swami N's podcasts?' Cecilia asked.

'Yes, do you know him?' breathed Wendy. 'He's wonderful. I go to his classes on Tuesday nights at the community centre.'

'He's courteous,' Cecilia deliberated. 'And I can imagine his classes would make you feel more peaceful.'

'He's changing my life! He's giving me the confidence to be the real me.'

'That's nice,' said Cecilia. 'Talking of changing lives, we have to do something about the Dysons' habitat. I need to see Mr Dyson today. I've tried phoning him, but he refused to talk to me. The hospital is going to discharge him soon, and he must know I've slapped an order on his house.'

'Where will he go? Isn't that a bit harsh, keeping him out of his own home?'

'Harsh? You saw the state of the house. The toilets weren't working, and the kitchen was unusable!'

'But they did have Meals on Wheels.'

Cecilia shook her head. What planet was Wendy on? One with a waterfall and no disgusting toilets, obviously. 'In Australia, we have legal standards for sanitation. Functional bathrooms and kitchens are essential. Otherwise, diseases will spread.'

Wendy looked miserable. 'Am I going to have to find him somewhere to live while his place gets cleaned up?'

'Isn't that elder care?'

'I've never done anything like that before.'

'We'll think of something.'

Wendy gave her a weak smile. 'Normally, I organise volunteers to drive the community bus, or take old people out on outings, and the new elder travel program is proving popular.'

'Elder travel?'

Wendy brightened up. 'Elder travel is when you team up a frail aged person with a volunteer. They go on short trips, like a riverboat cruise, or a tour bus trip. It's a lovely program.'

'There you go! Put our old man from Florence Street on a boat while his place gets cleaned up.'

'Unfortunately, not all of our elderly citizens can find travel companions.'

'Because they're crazy?'

Wendy was horrified. 'We don't use words like that. We say our clients have challenging behaviours.'

'I'll pick you up in an hour.'

Cecilia returned to her office and rang Aldo. 'Mr Dyson is being discharged soon. He can't move back home until it's cleaned up and the plumber and the electrician have been. It's a big job. It will take weeks to fix. What's the phone number of Auntie Mavis? Isn't she's a relative of the Dysons? Maybe she will take him in?'

'Cee-Cee, I can give you her name, but not her phone number … but you can find it in the white pages.'

'Sorry, I forgot about privacy regulations. A name will do just fine.' Cee-Cee? He had started using the nickname that only her sister used. What was happening here?

'Thanks,' she managed to say.

'Wait,' he added. 'For your clean-up, you need to know the old man made a lot of money during his working life. He was a well-known jeweller.'

'Oh no!' she howled. 'I'm not going to spend three weeks watching cleaners, plumbers, and electricians in case they find a hidden cache of expensive jewels.'

'I'm sure you will find a way around that problem.'

'It's going to be tricky.' She and Wendy would do flyby visits—not that Wendy would be able to deal with any looting. Maybe Cecilia could talk to Mr Dyson about removing any valuables. But if Mr Dyson were in charge, everything would be valuable.

'Did you speak to Old Ron?' she asked. 'Did you find out what time he visited Phil on the night of the murder?'

'Ron is not at home. He's gone to Tennant Creek to look at camels.'

'That's convenient. Who's looking after his place?'

'Auntie Mavis's son, John. He showed me a note from him.'

'Did Ron take his dummy female camel with him?'

'Excuse me?'

Cecilia allowed some silence to pass while she savoured her pleasure at shocking Aldo. 'Ron uses a dummy camel to collect semen. Extracting camel semen is a difficult and complicated business.'

'Do I need to know that?'

'Probably not,' said Cecilia cheerfully. 'I am just giving you background information on the contents of The Vegan Café's freezer.'

'Thank you.'

'My pleasure!'

Packing up her handbag and fetching the keys to a car, Cecilia swept Wendy up in her wake and descended on the council's car park. They drove into the city and parked in a parking lot on North Terrace. It was a ten-minute hike to the Royal Adelaide Hospital. Wendy scuttled behind her, muttering about how difficult it would be to find a travel companion at such short notice, especially if Mr Dyson was unsanitary.

Cecilia did not think that was an insurmountable problem. 'Mr Dyson shaved regularly and he was organised. He had a blue bucket containing disposable razors, a small mirror, shaving cream, and a metal cup for water. He just didn't have a functioning toilet or kitchen.'

They arrived at the hospital and found Mr Dyson in a single room, sitting in a chair next to his bed. He was tall, beady-eyed, and his skin was peeling and scaly.

Cecilia introduced herself and Wendy as officers from Glenelg Council. He glowered at them. 'What do you want?'

'Your house is unfit for human inhabitation. You can't return home until the sanitation requirements are fulfilled,' Cecilia informed him.

'What does that mean?'

'Before you can go back home, you must get your toilet, bathroom, and kitchen working, and get rid of the junk.'

'It's not junk.'

'We know this must be a difficult time for you,' said Wendy tremulously.

Mr Dyson eyed her like a kookaburra spotting prey. 'Difficult, yes! That's what you are doing, harassing a poor old man with a sick wife. Now, you're telling me I've no home to go to.'

'Can't you stay in a motel until the place is cleaned up and the plumbing is fixed?' said Cecilia. 'It may take a couple of weeks.'

'How could I afford a motel? I'm not made of money.'

'Could you stay with a relative?' Wendy tentatively suggested.

'Relatives!' Mr Dyson scoffed. 'My only son was murdered, my daughter won't speak to me, and my wife has had a stroke. The doctor has told me she can't talk or get out of bed on her own. She'll have to go to a nursing home. And now you're kicking me out of my own home! I think I might be talking to the press about my local council's strong-arm tactics.'

'Oh dear,' gulped Wendy.

'Go ahead,' Cecilia invited him. 'Then the world can see more footage of what your house is like. Especially the toilet.'

He pursed his lips.

'Why don't you stay with your sister while the house is fixed up?' asked Cecilia.

'She'd charge me for board. She's always after the money, that one.'

'Perhaps you would like to go on a cruise down the River Murray with our elderly folk?' Wendy suggested with a wobble in her voice.

'What? A cruise? Are you nuts? Why would I want to be around a bunch of old people on a riverboat?!'

Cecilia folded her arms. 'There is always Ward 4G.'

'What's that?'

'The psychiatric ward.'

'I'm not mad!' Mr Dyson spat. 'And I'm certainly not going to be stuck in a hospital ward with a bunch of lunatics!'

Cecilia held out her hand and counted down on her fingers. 'These are your options: a motel, stay with relatives, take a cruise down the

River Murray, or stay in the psychiatric ward. My colleague and I will be reporting to the hospital's social worker.'

'You're a tough one,' he complained. 'No heart.'

'Merely doing my job, Mr Dyson.' Cecilia beckoned to Wendy that it was time to leave.

The social worker was somewhere in the caverns of the hospital. Wendy left a message for her to call her.

'That went well,' Cecilia told her on the walk back to the car.

'Well?' Wendy was appalled.

'He now knows what he is up against.'

'What? You?'

'I uphold the sanitation laws of this fine country we live in,' said Cecilia, neatly avoiding a bumpy paver that might've caught her yellow polka-dotted heels.

'What on earth are we going to do with him?' Wendy stumbled on the paver and Cecilia caught and steadied her.

'We're going to visit his sister.'

'Oh my god!' Wendy pressed her fingers to her temples. 'I don't know if I can cope with this anymore.'

'You'll be fine. I've met Mavis. She's not rude, and you might even get a nice cup of tea and a biscuit.' Cecilia was looking forward to having a chat with her. She hoped she would cast some more light on the mysterious death of her nephew.

***

Cecilia parked the council's white Holden out the front of Auntie Mavis's 1960s house in Glenelg East. A little yellow-brick wall separated the house from the footpath, and standing behind the wall was a neat row of white roses, flanked by a patch of tidy green lawn. A long driveway stretched to an even longer backyard.

Cecilia pressed the doorbell, which chimed pleasantly.

Mavis appeared at the screen door. She did not open it. Cecilia introduced herself and Wendy, explaining they had come to talk to her about her brother.

Mavis sighed and beckoned for them to come in. She led them down the back and into the kitchen, where a pine table displayed a glass bowl brimming with shiny lush fruit. Cecilia noticed with pleasure that the kitchen was clean and there were no dishes in the sink. A large young man sat at the table. He was sharpening a kitchen knife on a stone.

'This is my son, John. He's Phil's cousin, and they were best friends. He's distraught about Phil's death.'

'I am so sorry for your loss.'

John looked at his mother, who began signing.

'John is deaf and mute,' explained Mavis. 'But he's not dumb. My John is smart.'

John signed again, pointing at Cecilia.

Mavis shook her head.

'What's he saying?'

'He wants to know if you are from the police.'

Cecilia passed him one of her business cards.

John looked at it and stuffed it into the pocket of his denim jeans. He got up, rinsed the knife, and put it and the stone away in a drawer. Then he left the kitchen.

Mavis offered them a cup of tea. Cecilia accepted and, after some hesitation, Wendy chose chamomile tea.

'Mrs Thompson, we have a problem with your brother's house,' Cecilia said.

'Call me Mavis.' She pushed the plate of biscuits towards them.

'I had to put a sanitation order on the house. Your brother can't move back in until the place is fixed up.'

Mavis frowned. 'That house is awful. John and I tried to help, but my sister-in-law wouldn't let us in and said it was none of our business, although my brother asked me and John to shop for them. He gave us a weekly shopping list. We would take cakes, baked beans, shavers, clothes, and drop them off out the back. She was always inside, but my brother liked to sit on the back porch.'

'Was Mrs Dyson the main hoarder?' Cecilia asked.

'Hoarder? What do you mean?'

'People who never throw anything away and live in squalor.'

'My son puts out the blue bin for them once a week.'

An unwelcome vision of the bags of poo swam into Cecilia's consciousness. She deleted that thought. 'Mrs Dyson will probably be going into an aged care facility. She's had a bad stroke and is incapacitated.'

'Incapacitated? That's nothing new. She never did anything before. She expected everyone to wait on her and squatted in that house like a big cane toad, ordering everyone about.'

'Not now. She can't speak.'

'That's a nice change. She was always telling her kids to cook and clean while she sat in front of the TV and ate cakes. She wasn't how a mother should be.' Mavis dabbed her eyes with a clean, embroidered handkerchief.

Cecilia gently switched focus. 'And the dog?'

'We only bought the best quality food for him. My brother looked after the dog properly. He took him for walks, and that was the only time my brother left the house. He was caught up in the spider web she had created.'

Cecilia had difficulty imagining Mr Dyson as a poor, helpless man too weak to stand up to people. It was not the impression she'd received at the hospital. 'Why didn't your brother call in a plumber and fix the toilet and hot water service?'

'He didn't want anyone to see what the house was like.'

'He is going to be discharged from hospital soon. Can he stay with you until his place gets fixed up?'

'I don't know if I can afford another mouth to feed. I'm on a pension.'

'Charge your brother board.'

Mavis nodded thoughtfully. 'He does have plenty of money.'

Cecilia thought about the security problems with the clean-up. 'Where did he keep his valuables?'

'He brought the safe back from work when he retired. God knows what he has stashed in there. He was a wealthy jeweller.'

A safe. How wonderful. If the cleaners bothered to go through the bin with the scratch and win cards, good luck to them. At least Cecilia didn't have to sit there all day making sure they didn't pocket a cache of expensive jewellery. 'How did you and your son pay for your brother and sister-in-law's shopping?'

'My brother gave us cash. The ATM is only a few minutes walk from his house.'

'Why was it left up to you to care for your brother and his wife? It mustn't have been easy for you. His son lived in Glenelg, too. Why didn't he help?'

Mavis ate a biscuit. 'Phil was mortified by his parents and the way they lived. He had to escape from her—his mum. He moved in with me when he was ten years old.'

Cecilia sipped her instant coffee, looking around at Mavis's spotless kitchen.

'He made marmalade the first year he was here. He put little red-and-white checked cloths on the jars and set up a table on the footpath with a *For Sale* sign. He was always the entrepreneur and keen on cooking. I taught him a lot.'

'What was he like?'

'I can't imagine anybody wanting to kill him. He was a generous boy, always wanting to please people.' Mavis twisted her handkerchief. 'I used to have chickens, but one night the foxes got in, and we woke up to a bloodbath of slaughtered chooks. I stopped keeping chickens after that. But look at my shelf.' Mavis pointed to a glass cupboard above the kitchen bench. The top ledge was crammed with ornamental chickens. 'Every birthday and Christmas, Phil would give me a chicken for my shelf. He was a sweet boy.'

'They're nice ornaments,' Cecilia said conversationally.

'Phil was a young man with his life ahead of him. He had a rough patch in his teens and early twenties with depression, but then he went on a health retreat, and it turned his life around. I'm not one for gurus and all that spiritualism, but it worked for Phil. He gained confidence, and when he was worried about paying his mortgage, he would meditate his way out of the anxiety. He got a job, made friends, and recently he had fallen in love, properly, for the first time. That poor girl! She must be heartbroken. John thinks we should invite her around for a cup of tea.'

Cecilia swished her coffee around in her cup. That would be Jessie. Had Aldo talked to her? She studied Mavis. She was smart about people and looked like an innocent old lady sipping her tea from a flowery mug, yet she had been growing marijuana in her garden, and her nephew was her dealer!

She put down her own empty mug, which bore a picture of an ocean liner sailing on the open seas. 'Have you been on a cruise?'

'My son and I like to go on cruises when we can afford it. Phil would add a little something to the cost.'

Perhaps that's where some of the marijuana cookie money went. Cecilia did not judge. She also liked going on cruises and holiday vacations.

Mavis agreed to see her brother and the social worker from the hospital. Cecilia rose to her feet, collected Wendy's cup, and took it to the sink with hers. She thanked Mavis for her hospitality, with Wendy echoing her as they said their goodbyes.

'It's been a successful day,' said Cecilia cheerfully in the car on their way back to the town hall. 'We have achieved things.'

'I've got a headache,' moaned Wendy.

'Well, at least you don't have to find a travelling companion for Mr Dyson to go on a cruise. Mrs Dyson is safely locked up in the hospital, and today is Friday, so it's the weekend. Time for some peace and quiet.'

'But who killed the cook?' Wendy asked fearfully.

***

I am in a cellar. There is a blanket on the floor, a bottle of water, and some boxes. The cellar smells of sweat. I sniff my armpits; the smell is mine.

I try to open the solid wooden door, but it's locked. I bang and bang on the door, calling for help. There is no reply. What am I doing here? Am I trapped in the cellar at the mercy of whoever has kidnapped me? Is he a rapist, a serial killer, or a collector?

I reach into my pocket for my phone, but I am in my nightie, and it has no pockets. My feet are bare, and the stone floor gives off an icy, buzzing sensation.

What could I use as a weapon against my kidnapper? I search the boxes in the cellar. One is filled with small jars of marmalade, adorned with red-and-white-checked cotton tops. Could I use one to slash whoever is out there? I smash a jar and then tear a piece of blanket, wrapping a shard of glass in it. Then I wait behind the door.

Slowly, the handle inches its way into motion. I scream and scream, lunging with my glass shaft—terror and rage course through my body.

With a tearing wrench, the sound of my screaming wakes me up.

***

Cecilia stood in her walk-in wardrobe, frocks gently swishing against her face.

I've been sleepwalking again. Goddamn it! she raged, and angry tears pricked her eyes, then a small comfort emerged. *At least I haven't left my bedroom.*

However, the sensor buzzer had failed to wake her; instead, it had become woven into her nightmares.

Is that what happened to Grandma Snow? Someone kidnapped her and kept her in a cellar?

It wasn't just young girls who went missing—older people could, too. All Cecilia's fears as a young girl came flooding back.

She pressed her face against a soft silky dress and waited for her tears to subside.

6

Vince hurried over to Cecilia's side as she was browsing the tomatoes for her weekly shop.

'The mayor, the big shot, he tells me the council will put up new parking signs for my shop. The mayor says the parking inspector is a bad man to be blackmailing poor old Vince.' He clapped his gnarled hands together with a smack. 'No more parking inspector!'

Cecilia was delighted; Ian had been sacked. The CEO must have been beside himself, having a corrupt parking inspector who he'd previously protected to get inside information on the staff, and now the mayor was on his back and hounding him. Vince tried to drop some extra tomatoes into her basket, but she firmly refused.

On her way home, she drove down Moseley Street and past the Sun-Kissed Motel. Mr Jones and his troublesome kombi van had settled into a campsite he had erected out the front of the motel. He had a sandwich board with a map of Australia covered in red dots, where presumably he'd found faulty parking signs, and he had a couple of chairs and a small navy-blue fold-up table. He also had a guest; a woman in a short black leather skirt was sipping something from a coffee mug. Mr Jones was pointing out places in Western Australia, and the woman was smiling and nodding. It all looked very homely. No doubt sex workers were like everyone else and enjoyed a holiday, seeing the sights around Australia.

At home, she set out the fruit in a large glass bowl on the kitchen bench and stashed the vegetables in the crisper.

Hannah wandered into the kitchen with the puppies. 'That fruit bowl looks lovely.' She nibbled on her finger. 'I feel like drawing, but I usually do people.'

Cecilia passed her laptop over and brought up a picture of Phil Dyson taken from his Facebook site. 'What's he like? You're a portrait artist. Maybe you'll see something we missed.'

Hannah studied the picture carefully. 'He has a symmetrical face and a nice straight nose, which make him good looking, although I don't think he always has been. I think he was dorky when younger. There's an uncertainty about him. You can see it in his eyes.'

'He had a terrible childhood.'

'Maybe that's what I'm seeing,' mused Hannah.

'His parents are awful. They lived in that hoarders' house. The one all over the news recently.'

'I remember that house,' said Hannah, looking up from the photo to her mother. 'When we were kids, we called it *The Crazy House*. We used to dare each other to go into the yard. A hugely obese woman lived there. Once, she caught us and threw a broken car mirror. Luke nearly got hit in the head. That mirror could have caused serious damage. We were terrified and never went back. It's weird to think she's Phil's mother. Poor guy. She was mad as a cut snake. He must have been so lost as a child.'

Propping a fist under her chin, Hannah returned to her examination of Phil's photo. 'I think I might draw him. He needs to be remembered.' She left the room and returned with her easel, drawing paper, and tin of pencils.

The puppies did not mind a stationary Hannah as she stood in front of her easel. They lay down back-to-back and were soon fast asleep.

Cecilia cleaned her cup under running water, pleased with Hannah. At last, it seemed she was returning to her usual self. If she could start drawing and painting again, maybe the depression would lift, and she would be no longer be a ghost who floated on the sofa.

As usual, on Saturday night, Cecilia settled down to watch television—but her mind was on other things. Who had visited the café after ten o'clock at night? Ian had been and gone. There was Old Ron with his camel semen. What time did he arrive? And who else visited Phil?

Even allowing for the bottle of vodka and the crate of fruit and vegetables that should have been packed away, the café's kitchen had been impeccably clean and uncluttered. Phil had time to give the café that extra gloss of cleanliness in readiness for her inspection, despite his visitors.

And Aldo? What about him? He was sending out strong signals that he liked her, calling her Cee-Cee and saying she was beautiful. She enjoyed being with him. He made her laugh, he listened to what she had to say, and when he touched her, it felt nice—really nice.

Why was she keeping him at arm's length? Why couldn't she have a fun affair? Was it because the symptoms of her sleepwalking and PTSD were growing stronger? They made her feel helpless and vulnerable. She was frightened she was losing control of her mind. Sometimes she had an almost overwhelming urge to burst into tears. What if it spilled out into her waking life?

Cecilia frowned at the conundrums her inner world was creating. It was not fair. She was not that scared person in her dreams. Far from it!

***

Cecilia and Angel entered Marigold Nursing Home's reception area. It was a vast space, tiled, with a smallish round mahogany table in the centre featuring a large vase filled with fresh lilies. They greeted the receptionist, signed in, and rang the doorbell for the locked dementia unit. A familiar nurse answered the door. It was Daphne, Garth's wife; she was a large middle-aged woman with an easy-going attitude.

'Oh, I'm so glad you're here,' said Daphne, smiling ruefully. 'I was going to ring you about Miss Archer's accident.'

'What's she done now?' Angel despaired.

Once a month, Cecilia and Angel visited their aunt, Army Auntie, a retired major. Army Auntie had never married or had children. In her late seventies, she developed Alzheimer's disease and had to retire to a nursing home. Cecilia and Angel were her closest living relatives. It was a chore to visit Army Auntie, who was uninterested in visitors, but the sisters made up for it by treating themselves to dinner afterwards.

'Miss Archer has a big bruise on her hand,' said Daphne. 'She got into a fight with a seagull.'

'Who won?' Cecilia asked.

'Oh, Cecilia,' Angel scolded. 'Seagulls can be vicious.'

'Army Auntie can be, too.'

'What happened?' Angel asked. 'Poor Auntie. She must have been shaken by the experience.'

'Well,' continued Daphne, 'she did shake her walking stick at the seagull.'

'Huh?' Angel was perplexed. 'Do seagulls come into the nursing home? Into the courtyard?'

'Since it was a sunny spring day, we thought we'd take a couple of our residents to Moseley Square for ice cream. We were all set up on the lawn when a seagull tried to snatch Miss Archer's ice cream.'

'Did the seagull survive?' Cecilia asked.

'It flew off in a hurry, with Miss Archer pursuing it and trying to smack it with her walking stick. It took another ice cream for her to calm down and to stop whipping her walking stick at any seagull who was passing by. We were worried Miss Archer might have a fall.'

'Why can't the council do something about all the seagulls who plague Glenelg?' Angel asked. 'They're pests.'

'Seagulls are protected under the *1972 National Migratory Bird Act*.' said Cecilia.

'How do you know that?' Angel asked. 'I've never thought of you being a bird sort of person.'

'Some of my restaurants, especially the new ones, come and see me about deterring or getting rid of seagulls. They're a nuisance in the outdoor dining areas.'

'I'll bring you the paperwork for Miss Archer's accident,' said Daphne, heading for the office.

In the dining room, Cecilia and Angel found Army Auntie, a tall, gaunt woman who wore her hair in a severe grey bob, and whose appetite was not reflected in her figure. She sat at a table, wolfing down a roast dinner of lamb, peas, and potatoes when Cecilia and Angel pulled up chairs and sat down next to her.

'How are you, Auntie?' Angel asked.

There was no reply. Army Auntie was too busy eating to have registered their presence.

Looking around the table, Cecilia noticed a thin woman wearing a black T-shirt and a rose tattoo that wound its way up her arm. Her face was blank, and she was sitting with her roast dinner untouched.

Army Auntie pushed her dinner plate away and scooped up a bowl that contained custard and tinned fruit. She smacked her lips and dove in.

'Oh my god!' Angel nudged Cecilia in the ribs. 'Look who's come in!'

A biker with grey hair pulled back in a stubby ponytail and wearing a weather-beaten leather jacket was walking towards them. He sat down next to the woman with the rose tattoo and put his arm around her.

'Hello, Mum,' he said.

She gave him a sweet smile and stroked his cheek. He picked up the knife and fork and began cutting up the meat, spooning it into her unresisting mouth.

'I guess bikies have mothers too, who have to live in nursing homes,' Angel whispered to Cecilia.

'Don't whisper,' replied Cecilia. 'It's rude.'

'Okay, Miss Bossy Boots.'

'Oh no!' exclaimed Cecilia. Having finished her custard, Army Auntie had snaked out a hand and swept up the bikie's mum's custard.

'Oi! That's my mum's custard!'

'It's mine now.' Army Auntie wrapped a protective arm around the bowl of custard and glared back at him.

'Give it back, Auntie,' Angel pleaded. 'Or you'll be in trouble with that man in the leather jacket.'

'Him?' Auntie snorted. She wasn't scared, not one bit. *All those years in the army,* thought Cecilia, *has made her used to dealing with tough men.*

From her bag, Cecilia pulled out a small box of chocolates. She dangled them in front of Auntie. 'If you give back that dessert, I'll give you some yummy chocolates.'

She went to snatch the chocolates, but Cecilia was quicker and put them behind her back.

'Well? They're your favourites.'

While she deliberated, Cecilia noticed the bikie had a small smile tugging at his mouth. Finally, Army Auntie pushed back her chair, leaving the bowl of custard. 'I'll take the chocolates to the TV room,' she announced.

Cecilia looked at Army Auntie's cardigan pockets. One of them bulged.

'What have you got in your pocket?'

'None of your business.' Army Auntie put a protective hand over it. Cecilia peered more closely. The pocket had small, jagged bits of paper sticking out. They were packets of sugar. She let it be. Another argument with Army Auntie was not worth the bother, and she was sure that the nursing home could afford extra packets of sugar.

They all trooped off to the television area, where *Bachelorette* was playing. After fifteen minutes of watching young people behaving badly—which had Angel entranced, Cecilia bored, and sent Auntie to sleep in a chocolate haze—they left to go out for dinner.

Hannah was babysitting Angel's kids, and Cecilia and Angel had made plans to go to an Indian restaurant in Hyde Park. Cecilia preferred not to have dinner in her area; it was too much like work to eat locally, and it made the chefs nervous to see her.

After having studied the menu, they decided on a buffet, placed their order, and fairly quickly, the wine and water arrived.

Cecilia said conversationally, 'I met a guru recently.'

'A guru?' Angel considered Cecilia. 'I can't imagine you with a guru.'

'No, not like that. I met him through work. He owns one of my cafés.'

'A guru,' Angel pondered. 'I once had a date with a guru.'

Cecilia was astonished. 'Do gurus use dating sites?'

'This one did.'

'What did he look like?'

'He was okay-looking. Tall and a bit skinny, but he wore his hair in a ponytail, and you know what I think about ponytails.' Angel pulled a face. 'Although, I don't mind men wearing a top knot.'

Cecilia considered this. Was it the same guru? The Vegan Café guru was no longer sporting the ponytail look: now he was into wavy, shoulder-length hair.

'Did he have blue eyes? Like, really blue.'

'Yeah, and he sprouted little sayings and expected me to be amazed by his worldly knowledge. He kept banging on about the benefits of meditation. That's so not me. I'd rather clean the front porch than go to a meditation class.'

'I think your guru is my guru. Was he an Adelaide man or from somewhere else? He has a slight accent.'

'His parents were Italian. He grew up on a battery chicken farm in Queensland.'

'Battery chickens!' Cecilia was appalled. 'Imagine waking up to the squawking noise of hundreds of terrified chickens in your backyard every morning. It would be traumatic.'

'Well, yes. He had some kind of breakdown in his twenties and went to India to find *The Truth.*'—Angel made air quotes with her fingers—'He trained under several gurus, and then he had a vision that he should come back to Australia and spread the light.'

'For one date, you got a lot of information out of the guru.'

'That's what I do when I go on a date—I get him to tell me his life story. Guys like talking about themselves, and it helps me figure out if I like them or not. For example, I never go near a man who hates his mother.'

'Aldo lives with his parents.'

'What!' Angel raised her eyebrows. 'That's a bit suss—a middle-aged man living with his parents.'

'He has a disabled son, and sometimes he has to go out at night for work.'

Angel refilled her plate. Cecilia eyed her with wonder; Angel ate twice as much as a normal person and remained slim. Cecilia only had to look at a bowl of jasmine rice and she gained a couple of kilos.

'Okay,' said Angel, between mouthfuls. 'What are Aldo's hobbies?'

'He's a magician. He tried to impress me by producing a rose from behind my ear.'

'That's a different chat-up line. I'm longing to meet your policeman.'

'It was a plastic rose, and I gave it back.' Cecilia pushed her rogan josh around her plate. She could not eat another mouthful, and Angel had ordered far more food than they could possibly eat. 'I think he's a flirt,' said Cecilia. 'And I don't do flirts. I'm not sure about this pickle either. The eggplant is bitter.'

'Dating is good fun. I had coffee with a tree climber last week, and he had an amazing body. You could see his muscles rippling under his T-shirt.'

'What's a tree climber do?'

'Climb trees!'

'Duh!'

'He saws off branches that are high up.'

'You're a serial dater, Angel. You collect dates. In fact, the more the bizarre their jobs, the more you're interested.'

Angel patted her phone, sparkling with fake diamantes, which she had kept on the table in case there was a crisis with the kids. 'I don't have sex or anything with my online dates.'

'Did the tree climber have any weird hobbies?'

Angel's face lit up. 'He's a pet-food taster. A friend of his has an organic pet food business.'

'Yuk,' said Cecilia. 'I do not want to eat pet food. That's disgusting.' Then she thought for a bit. 'Why do dogs go nuts about canned food? The puppies love it, much more than the dry pellets.'

'The tree climber said it was the sweet fruit powder they mix in with the gelatine in cans which gives it the taste dogs love.'

Cecilia laughed. 'You are a magnet for the whacky,' she told Angel.

'I know,' said Angel, dabbing her mouth with a napkin. 'It's so much fun.'

At bedtime, Cecilia took a while to get to sleep. She needed a rest from her head, which was jumping around with thoughts. She did not want to think about her feelings for Aldo, horrible houses, and the unexplained death of the vegan cook. She listened to rainforest music and told her subconscious there was nothing to worry about—and there was no need to go walking in her sleep.

***

'You're ruining a poor old man,' whined Mr Dyson.

He sat at Auntie Mavis's dining table examining quotes from electricians, plumbers, and cleaners. Cecilia had put them in a new folder and deposited them in front of him.

'Why don't you find some volunteers to clean my house, like the ones you were yammering about—the ones who take old people on cruises. Or you could dig up a retired plumber who wants to be useful.'

'No volunteer would want to clean your house,' said Cecilia. 'It's a disaster zone. This needs professional work.'

The cleaners had said it was a terrible job and they would have to fill at least eight super-sized skip bins, the plumber wanted to put in a new toilet and replace the kitchen sink, and the electrician said the house needed rewiring and smoke alarms.

Then there was the question of the big shed out the back. She and the cleaners had peered into the gloom when planning the clean-up.

'It's a bit smelly,' Cecilia had said, 'but it's outside my jurisdiction. Leave it.'

'What about the cars?'

'They're not a sanitation issue. Only the weeds need to be cut back in case they harbour rats or snakes.'

Mr Dyson pushed the paperwork back across the table to Cecilia. 'Hire the cheapest one.'

Cecilia grabbed it and made a hasty retreat in case he had more arguments against the clean-up.

Mavis followed Cecilia to the front door. 'Hang on for a minute,' she told Cecilia breathlessly.

Cecilia stopped by the front door. 'What's up with John?' she asked. He'd been lying down on the sofa when she walked past the lounge.

'He hurt his back while working for Old Ron.'

'Oh,' said Cecilia. Unwelcome visions of a dummy camel being humped by a live one swam in her consciousness.

'He's had to take a week off from his cleaning job at Glenelg Primary School. At least it's stopped my brother using him for free in the clean-up. I've made sure of that!'

Cecilia walked through the front door and stood on the front porch. 'Like Phil, John works at a few different jobs.'

'I don't know what you mean.' Mavis was wide-eyed with innocence. 'My son and I live a simple life. I'm on a pension, and John works as a cleaner.'

Cecilia gazed thoughtfully down the driveway. She was guessing the marijuana plantation was behind the shed. 'You have a lovely garden,' she said.

'It keeps me nimble,' said Mavis smiling, like a sweet old lady. 'I love growing things. Phil used to say it was good karma.'

An answering smile tugged at the corner of Cecilia's mouth. She was sure Mavis had nothing to do with Phil's murder, and Mavis's gardening activities were none of her business—but she wasn't sure about John. Garth said he was hot-tempered and he was so big. Perhaps he got into an argument with Phil, and it got out of control.

***

'Hey, Cecilia,' said Garth, opening the lunchroom door. 'You been busy?'

Cecilia nodded as she chewed slowly on a piece of carrot.

He fetched a plate and sat down opposite her, tipping a pastie from a paper bag onto a plate. 'Guess what?'

'What?'

'Ian has moved down south and is working as the lollypop man for traffic works.'

'Are they the ones who hold the stop and go signs?'

'Yes, and they get a good income.'

'Just for holding a sign?'

'It's danger money. Lollypop workers can get hit by cars.'

'Maybe Ian will get clobbered by the karma bus,' said Cecilia, closing her lunch box with a snap.

Garth squeezed tomato sauce over his pastie. 'I thought of something else after talking to your cop friend. Phil had two wallets; one was a normal black one with his credit cards, his driver's licence, his Medicare card, and stuff; the other was a large, tan-coloured pouch with a zip, about the size of a pencil case. I think John gave it to him after he went on a cruise to New Zealand. Phil used to keep the money he made from his various business enterprises in the pouch. I saw it one time when one of the green clean customers came into the pub and needed change. When Phil unzipped the pouch, I saw it was crammed with bank notes.'

'Maybe it was a robbery?' Cecilia wondered why she hadn't thought of that before. It was such a common motive. Perhaps one of Phil's customers stole it. 'You should tell Aldo.'

'Why don't you?' Garth gave her a cheeky eye roll. 'I've seen you with him on the South Esplanade's bench. He even had you eating chips, which is a wondrous thing considering the rabbit food in your lunchbox.'

'Can't a woman get some privacy around here? Anyway, I'm not an eye witness to the mysterious tan pouch; you are.'

'Okay, I'll talk to him. You know, Cecilia, I'm doing my best to find out who knocked Phil off.'

'Me too,' said Cecilia. 'I want justice!'

***

Towards the end of the week, Cecilia cornered Wendy in her office. 'We have more problems with the Dysons.'

Wendy hid behind her fringe. 'I don't think I'm going to like this.'

'We have to visit Mr Dyson to see if he needs assistance in arranging his son's funeral.'

'Oh no!' Wendy exclaimed in horror.

'We've got no choice. The sergeant from the local police station rang me because Mr Dyson is refusing to answer his calls. The coroner is discharging Phil's body tomorrow, and a funeral parlour must be found. We have to visit Mr Dyson and make him sort something out.'

Wendy trembled. 'I don't think I could convince Mr Dyson to do anything!'

'Phil's body can't be left in limbo. Would eleven o'clock suit you?'

'I do nice things for old people,' moaned Wendy, as they stood at Mavis's front door. 'I put on morning teas with cupcakes for the old folk, and I organise volunteers and arrange excursions. I have never had to deal with funerals and squalor.'

'There's a first time for everything,' said Cecilia encouragingly, patting Wendy on the shoulder.

***

John answered the door and gestured for Cecilia and Wendy to wait at the front porch. A few moments later, he returned with Mavis.

'We've come to talk about the funeral,' said Cecilia. 'The coroner is releasing Phil's body tomorrow. Do you know if Mr Dyson has made any plans for a funeral or cremation?'

Mavis eyed her with a wry smile. 'You don't give up, do you, dearie?'

'We're just doing our job.'

'We want to help,' said Wendy meekly.

'You'll find him at the kitchen table, sifting through bills and thinking up ways to not pay them.'

They walked down the passageway and into the kitchen. Mavis invited them to sit, offering them tea, which Cecilia refused. She was getting ready for battle.

'You again,' growled Mr Dyson. 'You're costing me a fortune. Don't clear the shed. There are valuables in there.'

'You need to think about organising a funeral for your son. The coroner is releasing his body tomorrow.'

'Are you saying I have to pay for a funeral? Good god! Do you think I'm made of money? The way you make me squander money on this so-called clean-up is outrageous. The media is going to hear about your antics, girlie. Besieging an old pensioner in his time of grief!'

Cecilia glared right back at him. 'You're not an old-age pensioner, are you? You have superannuation.'

'I've worked hard.'

'Are you going to give your son a funeral?' Cecilia could feel the rage boiling inside her. But she was not going to lose her professional focus.

Mr Dyson folded his stringy arms.

Cecilia searched in her handbag and produced printed sheets listing the names of funeral services; the most inexpensive ones she'd been able to find on the internet.

She spread them out on the table. 'Contact one of these. They don't offer coffee and cake afterwards, but they are cheap.'

Slapping his hand on the table, he shouted, 'Are you calling me a cheapskate, when my only son has died? I'm a vulnerable person and deserve support!'

Cecilia did not flinch. She glared right back at him. 'Would you like some counselling? I'm sure my colleague could arrange that.'

Wendy's head bobbed up and down in agreement. 'There are bereavement services available for our elderly folk.'

'Counselling?' Mr Dyson scoffed. 'I'm not soft in the head. I just don't see why I have to spend my hard-earned cash on all this palaver.'

'You don't qualify for government support for the funeral,' Cecilia told him, gritting her teeth.

'My son owned a nice flat on the esplanade,' he mused. 'I've heard developers offered good money to the owners. Phil must have made a tidy sum.'

'How did you know that?' Cecilia narrowed her eyes.

'Just the other day, the developers came to see me because I'm Phil's closest relative. They want to clear out his flat. Maybe you could do that, seeing as my health is failing.'

Cecilia wanted to clock Mr Dyson with her handbag. No wonder Phil had opted for the spiritual life and looked to Swami N as a father figure. His own father was monstrous.

Mavis was having an animated conversation with her son using sign language. He picked up the paperwork his uncle had ignored, pulled out his laptop, and began tapping, showing his mother the results of his search.

Mavis was agitated and continued signing, but John was insistent.

'What's going on?' Cecilia asked.

'My son wants a nice funeral for his cousin and is prepared to pay for it.'

'That's a good idea,' said Mr Dyson. 'Family should help each other out.'

Cecilia stood up and planted both hands on the table. His nephew was offering to pay for the funeral of his son; it was outrageous. He didn't seem to care about Phil's death; he was only concerned with how much it would cost to have him cremated.

Mr Dyson smirked at her.

'Who killed your son?' She didn't care if she sounded brutal.

'A fanatic.' Mr Dyson shrugged.

'How do you know?'

'He joined that weird vegan cult, grew his hair, and did those funny exercises at dawn on the beach.'

'You mean tai chi.'

'Whatever. He wasn't quite normal, that boy.'

'With you as a father, I'm not surprised!' Cecilia knew she had to leave. She could not take any more of Mr Dyson and was not going to get into a slanging match with him. She gathered up Wendy and stormed out of the house. Mavis hurried out after them.

'Why should my son pay for his cousin's funeral?' Mavis was almost spitting with rage. 'My brother is filthy rich. I'm going back inside to tell that horrible old man he can't stay at my place any longer. I know he's my brother, but there are limits. To take advantage of my son has crossed the line.'

'Good idea. Make him pay for a room at the Sun-Kissed Motel. They have cheap rooms. If you can't move him out, ring the police.'

Wendy yanked and yanked on the handle of the car door before Cecilia had a chance to click the key fob. Wendy fell into her seat. 'I need some chamomile tea,' she whimpered. 'That was truly dreadful.'

'Aged care is not always about tea and scones and a trip down the Murray River.' Cecilia pulled down the mirror from the sunshade. She applied lipstick and powder, considering her reflection. 'I'm not done yet.'

***

Cecilia rang Aldo as soon as she returned to her office. 'Mr Dyson refused to pay for his son's funeral. Can you believe it? What's worse, his nephew is going to pay for it. Talk about taking advantage of someone's kind nature.'

'Phil made out a will,' Aldo told her.

'Really? He was so young. Why did he bother?'

'He was a meticulous man, our vegan cook.'

'Who benefits?'

'It's not public knowledge until tomorrow. I think you will find it interesting; it has justice to it.'

Maybe Phil has left his money to Jessie, Cecilia wondered. 'It's a shame you can't work up a case against Phil's father.' Cecilia was still feeling the rage. 'He's a nasty piece of work.'

'Are you having trouble getting him to clean up the house?'

'Am I ever! He goes around to the house and takes things, like plastic buckets, out of the skip bin. He must have had about forty buckets. He's driving the cleaners bonkers.'

'But not you, Cecilia.'

'The old man isn't an early riser, so I've organised the skip bins to be emptied before he has time to get there. I'm sure he has heaps of money. But I feel as if all this cleaning up is a distraction to what happened to Phil.'

'Sorry, Cee-Cee—I have to go. Someone needs me.'

She put down her phone and stared at her computer, which had at least a dozen emails, unanswered from the state government health department. There must be somebody in the public service who had nothing to do but fill up Cecilia's inbox.

***

The coffin was polished pine with gilt handles. Cecilia was glad John, who worked hard dealing with horny camels and school toilets and classrooms, hadn't spent all his savings on a fancy coffin.

Mavis sat up the front and signed to John what the funeral celebrant said about Phil.

After a prayer, Mavis and John got up and walked to the pulpit. John, wearing black trousers and an impeccably ironed white shirt, stood in front of the congregation. His shoulders were hunched, and he looked as if he was trying to make himself appear smaller, which was difficult for such a large man. He looked at the congregation nervously, closed his eyes for a few seconds, and then began his story with his hands and face. Mavis, subdued in a navy-blue jacket, and dress, translated quietly into the microphone. All eyes were on John, who gathered up confidence and came alive, hands flying and a steady flow of a myriad of facial expressions, as he progressed with his eulogy.

'Phil was like a brother to me, except we never quarrelled. He learnt sign language, and as kids, we were always looking for a way to make a dollar. We cleaned cars, delivered the local paper, and we were even teddy bear surgeons for the childcare centre, sewing up legs and heads and then re-stuffing them.

'Later, when we were adults, we would go to the pub and watch the footy. Phil included me in the conversation. He always had time to explain what I was saying to other people. "I don't want you to be invisible," he said to me.'

John rubbed his eyes and, after a few deep breaths, he resumed his signing. 'Phil was my best friend, and I am going to miss him. He shouldn't have died.'

Tears sprung to Cecilia's eyes, and she heard a few muffled sobs from Jessie, who was sitting next to Daphne, who put a comforting arm around her.

When the service had finished, guests filed past Phil's coffin and laid down offerings. Cecilia sat back and watched as a skinny girl with pink hair tossed a bunch of soursobs, yellow weeds, and Garth laid a miniature bottle of vodka. Then a large, muscular woman with lank blonde hair scraped back in a ponytail placed a sparse, lacklustre bunch of flowers on the coffin. Cecilia wondered if this was Phil's sister; her overdeveloped arm muscles strained against an ill-fitting black jacket.

In matching cream-and-green kaftan and dress, Swami N and Astra floated through the guests. Some of them looked like Swami N's devotees, given the reverent bowing he received.

Aldo stood at the back of the chapel.

Over refreshments, Old Ron beetled up to Swami N. Cecilia edged closer in time to hear Ron say, 'I've got something in the freezer drawer at your café. I need to get it back.'

'What drawer?' Swami N was suspicious.

'The liquid nitrogen one.'

'I don't know anything about that.'

'The stuff in there is mine,' said Ron firmly. 'I had to hammer my old ute back from the Northern Territory to come and get it.'

'What stuff?' Swami N flashed his piercing blue eyes at Ron.

Ron was unmoved; maybe because he had dealt with camels all his life and they had the same beady-eyed stare.

'It's my property. I want to collect it this afternoon.'

'I am interviewing potential cooks this afternoon.'

'I'll nip in and collect it. I won't be in your way.'

'What have you been keeping in my freezer?' demanded Swami N.

'Camel semen,' said Ron. 'It's totally legal.'

Cecilia sniggered, waiting for Swami N's reaction.

'Camel semen!' Swami N seethed. 'That's disgusting. What is camel semen doing on my premises?'

'I had an arrangement with Phil. I'm coming this afternoon to collect what is mine.'

'No. I will go to the café and immediately throw it out!' Swami M responded angrily.

'No, you won't,' said Old Ron. 'I know things about you; secrets you wouldn't want anyone to know.'

Swami N stormed off in the direction of his wife, who was surrounded by adoring young male acolytes.

After he'd left, Cecilia sidled up to Ron. 'Remember me?'

'Are you the council girlie who made me get in a camel poo cleaner?'

'That's me.' She smiled. 'What secrets do you know about Swami N?'

Ron shrugged. 'I've no idea. But people like him always have something to hide, so it was worth taking a punt. Besides, it took a lot of effort to get that semen, and I'm now ready to export it to Saudi Arabia.'

'Did you visit Phil the night he was killed?'

'I had a delivery, so I dropped in about nine-thirty. He was busy getting the place spotless for that finicky health inspector.' Ron gave Cecilia a sly grin, which she ignored. 'I had a quick vodka and left him to his cleaning.'

'How did he seem?'

'Excited. He was in love, he was moving to the country, and he had a brand-new life ahead of him. It's bloody awful someone took everything away from him.' Ron reached into his coat pocket, took out a flask, and swigged from it. 'I'm going outside for a smoke.'

Cecilia turned to watch the girl with pink hair and the crazy chicken T-shirt, who was making a fuss about something with the caterers. Cecilia surmised she was Vee, Amy's sister—the one who Hannah had said was a cannabis cookie customer.

'Why aren't the biscuits?' Vee shouted. 'This should be a vegan funeral!'

Cecilia sidled up to her. 'I know you, don't I?'

Vee frowned. 'I don't think so.'

'You're the one who does such good work in protesting about animal cruelty and goes to climate change rallies. I'm sure I've seen you at demonstrations.'

'So?' Vee was rude. 'It's you old people who have made a mess of our planet.'

'I know,' said Cecilia sadly. 'Have you got a tissue?'

Vee rummaged around in her tapestry bag, found a packet of tissues, and grudgingly passed one to Cecilia.

Cecilia peered into her bag. Just cigarettes and a tin box. She thanked Vee and then moved on to her next target, the muscular Kylie. 'You must be Phil's sister. I didn't quite catch your name.'

'Kylie.'

'This is such a sad occasion. I am sorry for your loss.' Cecilia looked down at the woman's black bag, which was open. She was almost sure she saw something tan-coloured.

She moved back from Kylie, mapped out her moves, and then faked a trip, falling on top of Kylie and stabbing her calf with her stiletto heel while sweeping her large muscular legs off the floor and slinging her handbag loose.

'Ouch! What the hell?' Kylie shouted in outrage as she lay prostrate with Cecilia on top of her.

'I'm so sorry; I must have tripped over,' said Cecilia, rolling off her. 'I shouldn't be wearing high heels. Are you alright?'

'You stupid bitch!'

Aldo came over and helped Cecilia to her feet.

The contents of Kylie's bag had spilled all over the floor, including a long tan pouch with a picture of a cruise liner.

Aldo picked up the pouch. 'Where did you get this?' Then, unexpectedly, he handed it to Cecilia. 'I don't have a warrant to open it.'

Without hesitation, she unzipped it. It was stuffed with money. She passed it back to Aldo.

Kylie seemed to grit her teeth. *Aldo was going to have a tough time getting Kylie to talk,* thought Cecilia. Those jaws were not going to be opened easily.

Aldo showed Kylie his police badge. 'I think you better come down to the station for a chat with me.' He took her by the arm and Kylie limped off.

The funeral guests were agog at the sight of a possible arrest amid the tea and biscuits. John signed questions to his mum, and Mavis answered, looking wide-eyed and shocked.

Garth approached Cecilia, who was sitting down on a chair. It had been a complicated judo move.

'Are you okay? Those heels you wear are lethal.'

'Aren't they gorgeous? And useful, too,' she said, looking with pleasure at her bright red shoes with their long pointy silver heels, which offset her subdued, plain black dress.

Wendy joined them. 'It's just not nice,' she complained. 'Funerals should be respectful occasions.'

'It sure is one hell of a funeral,' said Garth. 'Fights breaking out everywhere. Worse than a bunch of seagulls fighting over half a burger.'

Over the chatter, Mr Dyson shouted at Mavis that John had inveigled himself into Phil's life. 'I should have been the beneficiary of my son's will, not John. He's too retarded to know what to do with it.'

'My son is not retarded,' Mavis spat. 'You are! Living in chaos and filth is bonkers. You should be locked up in a lunatic asylum.'

Cecilia was delighted to hear John was the primary beneficiary of Phil's will. She stood up. 'This funeral is a circus. I'm going to give John and Mavis my condolences and then I'm leaving.'

Twisting her handkerchief, Mavis turned to Cecilia on her approach. 'Why was Kylie arrested?' Mavis's hands were shaking, as she wrestled with her handkerchief. 'She couldn't have killed her own brother. Could she?'

Cecilia enveloped her in a hug. 'Let the police worry about that. They will find out what really happened.' She gave her Hannah's drawing of Phil. 'My daughter drew this. She said if you don't like it, that's okay, just bin it.'

Mavis showed it to John, who gently stroked the edge of the paper.

7

Cecilia lay back on the sofa with her laptop propped on her knees. She was doing some overdue research, checking out Swami N's website. There were several YouTube videos of him taking a meditation class. Cecilia listened to one and felt more relaxed than she had in a long time. Swami N had a lovely deep, soothing voice. Maybe she should go to his classes. They might even help with her sleepwalking. She looked at his program. He held classes regularly at Glenelg East Community Centre, and also did some country ones. He went to Whyalla once a month. His testimonials also interested her. One, in particular, read:

> *Swami Nardhamuni changed my life. I'd always felt different to everyone else. I was a lonely child, and in my teens, I had a really bad case of pimples and was called 'pizza face'. The job I had when I left school was cleaning public toilets for the council, which meant I didn't have to socialise. Then I lost that job because I kept calling in sick. I got so bad I couldn't get out of bed and all I did was smoke dope.*
>
> *One day, I picked up a pamphlet from Happy Herbs about a meditation retreat on Kangaroo Island. I was desperate and went without much hope. But a miracle happened to me during that retreat and it changed my life. Swami Nardhamuni taught me to change my mindset, just by reaching for the spiritual stillness within. I'm now a happy person, I have friends (even girlfriends!), my pimples have disappeared, and I am inspired to try to make the world a better place by living the vegan way. Phil, June 2017.*

Wow, thought Cecilia. Phil was an acolyte of Swami N—and a happy one, too. The passageway door opened, and Luke walked in.

'How did the interview go?' Cecilia asked, looking up from her laptop. Luke had applied for the position of cook at The Vegan Café, something Cecilia was not entirely happy about.

Luke's face lit up. 'I got the job! I fed the owner all the right lines about being a vegan.' Hannah had coached him before his interview. 'The pay is minimal, but at least I'll have a social life. I'm tired of working nights, and in a couple of years, I'll get a more serious job. Although, this one does have potential. If the café widened its menu, it could get more lunchtime customers. Currently, they just sell pies, cakes, and ice cream. I think the previous cook took it easy. He had plenty of time to go nuts with cleaning and making cannabis cookies.'

The puppies, who were outside, began hurling themselves against the back screen door. Hannah must be home from her dance class. Cecilia shouted at them and then got up and sprayed them with water.

Hannah walked into the family room and threw herself on the sofa. 'I'm pooped. Can we let Ziggy and Stardust in?'

'I've just told them off for scratching at the screen door. I don't want to reward them for bad behaviour by letting them inside straight away. How about in ten minutes?'

'Okay,' said Hannah, and turned to Luke. 'Did you get the job?'

He nodded, taking a swig of beer.

Hannah looked at the bottle. 'Did you know that Guinness used to include fish guts in their beer? As a gelatine?'

'Yuck,' said Luke, looking at his beer dubiously.

'In 2017, they switched in order to be vegan friendly,' Hannah continued. She punched up a fist in the air. 'So, yobbo beer drinkers are now vegan friendly!'

'Thanks a lot! I'm not a yobbo.' Luke was indignant.

Hannah laughed. 'Gotcha!'

He flipped her a finger.

'What did you think of the owner, the guru?' Cecilia asked him.

'Guru?'

'The café owner, also known as Swami N.'

'Oh, yeah, him.'

'Well?'

'For starters, he wears a kaftan, which is so last century, and he's got this weird way of looking at you; he stares at you without saying a word. I think it's rude to look at people like that.'

'That's because you're not good with eye contact,' Hannah told him. 'Remember that staring game we used to play when we were little? Whoever blinked first lost. I always won.'

'That was the only game you won, because you were a little squirt.'

Hannah poked her tongue out at him.

'How do you think you will go as a vegan cook?' Cecilia asked.

'Okay,' he said. 'I looked at some magazines in the café today. There were photos of sheep being jammed into trucks and you could see the whites of their eyes rolling in fear. There was another one of a pig being tasered. Bloody hell! It's disgusting. I don't want to eat animals who have been tortured.'

Cecilia was impressed at how quickly Luke was embracing the concept of veganism. Normally ideas took a while for him—and he had just come from working at the Broadway, where most meals were huge slabs of meat or fish covering the entire plate, decorated with the odd twig of parsley or spoonful of coleslaw as a nod to vegetables. Maybe his family home life had rubbed off on him more than she had realised.

'A weird thing happened at the end of the interview,' Luke added. 'Swami N had been so Zen and calm, but when that old camel guy, Ron, walked in with an esky to collect something, Swami N switched. He looked like he was going to lose it. His face went bright red, and he clenched his fists. I thought there was going to be a fight!'

Cecilia nodded. Swam N was very protective of the vegan way, and the camel semen in his freezer was definitely a forbidden item.

'Ron was like an ancient warrior. He stormed in, raced into the kitchen, snatched some containers from the freezer, and flew out. It was over in seconds. Do you know what was in those containers?'

'Camel semen. Ron and Phil had a deal to store it.'

'What?' Luke was incredulous. 'No wonder the owner was furious, having animal products stored in his vegan fridge. But camel semen? Who wants that?'

'Arabs do. Australian camel semen is in hot demand in the Middle East where they take the breeding of camels very seriously,' said Cecilia, a recent and reluctant camel expert. 'Camels cost a lot of money over there. In Saudi Arabia, they even have camel beauty pageants that boast millions of dollars in prize money.'

'Camel beauty pageants?' Hannah catapulted herself into the conversation and switched her phone on. 'How fascinating!'

'Why the hell did Ron store the camel semen at the café? Everyone has got a fridge, right?' Luke asked.

'The café's fridge also has a liquid nitrogen freezer drawer, which is hard to find unless you want to pay big bucks. It's used for when you want to store biological materials at minus one hundred and fifty degrees, and it's also good for making vegan ice cream.' Cecilia had done her homework.

'Look at this!' Hannah was waving her phone. 'Aren't these camels gorgeous? Here are last year's winners of the Miss Camel beauty pageant in Saudi Arabia.'

Cecilia and Luke peered at the photos.

'They have got big lips,' said Luke.

'Ooh, look at their hump cloths; they're made from intricate embroidery. I like the tassels too,' said Cecilia. 'Very stylish.'

'To be a winner in a beauty pageant,' Hannah read aloud. 'Camels are judged by their graceful walk, their humps, and lips. But guess what?'

'Oh no,' groaned Luke. 'Not more crazy information.'

'Several camels got disqualified last year because their owners used Botox on their lips!'

Luke frowned. 'How did Ron persuade Phil to store the semen? Phil was a vegan, right?'

'A little personal blackmail, and it's not as though the semen was for human consumption.'

'Consumption? Are you bonkers? No-one cooks with semen. That's disgusting. I'm not storing camel semen for Ron. He can find another freezer.'

'I'm sure that side of the business is gone.'

'And the same with marijuana cookies. I'm not doing that either.'

Cecilia was pleased Luke was not taking on the cannabis cookies business, but she was worried about him working for The Vegan Café. However, it was a done deal now. Perhaps it would be okay now Kylie was in the frame for murder. She had the ferocity, she hadn't liked her brother, and she had stolen his money.

Hannah's phone pinged, and so did Luke's. They looked down.

'Bloody hell!' said Luke, looking up at Cecilia.

'Oh my god!' said Hannah. 'Is that you, Mum?'

'It is!' said Luke, pointing. 'I'd recognise her outlandish red stilettos with the silver heels anywhere.'

'Show me!' Cecilia held out her hand.

There was a photo of her lying on top of Kylie at Phil's funeral. *Police make arrest at vegan cook's funeral* the headline read.

'Who is that enormous woman, Mum?' Hannah asked.

'Phil's sister,' said Cecilia. 'She stole his money, and I was helping the police with their enquiries.'

'The Instagram photo looks great.' Hannah punched her phone up in the air. 'Mum is pinning a murderer down, and it's going viral. Look! It's already got a thousand hits.'

'Honestly?' Cecilia looked at the picture again. she felt it was undignified to be viral, but at least it didn't show her face; the image focused on the insane rage on Kylie's.

Luke studied the photo. 'She is three times the size of you, Mum. Did you take her legs down first and then fall on top?'

'Yes.'

'That's a classic judo move. I'm impressed.'

'Why did you do that?' Hannah asked. 'Is she a thief, a killer, or both?'

'I don't know, except she pinched a lot of money from her brother. It was in a tan pencil case that he carried around with him, which somehow managed to end up in Kylie's possession.'

'Why did she want the money?'

Cecilia shrugged. 'For a TV? For bodybuilding? She spends a lot of time with weights.'

'I'm going to check her out on Facebook,' said Hannah. 'What's her name?'

'Kylie Dyson.'

A few minutes later, Hannah surfaced from Kylie's Facebook site. 'She's a serious bodybuilder and has won prizes in gladiator championships. In some photos, she is wearing a glittering bikini, a fake tan, and showing off her biceps. Oh, this is interesting: she writes, *bodybuilding is not just a beauty contest, it helps to harness your willpower and mental strength.*' Hannah stopped to draw breath. 'And she is crowdfunding, too. She says she wants to go to Bali for a bodybuilding contest and to bring back bodybuilding as an Olympic sport. Maybe that's why she needed the money? For plane tickets and a spray tan?'

'No way,' said Luke. 'Who would kill someone to buy a fake tan?'

'Some women go nuts about their bodies,' said Hannah. 'They want control, and, if they have been fasting, anything can happen. I remember when Vee, Amy's sister, did a juice fast; she went on a spider-killing spree. It was scary the way she stormed around the garden looking for spiders to stomp on, which is so non-vegan. Spiders have a right to live, too.'

Was Kylie crazy enough to kill her brother? Cecilia could only speculate.

***

A complaint about the potato salad being off at Bay Charcoal Chickens meant Cecilia had to delay her return to Sun-Kissed Motel to check the pH levels, which had been askew on her last visit. The chicken shop was in chaos, which surprised her. On previous occasions, it had scored high on the cleanliness scale. Out the back, the kitchen benchtops were littered with bowls of chopped veggies and even sliced bacon lay unrefrigerated on the bench. The sinks were full of dirty dishes.

'My wife,' said Christos, 'has the cancer. I have no time for chicken and salads. I must be with her when she has chemo.'

'I'm sorry,' Cecilia said. 'It must be a difficult time for both of you.'

'And my assistant cook leaves me and goes off to work at that fancy vegan café. I paid him good money but he said he couldn't be involved in the slaughter of the innocents. What a thing to say! I was hurt. All my chickens are free-range.'

So, that's why Bay Charcoal Chickens previously scored high on the cleanliness scale. Cecilia did not know Phil had worked there.

'Phil was a super-clean cook and then he goes and gets himself killed! What is it with vegans?' Christos demanded. 'They must be some weird cult.'

Cecilia bit back a comment that vegans were part of the new norm, and not a crazy sect. Christos had more important issues at hand.

He wiped his eyes with a corner of his apron. From her handbag, Cecilia handed him a tissue from her bag.

'An Indian family want to buy my chicken shop, but they're being cheap. My shop is worth more money.'

'Why don't you close?' she said gently. 'Then you can concentrate on helping your wife.'

'But will I still be able to sell the business?'

She considered the question carefully. 'I think your business is about location. You have a prime position on Jetty Road. That is why your business is saleable.'

'My wife and I have worked hard all our lives, and now it's time for us to take it easy. We would like to take a caravan trip around Australia.'

'I wouldn't mind taking a caravan trip, too, one day,' said Cecilia enthusiastically, hoping to calm him down with nice thoughts.

Christos brooded in silence.

'Are you worried if you put up a *closed* sign, the buyers might drop their price for your business?'

He nodded.

'If you put a *closed* sign on the door, you could concentrate on cleaning up the place. If a potential purchaser saw the mess, they would lower their offering price.'

'I can manage,' he said. 'I don't want to close down. That makes the business look like a failure.'

'You need to clean up before you sell any more salads and chickens. I can't risk food poisoning.'

Christos collapsed. 'You're right. I can't go on.'

She stayed a little longer, reassuring him he was doing the right thing, and it would be much better if he presented potential buyers with sparkling clean premises. She suggested he could tell them he was selling because his wife had a serious disease; that would make the closure understandable.

Cecilia drove back to the council and parked the car. Someone called her name. Aldo was getting out of his car, holding a bag of hot chips.

He shook the bag at her, rattling the chips, and pointed to the bench where they usually sat. Cecilia resisted the chips and produced an apple and a muesli bar from her handbag. A pack of militant seagulls hovered around them.

'Shoo!' Aldo produced an ironed navy-blue handkerchief from his pocket to wave them away.

'Look them in the eye,' Cecilia advised. 'Seagulls don't like eye contact.'

'Show me how?'

Cecilia switched on her alpha glare, and Aldo laughed. 'I wouldn't like being on the receiving end of one of those looks.'

Cecilia crunched on her apple.

Aldo picked up his bag of chips and held them while he ate. 'I want to look at you, not at seagulls. Although, a strange thing happened the other day,' he continued. 'The sergeant and I found two seagulls in a box on the station's front doorstep. Their legs had been tied together.'

'What?'

'People drop off all sorts of things at police stations.'

'Like babies?'

'And even a shark. One of our country coastal police stations found a shark in a box on their doorstep.'

'A shark?' said Cecilia mystified. 'It must have been a small one.'

'Sharks scare off the tourists. I think it was a message from one of the tourist operators.'

'Well, I know our local eateries find seagulls a nuisance, but there's not much to be done about it. They're protected by the migratory bird law. What did you do with the seagulls in the box?'

'I untied them and they flew off.'

'Do you like seagulls?'

'No, but every life is important. They looked so sad and terrified. I couldn't just dump them in the bin and let them die a long, painful death.'

'What a kind thing to do.' Cecilia was impressed. 'I wonder who trapped them? An annoyed restaurant owner? They should all know seagulls are protected, and you can go to jail for cruelty to animals or birds.'

Aldo retrieved a long chip and opened his jaws wide. He then sighed with contentment. 'Look around. Isn't it a lovely day?'

The council had turned on the play sprinklers in the square; small children rushed around, squealing as the water shot up. A golden retriever was playing, too, shaking his shaggy coat when it got squirted. It was not on a leash, but it seemed to be attached to a small boy in lime-green shorts.

'I was most impressed by you at the funeral,' he said with a smile. 'You took down a woman three times your weight and you didn't even mess your hair.'

'Judo comes in handy,' said Cecilia. 'Did she confess?'

'Confession is a complex process.'

'But you do it all the time. You get people to own up and tell you their secrets.' That was a part of Aldo that Cecilia was not sure if she trusted; he got people to tell him things. Cecilia had told him a lot, except about her PTSD and spooky sleepwalking.

'Let me guess,' said Cecilia. 'Kylie is no longer pretending she was working the night Phil was killed. Maybe she swapped with someone on the roster and drove to town to see Phil and borrow some money from him. She wants to go to a bodybuilding contest in Bali and perhaps she didn't have enough money. Maybe he refused and they got into a fight. Am I right? Or am I right?' A smile tugged at Aldo's face. 'Fancy killing someone for a fake tan and a trip to Bali. I took the kids there one Christmas holidays. It was so pretty, with all that greenery and the little shrines with flowers. We had a lovely time.'

Aldo crunched on a chip. She stole a look at his face. She was not going to get any more information from him until he finished that chip. *Why didn't Phil use a bank?* she wondered. It was risky carrying that amount of cash. Or maybe it was because he did not want the tax department to know about his additional income.

'I think Kylie could be violent,' Cecilia pursued Aldo. 'Did you see that photo of her on Instagram? She looked deranged.'

Aldo smiled broadly. 'One of the younger police officers showed it to me. It was a fine photo of you, too.'

Cecilia glared at him. Her backside had been on display.

Aldo cocked his head to one side and looked at her. 'Will you come to the movies with me?'

She held her breath and then let it out slowly. She would love to sit in a dark cinema with Aldo, sitting close and perhaps holding hands with their shoulders touching.

'What kind of movies do you like?' she asked, playing for time.

'The movies you like,' he said promptly.

'Romantic comedies?'

A shadow of doubt crossed Aldo's face. 'I like slapstick.'

'There's a film coming out soon. It's had rave reviews. It's about a nun in the twelfth century, and she lives in a small cell and does not see or speak to anyone.'

'Say what?'

'It's called *A Nun in a Cell.*'

'You sure are a hard nut to crack.'

Cecilia laughed. 'Okay, just kidding. What about the new James Bond movie?'

'It's a date!'

***

On her return from apples and chips on the bench, Cecilia received a summons from Tristan to meet him in his office.

She knocked on his door and stepped in. He gestured for her to sit down and continued typing, showing his authority by making her wait, so she whipped out her phone and checked her messages. There was one from her sister, Angel, who was having difficulties with Bazza. He had stolen some birdseed from the pet shop and the family didn't even have a bird.

Finally, Tristan emerged from his computer. 'How is the clean-up going at Florence Street?'

'It's done. Mr Dyson can move in when he pays the bills.'

'I thought he was going to a nursing home.'

'No, he is staying at the Sun-Kissed Motel. It's Mrs Dyson who has moved into a nursing home.'

'Will Mr Dyson pay his bills?'

'If he doesn't, then the debt collectors will come after him.'

'Are you hounding one of our poor elderly folk?'

Cecilia sniffed. 'There is nothing poor about Mr Dyson, except a reluctance to pay his bills.'

'What about the murder of The Vegan Café's cook? I heard you went to the funeral.' Cecilia groaned inaudibly. He hadn't seen the photo, had he? 'I don't want the council to be involved in sordid murders.' He tapped his phone.

'I went to the funeral in my time, not the council's. I felt sorry for him.' Cecilia touched the corner of her eye. 'It's such a tragic event—a young man's life cut short in such a brutal way. I keep seeing his body lying on the kitchen floor. I was the first one to find him, and I'm still in shock.' She squeezed her lips shut. She was not going to have a meltdown in front of Tristan.

Tristan squinted, puzzled. Typically, he was lucky to get one sentence out of Cecilia.

'It looks bad for our community,' he said. 'People will think Glenelg is not a safe place. We will lose our position as the diamond in the crown of Adelaide's beach suburbs!'

The diamond in the crown? How corny. Tristan was incapable of producing effective results unless he used the public relations officer.

'Hopefully, the police have now got his killer.' He looked at her, then down at his phone.

'I hope so, too.' She gritted her teeth, waiting for him to discuss the Instagram photo.

Then, unexpectedly, he leant forward. 'You look tired. I can't have my staff running ragged. I've got a duty of care to make sure you're not overloaded.'

Cecilia's mouth dropped open, and he gave her a fatherly wave as she left the office.

***

Luke walked into the family room while Cecilia was pouring herself a large glass of sauvignon blanc after an unexpected bout of sobbing in the bathroom. What was happening to her?

'Hey, honey,' said Cecilia. 'How was your first day at work?'

'It's a nice place to work, Mum. The café is custom-built, so I have a decent-sized kitchen, and the ingredients have to be organic and fresh, which means it's a different style of cooking … but I like it.' Luke pulled open the fridge door, grabbed a vegan beer from the side door, and headed for his favourite recliner. Cecilia joined him with her glass of wine. 'You met the owners of the café, didn't you, Mum?'

'I sure did.'

'Astra is over the top,' said Luke.

'That's one way of putting it,' said Cecilia snippily.

'When her husband is not there, she hangs around the kitchen and tries to come onto me. I think the hardest thing about this job is going to be dealing with the owners.'

'You need to sort her out. Tell her you are not a player with women.'

'Yeah, that's not me.' Luke swallowed a mouthful of beer. 'Who do you think killed Phil? Was it his sister?'

An uneasy feeling crept over Cecilia. Her wine tasted sour. Perhaps she should have made herbal tea instead. 'Kylie wanted money, and he must have refused her.' Cecilia ran her finger slowly around the top of her wine glass. 'I guess they had a fight.'

'It must have been one hell of a fight.'

'I know,' said Cecilia unhappily. Killing someone over a couple of thousand dollars to buy a fake tan and go to Bali for a bodybuilding contest seemed farfetched, but Aldo had said people kill for crazy reasons and that most murderers had mental health issues.

And Kylie had looked crazed in that Instagram shot—her teeth were bared in a white-hot rage, as if she was possessed by something sinister.

**

After a morning of routine inspections that ticked all the boxes, Cecilia returned to the office and found the town hall suspiciously quiet. Anne was not at the front desk, nor was the building inspector in his office opposite hers, so she walked down to the lunchroom. Most of the staff were there, looking at their mobile phones, their faces shocked and intent. The sounds of crashing and screaming poured out from their phones.

Cecilia made her way to Garth's side. 'What's up?'

'Someone drove their car onto the pavement of Jetty Road,' Garth replied.

She peered into his phone. A white station wagon had climbed up onto the footpath, ploughing its way through a gaggle of shrieking people, and ending up smashed halfway inside a shop. The news feed played the same sequence again and again.

'Is it a terrorist attack?' Cecilia asked.

'Those bloody Muslims,' said Tristan. 'They should all be deported back to where they came from.'

'Do you mind?' Cecilia said angrily. 'Someone in your position should not be making racist comments.'

'Who do you think you're talking to?' Tristan's face was bright red.

An idiot, thought Cecilia. She got out her own phone, trying to work out which shops the car had crashed into. At first, she thought it might be Vince's Fruit and Veg, but on closer inspection, it looked like Happy Herbs had taken most of the damage.

Happy Herbs was not on her list as a food outlet. It sold bongs and herbal remedies, but not marijuana; though most of its products were involved in the grinding, processing, or smoking of marijuana.

She studied the footage again, then pressed pause on the phone and looked closely at the driver. She enlarged the picture. The driver was an older man and had a strong resemblance to Mr Dyson.

She showed it to Wendy. 'Check this out. Don't you think the driver looks like Mr Dyson from Florence Street?'

Wendy studied the picture. 'It looks like him, and he owns a white station wagon, too. I've seen it in his driveway. It was the only car that seemed in working order.'

'Okay, everyone,' Cecilia told the lunchroom. 'Listen up! This may not be a terrorist attack. It could be one of our senior residents who lost control of his car.'

Mutterings wafted around the lunchroom as staff zoomed in on the pictures on their phones.

'What shall we do?' Cecilia asked Wendy. 'Shall we ring the cops?'

Wendy gnawed on her bottom lip. 'The police will find out soon enough that this is an elderly driver issue and not a terrorist one.'

Cecilia was taken aback. Wendy was becoming sensible. 'We do nothing?'

'Well, currently, it's about dangerous driving, and that's a policing concern. There's not much we can do.'

'It's weird that Mr Dyson keeps popping up at the moment,' mused Cecilia.

'Yes,' said Wendy. 'He's in for a lot of publicity, which will annoy him.'

'I can imagine that. He has a limited range of emotions, and being annoyed is at the top of his list. He only cares about himself. He didn't even seem too concerned his son was murdered.'

'It's the hoarding,' said Wendy sadly. 'It's an addiction he can't think past.'

'Huh?'

'I've been doing some reading,' Wendy shyly explained. 'Hoarding is an offshoot of obsessive-compulsive disorders. A lot of older people have it. OCD is a control thing.'

Cecilia thought about Army Auntie, whose cardigan pockets were full of little packets of sugar she'd nicked from the dining room table at Marigold Nursing Home.

'Do you think he was strong enough to bash Phil?'

Wendy's worried look returned. 'He's fit, and I don't know what lengths he would go to maintain his hoarding lifestyle.'

***

'I see the babies ate their bed again,' said Cecilia, walking into her family room.

Hannah emptied a dustpan full of white fluff into a bin bag. 'We only bought this bed a couple of days ago.'

'We'll get another trampoline dog bed for inside,' Cecilia decided. 'Ziggy and Stardust can't trash those.'

Hannah tied a knot in the bag. 'I think I've got all of the fluff.'

'Are you going out?' Her daughter was dressed in a short black skirt, black tights, and a soft grey shirt. It was a nice change from grubby tracksuit pants. Her long rainbow-coloured hair was piled up in a loose knot.

'I'm going to a vegan festival.'

'You look lovely.'

She blushed. 'I don't look too tacky?'

'You look like somebody I would want to meet: interesting and arty, but not tacky.'

Hannah left, and Cecilia lay on the couch, eyeing the puppies who were playing tug of war with an old rope. They were noisy, and she could hardly hear the television. She wanted to watch the news to see if it was Mr Dyson whose dubious driving skills had trashed the lower end of Jetty Road.

Cecilia got up and collected two apples from the fruit bowl. She led the puppies outside with caressing words, gave them each an apple, and then shut all the doors, including the doggy door in the laundry.

The coverage of the accident appeared halfway through the ABC news. An elderly man had lost control of his car and drove into a shop on Jetty Road, Glenelg. Luckily, he had been driving slowly and nobody was hurt, just a few cuts and bruises, but Happy Herbs, which had borne the impact of the station wagon, would need to replace its front window and door.

Mr Dyson seemed to have survived the accident unscathed and was furious with the attention of mobile phones and journalists. 'Go away! You're harassing a poor old man!' He waved his walking stick which he had retrieved from the wrecked car and swung it wildly, which only encouraged the camera clickers.

Cecilia smiled happily from her sofa in her living room. Hopefully, Mr Dyson would be mortified by the publicity, which served him right. She sipped her wine. It was Friday night—the weekend, and what better way to finish a working week.

At about eleven o'clock that night, after she had made her preparations to prevent sleepwalking—the doorbell was hung over her door, the sensor pad was switched on, and she had completed her session of self-hypnosis—there came a knock on her door. She turned on her bedside table lamp. Her bell jingled, and Hannah stood in the doorway; her hair was ruffled, and her eyes were ringed with black smudges.

Cecilia sat up in bed with a jolt. 'What's wrong, honey?'

'I got attacked at the vegan festival!' Hannah sobbed.

'What?' Cecilia leapt out of bed and rushed to her daughter, enveloping her in a hug. Terrible thoughts raced through Cecilia's head and she felt sick.

Meanwhile, Ziggy and Stardust whined and scratched at Cecilia's bedroom door.

'The babies, Mum.'

'Oh, yes … the dogs.' Cecilia knew she had to pull herself together. 'How about I make you a hot drink, and you can be with Ziggy and Stardust?'

'I'd like that.'

Cecilia was desperately trying to keep her emotions under control as she busied herself in the kitchen. She selected Hannah's childhood mug—the one with bunnies on it—then she worried her daughter might feel like she was babying her, so she put the bunny mug back and picked up the pink one with the love hearts that said 'V is for Vegan'. Something had gone terribly wrong at the vegan festival, so Cecilia dumped that mug, too. Finally, she chose a generic white one and made a hot cacao drink with almond milk.

Hannah sat down on the sofa, and the puppies jumped on her lap and began licking her face vigorously, perhaps sympathetic for her tears. Or perhaps they liked the salt.

Cecilia made herself a coffee and put it on the side table. She sat down on the sofa next to her daughter and began soothing the puppies so Hannah could drink her hot drink without the dogs spilling it all over her.

'Talk to me.'

Hannah took a deep breath. 'Vee, Amy's sister, was scary-crazy. She attacked me. Physically!' Hannah's eyes were still round with shock. 'I was with a group of friends, and she pushed her way through and screamed at me that I was a slut. Then she really lost it and slapped me.' Hannah wiped her nose on her grey shirt while Cecilia fetched the tissues. 'She kept shrieking that I had taken Phil away from her and that he had been her boyfriend until I screwed things up between them.'

'Was Vee Phil's girlfriend?' Cecilia asked.

'I don't know. Maybe they had something going on. At least, Vee seemed to think so. But why would she accuse me of taking him away from her?'

'That's nuts. You hardly knew him! Besides, it was Jessie who he fell in love with. It makes no sense.'

'I know!' Hannah knuckled her eyes. 'If he hadn't got killed, I wouldn't have remembered him. I just try to be friendly to everyone I meet; it's good karma. She must have been in the café when I was talking to him about veganism.'

Cecilia gave a half-smile. Hannah always talked to people in shops and cafés.

'The trouble is, Vee has never liked me. She knows that I know she's not a true vegan.'

'Okay,' said Cecilia uncertainly. Sometimes young people's relationships seemed complex and baffling. Had Phil told Vee he had fallen in love with someone else but not said who it was?

'Vee's crazy, Mum. All that dope she uses has made her paranoid.'

'Phil's dead. What does it matter? He's nobody's bloke now.'

'I didn't do anything.'

'I know you wouldn't try to steal someone's boyfriend.'

'Yes, but what I meant is I didn't do anything. I was passive and frozen with fear. I let Vee slap me around and just lay on the ground, curled in a ball, while she kicked me.' Tears trickled down Hannah's cheeks. 'My friends pulled her off me, and one of them, the guy who does wood carving, he drove me home.'

Cecilia was outraged. Physical violence should not be tolerated. 'We should call the police and charge Vee with assault. Do you want me to make the call?'

Hannah wavered. 'I don't want to be afraid, and I don't want to be the kind of person who gets picked on.'

'Are your ribs okay? Do you think she broke any of them? Does it hurt when you take a deep breath?'

'I don't think so. Maybe I am making a big deal about it. I don't think calling the police is necessary.'

'But she slapped and kicked you! I can see a red mark on your face. You can't let her get away with it.'

'Sorry, Mum. I didn't mean to disturb you. I think it was the shock because I've never been hit before.' Hannah swallowed the last of her drink. 'I want to take the puppies and go to bed and forget anything happened.'

Cecilia bit her lip. She was able to protect Hannah when she was a child: shield her, advocate for her. But not as an adult. With difficulty, Cecilia was learning to let go of her parent role. Hannah now had her own trajectory to make; she was beyond reach and all Cecilia could do was stand on the sidelines and watch, even if things did go wrong. Cecilia couldn't make Hannah go to the police—no matter how much she wanted her to report it.

She lay in bed, wondering about Vee. How violent was she? Could she kill? Phil must have told her he wasn't going to see her anymore because he had found his true love, whom he didn't name. Why else would Vee attack Hannah?

Could that have provoked an insane murderous rage?

***

On Saturday morning, Cecilia wrote down her shopping list on the back of a pamphlet that advertised a tournament in which she and her bridge partner—Don, a dapper eighty-seven-year-old and a retired neurosurgeon—were competing that afternoon.

She collected the shopping bags from the laundry, drove to Jetty Road, parked in the supermarket car park, and then before shopping, she decided to take a stroll and check out the devastation that Mr Dyson had caused.

Arms folded, she stood in front of Happy Herbs. The shop normally showcased a Hindu god, a large blue, multiarmed Vishnu in the window but, instead, brown slats of wood were now nailed to the frontage, momentarily banishing the god. Next door was a *closed* sign on Vince's shop. As she peered inside the window, she saw all the produce had been removed.

The damage was worse than it seemed on television. The shared wall between Vince's and Happy Herbs was cracked, and she guessed debris had found its way into the fruit and vegetables. She hoped they both had good insurance.

She crossed back over the road again and browsed the supermarket shelves, thinking of what to make for tonight's dinner. No matter what happened—bashing, car crashing, theft, or murder—there was always the question of what to make for dinner. She decided to make veggie burgers and wedges: carbohydrate comfort food.

Cecilia drove home, put away the shopping, and turned on the kettle. Hannah had set up her easel in a sunny part of the lounge. She had a photo of Kylie positioned to the side of her easel and was drawing her using colour and glitter pencils. It was not complimentary. Hannah had even managed to draw the veins sticking out from Kylie's biceps and her bikini glittered in a vile blue.

'Do you think I'm mean about Kylie? It's just that … well, she could have murdered Phil,' said Hannah anxiously. 'Or maybe I'm unfair about female bodybuilders. Maybe female bodybuilding is a symbol of resistance to male expectations of what a woman's body should look like. But it does seem to me a rather extreme way to express femininity.'

'Well, I don't know about that,' said Cecilia. 'Except I'm not too keen on male bodybuilders, either. All those veins sticking out and emphasising muscle definition remind me of biology classes at school.'

'I don't like this portrait,' Hannah declared. 'It feels yuck, and I don't understand her.' She ripped the drawing from the easel and threw it in the bin.

'Why don't you draw Vee?' Cecilia asked. 'It might help you to get over the attack.'

Hannah turned around to face Cecilia. 'You mean as therapy? I *am* doing something about it, but I'm not going to the police. It's not that serious. I just don't want to be a person who gets picked on—someone who's afraid.'

Cecilia frowned at the sight of her daughter's face. There was a purple bruise as big as two knuckles on Hannah's cheek. Cecilia could no longer keep quiet. 'That's why so many people don't report their assault to the police: because they say, "It's not that serious".'

'Walk a mile in my shoes!' Hannah shot back.

Biting her lip, frustrated and helpless, Cecilia retreated to the front lounge with her chamomile tea. As a distraction, she began to plan her wardrobe for the bridge competition. She decided on a sky-blue dress, a turquoise Aztec beaded necklace, and her black pumps.

***

At bridge, Cecilia and Don scored well, making fifty-two percent, and came third. A couple of times during a break in play, she checked her phone for a message from Aldo, but there was none.

At home, she discovered both Luke and Hannah had gone out. Cecilia felt relieved. It was good Hannah had decided to go out, despite her shocking experience the previous night, and she was drawing and painting again, which was a relief. Hannah was handling it in her own way, and Cecilia had to leave her to it.

Now, what was for her dinner? The veggie burgers could wait for when the family was home. But just for her, she would have a simple meal, she decided, opening the fridge door and examining its abundant contents from her weekly shop. She fetched a frying pan and made spicy scrambled eggs with chilli and rocket. With a table mat to balance her bowl, she sat down on the sofa and turned on the ABC news. Being Saturday, it was mostly sports news, which bored Cecilia. She switched to a period piece drama on Netflix.

Her phone was next to her on the side table; there was still no phone call or message from Aldo. Exasperated, she dumped the phone on the hall table bowl that also served as a place to put keys. She was cross with herself for constantly checking if he had texted. It seemed unlikely there was going to be a movie date with him this weekend. Perhaps it was a good thing. She wasn't sure if she was ready for that kind of intimacy, especially when she was struggling with sleepwalking.

At around eight o'clock, she phoned Bruce, an old school friend.

'Do you fancy a cruise sometime?'

He replied that it sounded like a fabulous idea and he would run it past Freddie, his partner. Then Cecilia retired to have a long bath and daydreamed about blue oceans, creamy scented massages, and no dead bodies—or injured daughters.

***

Cecilia dipped small rectangles of sponge cake into a chocolate sauce and sprinkled grated coconut over them; she was making lamingtons for afternoon tea for Angel and the kids.

At three o'clock, Angel parked outside Cecilia's house, and the kids poured out equipped with water pistols. Cecilia stood in the passageway, watching them race through her house and out to the backyard in dismay. Angel kicked off her shoes and snuggled up in her favourite green-and-pink armchair in the front lounge.

Cecilia walked down the back and fetched a jug of cordial, plastic cups, and a plate of lamingtons from the kitchen. She put them on the outside table. 'Take your shoes off before coming inside,' she told the kids. 'Or better still, don't come inside.'

'Aww, Aunty Cee-Cee, these are really cool water pistols,' said Bazza. 'Do you want to have a look?'

'No,' said Cecilia, and returned to the kitchen to pour boiling water into a teapot. She set down the tray on a mahogany side table in the front lounge. 'Really, Angel? Water pistols? Why? They'll get soaked.'

'I've told them they can only use them outside and they have to take their shoes off when they come inside. Anyway, it's a lovely spring day. They'll dry off.'

'That's small comfort.'

'The water pistols are about no body contact, because I don't want any more wrestling,' Angel explained. 'The kids were playing this game where if you pinned someone to the ground for more than twenty-two seconds, then that person was dead.'

'Why twenty-two seconds?'

'I have no idea. Anyway, I had a teacher ask me in for a little chat about Timmy.'

'Did Timmy beat someone up?' Timmy was the middle brother—a wiry, tough ten-year-old with spiky hair, who could punch well above his weight.

'No, it wasn't that. His teacher wanted to know about the bruises on his arm because she thought I was abusing him. I've never been so embarrassed in my life! I've put my foot down with the kids. No more body contact in games, or else the PlayStation goes out in the street, never to be seen again.'

Ziggy and Stardust were also dismayed by the water pistols and huddled up to Chloe in the front lounge. Normally, they said hello to the kids, receiving pats and adoration, before retreating with Chloe and the sisters. Not this time. The puppies hated getting wet.

'How's the murder investigation going?' Angel asked, sipping her tea with two sugars. 'I see you're still involved in it.'

Cecilia sighed. 'I want it solved.'

'And you've gone viral!'

Cecilia scowled.

'Sally showed me your Instagram shot.' Sally was Angel's oldest and the only girl. 'You're amazing, Cee-Cee,' Angel continued. 'Fancy pinning a gigantic woman down to the floor in a funeral parlour! The kids were most impressed. Then we argued because the kids asked "if Aunty Cee-Cee can squash people, why can't we?"'

'Just tell them I was assisting the police with their enquiries.'

'Who was she?'

'The cook's sister. It looks like she stole several thousand dollars from him, perhaps on the night of his murder. She's into bodybuilding and wants to go to a contest in Bali. Maybe she needed the money for that.'

'Hmm, bodybuilding.' Angel ran a finger around the rim of her teacup. 'No, I don't think I have had a date with any of those.'

'She's one of the suspects now.'

'She looked certifiably crazy in that Instagram.' Angel picked up a lamington and put it on her plate. 'You're a good baker, Cee-Cee.' She broke it into quarters and wiped her hands on the cloth napkin Cecilia provided. 'How are things going with Investigator Aldo?'

'I don't know.'

'What do you mean, you don't know? Has he asked you out again?'

'Again? Well, he's asked me to the movies at some unspecified time. But I'm not sure if—'

'If what?' Angel leaned forward in her seat. 'Are you backing out?'

'There's a murder to be solved, and that's more important,' said Cecilia, sidestepping her sister's questions.

'Since when have you been so shy around men?'

'Since I started sleepwalking again.'

'Oh, no!' Angel dropped her half-eaten lamington in horror.

'I'm barricading myself in my bedroom. I have bells, alarms, and whistles. Oh, and I'm seeing a psychiatrist.'

'Jeez, Louise! Now I am really worried about you. God knows where your sleepwalking will take you this time.'

'My bridge club?' suggested Cecilia, and took the remaining lamington.

***

Cecilia's Monday morning crawled along. She rearranged her filing cabinet, cleaned out her desk drawer, and kept reviewing her conversations with Aldo. He'd told her she was beautiful. He'd asked her out for fish and chips on the esplanade, and if she wanted to go to the movies with him. He was attractive, and she felt little skips of excitement when she spoke with him. She enjoyed the feel of him—bulky and warm—when their shoulders had touched on the bench.

But what did he want from her? Was it merely sex? She was not the sort of person who would have sex simply on a physical basis. Not at her age. In her twenties, she'd had a few one-night stands, but at fifty-three years old, casual sex was not on her agenda.

Garth stuck his head around her office door and squinted at her from under grey bushy eyebrows. 'Are you okay? You look a bit washed out.'

'I feel flat. Maybe because everything seems to have stopped in the investigation.'

'It's got me stumped, too.'

'How's Jessie?'

'She's coping. She had a nice cuppa tea with Big John and Mavis. I think Jessie and John wanna take over Phil's green cleaning business and expand it. Phil had over fifty customers. Can you believe it? I thought he only had a dozen customers, but these days lots of people are worried about all the chemicals in cleaning products. They say cleaners have a rotten high risk for cancer. I suggested to my Daphne that she try green cleaning, and she suggested that I try it on the toilet.'

'I use eucalyptus oil and baking soda mostly,' said Cecilia absently.

Garth's phone rang. 'Yep,' he answered. 'I'll be over to pick it up.'

'A lost dog?' Cecilia enquired.

'A British bulldog. It should be easy to find its owner. Do you know British bulldogs can fetch up to nine thousand dollars? The owners will be in a hurry to get it back.'

'Wow,' said Cecilia. 'That's a truckload of money tied up in a dog.'

Garth disappeared, and Cecilia returned to her computer. She scrolled through her emails. There were some new guidelines from the state health department about the positioning of restrooms in cafés. She thought of Industrial Coffee, the place where she'd taken Jessie. It was a converted garage, and to access its restrooms, you had to go through part of the kitchen. They had saved on plumbing costs by keeping the garage's old bathroom.

Industrial Coffee was going to be annoyed about moving the toilets because it would be expensive. She wondered if putting a wall between the kitchen and the passageway to the bathrooms would meet the guidelines. She would have to talk to the building inspector, and they would do a joint inspection.

She brought up her spreadsheet of food outlets to see if any of them came to mind for having oddly positioned restrooms, but found it hard to concentrate.

Was Kylie really the murderer? Had she confessed? Aldo had the reputation of being good at getting confessions.

Cecilia had come across many connections since she found Phil dead on the kitchen floor—a fruit and veg blackmail racket, a boutique cannabis cookie business, the harvesting of camel semen, a hoarders' house, and a more expansive knowledge of peculiar hobbies. Did any of them have a bearing on why Phil had been killed? Were they clues?

And at the back of her mind were her feelings about Aldo which wouldn't go away.

She squirmed in her seat. Maybe she was too keen on him, and she could not afford that. A brisk walk down the main street would do her good. She needed to think about restrooms, not Aldo.

All was quiet outside the police station. Cecilia could not help but feel disappointed, and then she scolded herself for having such thoughts.

As she walked down Jetty Road, she was pleased to see several new cafés opening up, which promised good business for the summer tourist season. However, no ill-positioned restrooms sprang to mind— although, a clothes business was now a gourmet burger outlet, which would need an inspection soon. She walked back to her office.

Garth whistled for her as she walked down the corridor. After she entered his pocket-sized office, he gestured that she should close the door.

'Have you heard the news?' he demanded.

'What news?'

'Tristan has got a promotion. He's going to be CEO of Treeside Council.'

'Well, fancy that. Treeside Council, eh?' Cecilia laughed. Treeside council was notorious in South Australia's local government world for having the highest turnover of staff.

'Tristan is really happy. He says he's gonna get a lot more money working for a bigger council.'

'And a lot more trouble too,' said Cecilia. 'Wasn't the last CEO found hiding under his desk, clutching a whisky bottle and babbling about seeing pink koalas?'

'Yep, and there are heaps of other shenanigans going on among the elected members and senior staff. Bullying, sexual harassment, you name it. They've even got a court case going about it.'

'Tristan is going to be so stressed out,' said Cecilia happily.

'Oh no,' said Garth, his eyes wide with feigned innocence. 'Tristan has told me he's going to make a difference. He's gonna be the new vacuum cleaner.'

Cecilia shook her head. 'He can't even handle parking regulations.' She lolled back in her chair. 'By the time Glenelg Council finds a replacement, with a bit of luck, we should be without a CEO for at least four months. 'Oh, the bliss …'

'I helped him get the job.' Garth looked smug. 'When I saw the job advertised, I encouraged him to go for it. I even offered him a reference and encouraged him to apply. A reference from one of the First Nations People carries a bit of weight these days. It shows Tristan is "culturally sensitive".'

Cecilia snorted.

Garth snickered and continued. 'Tristan was thrilled with that, and the prospect of an extra hundred thousand dollars a year in his salary. I figured a reference was a small price to pay to get rid of him.'

Cecilia frowned. 'I don't know why a CEO's wages are tied to the amount the council receives in rates. The bigger the council, the bigger the pay cheque for the CEO.'

'But not us humble workers,' said Garth. 'Our salaries are capped.'

***

Cecilia woke up with a runny nose. She reached for the tissues, blew, and took another one. She felt around her body with her mind. She was hot and her muscles ached. Maybe she was coming down with the flu that had been going around the town hall.

She got up and made herself an espresso but she still felt awful. There was nothing at work that couldn't wait. She phoned in, said she was sick, and headed for the sofa.

Hannah had started drawing early in the day. She'd put her easel up in the sunny part of the family room, and was working on a portrait of Vee. It was dark and menacing, and Hannah was using thick charcoal strokes.

'Don't forget the pink hair,' said Cecilia. 'Make her look silly and stupid. She's just a bully.'

Hannah scowled at her drawing.

Cecilia sighed. Was Vee insane enough to kill? It was a terrible thought. But so was thinking Kylie, Phil's sister, was a killer, too. Cecilia had googled fratricide and learnt that it was the least common form of family homicide. Maybe she didn't want anyone to be a killer. Not in her community. It was a shame Phil hadn't just slipped on the floor and hit his head.

After a small lunch, she retreated to her bedroom, where she slept on and off during the afternoon.

Hannah made her cauliflower and cashew soup for dinner, and they ate in front of the television. Luke was at a mate's place.

'Dad's moved back to Adelaide,' Hannah said suddenly, fixing her eyes on the creamy soup, avoiding looking at Cecilia. 'He's got a job selling cars for BMW.'

'Oh,' said Cecilia carefully. 'Where's he staying?'

'He's renting an apartment in Adelphi apartments. It'll be nice to have him living close by.'

'Have you been there?'

'Yeah.'

'What's his flat like?'

'It's got lovely views of the sea, but it's small. There's only one bedroom.'

'They crammed the apartments in those high rises,' said Cecilia. 'A lot of retired people live there.'

'Dad's flat would be too small for two people.'

'Oh well, you're too old to worry about having sleepovers at your dad's place.'

'I want him to meet the puppies.'

Cecilia hesitated. 'Do it when I'm not here.' She had to draw boundaries without slanging off at Steve.

'Luke is pleased, too, that Dad has moved to Adelaide. He wants to do guy stuff with him.'

'Like what?'

'Watch sports on TV and do gaming with him.' Hannah looked at Cecilia sideways. 'Dad also wants to catch up with you. He says you were lots of fun.'

'Fun? Not with this flu. I feel like one of the puppies' old toys. All chewed up and soggy.'

'You both have a great sense of humour.'

Cecilia shook her head and got up off the sofa. No romantic reunions were going to happen between her and Steve. She took her phone and went back to bed. There was still no call from Aldo. She was beginning to wonder whether she had misunderstood him. Maybe he was a flirt, like Steve.

Her doubts grew about Aldo throughout the day. She watched the mini-series *The Little Drummer Girl* and was fascinated to see how the main female character, Charlie, was groomed by an Israeli spymaster. He wooed her, kept her on a tipping point, just out of reach, but with the possibility or promise of a mysterious romance in the offing. Had Aldo done that to her? Had he built a relationship and made an emotional connection with her so she would tell him everything she knew about Glenelg? Was he manipulating her to be his informant? Was she a lonely divorcee? An easy target?

Cecilia blew her nose loudly and tossed the tissue into the overflowing wastepaper basket.

Sod that for a joke. Now she knew the playing field, he would not find her a soft touch. Nevertheless, it was not going to detract her determination to find justice for Phil. The information conduit from her and Aldo could go two ways.

It had been four days since she had seen him. But who was counting?

8

By Saturday, Cecilia had recovered from her flu and went to her bridge club in the afternoon. She played reasonably well but had a couple of brain fades when she forgot to count the trumps properly.

During a break in the play, she told her partner Don about Phil's murder. She thought he might have a medical take on the murder. Don steepled his long tapered fingers, donned his neurosurgeon's hat, and asked how many blows to the head had Phil received.

'Several, I think.'

'I have seen a few murder victims in my time caused by subdural hematomas. Multiple blows to the head usually mean the killer was in a frenzy, in a heat of passion, and it's not a premeditated crime.'

Cecilia was not sure if that it made it better or worse. Phil didn't seem to be the type to make enemies. He wasn't an egotist, and from all reports, he avoided confrontations. But someone had been seriously annoyed with him.

She arrived home feeling stiff and needing some exercise after sitting for three hours. She found Hannah sipping herbal tea in the kitchen, dressed in her fairy costume, which was a skirt made of a leafy rainbow-coloured gauze and a pink leotard on top.

'How was work? The little kids' party?' Cecilia asked.

'Every girl was dressed in pink. It must be a genetic thing. I think girls are programmed in their DNA to like pink. I need to get out into the fresh air after being cooped up in a shop full of squealing girls. Shall we take the puppies for a walk?'

'I'll just get changed,' said Cecilia, wanting to keep her red-and-white roses dress clean from puppy paws. She pulled on some leggings and a loose black top, then returned to the living room to find Hannah still in her fairy costume.

'Aren't you going to change out of your costume?' Cecilia asked.

'There's no point. It needs a wash anyway. The birthday girl managed to tip her red cordial over me.'

Ziggy and Stardust were leashed up. Cecilia took Ziggy and Hannah took Stardust. The puppies jingled as they walked; Hannah had bought them tiny bells. Cecilia approved of their new repertoire. There had been an unfortunate incident with a baby bird, which Hannah had discovered. Warning of an imminent dachshund attack was required for the safety of birdlife in the backyard. There was another advantage, too—Cecilia could now hear them in the house if they broke into one of the bedrooms.

They ended up at the park surrounding Partridge House, a grand old villa owned by the council. The playground was occupied by small children, parents, and, unexpectedly, Aldo and a young man—perhaps Aldo's son—sitting on the park bench.

Aldo waved vigorously to her as they approached. She felt a rush of pleasure at the sight of him and then reined it in. He stood up and produced one of his spectacular smiles. His son remained seated on the bench.

Cecilia looked at Aldo's son in wonder. He was breathtaking. He had white skin, ruby lips, and shiny black hair pushed back but falling in soft curls around his neck. His long, slender legs were covered in black jeans, and he wore a simple ironed white T-shirt. He was sitting still, his eyes drawn to the antics of small children in the playground.

Hannah, too, was entranced by Leon. She danced around him, examining him from every angle. 'Can I draw you?'

Leon did not react. Motionless, he stared at the park.

'Are you an artist?' Aldo asked Hannah.

'I try to be,' she replied shyly.

Aldo turned to his son. 'Do you want this girl to draw you? Do you want to be a portrait?'

'I don't like dogs, and I'm not sure about fairies either.' His voice was soft.

Hannah flipped a pink segment of her skirt dismissively. 'These are my work clothes. I work as a fairy for children's parties. I could come to your place and look ordinary. You won't even notice me. And, of course, I wouldn't bring the dogs.'

Cecilia's eyes widened. Hannah could be pushy when it came to her art.

'How will you draw me?' Leon asked.

'Sitting.'

'Do I have to talk?'

'Only if you want to.'

'I don't do talking,' said Leon, 'but I can sit.'

'Tomorrow?' Hannah asked.

'You can come too,' Aldo told Cecilia. 'I have a new coffee machine, and it makes proper Italian coffee. You'll love it.'

'I'm a sucker for good coffee,' said Cecilia.

All her promises to herself to keep away from him were dissolved.

***

After dinner, Cecilia made herself comfortable in her bedroom. She piled up the pillows on her bed, settled in with a cup of peppermint tea, and rang Angel. 'I can't make afternoon tea on Sunday,' she said. 'I'm going with Hannah to Aldo's house. Sorry about the late notice.'

'Why are you taking Hannah? You won't be able to be cosy when she is around.'

'Cosy?'

'You can't fool me,' said Angel. 'Your favourite detective!'

'It's not about me, it's about Hannah and Leon.'

'Who's Leon?'

'Leon is Aldo's son. He's breathtaking, and Hannah wants to draw him.'

'I'm glad Hannah is getting back into her art.'

Cecilia looked down at her toes. Her nails were too long; she needed to find time for a pedicure. 'How are you?' she asked Angel. 'Any interesting dates?'

'I'm too busy to date. The kids have joined the Tigers football club. Even Sally wants to be an AFL star. I spend so much time driving them to football and then to the hospital. Three out of the four kids have had broken arms and fingers in the last six months! Why couldn't I have bred nerds who sit around gaming? Nerds don't need trips to the hospital.'

'At least with football, your kids have found an outlet for their biffo,' said Cecilia. 'It's organised aggression, and it hasn't done Luke any harm. Well, maybe a broken toe and finger.'

'Luke is their hero.'

'He loves his footy.'

'Maybe I should forget about finding the right guy for me and chill out and watch TV. There are some good series on at the moment.'

'I bet you last two months before going back to dating,' said Cecilia.

Angel laughed. 'You should talk, with all your favourites!'

'What? TV shows?'

'You know what I mean. You collect men too.'

'As friends,' said Cecilia. Then she remembered something and frowned. 'Steve has moved back to Adelaide.'

Angel gave a small hiss. 'How's it going?'

'The kids are pleased. Hannah is hoping Steve and I will get back together.'

'What about your policeman?'

'I am just his informant.'

'Not *just!* He sounds like a sweetie. You must do something with him.'

'I know, but I'm not sure if he's a player—the sort who plays around with a few women.'

'Have you seen him do that with anyone else?'

'No, but …'

'Is it the sleepwalking again?' Angel asked. 'Is that what's stopping you?'

'Yes; it's embarrassing. I do weird things.'

'For someone who likes to be in control all the time, this sleepwalking is curious,' Angel observed. Then she homed in for the sister kill. 'You have to take your medication. It was the only thing that stopped you from wandering around in your sleep when you were a teenager. Mum and Dad were so worried about you. I don't know why you make such a fuss about medication. Maybe it's because you're a vegetarian. You're so pure about what you put in your body.'

'Thanks, Angel! I must check my anti-depressants and sleeping pills for traces of animal products.'

'I don't know why you are so gun-shy about Aldo.'

'He's a homicide detective,' Cecilia replied. 'I don't think I could cope with asking how his day went.'

Angel sniggered. '"How was your day, love?" "Oh, a man carved up his wife into tiny pieces—what's for dinner?"'

'Don't!'

'Sorry,' said Angel. 'That was a bit crass of me. Couldn't you just be friends with benefits? Maybe that's what you need. Let your hair down and have fun sex.'

Cecilia winced. Was she so uptight and repressive of her feelings? Perhaps they had to come out somehow. Was that why she had sleepwalked and had terrible dreams?

***

Opposite the racecourse, Cecilia and Hannah pulled up in front of a yellow-brick, two-storey house built in the sixties in Morphettville, an adjacent suburb to Glenelg. Next to the house was a construction site. It looked like two townhouses were being built.

Cecilia popped the boot with her key fob and waited for Hannah to pull out her easel and a large Christmas-cake tin filled with pencils, rubbers, and cloths.

Loaded up, Hannah turned and looked at Aldo's house. Her eyes lit up. 'Check this out, Mum!' she squealed, pointing to the little yellow-brick wall. 'The pillars have got lions on them!'

'Oh, that's sixties Italian-Australian,' said Cecilia, putting her keys back in her woven straw bag.

'Wow, they're so cool and retro.' Hannah leaned against the boot, squinting at the yellow lions.

Cecilia lifted an eyebrow. When she was Hannah's age, stone ornaments in the front garden—like pink flamingos, gnomes, and lions—were so *not* cool. How times had changed.

She rang the front doorbell and a little *ding-dong* tune played.

'Hello! Hello!' Aldo greeted them, opening the door. He was wearing his beige chinos and an ironed black polo shirt.

'Did you see next door?' He pointed energetically at the construction site.

'Umm,' said Cecilia uncertainly. 'Are you not happy with it?'

'What? Of course, I'm happy with it!' Aldo sounded surprised. 'One townhouse is going to be my place and Leon's, and then I will rent the other one out. It's going to be splendid. Everything will be new, and I will have plenty of room for Leon.' Aldo led Cecilia and Hannah to the building site, from which a wooden skeleton ascended, marking off different areas. 'See! The rooms are big, and I will have two living areas. If I'm at work, and Leon is distressed, he can walk next door to Nonna and Nonno's house.'

Cecilia returned to the pavement and examined the billboard in front. It had a big picture of the townhouses, which were shaped with blocks stacked up haphazardly and decorated with a mixture of materials: wood slats on one block, black-painted plasterboard on the others, and a broad line of sliced slate at ground level. The front door was bright red.

'What do you think? Isn't it special?'

'It's very modern and bold, and I like the red front door,' said Cecilia, thinking she had seen a lot worse in Glenelg North.

'I want my house to stand out and flourish like a red rose, not be boring,' said Aldo.

Hannah was tapping the lions, checking what they were made of.

'Come on inside!' Aldo hurried Cecilia and Hannah into his parents' house and stopped at the formal front lounge room, where his parents were watching a soccer match. Introductions were made. Nonna smiled a lot, and Nonno stayed focused on the soccer game. He had a fine head of white hair, slicked back in the same style as Aldo. Even Leon had his hair pushed back, Cecilia remembered, but his hair fell in wavy curls around the nape of his neck. She wondered if the Giovanni men all went to the same barber.

Aldo showed Hannah to Leon's den, where he was playing a computer game on the television involving trains. Hannah set up her easel and turned on all the lights. Leon ignored her activities, remaining focused on his game.

Aldo then led Cecilia through a sunlit kitchen and out to a cement patio that looked onto a sizeable and busy-looking backyard. Chooks picked their way around a chicken run, lemon and orange trees had almost finished their fruiting, and nets were spread over parts of vegetable patches. Cecilia was impressed by the family's working garden.

Aldo gestured for her to sit at an old wooden table with a faded plastic floral table cloth and a bench, flanked by half a dozen unmatching chairs. Cecilia chose a spongy comfortable one. She wondered if the pergola was Aldo's retreat; there were several motor-racing magazines on the table. Perhaps car racing was his hobby.

'How do you have your coffee?'

'Milky white.'

Aldo brought out a tray with a steaming espresso pot, a jug of milk, blue-and-white-striped mugs, and a plate with four chocolate biscotti.

Cecilia was impressed. He was domesticated, even if he still lived with his parents.

'How's the investigation going?' Cecilia asked. 'Or shouldn't I ask?'

'Somehow, you are always in the picture.'

'Professionally, of course,' Cecilia interrupted. 'I choose to keep my community safe.'

Aldo ate a whole biscotto in two mouthfuls and munched with a blissful expression on his face.

'I'm going to be straight with you. I need help,' he said. 'Kylie is not budging from her story. She says she did visit Phil at about ten o'clock on the night he was killed, and they had an argument. She swung a fist at him, knocking him down, and that's when the pouch sort of fell out of his pocket. She grabbed it and ran. She said he was alive when she left him. The autopsy report showed bruising to Phil's jaw. She could be telling the truth.'

'Mmm,' said Cecilia, sipping her coffee. It was strong and rich. 'Kylie did seem uptight at the funeral. I watched her during the service. She didn't smile once during John's eulogy.'

'Kylie is not good at expressing her feelings. After some prodding, she broke down and cried. She loved Phil in her own way. He was the only one who understood her because he knew first-hand that her childhood was horrible.' Aldo offered Cecilia a chocolate biscotto, which she took to be polite and then discovered it was crunchy and delicious. 'I felt sorry for her,' Aldo continued. 'Her childhood warped her and made her hostile to everyone.'

'Yeah, it must have been tough.' Cecilia imagined growing up in a house where food came in boxes or tins and having no friends but the television. Bodybuilding would give Kylie a sense of control to make up for the madness of her childhood.

Something was going on in the chook yard—a battle of sorts. Feathers were flying and there was a lot of squawking.

'Shouldn't you do something?' Cecilia asked. 'Like throw a bucket of water over them?'

'Nonno bought a new hen at the markets yesterday and now the chooks have to sort out their new pecking order. It's not a bad fight.'

When the racket died down, Cecilia said, 'As I get to know Phil, he seems like an ordinary bloke doing his bit for the planet. And it takes a lot of work to be a true vegan. There were a few women in his life. But I can't make the connection to him being a murder victim.'

'You're amazing, Cecilia. You are a magnet for information on Phil's homicide, which makes it easier for me to talk about it. But I don't want you to be stressed out. It's my job, not yours.'

She shrugged. 'My job is to feed you information.'

'I wish you would trust me.'

'I do—I think you are a good cop.'

'That's not what I meant.'

The biscuits bothered her. He was onto his second. She changed the subject. 'I hope we didn't bully Leon into sitting for the portrait.'

'It's okay. He wouldn't do it if he didn't want to.'

Cecilia asked the question which had been bugging her. 'Does his mother see him?'

'She does, now he's stable. They go to the same bistro together every Wednesday night. He doesn't have meltdowns unless he goes somewhere new. I used to try to take him on holidays, like Bali, but he couldn't cope, and there are no trains in Bali.' Aldo tapped his head. 'I don't know what I was thinking. Not one of my brighter ideas. Anyway, he does go out a bit. We catch the tram to Partridge House on the weekends. He loves the tram and ringing the bell for the next stop.'

'Do you think he will be able to live independently?'

'Why? He is family! Aussie Italians like to live together. But the social worker says he still needs to know how to clean and cook.' Aldo gave a big sigh. 'It's true. If something happened to my parents, which it eventually will, then he has to be more independent. But he doesn't like cooking because he can't bear to handle raw meat.'

'He could cook vegetarian meals. Or even vegan!'

'I hadn't thought of that. I have always assumed meat is part of every evening meal.'

Cecilia let that one pass. 'Did your wife remarry?'

'She married her podiatrist, who she met when she had an ingrown toenail. Now they have a little girl.'

'Like Leon? Black hair and white skin?'

'Yes—she got it from their mum.'

Cecilia was not surprised. Aldo was handsome—of course he would have an attractive ex-wife.

'She is difficult. She likes to present as being picture-perfect— especially in hosting dinner parties—and then in the middle of one, I would be called away to work. She didn't like me working on murder cases. She found it distasteful and was embarrassed by it. Also, she found Leon hard to cope with, too. She was mortified when he had a meltdown in the supermarket. I told her not to take him there, but she said he should learn to be normal.' Aldo scowled. 'What's "normal"?'

'I don't know,' said Cecilia. 'I'm more interested in right or wrong. I'm a letter-of-the-law sort of person.'

Aldo nodded. 'Me too.' He switched moods and turned on his smile. 'Why are we talking about all that? We should be talking about us and how beautiful you are.'

Cecilia blushed.

He reached out, then dropped his hand. His mobile phone was buzzing on the table. He frowned as he looked at it and briefly answered it.

Cecilia rose to her feet. He was going to kiss her. She knew it. Thank god for the mobile phone. She did not think she would be able to resist him.

He stuffed the mobile phone in his pocket. 'Sorry, *bella*, work calls.'

Cecilia rose to her feet. 'Let's see how the drawing is going.'

They went into Leo's den. He was sitting, hands busy playing his computer game, while Hannah busied herself around her easel.

'I think I'm done for the moment,' Hannah told Leon. 'But do you mind if we have one more session? Could I come next Sunday?'

'I don't mind sitting for you, Hannah,' Leon said, without looking at her. 'You don't talk.'

Hannah blushed at the compliment. 'Thank you.' She began gathering up her things.

'Yes,' said Aldo, looking at Cecilia. 'Next Sunday.'

She felt a thrill of anticipation.

***

'Mum,' said Hannah, on the way back from portrait sitting. 'I'm worried about something. I'm not sure if I should tell you, because it doesn't seem like our business. You know, I don't like to gossip, but …' Her voice trailed off.

Cecilia caressed the steering wheel with her thumb and waited in silence. Hannah often approached things in a round-about way, rather than zeroing in.

'Amy came to see the puppies and me the other day, and she was wearing this purple-and-blue scarf around her neck. I've never seen her in a scarf before. Anyway, even though she loved playing with the babies and saying how sweet they were, I noticed she was looking tired and wondered if she regretted breaking up with Luke. But she said it wasn't that; she was scared of Vee, and then she burst into tears. Like, full-on sobbing and hysterical.'

Cecilia paused at the traffic lights on Brighton Road.

'Amy pulled off her scarf and showed me the bruises around her neck. They were horrific. I took photos, which I can show you later.'

'Poor Amy!' Cecilia was shocked. 'What on earth happened?'

'Amy walked into Vee's bedroom one night and saw Vee sitting on her bed munching, her cheeks stuffed with a big mouthful of biscuits. There was a big jar of them on her bedside table and it was the same jar

Phil used on trading night—a big square canister with a bamboo lid. Vee jumped up and grabbed Amy by the throat and said she would kill her if Amy told anyone about the marijuana cookies.' Hannah hunched up in the passenger's seat. Cecilia gave her a brief glance but kept her eyes on the red traffic lights.

'I told Amy that Vee is a violent nut case and should be stopped. But Amy doesn't want to dob Vee into the police because she's her sister. We both wondered about Phil's death. Then Amy back-tracked, saying Vee had anger management issues and she needed to attend some of Swami N's workshops.' Hannah took a hair elastic from her wrist and tied up her long hair in a loose bun. 'What do you think, Mum? I feel sorry for Amy, but Vee is a psycho. Remember what she did to me?'

The lights changed to green and Cecilia accelerated.

'What do you want to do?' Cecilia asked, playing for time. She felt sick about the violence and was concerned for Amy.

'Can you have a quiet word with Aldo? Tell him what Vee did to me. But I want to leave Amy out of it. She's freaking out.'

'I think Vee's violent attack on Amy and being discovered with Phil's cookie jar is far too important for us not to tell Aldo. Screaming at caterers at a funeral, punching, kicking you, and now half strangling her own sister is vicious, criminal behaviour. And it seems to be escalating. She needs to be stopped.'

Hannah heaved a sigh. 'I guess so.'

At home, Cecilia took her phone into her bedroom and called Aldo to tell him about Vee. 'I've just been talking to Hannah and she fessed up about Vee. She slapped and kicked Hannah at a vegan festival, and then half-strangled her own sister when she was discovered with Phil's cookie jar. Vee is dangerous and scary.'

'Vee? The one with the pink hair?' he asked.

'That's right. Hannah says Vee thought she was in a relationship with Phil. Could Phil have told her he had fallen in love with someone else and Vee went crazy and bashed him? I think Phil thought they were having casual sex, but perhaps Vee thought it was more significant.'

'Interesting,' pondered Aldo. 'Phil's cousin, John, backs that up. Well, at least in terms of Phil having regular casual hook-ups. He was popular with girls, but Jessie was the first one he had lit up for.'

'Did Mavis translate?'

'Yes, somewhat disapprovingly.'

Was Phil promiscuous? Cecilia wondered, disappointed with him. 'Did you interview Vee?'

'I interviewed all of Phil's friends, including Vee. She's an aggressive little thing, like a small rabid dog. She said she didn't go to The Vegan Café that night and had gone clubbing instead. She was quite open about being a cookie customer and said that she had been in a relationship with Phil. She also said I was stupid to think she would get rid of her dealer and sex buddy.'

'Stupid?' Cecilia stifled a laugh.

'Yes,' said Aldo cheerfully. 'However, she has a potential alibi. She used her debit card to buy drinks at a club, so we can check that.'

'She could have given her card to someone to buy drinks.'

'Huh?' Aldo sounded disbelieving. 'What young person hands over their debit card?'

'Maybe there were only a few dollars on the card, just enough to buy one drink.'

'There's a possibility, I've not thought about that. This homicide is difficult,' Aldo complained. 'I have gone through a big tub of chocolate gelati in the last few days. Some cops do alcohol, but I do ice cream. My doctor says I need to lose weight and my blood tests show I have diabetes. Mamma mia! Who would think ice cream would be so deadly? I told the doctor I have no time for diets and exercise and he should give me a tablet instead.'

Cecilia remembered the chocolate biscuits; he had eaten three of them. He was overweight but not obese. She sighed. She did not need another of her lovers to die on her. It had taken her several years to get over Ivan the violin-maker's sudden death in the supermarket. Aldo must know how to keep healthy but was ignoring it.

'Something has to be done about Vee,' she insisted. 'She brutally attacked Hannah and Amy.'

'Don't stress. We are testing all the alibis. There may be holes. We are not ruling anyone out. We are doing the ABC.'

'What's that?

'Assume nothing, believe nothing, and check everything.'

***

Cecilia retrieved the keys to a council car from the receptionist and drove to The Vegan Café. They had a car park around the back, so there was no hustling to find a park on Jetty Road. A few cars were parked there, including Swami N's, who had the bonnet open of his Mazda 2 and was poking around. She hadn't pegged him as a practical guru. Not wanting to disturb him, she walked briskly around to the front of the café.

Behind the counter stood Astra, looking lovely as usual. She was wearing a long dress, a white bodice, and a smile.

She recognised Cecilia and the smile disappeared. 'What do you want?'

'A pie,' Cecilia answered. 'What sort of pies do you have?'

'Luke, darling!' cooed Astra. 'Can you come and tell this … lady what sort of pies you have? I know you have made some delicious new varieties.'

Luke came out, wiping his floury hands on his apron. He appeared startled when he saw his mother, but Cecilia maintained her bland smile as if she didn't recognise him.

He recited the range of hot pies.

'There is so much to choose from now we have Luke,' gushed Astra, cosying up to him.

The doorbell tinkled, and Swami N slid in, his kaftan swishing around his legs. Immediately, Astra jerked away from Luke and began straightening the jars of Swami N's signature tea on the shelf.

'Ah, the health inspector,' said Swami N gently. 'How can we help you?'

'I'm just buying my lunch.'

'It will be a pleasure to serve you, won't it, Luke?'

Luke went bright red with embarrassment and passed her a brown paper bag.

Cecilia ate the lentil pie in the council lunchroom; it was delicious. Just as she was dusting out the bag for crumbs before putting it in the recycle bin, Garth walked in with his burger. Cecilia made herself a chamomile tea.

They sat in silence. Finally, Garth asked, 'What's wrong, Cecilia?'

'It's The Vegan Café. My son is working there now, and I'm not sure what's going on. Something feels odd.'

Garth scratched his beard. 'Now, would your son be a big fella, with short blonde hair and built like a brick wall?'

'Yes.'

'I've seen him down at the Broadway. When he was their cook, the owners would bring him in to break up brawls. Your lad sure knows how to fight. He could easily handle any bloke who was wielding a frying pan at him. Especially a scrawny vegan.'

'I know Luke can take care of himself in a fight but it's the wife— Astra—I'm worried about. She could cause a lot of problems for Luke.'

***

'Mum, what happened today?' Luke asked as he walked into the family room. 'You acted like you didn't know me when you came into work.'

Cecilia was setting the table for dinner. 'Astra doesn't like me. She says my chakras are screwed.'

'Does Mum have chakras?' Hannah wondered aloud.

Cecilia ignored Hannah and zeroed in on Luke. 'I've got a funny feeling about you working at The Vegan Café.'

'Don't fuss, Mum.' He threw himself onto the recliner.

'I don't, normally.' Cecilia fetched three blue napkins from a drawer.

'Swami N says he's a pacifist and abhors any kind of violence. He even said that footy should be banned, which is absurd.'

'And his wife?'

Luke sighed. 'She thinks she's attractive, but I'm not interested.'

'She appeared interested in you.' Cecilia looked at the creases in the napkins. She was not going to iron them, despite her urge for neat and tidy things when she was stressed.

'It's not just me. Any young bloke who comes into the café gets the full-on treatment. She's over the top.'

'Like Dad,' said Hannah. 'I couldn't believe the way he carried on with the waitress last night at dinner. It was so embarrassing.'

'Dad's not like that,' Luke objected. 'He's just a friendly guy.'

Hannah looked at Cecilia, who avoided eye contact. Cecilia bent down, reached into the saucepan cupboard, and pulled one out. She took out her polishing cloth from another drawer, not wanting to be part of a conversation about Steve.

'I don't know why you two have got it in for Dad,' Luke grumbled.

'He's nice and normal to you because you're a bloke,' said Hannah sadly. 'But he's different around women.'

Cecilia's saucepan was now gleaming.

'You're just making something out of nothing,' Luke told Hannah.

'He treats me as if I'm some dumb girl who knows zilch. He even booted Ziggy!'

'If Dad hadn't, he would have tripped over him, then they both would have been hurt.'

'You don't kick dogs!'

'It was just a nudge. Not everyone is in love with your feral pets.'

Hannah ran out of the family room with her puppies in hot pursuit. Cecilia let her be. Dinner could wait. Hannah had to get over her disappointment and shock that her dad was a misogynist and not the man she'd thought he was. She put her saucepan back in the cupboard.

'I really like making vegan food,' said Luke. 'At home, we're mostly vegan, and it feels right.'

'Yes, but we don't go bashing each other over the head with frying pans.'

'What's that got to do with the café? I thought Phil got killed by his crazy sister.'

Or a criminally insane vegan, thought Cecilia.

'I would love to turn it into a real café,' said Luke. 'They put too much effort into selling books, vegan make-up, shoes, and mock animal food. Plus, their products are way too expensive for the vegan market. If they concentrated on having a better menu, the café could be a right little goer. Swami N showed me the receipts and a tally of the takings. The café is only just breaking even.'

'Was he businesslike?'

'Oh yes, and he had spreadsheets. He's computer savvy.' Luke got up, took a beer out of the fridge, and returned to the recliner.

Her mobile pinged. There was a message from Aldo to call him. She decided to wait until after dinner; she had some issues with her kids to sort out first.

She knocked on Hannah's door. 'Dinner is on the table.'

Her daughter trailed down the passageway, flanked by the watchful puppies.

'Your dogs are crazy,' said Luke.

'They are not! They're just happy little dogs. Why do you have to be so mean to me?' Hannah ran away again in tears.

Cecilia decided it was time to intervene. She put her hands on her hips and went full frontal on her son. 'Why pick on Hannah? It didn't go well with Hannah and Steve, and that's sad.'

Luke slouched in the recliner. 'She's oversensitive. I'm just telling the truth. Is that wrong? I'm an honest guy. I don't do bullshit.'

'Bullies say they are just being honest so they can say any mean thing they like.'

Luke jumped to his feet. 'Are you calling me a bully?'

Cecilia gave her son the full beam of her glare. She was still the alpha dog in the house.

A door banged and Hannah marched into the kitchen. She was holding a spear the same height as her, and it had engraved runes on the wood. She banged it on the floor. 'You will not be rude and unkind to my dogs, or me.'

'Say what?' Luke started, half-rising from his chair.

'Well, Luke?' She thumped the spear again.

'You're nuts.'

She swung around and smacked his arm with it.

'Ouch!' exclaimed Luke.

'Hannah!' said Cecilia. 'Put that spear away.'

'Not until my stupid brother apologises.' Hannah lifted the spear and assumed a warrior pose, pointing the spear directly at Luke.

Cecilia didn't know what to do. It was great Hannah was getting in touch with her inner warrior, but with a spear?

The puppies picked up on the mood and stood on either side of Hannah, guarding her and watching Luke with big eyes. Was Hannah now the alpha dog?

Luke flopped back down in his chair, his brow furrowed. 'I'm sorry, Hannah,' he mumbled, a blush spreading over his face. 'I was insensitive to your feelings.'

'Where did you get the spear?' Cecilia asked Hannah.

'An art student friend of mine made it.'

'It's cool,' said Luke, recovering quickly from his embarrassment. 'Can I have a look?'

'Maybe later,' said Hannah. 'But now, I'm hungry.'

The puppies were lured outside with treats. Hannah and Luke were quiet during dinner, and Cecilia let them have time to ruminate.

After dinner, Hannah and Luke moved into the living room. Hannah showed Luke the spear, and arguments were forgiven, much to Cecilia's relief.

Hannah laid the spear down on the floor alongside the sofa and then had to pick it up again. The puppies were investigating the spear with their teeth, perhaps thinking it was a very big chew stick, so Hannah put the spear out of reach on the kitchen table.

'How's work?' Hannah asked Luke, plonking herself down again on the sofa.

'Yeah, good. However, I would like to know more about the business side of things. Why isn't the café making money? One day I'm going to own a café or restaurant.' He got out his laptop and began tapping.

'What are you checking?' Cecilia asked.

'I'm going to research The Vegan Café,' said Luke, 'and see if it's a franchise. They can be ridiculously expensive.'

Cecilia joined Hannah and the dogs on the large sofa.

'It's not a franchise,' said Luke, looking up from his laptop. 'But there is a wholesale company called the Vegan Aussie, and they supply all those vegan products we have on our shelves.'

'What does the internet say about the Vegan Aussie?'

'Their website looks professional, and they have a wide range of products. I imagine wealthy vegans own it. Not all vegans or vegetarians are skinny, impoverished animal activists. I'm a footy player and an almost vegetarian, and Mum, you're …' Luke's voice trailed off.

'Plump, middle-aged, and a health inspector,' Cecilia finished for him.

'I don't think your favourite policeman thinks that,' Hannah interjected.

Cecilia blushed, laughed, and blew Hannah a raspberry. Then she realised she hadn't phoned Aldo back. 'I'll leave you to your research,' she told Luke, who had Hannah hanging over his shoulder, pointing out vegan violations.

In her bedroom, Cecilia rang Aldo, but it went to voicemail. She was relieved, now able to concentrate on her new nightly routine which involved medication, meditation, bells, and sensor pads on both sides of the bed. She was equipping her subconscious—her sleeping self—with every tool she possessed in order to stop the sleepwalking.

This was war, and she was not giving in.

***

After a night of uninterrupted sleep, Cecilia woke refreshed and ready for work. A client of Luscious Nails had complained they developed a fungal infection after treatment, so Cecilia visited the salon and checked their routine for sterilising instruments. It came up fine, although the beautician was annoyed. 'Just because we are Chinese, people think we cut corners. We are very clean.'

'Maybe your client got tinea from not drying between her toes properly,' said Cecilia.

Someone called her name as she was leaving the beauty shop—it was Jessie, and she was carrying a big box in a cotton bag. She seemed less defeated and had managed a smile.

'Hi Jessie,' said Cecilia. 'How is it going?'

'Not too bad. Would you like a coffee? I owe you one.'

Why not, thought Cecilia. She could have a talk afterwards with the owners about the position of their toilets.

They crossed Jetty Road, walked past a couple of shops, and entered Industrial Coffee.

After they had settled themselves, Jessie scrutinised the sweets and chose a slice of banana cake with thick butter icing.

'You're not a vegan?' Cecilia asked.

'I wish,' answered Jessie. 'But cakes are my undoing. Especially ones with eggs and butter. Yum!'

Cecilia smiled and asked, 'Have you been shopping?'

'Yes, I've just come from Happy Herbs. They've reopened.'

'Do you like incense? I'm a scented candle sort.' Cecilia thought the bag was far too big for candles or incense. She must have something else in there.

Jessie looked around to see if anyone was listening. 'I don't have a candle or incense in the bag. I have something else.'

'Oh?' Cecilia smiled politely.

'It's a long story.'

'No rush,' said Cecilia, intrigued by the contents of the bag.

'Did you know I am boarding with John and Mavis until I can find a place?'

'Garth told me you had moved in. How's it going? Mavis seems like a nice person.'

'Yes, she's a sweetie, and being on a pension, she's happy to get some extra cash; I pay her board money. And they don't mind my parrot, Percy, even though he does talk a lot—which was tough on Daphne when she was sleeping through the day after working night shifts. But Mavis is a bit deaf, and John, well, he can't hear at all, so Percy isn't a problem. John and I are fitting out the shed to make green cleaning products and oils.'

'John sure is multi-skilled,' Cecilia observed. 'He can handle camels, too.'

'He is incredibly good with his hands, and he makes me laugh.'

'I heard he was a good mimic.'

'Yes, and I don't feel sad when I'm around John. I'm learning sign language, too. It's fun—it's so expressive.'

Cecilia was intrigued. Was this a love affair in the making?

Their coffees arrived with a sponge finger biscuit for Cecilia and banana cake for Jessie. She took a fork and chopped off a large piece, eating the icing first.

'What's Mavis going to do with her marijuana plantation?' It was a bold question, but Jessie must have seen it if she was using the shed out the back. 'I heard that she used to help Phil with his cookie business.'

Jessie huffed. 'So, you know about that? Well, I didn't, not until I saw the marijuana crop on my way to the shed. Phil didn't tell me.' Jessie frowned slightly. 'There was a lot about Phil I didn't know. Like growing up in the 'House of Horrors'. Mavis was upset because she doesn't know what to do with the marijuana plants, and she has lost a source of income. She and John like to go on a cruise once a year. But neither John nor I want to sell marijuana, so we were going to burn it. Then Mavis heard on the news that marijuana oil was legalised for pain relief, but hard to source.' Jessie pointed to her box, which was next to her chair. 'I bought this extracting machine from Happy Herbs and Mavis is going to make marijuana oil.'

Cecilia nibbled on her biscuit. 'You'll need to get accreditation as suppliers.'

'I'm a nurse, and I'm sure I can work my way around the forms. If it's too complicated and we can't get accreditation, we can start up a little cottage business with Mavis' over-sixties club. Many of them are in chronic pain from arthritis or something, and marijuana oil is supposed to be good for pain relief. Mavis is thinking of switching from the vegan market to an informal cottage business for old people. CBD oil makes good money.'

Cecilia wondered if marijuana oil would come under her jurisdiction and whether she needed to check what insecticides were being used. Then, she decided it would probably end up with the state department of health and not be a local concern. She also ignored the possibly illegal over-sixties market. It was not her business.

They said their goodbyes, and Jessie hugged her. They hadn't talked about who killed Phil. Cecilia had chosen not to bring it up. She didn't want to spoil the new life Jessie was building for herself. Things could end up right sometimes.

***

Another day passed with no call from Aldo. Cecilia refused to ring him because she was battling romantic thoughts. He kept popping up in her mind, and her rational self was annoyed he was occupying so much head space. She was an independent woman, not one who needed a man around to make her feel good about herself. But he was attractive, laughed easily, was compassionate (even to seagulls!) and was intelligent. She was hooked despite her inner arguments. She had even looked at her underwear the previous night and thought she could do with a refresh!

Tonight was Luke's turn to make dinner. Cecilia and Hannah were hanging around the living room, waiting for him to come home.

'It's nice to have a live-in chef,' said Hannah.

'He makes yummy pies,' agreed Cecilia.

The passageway door opened, and the puppies leapt into action. Everyone was home now!

Luke carried a tub of vegan ice cream and a frozen vegan pizza. Cecilia shooed the puppies away from the kitchen, and she and Hannah looked at the pizza box dubiously.

'I want to see what it's like,' Luke said, turning on the oven and putting the ice cream in the freezer. 'I'll make a nice salad to go with it, and we'll have fruit salad for dessert.

Cecilia took the pizza box and studied the back of it. 'It's made by a company called Vegan Haute Cuisine.' She took out her laptop and tapped away. 'They have quite a history.'

'They do a lot of mock meats,' replied Luke, slicing carrots into thin match sticks. 'Like vegan hot dogs, burgers, and nuggets—and they're pricey, too.'

'Did you know bigger companies often own smaller companies, and then they too are owned by even bigger companies?' Cecilia stomped on the pizza cardboard box, making it small enough to fit into the recycling bin.

Luke frowned. 'I didn't find anything questionable about the Vegan Aussie.'

'No, but who owns Vegan Haute Cuisine?' Cecilia tapped away. 'Bingo! It's owned by a mega food distribution that also sells chicken.'

Luke's mouth dropped open.

'How could they?' Hannah jabbed her finger at the box. 'That's cheating vegans.'

'Maybe you could make your own pizzas and freeze them,' Cecilia suggested.

'I wonder if the boss knows about this,' he muttered, soaking the carrot sticks in a Vietnamese pickle sauce he had whisked up using vinegar, sugar, sesame oil, and a sprinkling of fresh green coriander.

'I'm sure he would be very upset,' said Hannah.

'How did Swami N get the money together to build a new café?' Cecilia asked. 'It would've cost a fortune. I know he took meditation classes and retreats before going into business, but I can't imagine he would have made hundreds of thousands of dollars from them.'

'They used the wife's money. Her parents owned a chain of car yards, but then they died in a car crash, and she sold the car yard businesses and made a packet of money. She had to tell me, as if I would be impressed by how wealthy she was.' Luke rolled his eyes in displeasure.

'Are they new to the food business?'

'They sure are. Phil managed the café. He must have set it up as well. He did a good job. I think it would be a dream to custom-build a café and a shop.'

'If it weren't for Phil's vegan pies, would the café have been a flop?'

'Yeah,' said Luke. 'There would be nothing but pamphlets and tofu.'

The timer beeped on the oven, and donning some oven mitts, Luke pulled out the pizza. Using the rocking pizza cutter, he sectioned it into neat slices.

'How do you tell a woman that you're not interested in her?' Luke asked while they were having fruit salad and ice cream. There was a consensus that the pizza was rubbery and tasteless.

Cecilia forked a piece of watermelon. 'Are you having trouble with Astra?'

'She's so old. She must be at least ten years older than me, and she keeps coming on to me. I just want to do my job, but she invents all these excuses to come into the kitchen.'

'Tell her you have a girlfriend, and you're not interested,' advised Hannah.

'I don't have a girlfriend.'

'Don't you know how to pretend?' Hannah asked.

Luke shook his head. 'I'm no good at bullshitting.'

'Get a new job,' Cecilia said. 'One where cooks don't get bashed.'

'The husband won't come at me with a frying pan, Mum. He knows he would come out a loser. I'm way stronger than him. Anyway, he doesn't know what his wife is like. She never pulls any stunts when he is around. With him, she behaves like a little girl.'

Cecilia picked up the dessert plates and the fruit salad bowl. Luke was so literal and unembellished; he didn't see the sneaky stunts people pulled until they hit him in the face.

He retired to the recliner chair and opened his laptop while Cecilia and Hannah did the dishes. Everyone took it in turns to do them; it was a routine Cecilia had established years ago because it encouraged family conversation.

'I am looking forward to seeing Leon again,' Hannah confessed, drying a plate. 'He has been so interesting to draw. Kind of difficult too, because I've never drawn someone like him before. He is completely unconscious about how he looks.'

'Does he ever smile?' Cecilia asked, scrubbing the pizza tray, wondering if Leon had inherited his dad's radiant smile, which was large and expansive, and made Cecilia feel special.

'When something good happens on his game, he does. However, it's more of a flickering smile. You have to be watching to see it.'

'Do you want to capture Leon's fleeting smile or his vulnerability?'

'Vulnerability?' Hannah pondered. 'I didn't see that. He seems self-assured, like he has nothing to hide and nothing to manipulate. He's fascinating, Mum.'

Cecilia sprayed the kitchen sink with a bottle of diluted vinegar and scrubbed it clean. 'I went to school with an autistic boy. You would think he would get bullied, but he wasn't. The kids left him alone. He liked to look at the sky, and the teachers always let him have a window seat.'

Hannah hung up her tea towel. 'Are you are coming next Sunday?'

'You don't need me. You know the family now.'

'You're needed.'

'Why?'

Hannah gave a cheeky grin. 'Because your favourite policeman wants to see you.'

Cecilia grabbed a tea towel and flicked it at her.

'It's so obvious he likes you. Why don't you give it a go? I felt really upset when Kim dumped me, but remember the art student who carved my spear? He's from Sudan. And I think we might be dating soon.'

'It's different when you're twenty-one,' said Cecilia.

'Why?'

'You're more cautious about engaging with someone at fifty-three,' said Cecilia, thinking of her most recent session with Dr Davidson when he'd discouraged her from dating. A new romance, although wonderful and exciting, was a high-stress trigger point, he had told her.

'It encourages obsessive thoughts about someone; you keep replaying every conversation and attaching meaning to it,' he'd said.

Cecilia had sort of agreed that she was thinking about Aldo way too much.

Hannah was puzzled. 'What is there to be cautious about with Aldo? He's a nice guy.'

***

Outside the Sun-Kissed Motel, on the pavement where Mr Jones' campsite was set-up, two grey-haired men were sitting on deck chairs and studying something on the table. Cecilia parked behind the kombi, popped open the boot lid and retrieved her pool testing kit.

'Hi, Christos,' said Cecilia, wondering what the chicken shop owner was doing with Mr Jones. She looked over their shoulders and saw a large geological map spread over the fold-up table; it looked as though it had been hand-made by a professional cartographer. It showed every brown creek, winding paths, and tracts of land covered in green trees. It was of Deep Creek Conservation Park.

'What a lovely map,' she observed.

Christos looked up from the map and beamed. 'My wife and I are planning a camping trip in between her treatments. Mr Jones says the Deep Creek Conservation Park is scenic. I was walking past his campsite,' he pointed to Mr Jones' sandwich board, with its map of Australia and red dots, 'and I thought to myself, *Here is a man who travels a lot. I'll talk to him about nice nature places to visit.*'

'I've been everywhere,' boasted Mr Jones. 'Except for Tasmania. A lot of people from the motel come and talk to me about travel.'

Cecilia thought about the last occupant of Mr Jones' guest camp chair; the lady wearing a short skirt. She had been interested in camping, too. Cecilia smiled and left the men to it. She entered the front office of the Sun-Kissed Motel and rang the bell.

The owner came out, smirking. 'I tested the water in the pool early this morning, and it's correct.'

'Let's go and see,' she said.

At the side of the pool, she unpacked her bag of testing equipment by the pool and took samples. Her five-way 'pool essential collection kit' showed the correct results.

'Is Mr Dyson still staying with you?' she asked.

'Of course. Why would he want to stay in that filthy house when he can stay in a nice clean motel?'

'Is he here now?'

'Yes, but Mr Dyson is not an early riser.'

'It's a shame about his son, Phil,' said Cecilia, automatically probing.

'Yes, a terrible thing to happen. He was only young.'

'You knew him?'

'He was a regular guest. He would come here on a Wednesday afternoon.'

Cecilia caught her breath. Was Phil part of the sex trade at the Sun-Kissed Motel?

'Did he meet someone?' she asked casually.

'A very pretty woman. She never came through the front door, but I would see her on the CCTV going to his room.'

'What did she look like?' Cecilia couldn't imagine Phil consorting with sex workers—not when he had so many girls taking an interest in him.

'She was attractive in a natural way. She had …' An uneasy expression crossed the motel owner's face. 'It's not my place to talk about my guests.'

Not a sex worker, thought Cecilia. 'Have you told the police?'

'Of course not. I don't poke my nose into other people's business, unlike some!'

A smile twitched on Cecilia's lips. She didn't care what he thought of her—being nosy got results.

'I'm sure the police will be interested,' Cecilia told him. 'It may be important evidence.'

'I don't want police buzzing around and upsetting my guests.'

'I don't think you have a choice.' She breezed off and knocked on Mr Dyson's door on the ground floor.

Mr Dyson stood inside the door and wouldn't let her into his room, but Cecilia didn't care. She knew how awful the rooms were, with their stained purple bedspreads and orange net curtains.

She presented him with a fistful of unpaid bills. His eyes bulged when he saw the final tally. 'I can't afford this. It's thousands of dollars.'

'We had to get special cleaning units in. The dumping fees were high and so were the costs of plumbing and electrical work. These bills are overdue.'

'You're pestering a poor old man.'

'If you don't pay, then the debt collectors will come in. They will see what's in your safe and value your house for sale, or you can take out a reverse mortgage. I imagine your house would have a certain historical value.' *And notoriety, too,* she thought to herself.

'You don't give in, do you, missy?'

'No.'

'Seeing as I am bereft of a wife to help me look after the house, I think I might move into one of those retirement villages where they do everything for you. But I want to keep my dog.'

Bereft? Cecilia scowled. What did Mr Dyson do around the house? Nothing!

He wiped his nose on his sleeve. 'I've been to see the bank. That's why I was driving down Jetty Road when my brakes failed. It was a terrible shock for me. It gives me the shakes just thinking about that accident.'

How many other prangs had Mr Dyson been involved with? She thought of all the broken-down cars in his front yard.

'These days, normally, I don't drive, and I can't ask John to take me; not after he made off with all my son's money. I still keep one car working for emergencies. I had it serviced a few months ago and everything was supposed to be okay. I should sue that mechanic. He's caused me a lot of grief and rude publicity with my little car accident.'

'Is that so?' Garth had told her he'd heard from one of his paramedic friends that Mr Dyson's foot had got tangled on the accelerator. But nothing ever seemed to be Mr Dyson's fault.

'I'm seeing real estate agents this afternoon,' he said grandly. 'Come back in half an hour.'

'Why?'

'I will give you the cheques.'

That was easy, thought Cecilia. But why couldn't Mr Dyson walk to the post box which was only five minutes away? He was not infirm. But she did not quibble; she wanted an end to her relationship with him. She sat in her car and caught up with her emails on her phone. When she returned, Mr Dyson had a fistful of envelopes.

'I want my dog back,' he said. 'You need to get your skates on and post these.'

She looked at the envelopes. There were no stamps. 'You want me to pay for the postage? It's over a dollar a letter these days.'

Mr Dyson showed some yellow teeth.

'Just give them to me,' she said impatiently, losing interest in postal costs—anything to get Mr Dyson out of her hair.

From an ancient, cracked leather brown wallet, Mr Dyson gave her a ten-dollar note. 'I would like a receipt.'

***

Cecilia drove to the post office, then popped in next door to a coffee shop and bought a large takeaway latte. Back in her office, she sat at her desk looking out at the ocean and sipped her coffee.

This case was starting to unveil more of its mysteries. A clandestine girlfriend? She rested her chin on her knuckles and thought. Who was the woman Phil had assignations with at the motel? Possibly married because she didn't want to be noticed and took the back entrance.

She had to tell Aldo—but first, she wanted the facts on Vee. She phoned him.

'Vee is off the grid at the moment,' Aldo said. 'She's in a rainforest somewhere in Queensland, according to her friends. I've got the Queensland police looking for her.'

'I went to the Sun-Kissed Motel today. The owner said Phil was a regular there on Wednesdays, and he met *a pretty woman in a natural sort of way*—his words. She also didn't want to be spotted at the motel and ducked around the back.'

'Another woman!' exclaimed Aldo. 'And a surreptitious one, too? I wouldn't have placed Phil as a customer of Sun-Kissed.'

'Perhaps it was Astra, the café owner's wife. I don't think she uses make-up.'

'I'll get an ID photo of her and show it to the motel owner.'

'My son is working at The Vegan Café now,' Cecilia added. 'Do you think it's safe?'

'I don't think we have a serial killer of vegan cooks on our hands.'

'Duh,' said Cecilia, annoyed at what sounded like flippancy. Nevertheless, she was thinking about taking another look at the owners of the café.

'Leon liked sitting for Hannah,' said Aldo. 'And I enjoyed having coffee with you.'

'It was nice,' said Cecilia, and then wanting to avoid an intimate conversation, she wound it up. 'I must go because I'm doing my rounds on food outlets this week, handing out pamphlets on five easy steps to washing your hands.'

'Five easy steps?' Aldo sounded confused.

9

The next day, Cecilia visited the Sun-Kissed Motel with Mr Dyson's postal receipt and fifteen cents change. She was going to shove the envelope under his motel door, but he opened it.

'Good morning, Mr Dyson,' said Cecilia breezily. 'I posted your cheques yesterday, so you should be all paid up now. Here is your receipt and fifteen cents change.'

He studied the receipt and counted the coins, then stuffed them into his pocket.

'All right then,' she said, turning to go.

But Mr Dyson was not finished. 'I've bought a nice little unit in a retirement village at an excellent price, and I can keep my dog.' He puffed out his bony chest and showed his yellow teeth. 'The real estate agent is fixing the old place up, getting it painted and polishing the floorboards, and then they are going to stage it—put in beds and lounge room furniture, like how you see on those TV house makeover shows.'

Cecilia thought it would make an interesting before-and-after renovation show: *From House of Horrors to Glorious Heritage Home.* 'It would make fabulous television footage, like a fairy tale; from ashes to a ballgown. And they could do a section on you, about how difficult it was for you, a helpless old man, to live in such dreadful circumstances.'

'What?' Mr Dyson spluttered. 'Be on TV? No way! I'm a private person.'

'Well, you've been a regular feature on the news recently.'

'Too right, I have! All those journalists, pestering an old man in his time of grief.' He held out a mottled hand to her.

Cecilia stepped back out of reach. Did he want to shake hands with her? No way!

'Have you got the phone number for that clean-up service? I need to clear out the back shed.'

Cecilia took out her phone, scrolled through her contacts and found the number listed under *Horrible Houses Clean-up*. She wrote it out for him on a page torn from her notebook.

'How's the investigation going into your son's death?' She felt she did not owe Mr Dyson any favours; there was no need to pussy-foot around him, and she wondered if he had heard anything.

Mr Dyson's shoulders slumped. Gone was the cocky look. 'It's terrible. My son's life was cut short. He was barely twenty-nine years old.'

'Did he talk about the café?'

'We hadn't seen much of him in recent years. Kids want their independence, and their mother was not the easiest person to get on with. I walked past that café with my dog a few times. It looked smart, and the windows were spotlessly clean.' His voice quivered. 'My wife was not a good home-maker.'

Was he blaming his lifestyle on his wife, or was he having a delayed reaction to the grief of his son's murder? He had been too busy fighting his cleaners to have time to grieve. Now that it was almost all over, he had to face the stark reality of his son's death.

'Phil used to be a loner with his odd little hobbies, but he seemed to have settled down, got a proper job, and was doing well for himself. Some nights he would work late, and he would have visitors. My son had become popular!' Mr Dyson grew taller with pride and then collapsed into himself, like a cockroach withdrawing its legs. 'I can't believe someone killed him. I don't understand it. Why are psychos running riot in our town?'

'I'm sorry for your loss,' said Cecilia gently, and went back to her car.

The kombi was gone and so was the black cloth covering the 'no parking' sign. The council must have passed the signage at last night's meeting.

Cecilia was examining Astra's Facebook profile, which had videos of her standing on mountaintops and looking soulful, when Garth knocked on her door.

'Have you got five minutes?'

'Sure,' she said.

'You remember that fluffy little killer I brought in?'

'Councillor Johnson's dog? I thought you had a court order to have it euthanised.'

'We never even got that far. The elected members didn't pass the order because they wanted to keep Councillor Johnson sweet. They gave the dog another chance.'

'How corrupt! Did he fix his fence?'

'Yes, but the little bugger dug its way out and was hit by a passing car. That was interesting, too.'

'What do you mean, "interesting"?'

'Karma.'

'Huh?' Then her eyes narrowed. 'Whose car hit the dog?' She suspected Garth and his truck.

'One of our locals.'

'Who?'

'Phil's Auntie Mavis.'

'Poor Mavis!' Cecilia always shuddered when she saw dead animals on the road. She kept her fences tightly secured. It would be too horrible if one of the puppies escaped and got hit by a car.

'She was so upset she came to see me. She didn't know what to do with the dog's body and had stuck it in the back seat with one of those crocheted rugs around it. I had to fetch her a cup of tea and reassure her I would take the animal and explain it to the owner.'

'Did you tell her about the biting?'

'I sure did! I told her the dog had mauled a three-year-old child and should have been impounded. Mavis was so shocked a dangerous dog was allowed to be on the loose in Glenelg that she left in a much better state of mind.'

'I'm not going to ask what you've done with the dog.'

'It's in one of the cages. I've left an urgent message on Councillor Johnson's phone that he needs to pick up his dog.'

'Did you tell him it was dead?'

'I must have forgotten.'

***

Luke stormed through the door into the family room, wielding his super-sized sports drink of water. 'You'll never guess what happened today!'

Cecilia was sitting on the sofa, playing tug the rope with the puppies. Hannah was out, trying a new still-life art class.

'I got sacked!'

'What?!' Cecilia dropped the rope.

'Bloody Astra cornered me in the kitchen and was trying to kiss me behind the freezer when the husband walked in. He went crazy and said he was going to charge me for sexual harassment. That's so unfair. It was the other way around. Then Astra started to cry and said I had been coming on to her. It was my word against hers. What am I going to do? Swami N said he is going to file a police report. Who are they going to believe? A delicate weeping red-head, or a six-foot-two footy player?' Luke filled his water bottle with cold sports drink from the fridge. He took a swig of sweet grape flavoured sports drink. 'I shot back that his Vegan Haute Cuisine produce was dodgy and was owned by a fast-food chicken chain. That shut him up. You should have seen his face—he was red with rage. No serenity there.' Luke took a swig of water. 'I told him I would tweet and tell all the animal activists about the café's questionable produce.'

'And then what happened?' Cecilia asked.

'I thought he was going to have a fit—his eyes were bulging, and one of his blue contact lenses popped out. I was waiting for him to swing a punch, but he backed off. He knew he was beaten. Astra fluttered around him, patting him, and encouraged him to come out of the kitchen and into the café, where he sat down on a table. Then he closed his eyes and started that meditation breathing thing. I went back into the kitchen and tidied up. I had some lentils cooking on the stove, and I couldn't walk out and leave the stove on; the place might've burned down.'

'What happened then?' Cecilia asked.

'I walked out, and he wasn't there. Neither of them were. They sacked me and left me to lock up! How weird is that? But more importantly, how is it going to look on my work resume? Sacked!'

'Sexual harassment,' Cecilia reflected. During an inspection, she often asked the staff if there were any safety issues. Several times, a waitress confided that the male owner was sexually harassing her—but female-on-male was unusual. 'If you don't expose the café for having connections with caged chickens, he won't charge you with harassment.'

'But I didn't do it, Mum. I just made pies and sweets.'

'I know you didn't,' she said, sighing. 'But sometimes you just have to walk away.'

'I want to file for sexual harassment. I bet you that super-sexed wife tried it on with Phil.'

Ziggy and Stardust jumped on the sofa. Cecilia slowly caressed them, giving herself time to think.

'You could go to court, and you may have a good chance of winning. But do you really want to go through the fuss and bother? It could take several years of court proceedings. Wouldn't it be easier to forget about it and get another job?'

'It's not fair, Mum! Anyway, I have to go and get changed. I've got footy training tonight. I can let off some steam there.'

While Cecilia was having her breakfast the next morning, Luke marched in. 'I'm going to the café to tell them I'll report Astra for sexual harassment. I'm not taking this lying down. It's sexist.'

'It's your decision.' Luke was an adult now, and he always met challenges head-on. At least he wasn't going to continue working for The Vegan Café. Perhaps he could get a job at the Stamford Grand, renowned for its fancy restaurant. It would broaden his skills, and they might like a cook who could cook vegan cuisine.

***

After Cecilia had settled into her office and made plans for the day, she gave in about not contacting Aldo. She didn't want to seem needy, but there were things to be sorted out. She sent him a text, asking if Vee was safely locked up. Hannah and Amy needed to feel safe. He fired a quick one back to say Vee had been arrested in Cow Bay in the Daintree Rainforest and was in Brisbane's remand centre, waiting for extradition to Adelaide.

When she got home from work, Luke was lying on the couch. His breathing was rapid, and he was sucking down water from his sports bottle.

'I saw Swami N, Mum,' he croaked. 'He and Astra are going to sell the business, and after much soul-searching, he had discovered he was not a businessman, and that money was a distraction from the real world. They're going to move to Thailand and run meditation retreats.'

'He told you all that?'

'After I told him I was going to sue for wrongful dismissal and tweet about his dodgy produce unless he gave me four weeks' pay and a reference.'

'Good move.'

'He told me to come back in half an hour and he would have the reference ready and the money transferred into my account. I spent the time looking at cafés and restaurants on Jetty Road. The new burgers-and-beer restaurant is hiring, but there's no room for creativity. It's just heaps of stuff piled up on a bun.' Luke coughed. 'I feel dizzy and nauseous all the time, and I've got a whopping big headache.'

Cecilia got out her thermometer and took his temperature; it was dangerously high. She gave him a couple of paracetamol. If the fever was not down in an hour, she was going to take him to hospital.

Two hours later, she and Luke were sitting in the emergency room at Flinders Hospital. Luke was shaking and taking big swigs from his water bottle.

'It looks like alcohol poisoning,' said the doctor.

'I'm not drunk,' Luke objected. 'I haven't had a single beer today.'

'We'll run tests,' said the doctor.

Blood was taken by a middle-aged nurse. 'Nice muscles,' she said with a wink, causing Luke to blush. Then, with some difficulty, he managed to stagger into the bathroom and do a wee for a urine test.

They waited in a curtained cubicle. Luke lay on the narrow bed, tossing and turning, wanting more blankets and then throwing them off. Cecilia began to speculate about all kinds of diseases, particularly meningitis. Fever and nausea were symptoms of the disease. She felt dizzy with fear and tried to hide it from Luke. She stayed with him all night. The hospital staff were so busy. She wanted to be there in case his condition suddenly worsened. Occasionally, she would read aloud exotic vegan recipes, which seemed to soothe him, like story time when he was a kid. They were both impressed by a vegan version of haggis.

The doctors were baffled. The blood and urine tests had come back normal. They checked his kidneys, lungs, and appendix and all were good, but Luke's temperature remained precariously high.

Hannah came in mid-morning. 'Here's your favourite sports drink.' She flicked the lid and was about to pour it into Luke's bottle, when Cecilia stopped her.

'Maybe I should give it a clean,' said Cecilia.

In the visitors' room, she gave his bottle a good clean. Then she had a sudden unexpected thought. She googled poisoning. High fever and nausea were some of the symptoms.

Her eyes widened in shock. She rang Aldo, not caring about the implications. 'I'm sorry to bother you, but what do you know about poison? I think my son has been poisoned. He's in intensive care at Flinders. The hospital has run tests, but nothing has come up.'

'That's awful,' said Aldo. 'You must be so worried.'

'They don't know what is wrong with him.' She tried to slow her breathing down.

'I will come straight away.,' he said.

She brought back Luke's water bottle, filled with cold water, to her son's cubicle. A team of doctors and nurses were standing in front of her son's bed. A drip had been inserted in his arm and he was hooked up to a heart monitor.

Hannah rushed to her mother's side. 'What's happening, Mum?'

Cecilia put her arm around her. It was crowded in the hospital room.

Then, Aldo appeared at the cubicle entrance and the room was even more crowded.

'I think I need some fresh air,' said Hannah, her voice trembling. 'I'll be back in an hour.'

Cecilia hustled Aldo into an empty visitors' room and burst into tears. Aldo wrapped his arms around her and cuddled her as she sobbed.

'*Cara mia,*' he murmured, stroking her hair.

Eventually, she removed herself from his embrace. She switched from tears to anger. 'Luke could have been poisoned. How crazy is that?"

'I have been thinking about it, too,' said Aldo. 'It could be antifreeze. Does he usually carry around a drink bottle?'

'Yes, it's always with him. What's antifreeze?'

'It's an agent used in car cooling systems; it's clear and has a slightly sweet taste.'

'Oh' said Cecilia mulling it over. 'Luke has those sugary sports drink so he might not have noticed the difference.'

'Ethylene glycol poisoning is nasty. I have seen its results before. The symptoms look like alcohol poisoning, so it's difficult to diagnose, and you need to get the antidote as soon as possible.'

'Antifreeze? I have seen that so-called guru tinkering with his car.' Cecilia's eyes glittered. 'I'm going to find a doctor.' Then, she paused and looked Aldo in the eyes. 'Thank you.'

He cupped her chin with a large hand. 'Luke will be okay,' he reassured her.

The doctors ran tests on Luke's kidneys and found calcium oxylate. Aldo was right; it was ethylene glycol poisoning. They kept him on a drip and said he would have to wait for the poison to work through the rest of his body.

Aldo interviewed Luke intensively about his last twenty-four hours about what he drank and ate. His water bottle was the constant factor, and Aldo sent it away for testing. Cecilia hoped she hadn't done too good a job cleaning it.

'The wife was nuts,' Luke told Aldo, who interviewed him the following morning when he was much better. 'She kept coming onto me. It was embarrassing. She couldn't believe I was not interested in her. She thought everyone found her attractive. Once I crouched down and hid behind the flour bins when she walked into the kitchen.'

Cecilia smiled. Luke was so huge and visible. She couldn't imagine him hiding successfully behind a flour bin.

'It was all Astra's fault. She couldn't keep her hands to herself. I told Swami N that I had been sexually harassed by his wife, which of course he denied, saying that couldn't have happened because Astra is beyond body-bound matters and is enlightened. Whatever that means.'

'Maybe that sex is not important,' Cecilia suggested.

Luke scoffed. 'Oh yeah? She is a sex-starved bunny. Then she burst into tears and, in that weird baby voice she uses when she is around her husband, said I was saying mean and nasty things about her.'

'She certainly has a thing for young men,' said Cecilia.

'It's creepy,' said Luke.

'Did you find any trace of antifreeze in the water bottle?' Cecilia asked Aldo.

He shook his head.

'I wish I hadn't cleaned it.'

'I interviewed Swami N about Luke's poisoning,' said Aldo. 'He denied all knowledge of it. I have no evidence to link it back to him. He also said bad karma must have caught up with Luke because he misbehaved with his wife.'

'Bad karma? I'll bad karma *him!*' Cecilia clenched her fists.

'It could have been Astra who poisoned Luke,' Aldo observed. 'Luke had turned her down and blocked her sexual advances, which might have made her spiteful.'

'Yes,' said Cecilia. 'Astra knows about cars.' She turned to Luke. 'Do you remember saying her parents owned car yards? Maybe she poisoned you because you turned down her overtures. It's a shame we don't have evidence from the bottle. How I wish I hadn't cleaned it.'

'You didn't know that.' Aldo tried to comfort her.

Cecilia put her hands on her hips, still annoyed. 'It just shows that cleaning everything is not always a good thing!'

Aldo brought out his coin and began rolling it up and down his fingers.

'Where were Swami N and Astra on the night of the murder?' Cecilia asked.

'He was in Whyalla taking a meditation class and stayed overnight at a motel, checking out at eight o'clock the following morning,' Aldo answered. 'And Astra says she was seeing clients for aromatherapy and was exhausted from all that healing, and she had an early night.'

Cecilia could imagine Astra poisoning someone for karmic reasons, but frying pan bashing seemed too physical for her.

'And Vee?' Cecilia asked. 'Don't tell me she is on the loose.'

'I'm going to talk to Vee later this afternoon. She's flying in from Brisbane. Things were delayed because she had to go to court for biting a policeman's ear when she was arrested at Cow Bay. The policeman had to have stitches.'

'Bloody hell,' said Luke.

'She's a vicious little thing,' said Cecilia. 'At least there is one less violent person on our streets.'

Then Steve arrived. Hannah had called him after she and Cecilia agreed he should be notified. Cecilia took Aldo to the visitor's room. 'I will not be in the same room as my ex.'

At the visitor's restroom door, Aldo's phone pinged. He looked at it. 'I have to go. Sorry. Will you be okay?'

'I'm fine,' she answered, and hesitated, looking at Aldo, who had an expectant look on his face. She ducked a possible hug, suddenly feeling shy from an onslaught of attraction to him, and she waved him goodbye, thanking him again.

She made herself a cup of instant coffee and sat down on one of the navy-blue vinyl armchairs in the visitor's room, thinking. She was angry with Swami N, and she felt let down. She had believed in him and thought he was a healer, but there was more to him than his holy-guru façade. He must have wanted to protect his reputation as a spiritual leader. If Luke put out the story of The Vegan Café's connections to chicken farming, it would harm his holy status, but he was quitting the café business and could simply say he had to walk away from a corrupt vegan pizza chain.

She put down her cup, frustrated. It was too complicated, and she needed some decent coffee.

Hannah opened the visitors' room door. 'Any news about Luke?'

'He was poisoned with antifreeze,' Cecilia replied.

Hannah's eyes widened in shock. 'By accident?'

'Highly unlikely. Antifreeze is used in cars. It's not something you would find lying around in a kitchen.'

'Will he be okay?'

'Yes, when the poison works its way out of his system.'

'Did someone poison Luke?' Hannah asked slowly, adjusting to the news.

'It certainly looks like it. Maybe Swami N or Astra.'

'But Swami N is a holy man!' Hannah was disbelieving. 'He wouldn't do anything like that.'

'I know, poisoning someone is certainly not spiritual. *Sneaky* is more like it. Maybe there is more to Swami N than meets the eye. Unfortunately, there is no proof of who poisoned Luke.'

'Why aren't you with him?' Hannah asked.

'Your dad is visiting him.'

'I'll give them some time on their own then,' Hannah said, walking over to the sink to put the kettle on. Then she rummaged through the tea bags. Bringing her mug of tea over to one of the navy-blue armchairs, she sat down and looked around the visitors' room. 'What a depressing room. Look at that picture of a white swan flying over the blue lake. It's so fake. A misguided cliché for hope. That overextended swan's neck is not at all soothing. It's stretched to the limit. Unlike The Vegan Café. Now, that's a peaceful and serene environment, even if bad things have happened there.'

'I wonder if anyone will buy it,' mused Cecilia. 'It's a specialised business.'

'Did I tell you that Dad and I popped in there the other day? We thought it would be nice to see where Luke worked and try his pies. The owner's wife, what's her name? Oh, Astra. Anyway, she was behind the counter, and Dad started his chat-up line, boasting about how good Luke was with people because his dad was a famous actor.'

'As a purple grape,' said Cecilia snippily.

'Then Dad asked her out! I was amazed at his audacity. She's married to Swami N, isn't she?'

'Yes.'

'Mum, she seems so naïve, but she took him down in this little girl voice and told Dad she didn't go for old men!'

Cecilia snorted. 'How did Steve react?'

'I almost felt sorry for him. He was confused, but you know Dad— he pretended nothing had happened.'

'What do you think about Swami N? Do you know if he is popular with the animal activists?' Cecilia asked.

'Not only with them. Anyone looking for healing or something beyond their own lives are attracted to his classes.'

Cecilia was taken aback. She hadn't known Hannah had been exploring the spiritual side of life. 'Have you been to his workshops?'

'Only once, because his sessions were too expensive for me. However, I liked it and felt good afterwards.' Hannah put her hands in lotus pose and closed her eyes.

Cecilia looked at Hannah, incredulous. 'You realise he could have poisoned Luke?'

'It's such a shame,' said Hannah, opening her eyes and swishing her teabag. 'He's a wonderful spiritual leader. Perhaps he's a *borderliner.*'

'What's that?'

'Someone with a personality disorder. Maybe one minute Swami N is a spiritual conduit, and the next, he has an utter freak-out and goes around poisoning people. I think his wife has a lot to do with him being so unhinged.'

'Why?'

'Because she is pretty and naïve. She is a magnet for the kind of guy who likes to look after women, and that makes Swami N feel insecure.'

Cecilia stared at Hannah. 'When did you get so smart about people?'

'I have to notice things if I want to be an artist. Especially portraits. You have to see inside a person.' She looked at her cup in disgust. 'Why can't hospitals have decent tea?' She got up, walked over to the sink, and poured the contents of her cup down the drain.

***

The front door of The Vegan Café had a *closed* sign, but Cecilia peeped through the picture window and spotted Swami N sitting at a table, working on his laptop.

She ducked and hurried around to the back of the café. She took a few deep breaths and settled into her new persona. She knocked loudly on the screen door, and after repeated knocking, Swami N appeared in the doorway. His hair was messy, and he was wearing a dingy grey T-shirt, which was an unbecoming colour on him; his face looked dull and washed-out.

'What do you want? The café is closed, and I'm busy.'

'I'm sorry to disturb you,' fibbed Cecilia. 'But I am here to collect my son's tools. His name is Luke. He was your cook until he got sick.'

'Was Luke your son? That explains something that has been bothering me. The karma is not right in Glenelg. Everyone knows everybody. Even that crazy camel guy. It's suffocating. I've had to increase my meditations.'

Cecilia bit her lip. She loved the sense of community in her hometown. Swami N was the problem, not Glenelg.

'We're closing down. Your son will have to get another job.'

'That's why he needs his tools back.'

'Tools?'

'He uses his own knives.'

'Huh?'

'Some chefs like to use their own knives because they're better quality. Can you please look for them in the knife drawer? They're in a black case.'

'As if I haven't got enough to do.' Swami N ran his fingers through his greasy hair. 'Now I have to poke around looking for knives.'

'It's sad you're closing,' said Cecilia earnestly. 'It was lovely having a vegan café in Glenelg. Luke is also disappointed the café had to close. You seemed to be making a good trade.'

'I prefer the spiritual path, rather than a money-making one. There are so many bad vibes around money.'

'Do you think that's why your cooks get killed or poisoned, because the café has bad karma?'

Swami N gave her a piercing stare.

However, Cecilia was in prattle mode. 'Perhaps it's because your wife is so pretty. I just love her long wavy hair. I have never been able to wear it loose like that. I have long hair too, but I have to tie mine up in a bun or a plait.'

'Who are you, the local busybody?'

'I like my cafés and restaurants to be safe working environments; it's my job. Although I think, in your case, it's a human problem rather than an environmental one.'

'What on earth are you talking about? Why don't you just go away?'

'I want my son's knives.'

'Come in and get them.'

She studied his face. He was squinting and his fists were opening and closing jerkily.

'I'll wait here. You get them.'

Swami N disappeared inside the café. A few minutes later, he emerged holding a knife, which he pointed at her.

'That's not my son's knife.'

He edged towards her. Cecilia stepped back a few steps, not taking her eyes off him. She hadn't factored in a knife attack in her plans. She'd only wanted to unsettle him and maybe get him to tell her the truth. 'You have to be careful with knives,' she said, staying in her 'babble' persona. 'You can easily cut yourself. That's why a lot of chefs have blue plastic band-aids. Although Phil was a greenie, and when I looked in the first aid box, I noticed he had bandaids that were biodegradable—'

'Will you shut up!' Swami N yelled.

'This must be a difficult time for you. I feel so sorry for you. It's hard work to close a business down. I remember when the Chinese restaurant on Jetty Road had to close; it took months and months of paperwork and then they had to sell off all the tables and chairs. My bridge club bought the chairs; they are so comfortable because they're padded. But you've got plastic ones. Maybe they'll be good for an outdoors café.'

'Shut up!' he screamed and lunged at Cecilia.

She side-stepped. Swami N ended up stabbing the blue rubbish bin, but the plastic was so hard the knife bounced back. He turned towards her, brandishing the knife.

'Put down that knife.' A voice came from somewhere behind Cecilia. Aldo? What the hell was he doing here? She was distracted and didn't have time to react when Swami N grabbed her by the waist with one arm and held the knife to her throat with the other.

Holy cow! She had stuffed that one up. She considered various judo moves but she could feel the knife juddering against her throat.

Swami N turned, and Cecilia had a view of Aldo standing with his hands in his suit pockets.

'Take your hands out of your pockets and put them in the air!' Swami N screeched.

Aldo obliged, slowly and calmly he put his empty hands up in the air. 'It would be much better if you put down the knife and let her go.'

At that moment, police sirens blared, and a bevy of cars arrived.

The guru shrieked. 'I can't cope with all this *noise!*' He shuffled Cecilia through the back door of the café and locked it, and stood for a moment, marooned in the kitchen.

He still had his knife to her throat, and he was gulping and gasping for air, showing all the signs of a full-blown panic attack. The blade slipped and Cecilia felt a sharp pain on her neck. 'What shall I do? What shall I do?' he panted.

'Breathe,' said Cecilia quietly. 'One breath at a time.' She closed her eyes and willed her body to become still.

Gradually, their breathing slowed and became synchronised.

Cecilia's phone buzzed in her handbag.

'Don't answer it,' the guru muttered.

How could she, pinned down with a knife to her throat?

There was a knock on the back door. 'Hello,' said Aldo through the back door of the kitchen. 'Is everyone alright?'

Cecilia could feel Swami N's body tense up again. 'It must be extremely uncomfortable for you to be meditating in this position,' she whispered. 'Why don't we go into the restaurant and sit down?' She could feel a trickle of blood running down her neck.

The knife teetered.

'Reach for the stillness within,' she quoted from one of his meditation tapes.

Achoo! he sneezed. 'Your perfume is irritating my chakras,' he complained. He pulled her into the restaurant. 'Sit on that chair and don't talk.' Then, he climbed up onto the table next to her chair and sat cross-legged, placing his hands in a lotus pose with his eyes half-open.

Cecilia eyed his knife. It was now positioned between his legs.

'Are you ready to talk now?' Aldo called. His voice now muffled from the back door.

The guru's eyes flew open. 'What about?'

'Is the woman with you okay?' Aldo questioned.

'She's stopped talking.'

'Can you hear me, Cecilia?'

She could hear the panic in Aldo's voice. She looked to Swami N. He remained seated, but his eyes were now darting around, and he had picked up the knife.

She took a risk and, not taking her eyes off the guru, said loudly but without emotion, 'Yes, Aldo, I can hear you.'

'I need a cup of tea,' said Swami N suddenly.

'Let me be of service to you.' She placed her hands together and made a little bow.

The guru nodded, mollified by Cecilia's show of respect. 'Something soothing. Use my signature blend.'

Cecilia tiptoed behind the counter and turned on the kettle, her eyes searching a row of tins until she found *Swami N's Calming Tea*.

She stood at the counter, letting the tea leaves soak, silently watching Swami N. He had stopped fidgeting with the knife, but his eyes were still restless, shifting from the back door to the big picture window at the front. Cecilia looked too but couldn't see any sign of the police. When the tea was ready, she chose a cup with a peace dove for Swami N and dunked a chamomile tea bag into a plain white cup for herself.

Silently, she gave Swami N his cup of tea and sat down at his table.

'What do you want? How can we make this situation better?' Aldo shouted through the back door.

'I need silence, I need tranquillity, and I need serenity,' said the guru, blowing on his tea through puckered lips.

'I think we can provide you with that,' said Aldo. 'A nice place to rest and forget about your troubles.'

Cecilia stifled a laugh. A jail cell could provide that.

'Holding a woman hostage is not relaxing, especially with someone like her,' said Aldo.

Cecilia stiffened. What did Aldo mean?

'I know, she doesn't stop talking,' said Swami N.

Cecilia bit back a rebuttal. It was just an act she had put on for Swami N. She wanted to throw him off balance, which worked, but had consequences she had not foreseen. She dabbed at her neck and noticed her finger was stained with blood.

'Let her go, and then I will be able to help you. Keeping her hostage is making things worse.'

'Tell me about it!' Swami N glared at Cecilia. 'If she wasn't such a busybody, none of this would have happened.'

'You don't need a hostage,' said Aldo. 'Haven't you got a meditation class to run tonight?'

Swami N tipped back his head and drained the last of his tea. 'I'm not keeping her. She is a blot on my spiritual landscape.' He turned to Cecilia. 'The front door is not locked. You can walk out.'

Not locked? Goddamn it! How was she to know? She rose to her feet and without a backward look, ran out of the café.

Combat police officers surrounded her. She felt unnerved by their navy-blue outfits and serious expressions. They started talking but she couldn't hear them. Her tummy was roiling and churning. Desperately, she looked for a place to throw up. The garden next to the footpath would have to do. Cecilia heaved, and someone patted her on the back, until finally, she stopped. A paramedic passed her a cup of water and some tissues, and another threw a big blanket over her and led her to the ambulance. In the distance, she saw Aldo waving to her before returning to the back door.

From her position seated in the ambulance, she could see The Vegan Café was under siege and cordoned off with yellow tape. There was also a yellow-viz police presence, and their cars were everywhere. A couple of combat police crouched on the top of the roof of The Vegan Café, holding rifles. The general public was there too, curious and peering over the barriers while filming with mobile phones.

A paramedic examined her. 'It's just a cut; you don't need stitches.' He applied some disinfectant and put a dressing on her neck.

'Are we done here?' Investigator Hugh asked, appearing at the back of the ambulance with his chiselled jaw directed at Cecilia. 'I need to talk to her.'

'Yeah, she'll be fine.'

'Good,' said Cecilia. 'Now will you take me home? I need a long bath and a bucket of coffee.'

'We need a statement from you first,' said Investigator Hugh.

'Not here,' said Cecilia, looking at the peepers and the journalists. She could just see the headlines: *Health Inspector Held Hostage*.

'We will go to the police station.'

'Can't you interview me at home?'

'You need to make a statement.'

'I'm not walking out through all those people,' said Cecilia, pointing to the onlookers.

'I'll bring the car around.'

Even so, Cecilia had to walk a public path. Promising to return the blanket to the ambulance, she threw it over her head and shoulders to hide her face as she walked to Investigator Hugh's four-wheel drive.

In the car, she told him, 'You have to stop at a coffee shop and get me a takeaway. I'm not drinking police coffee.'

'I don't know if we have time for that.'

'Oh yes, we do.'

Fifteen minutes later, he hustled her into an interview room. She sat on one side of the table, cuddling her extra-large cappuccino, and he sat opposite her with his laptop.

'Why did you go to The Vegan Café?'

'My son had been fired from the café, and I thought he had left his knives behind.'

'Knives!' Investigator Hugh leant forward in his chair, his eyes eager. 'What's your son doing with knives?'

'It's nothing suspect. My son is a chef. I bought him a set for Christmas. They were expensive, too. They cost over five hundred dollars, and I don't want him losing them.'

'Why did Swami N hold you hostage?'

'Well, he's crazy—he's missing a few brain cells.' She felt irritated that she was stuck in a police interview room being interrogated when she could be home in a bath full of soothing bath salts. Her body ached from all the tension.

'What happened when he took you into the café?'

'He was agitated, so I told him to breathe. And I'll tell you, having your head pulled back and a knife held to your throat is not conducive to meditation! Anyway, he grumbled about my perfume, put down his knife, and let me make him a cup of tea. Aldo then talked him into releasing me.'

'Swami N charged at you with a knife, I heard.'

'That's right; he missed and got the blue rubbish bin, and it bounced back.' Cecilia was miffed with herself for misjudging the strength of the blue plastic bin.

'I don't understand why he attacked you.'

'He thought I talked too much.'

He looked at his laptop, then up to Cecilia. 'Have you got anything else to say?'

'I want to go home.'

'You are free to leave.' He got up.

'How? I'm not walking home. I've had a nasty shock. My car is at The Vegan Café, and I am certainly not going back there.'

He drove her home, saying that no doubt Investigator Aldo would want to interview her again, given the scantiness of her statement. Cecilia ignored that remark.

***

Lying in the bath, Cecilia let the tension seep out. Things had got out of control at The Vegan Café. Way out of control. What did Swami's N's psycho behaviour mean? Did he kill Phil? But he had an alibi. He was in Whyalla at the time, which was a four to five hour drive away. She rolled her head from side to side, relieving the stiffness in her neck from being thrust into an uncomfortable position with a knife for so long.

After her bath, Cecilia reclined on the sofa in her pink satin pyjamas with the puppies bookending her. She wore a soft pastel-blue scarf around her neck, hiding the dressing, unsure if she wanted Luke and Hannah to know about the knife attack. She was waiting in trepidation for the news.

On it came.

Breaking news: Hostage situation in Glenelg.

The footage showed the Vegan Café surrounded by yellow tape and men in navy-blue uniforms holding automatic weapons, looming on roofs or half-hidden by cars. There was also a yellow viz vest police presence, mainly to keep back the onlookers and journalists.

One journalist stated that The Vegan Café was also the site where Phil Dyson was murdered and posed the question of whether there was a connection.

Then Aldo's face appeared on the television. Cecilia was shocked at her own reaction. Something fizzed and crackled inside her. She could not take her eyes off him. He spoke well and said that there had been a hostage situation, but it was now resolved, and no-one had been seriously injured.

The journalists began firing questions.

'Who was the hostage?'

'Who took the hostage?'

'Why did it happen at The Vegan Café?'

'Is there a connection to the cook's death?'

Aldo brushed these questions aside and said he had no more information to give. Cecilia sighed with relief; he'd protected her name. That was what the mainstream press dealt with. Now, what about social media?

Much was made of the connection between the murder and the hostage situation. Swami N's name came up, and there was speculation that as a spiritual celebrity, he might have been held hostage by a deranged follower. Maybe even by the person who killed the cook. There was a lot of outpouring of sympathy for Swami N and prayers were offered for him online.

Cecilia snorted.

There was a fuzzy picture of her being led away and wearing her blanket. Social media pegged her as the hostage-taker. Fortunately, Cecilia had dressed down for a possible confrontation with the guru. She wore black leggings and flat shoes—no give-away floral frocks. But she hadn't meant the confrontation to be *that* public and involving such a large number of police.

They must have bundled up Swami N into a waiting van, out of sight from onlookers.

Hannah arrived home from her art class and the puppies abandoned Cecilia, throwing themselves at her and squeaking with delight at her homecoming.

'I thought you would be at the hospital visiting Luke,' Hannah said.

'Luke is being discharged tomorrow morning and he said some of his footy mates are visiting tonight.'

'What's for dinner?'

Cecilia stretched out on the sofa. 'I don't know. Pizza?'

'You look tired, Mum. Have you had a busy day?'

'Well, yes, it was a bit hectic. What's on TV tonight? I could do with a nice romantic comedy.'

Hannah looked at her phone. 'Unreal! Did you know about this, Mum? There was a hostage situation at The Vegan Café. No-one knows what happened, except a woman was led away by the police.' Hannah raised her eyes up from her phone and questioned her mum. 'What happened?' she asked.

Cecilia hedged, not ready to tell Hannah she had been held hostage at knifepoint. 'There's something weird going on at The Vegan Café, that's for sure,' Cecilia said, waving a casual hand. 'Maybe it's bad karma.'

Hannah scoffed. 'Since when did you believe in karma?'

'A lot of bad things have happened there,' Cecilia replied. She took a soft throw from the blanket box and cuddled into it, switching the television over to Netflix and finding one of her favourite shows.

She had a phone call from Aldo, which she ignored. No doubt he would want to tell her off for getting into a dangerous situation. Instead, she sent him a text, saying she was a bit overwhelmed at the moment and would call him tomorrow.

At the back of Cecilia's mind was the worry about how her unconscious mind would handle the day's events. Before bed, she armed up. She took her medication, checked the sensor pad by her bed, and hung the bell over the door. Then lying under her doona, plugged into her phone and accompanied by rainforest music, she doubled her self-hypnosis regime, which told her not to sleepwalk.

***

I dress quickly. I have to go to the police station. More police are needed for the search. I must convince that greasy investigator to widen his investigation. There are warehouses and abandoned small manufacturing businesses on the other side of Brighton Road.

Grandma Snow could have wandered in there.

A bell rings.

What was that? It's not a police siren.

***

'Mum! Mum!' Hannah appeared in the passageway, rubbing her eyes sleepily. 'I heard a bell ring. Why are you all dressed up, Mum? It's the middle of the night?' Then, she put a hand to her mouth. 'Are you going out on a secret date to see your favourite policeman?'

'I wasn't looking for him,' Cecilia said, her mind fuzzy. 'I was looking for Grandma Snow.'

'Is she the one with the long plait? I've seen her in one of your photo albums. But she passed away a long time ago.'

'Oh, yes …' Cecilia ripped herself back into the present. 'Oh, my goodness,' she said, looking at herself. She was standing in the passageway, dressed in her pink hibiscus frock and her pink heels. 'I was sleepwalking. I think I need to get changed back into my pyjamas.'

'Why are you sleepwalking?' Hannah asked.

Cecilia could see she was a little scared and knew she needed to be strong for her. 'Why don't you make us a hot chocolate while I change my clothes?'

They climbed on the sofa with the puppies. Cecilia cradled her hot drink, telling Hannah the story of how Grandma Snow vanished one Sunday morning, leaving a cinnamon tea cake in the oven, and never came back.

'That's so sad,' said Hannah, her eyes filling with tears. 'How old were you when she disappeared?'

'Thirteen.'

'Did you ever find out what happened to her?'

'No.'

She chewed her bottom lip, and Cecilia saw unspoken horrific possibilities tumbling around in her mind.

'I sleepwalk because I have PTSD from Grandma Snow's disappearance. It's a trauma that's never been resolved. My dreaming self is still searching for her.'

'Have you always sleepwalked?'

'Only as a teenager.'

'Why now?'

Cecilia stared at the puddle of chocolate at the bottom of her cup, sensing an overpowering feeling of foreboding, like something sinister was crashing at the back door of her subconscious.

Side-stepping Hannah's question, she ruffled her hair. 'Don't worry about me, sweetheart. I'll fix this.'

'I wonder where I'd go if I sleepwalked,' Hannah mused.

'Not to The Vegan Café,' said Cecilia, forcing a light-hearted tone.

Hannah smiled. Cecilia now felt like the mum Hannah knew, and not the shadowy one who lurked in dream time.

10

Cecilia sat at her desk writing her monthly report for the council. One minute she was a hostage with a knife held at her throat, and the next, she was telling the council about illegal restroom toilets. She gazed out the window and saw a familiar figure sitting on the bench where she and Aldo sometimes sat. It was Amy, Luke's ex-girlfriend, and her shoulders were slumped.

Cecilia felt a maternal pang. Amy had been part of her family life for more than four years. Not only had she spent time with Luke, but Cecilia had also mothered her, and Hannah treated her like a sister, bickering about the finer points of veganism.

Now that Amy and Luke had split up, Cecilia didn't see her anymore and she was worried about her. Vee's attack would have been traumatising, and Amy had no support. Her mother was the most self-centred woman Cecilia had ever met. She worked as a debt collector for the high end of town. She fought with numerous boyfriends, and at least three of them had taken out restraining orders on her for stalking. Mostly she ignored her kids, which was why Amy had been over at Cecilia's house so often. It was not just Luke who Amy had loved, but being part of a family home, too.

Cecilia picked up her mobile phone and left through the town hall's massive wood and glass front doors. She walked up the wide steps next to the monument and onto the green grass which stretched out along South Esplanade. She stood in front of Amy.

'Hey, honey,' she said to her. 'Do you mind if I join you?'

Amy burst into tears. Cecilia sat down on the bench and put an arm around her. Amy flinched, and Cecilia retreated, surprised. She had always hugged Amy. Eyes lowered, Amy adjusted her scarf. It was then Cecilia spotted the bruises and remembered Hannah's story of Vee half-throttling her. That was why Amy had jerked away.

'Where did those bruises come from, Amy? From your sister?'

Amy folded her arms around her tummy and rocked on the bench. 'My sister has been arrested and it's all my fault. I told the police about her.'

'Those are serious bruises.'

'I'm so worried about her. She stole Phil's big cannabis cookie jar on the night he got killed and now she's in jail.'

'Obviously, she has psychiatric problems and needs help and is obviously prone to angry, violent outbursts, but how far do you think she would go?'

'Do you mean … did she kill the cook from The Vegan Café?'

'Yes.'

'I don't know. Why would she?' Amy hedged.

'Somebody did.'

'She said she dropped into the café before midnight and saw the lights were on and the back door open. She went in and found Phil lying on the floor. She panicked, grabbed the cookie jar, and ran.'

'Did she know he was dead?'

'She wasn't sure, but she didn't want to stick around. She said she would be blamed for it because everyone blames her for everything. Maybe her story is true, because she made a big fuss when she heard Phil had been killed. She said whoever did it was going to get payback from her. But Vee makes things up, like saying she was in a relationship with Phil. It was more like drop-in sex.' Amy stared out to the sea. The waves were grey and choppy. Spring had taken the day off, allowing winter to have one last gasp before retiring for the season.

'You did the right thing, telling the police,' Cecilia reassured her.

'Do you think so? Mum is annoyed with me, too. She said I should have shut up and that it was embarrassing to have a daughter in prison.' Amy scrunched her eyes shut. 'I just want to leave all this behind me.'

'That's a good idea. It's time to focus on you, sweetheart. What are you going to do with your life? You have to put yourself first. You can't keep looking after Vee and your mum.'

'I miss you guys,' said Amy, a sad expression crossed her face. 'I know Luke and I are over and that's okay, but I always felt you were my other family.'

'What about a tree change? Move somewhere else.'

Her eyes widened. 'You know me so well. I have some school friends who have moved to Melbourne, and I think I can transfer my TAFE course over there. I'd have to get a job, but that's no drama. I'll do waitressing; I have plenty of experience.'

'You do that,' Cecilia encouraged. 'And don't forget you are always welcome to visit us.'

'The other day, I popped around to see Hannah and her puppies.' A smile lit up Amy's eyes. 'They're so cute!'

'And naughty!' Cecilia stood up and ruffled Amy's hair and said goodbye with reassurances that Amy was welcome to call her any time if she needed support.

Back at the office, Cecilia finished her report for the council. It was thrilling stuff, like sleuthing her food outlets for unlawful toilets. She pressed send on her report and leant back in her chair, sighing with contentment.

Today had turned out quite well, considering recent events. Amy was going to be okay, and both Swami N and—hopefully—Vee would be locked up, unable to kill or cause more harm. And Cecilia had found another wrongly positioned restroom! St Leonard's hotel, to maximise their pokies area, had erected an illegal restroom area for the gents in their new extension. It would have to be demolished. Cecilia was delighted. She loathed the pokies.

***

Angel texted Cecilia and asked if she could come around after dinner. It was a weeknight, and out of keeping with the sisters' normal routine. *Something must be up*, thought Cecilia.

The doorbell rang and Cecilia answered it. Angel stood on the stoop, looking dishevelled. Although her white jeans were spotless, she had panda eyes where her eyeliner had smudged. She was alone. The kids must have been dispersed to their various fathers.

'I'll get us a cup of tea,' said Cecilia.

Angel shook her head. 'Not tea. Wine.' She walked into the front lounge and flopped onto her favourite poufy chair, kicking off her shoes.

'Okay, I have a chardonnay open,' said Cecilia, and headed for the kitchen. She returned with the bottle, glasses, crackers, and basil pesto.

Angel took a big gulp of wine. 'Hey, Cee-Cee,' she said. 'I want to talk about Grandma Snow's disappearance. It's catching up with me, too.'

Cecilia took a cracker.

'What do you think happened to her?'

Cecilia fidgeted in her chair. She and Angel talked about everything, but they never talked about this. It was too painful at the time; they were scared and confused. Angel became way too skinny, and Cecilia started to have panic attacks and sleepwalked. Their parents spent a fortune on psychiatrists for them, which eventually helped.

'Well?' Angel pursued.

Cecilia stared into her coffee cup. 'I don't know, but I don't think she went surfing.'

'Why did her surfboard go missing the day she disappeared?'

'Maybe someone stole it?'

'The shed was locked and the key to the padlock was hanging on the hook rack in the kitchen where she and Grandpa kept their keys.'

Cecilia heaved a sigh. 'That board was made of wood and was so heavy. I can't see her being strong enough to carry it, let alone go into the surf.'

'Maybe she could have dragged the surfboard by the leg rope down to the beach?'

Cecilia's mouth dropped open. She had never thought of that, using the rope to drag the surfboard to the ocean. 'But she was wearing her red polka dot apron. Who goes surfing in a red and white pinny?'

'Maybe she forgot to take it off. That was the thing, wasn't it? Grandma Snow had early Alzheimer's.'

'But not so as you would notice.' Cecilia felt she had to defend Grandma Snow.

'She forgot my birthday the week before she disappeared.'

Cecilia did not remember that, but she did remember she was her word finder. 'What's the name of the hot box, Cee-Cee?' They would make a joke of it.

'She didn't want to go senile,' Angel said quietly. 'One day I saw her crying.' Cecilia said nothing, letting Angel talk. She was clearly troubled. 'I'm getting flashbacks.' She looked miserable.

'Oh, Angel! I'm so sorry.'

'Jack wants a surfboard for his birthday. A mate of his goes surfing down south, and his family have a holiday place there.'

Jack was Angel's oldest son. Cecilia had escaped the surfing scene with Luke and Hannah. There were no waves at Glenelg beach, Luke preferred ball sports, and Hannah didn't like the feel of sand between her toes.

'I don't feel it's fair if I say no,' Angel fretted.

'Get him lessons that teach him safe surfing. Find some spunky surfer to instruct him.'

Angel snorted. 'A spunky surfer? Yet another one to add to my list of dates?' Tears filled her eyes. 'I think I have a problem with commitment,' she said. 'I date, but I don't want a relationship. Maybe I'm scared they'll disappear like Grandma Snow.'

'Wait,' Cecilia told Angel. She walked out of the sitting room and into her bedroom. She bent down in her wardrobe and pulled out her blue memory box. On her return, she put it on Angel's lap.

Angel's face lit up as she looked at the photos and recipes. She shook the snow globe. 'I've still got mine which she gave us one Christmas.

Do you remember? Grandma was so busy talking, she drowned her Christmas pudding in gravy.'

'And remember her treasure hunts?'

'Yes, and the cakes she made were the best.'

The sisters shared memories; the happy ones, before Grandma Snow went away.

***

Cecilia walked into the family room and waved her car keys at Hannah. 'It's time to go,' she said.

'Mum! You look normal!' Hannah exclaimed.

'Well, thank you very much!' Cecilia was wearing a loose pink knit over leggings and subdued lipstick.

'I mean, I love your frocks and high heels, but they're not for casual wear.'

'I'm in a subtle mood today,' said Cecilia, thinking that the last time she had talked with Aldo, she had a knife held to her throat, and he was bound to make a fuss about it. Cecilia wanted to blend into the background.

'Why subtle?' Hannah asked, as she stashed her easel and art folder in the back of Cecilia's Subaru.

'I don't need to impress Aldo.' In fact, if Aldo hadn't sent her a text that morning about how he was looking forward to seeing her for coffee, Cecilia might not have showed up. She was embarrassed about causing a ruckus at The Vegan Café.

'Fair enough.' Hannah moved on to her own concerns. 'I think I've found what is missing from my portrait of Leon, but I need to see him again in case I'm wrong.'

'Is androgyny the missing piece?' asked Cecilia, turning the ignition on. 'He could be a girl or a boy.'

'Maybe.' Hannah shrugged, not sparking with this idea. 'I think Leon looks like he comes from another world. He has that ethereal quality to him. I hope he likes his portrait.'

'Are you going to give it to him?'

'If he wants it. People don't always like their portraits.'

'Don't forget to take a photo for your portfolio.'

'Maybe,' said Hannah. 'But at the moment, I'm feeling that I shouldn't hang onto my work. That would be materialistic. Real art should be cast out into the world like the Buddhists do when they make their sand mandalas. They place one grain of coloured sand at a time onto the mandala with tweezers. It takes them weeks! Can you imagine all that work? Then when it's finished, they look at it, say a few prayers, and blow it all away.'

'You've got to be joking! All that work going up in a puff of sand? That's certainly not my thing. I'm hopelessly materialistic. I'm not giving up my sofa, my air conditioner, and television.'

'You've just got to let go, Mum, and live in the present.'

Cecilia sighed. Was she hanging on to the mystery surrounding Grandma Snow's disappearance all those years ago?

At Aldo's place, everyone settled into their positions. Hannah joined Leon in his den, Cecilia sat with Aldo on the back patio and, after greeting Cecilia and Hannah, Aldo's parents retired to the front room to watch the soccer.

Cecilia was very aware of Aldo's presence. He was charming and protective, a combination she found hard to resist. 'How is everything?' she asked, putting on a bright and cheerful smile. He seemed relaxed and hadn't brought up the hostage situation. Yet!

He rocked back in his chair, put both hands behind his head, and smiled lazily at her. 'I'm done. I just have paperwork to do.'

'I figured you had two suspects—Vee and Swami N. What happened with Vee?'

'She threw a chair at me.'

'That's a good excuse to buy new chairs. Your chairs are so grotty. How old are they? Thirty years?'

'They have to be lightweight for safety reasons.'

Cecilia snorted. 'So, there's not much money in police décor budget?'

'We don't live in luxury like you do in the town Hall.'

Cecilia liked her office and changed the subject. 'Did she confess to killing him?'

'No, she kept telling me to piss off. Hugh and I took her out the back to the smoko area and fed her cigarettes. I told her she looked like a girl who'd been neglected. That's when she opened up and said her mother never loved her and she never knew her dad. She cried about Phil's death,' said Aldo, moving his hands from behind his head and placing one over his heart. 'She loved him in her own way.'

'Was love Vee's trigger? I'm surprised. She always comes across as a badass.' Cecilia sipped her milky coffee and eyed the plate of biscuits. Today there were only two chocolate biscotti.

'That's the thing with confessions: you have to find the switch—the button that shows the strong feelings inside a person. With Vee, it was love—or rather, the lack of it. Poor kid. Her childhood had twisted her. She said when she was little, her mum would drug her when she had men sleepover.'

Cecilia raised an eyebrow. Aldo was a compassionate man, despite working in homicide. 'So, Vee didn't kill Phil,' she pondered, looking out to the tomato patch. They were bright red and looked tasty.

'She just stole his cookies.'

Cecilia broke a biscuit in half and licked her fingers. 'So, Swami N must be the killer. I think I tipped him over with my busybody act. I showed what he was really like.'

With a snap, Aldo closed a racing-car magazine, which had been lying on the table half-open. 'Yes, but I didn't need you to put your head on a chopping block. He held a knife to your throat!'

'I miscalculated. If you hadn't arrived, I would have got away. Seeing you made him grab me as a hostage.' Cecilia was in attack mode. She was not going to defend her actions, because they proved that underneath that holy façade, a criminal lurked.

Aldo glared at her. 'You think it's my fault?'

'No real harm was done,' said Cecilia, thinking how lucky she was not to have her face plastered over social media.

'Don't be flippant,' he said. 'I've told you far too much about the case, and look what happens? You get taken as a hostage!'

His complaints fell on deaf ears. 'How did you get Swami N to confess? It must have been weird.'

Aldo sulked for a moment, eyed a biscotto, folded his arms, and then continued the story without picking one up. 'It took a couple of days to get a confession out of him. He refused to eat and only drank water. Jail doesn't cater to vegans and gurus. He sat cross-legged on his chair, doing his meditation thing and sprouting new-age platitudes to anyone who had the bad luck of interviewing him.'

'Is the spiritual life not for you?'

'I go to mass at Christmas,' said Aldo.

'How did you get the creep to confess?' Cecilia asked. 'What was his trigger?'

'An Italian cheese and tomato sandwich! I bought fresh bread—and not just ordinary bread either; it was Italian bread, which is the best with its crunchy crust. Then I layered it with tasty cheese and sliced tomatoes from Nonno's garden.'

'Say what?'

'I made him a special lunch and served it on a china plate.'

'You gave the guru a cheese and tomato sandwich?' Cecilia was incredulous.

'He fell on that sandwich like a starving man, like an alcoholic taking that first drink, like a diabetic eying off chocolate ice cream!'

'But real cheese? Vegans don't eat dairy.'

'Swami N is Italian. It is food from his childhood. How could he resist such a sandwich after days of fasting and constant questions? I let him eat in peace and did a crossword puzzle on my phone.'

'Huh?'

He shrugged. 'What can I say? I like words.'

'Then what happened?'

'Next on the menu were two cannoli with vanilla custard from the Italian café. My favourite dessert! One for me, and one for our vegan guru.' Aldo kissed his fingers. 'I could not resist and nor could he! You should have seen him, Cecilia. He wept as he ate his creamy cannolo. He even licked the custard from the paper. It was his breaking point.'

'Wow! He fell apart as a vegan and as a guru, and then who was he?'

'A small child. I asked him if he killed Phil, and he was so scared that he wet himself. I gave him a serviette to cover himself and suggested we prayed.'

'You what?!'

'I googled a prayer in advance. I adapted it. I knew I had to find a way to be intimate with him. I had to speak his language, and I needed more information for a valid confession.'

'Which prayer?'

'I chose a Catholic one. It is about telling the Lord I have sinned and asking for forgiveness. I know Swami N was brought up as a Catholic. He is an Italian-Australian, like me.'

'Won't he be answering to the criminal courts and not to the Lord?'

'Some people only confess to a higher power. I thought bringing one into the interview might make him talk.'

'Good heavens!' said Cecilia. 'A forgiveness prayer, a sandwich, and a vanilla twist made Swami N confess?'

'Yes,' said Aldo, leaning back in his chair. 'Then he was ready to answer questions. He said he didn't mean to kill Phil. It was anger that made him do it. He said he adored his wife and was terrified of losing her because she was so pretty, wealthy, and easy to manipulate.'

'She was his lovely cash cow,' said Cecilia. 'He wouldn't want to lose that.'

'He suspected his wife was having an affair with Phil, and then he heard Phil talking on the phone to his auntie, telling her he was leaving

Glenelg with his girlfriend and that they had to go far away because the woman's husband was the jealous type.'

'Oh, my god! He thought Astra was going to run off with Phil. Oh no! What a stuff-up. It was Jessie, not Astra.'

'Yes.' Aldo stretched back in his chair. 'After taking his meditation classes in Whyalla, he drove back to Glenelg.'

'That's a four- or five-hour trip.'

'He went to Phil's flat, but no-one answered the door. He then drove to the café and found Phil polishing a frying pan. He confronted Phil and asked if it was true that he was quitting his job. When Phil said he was leaving town with his girlfriend, Swami N lost it and grabbed the frying pan in a blind rage and hit Phil with it. Repeatedly. Then Swami N drove back to Whyalla, so he could check out from the motel the following morning. Oh, and we found a pair of rubber gloves stuffed down in the space between the driver and passenger seat.'

'The missing gloves turned up,' mused Cecilia. 'Why didn't he dump them?'

'I think because he did not believe he would get caught—he felt invincible as a guru.'

'He did a lot of driving that night,' said Cecilia. 'It must have been nine hours, but an effective alibi initially. It's crazy. Phil was killed based on the wrongful assumption that he'd been having an affair with Astra. What about Luke? Did Swami N poison him?'

'Yes. He was jealous of Luke, and he was scared of online exposure. He knew he couldn't bash Luke, so he opted for poisoning him and put the antifreeze in his water bottle. Swami N has a lot of repressed feelings. He talked about anger as if it was something separate from him. He said that anger was an evil spirit which had visited him from childhood.'

'Well, he grew up on a chicken battery farm. Imagine the terrified squawking and smell of thousands of chooks each crammed into tiny spaces. I've even heard they macerate and grind down live male chicks. It screws my head thinking about it.'

'Yuck!' Aldo was disgusted. 'You must try some of Nonno's eggs. They are twice the size of ordinary eggs.'

'My sister dated Swami N a few years ago. They met on a dating site. She thought he was more interested in being revered than having sex. Maybe that's why Astra came on to so many young men. Swami N could be light on with the sexual side of things, which may have frustrated Astra.'

'Your community connections are amazing.'

'Thank you.' She folded her hands tidily in her lap. 'But nothing compared to your confession techniques. What do you do with bikies?'

'Straight talking and a vintage World War II leather jacket.'

'What happened to Swami N after the confession?'

'I gave him some clean pants and he resumed his guru pose. He was calm and detached, as if someone else had committed the crimes. He sat on the chair with his legs folded under his bum, enacting his holy stance. He even recovered enough to give me advice about seizing the moment and searching for the divine within, despite the splotch of custard on his caftan!'

'You must be joking. He said that after his confession?'

'Yes,' said Aldo. 'Luigi Alfonsi is now in custody.'

'Who?'

'Swami N's real name is Luigi Alfonsi.'

Cecilia shook her head. She was still marvelling at Aldo's unconventional interviewing techniques. 'Where's Astra? Did you interview her? What did she say?'

'We caught her at the airport and brought her back for questioning. What a drama that was. I had to remove Inspector Hugh from the interview room because she kept doing a baby girl act with him, trying to get him on her side and saying I was a mean old man.'

'That sounds like classic Astra. Did she know her husband was a murderer?'

'No, she was definite about that. She was puzzled at first when she learnt Phil had been killed, but then Swami N told her it was a bikie killing because of Phil's cookie business.'

'Why didn't she tell you that during the investigation?'

'Her husband told her to keep quiet because they did not need more trouble with the bikies. He said bikies did whatever they liked, and the police couldn't stop them.'

'And she believed him?' Cecilia shook her head. 'Astra is more than a few stars short of a night sky.'

'She said she didn't like to think about nasty things. They mess with her chakras.'

'That's that, then. Case solved. I'm glad my community is now safe from psychotic vegans and murderous gurus.' She stared at her empty coffee cup. 'You're so … good to me,' she said quietly. She wanted to snuggle into him, feel his warm body and smell his nice aftershave.

'I would like to be *very* good for you.' Aldo stood up and so did she. He reached out and caressed her hair. She put her hands on his broad chest.

They were about to kiss when the back door opened. It was Hannah and Leon.

Leon held up a large drawing. 'Look what Hannah has drawn.' His eyes were bright. 'She has given me wings. I am an angel!'

Everyone smiled. Even Leon, for a moment.

Aldo put his arm around Cecilia. 'I think I want to interview you,' he whispered in her ear.

Cecilia blushed with pleasure. The case was solved, Glenelg was free of violent vegans and gurus, and Aldo hadn't eaten a single biscuit.

Surely, she could now allow herself to be seduced.

***

The black corded rotary phone rings.

I sprint down the hallway to pick it up.

A woman's voice speaks. She is the lady from the Broadway Kiosk on South Esplanade, where Angel and I sometimes buy ice creams. She says Grandma Snow has been spotted on the path, dragging a surfboard.

If I can get there quick enough, I'll be able to stop her from going into the ocean.

Strangely, our front door is locked. Someone has confined me to the house.

I run into my bedroom and find my handbag lying on the armchair in the corner of my room. I scrabble through it for my car keys. Yes! I have them.

My next job is to step around the booby traps and find an opening out of the house.

I find one, and now I am running out to my car. It feels slow and heavy to drive and I wish it would go faster; I have to get to the beach in time.

Finally, I arrive at the beach in Glenelg South and park my car. My hand is on the handle, yanking, ready to jump out and race down to the beach to rescue Grandma Snow.

Then a blinding light stings my eyes, and I put my hand up to shield them from the glare of a flashlight shining in my face.

A man's voice says, 'This is the police. Please get out of your car.'

***

Cecilia looked around her; it was dark, and she was sitting in her car, wearing her pink satin pyjamas. She could hear the crashing of the waves. The driver's door was wrenched open, and she stumbled out of the car to the waiting policemen.

'We've been following you,' said the older policeman. 'Your driving was erratic.'

Her thoughts were jumbled. She couldn't remember driving the car. The last thing she knew was that she was in bed.

'Please breathe into the breathalyser.' The policeman examined the reading. 'Zero. What are you doing driving around in your car at two in the morning?'

'I just needed to go to the beach. I wasn't speeding, was I?'

'Almost. Are you stoned? Maybe we should run a drug test.'

'I'm on anti-depressants, but not the kind that makes you too sleepy.'

'You look stoned. Why are you in pyjamas?'

'I think I was driving in my sleep.'

The policeman was stern. 'We should give you a ticket for dangerous driving. Are you getting help? Sleep driving is a serious problem.'

'I know,' she said, tears pricking her eyes.

'Is there anyone you can call who could come and pick you up?'

'Couldn't I just drive home? I only live four streets away.' She tried to sound competent and reasonable.

The policemen looked at each other and shrugged. One of them said, 'We'll follow you home and make sure you're okay.'

'Thank you so much.' She got back into her car.

In her kitchen, Cecilia made a hot chocolate and wrapped both hands around her mug. She was shaking. The words 'sleep driving' screamed around and around in her head. Was she going mad? It seemed she had this secret life, one which she had no control over. She could have crashed the car. She could have killed someone while driving in her sleep.

She didn't understand why the bell did not wake her up. She walked into her room and noticed the window was wide open. *Holy crap!* She had climbed out of the window in her sleep. The sensor pad was working, but what if she got out of the other side of the bed? She ran to the bathroom and threw up until there was nothing left.

Then she sat on her bed and burst into tears. Why had it happened again? The mystery of Phil's death had been resolved, so there was nothing to worry about. But still, her subconscious was restless and playing havoc with her mind. It felt so unfair that she had this disorder. She was competent. She fixed things, she fixed people, but she couldn't fix herself.

She couldn't bear to be in her bedroom. It was a reminder of her crazy self. She lay down on the sofa in the living room. What would happen to her? Hospital?

Certainly not a romantic evening with Aldo.

11

The alarm clock on her phone buzzed at 6.45 am. Cecilia looked at it. She wriggled her neck. It was sore from sleeping on the sofa.

She heaved herself upright, spilling two sleepy dachshunds to the floor, and staggered down the passageway to her bedroom. She sat on her bed and looked helplessly at the door to her ensuite. She felt too exhausted to have a shower. Perhaps she could skip that part and just get dressed. However, her wardrobe loomed at her, and she could not choose what to wear.

Her hands fluttered on her lap, and she could see they were trembling. She was unravelling. Anxiety flooded in, and she felt nauseated as tears trickled down her cheeks.

She decided to tell work she was too sick to come in. She was worried she had only taken time off work a few weeks before because of the flu, and then several more days when Luke was sick, but her work-self had blacked out, leaving her defenceless.

She returned to the sofa and waited for the clock to turn nine. She sent a text to the council's receptionist to say that she wasn't coming in, and then she called Dr Davidson's rooms. She used the magic words to force the receptionist to speak to her psychiatrist and to arrange an appointment straight away, instead of the usual four-week wait.

'I don't feel safe. I need an urgent appointment.'

'Not safe? Oh, dear. You hang on, lovey, and we'll organise something as soon as possible.'

Hannah and Luke appeared in the kitchen as Cecilia ended the call.

'Mum! You're still in your pyjamas!' Hannah was shocked.

Luke looked worried. 'Are you okay, Mum?'

Cecilia shrugged. Hannah hovered around, and Luke made her a cup of tea. Cecilia stared at the television in silence, willing them to leave her alone. She could hear them muttering among themselves, Hannah explaining something, and then they left the house; Hannah to go to TAFE, and Luke to visit the Stamford Grand Hotel to see about a job.

Cecilia watched a cooking show and a renovation show. She felt nothing. Her mobile lay on the table. Aldo texted to say hello. Cecilia left it.

Around midday, her phone rang. She looked at the ID. It was Scott from the clean-up service that had worked at Florence Street. She eyed the phone and listened to its ringing. It rang twice. Reluctantly, she answered it.

'Hi Cecilia,' said Scott, sounding anxious. 'I wanted to ask your opinion about something. You know how Mr Dyson asked me to clean out his shed?'

'Yes,' she said slowly. 'I gave him your number.'

'He was insistent that everything should be chucked out, which was weird because he kicked up such a fuss about throwing out all the junk from the house. Did you know he had forty-three torches? Most of them were working. They just needed new batteries.'

'Hmm.' She waited for him to come to the point of the call.

'I keep records of my hoarders' houses. My girlfriend and I are going to write a book one day.'

'Why have you called me?' Cecilia was losing patience.

'Because I've found some weird and interesting things in Mr Dyson's shed. I didn't know who else to call because Mr Dyson isn't answering his phone. There's a nice vintage surfboard I'd love to have. It's made out of hollow wood. It's one of Tom Blake's originals. It's exquisitely carved, and it could be worth a lot of money.'

She held her breath, then let it go. A wooden surfboard? The words clanged in her subconsciousness. 'Perhaps I should see it.'

'Would you? I would appreciate it. There is something else I want to show you. It's a long box.'

'I'll be over in ten minutes.'

She put the puppies out the back and tied her hair back in a ponytail. She operated on autopilot. She had to go to the shed—there was no way out—even though she had no idea why.

Scott's truck was parked out the front of the Dysons' house. The gaggle of broken-down cars was still there. Presumably, Scott was going to get the car wreckers in soon. He stood in some sunshine in front of the shed. He was a gangly young man with a shock of sun-bleached hair, and he wore a faded blue surfer's T-shirt. 'Thanks so much for coming over,' he said.

He beckoned her into the shed. A thin walkway wound its way through boxes piled up on either side. At the end of the line was a long box made out of heavy-duty cardboard with three old rope handles.

She closed her eyes briefly. 'Where's the surfboard?'

He pointed.

There it stood, shining in a corner. Jack must have dusted it down. Cecilia turned it around and recognised the initials immediately: *E.S.*

They were Grandma Snow's initials. It was her surfboard. Cecilia folded her arms tightly across her chest to still the shaking in her hands.

Scott turned his attention to the long box. 'I've got a bad feeling about this box. It looks like a coffin even though it's made of industrial cardboard, and it's got a padlock on it. There was something in it when I moved it. I heard rattling.'

Before Cecilia could object, Scott produced bolt cutters and snapped the padlock. He opened the lid, revealing a tidy setting of dusty bones, forming a complete human skeleton and a sprinkling of red polka dot scraps of material.

Cecilia recognised the pattern of Grandma Snow's favourite apron.

She ran out of the shed, her breath heaving, her eyes wild.

What the hell was Grandma Snow doing in the Dysons' shed?

***

Filling up Cecilia's bedroom with his large presence, Aldo lounged in the corner armchair. She sat upright in her bed with her hands folded tightly in her lap, unable to meet his eyes. He had come around to her house because she'd messaged him that she was not well enough to see him at the police station. Scott had called the police, and Cecilia had driven home and gone straight back to bed.

'When my old boss, Investigator Longbottom, retired, I inherited his cold cases and unsolved incidents,' Aldo told her. 'One of them was Mrs Snow's.'

She twisted her hands, a dull ache pounding in her head. A cold case? It sounded like something to be mused about, like talking about a murder mystery movie and taking apart the plot afterwards over coffee. From far away in Cecilia's mind, a voice snapped, *Grandma Snow had been a person, not an incident.*

Aldo leant forwards in the armchair, his brown eyes studying her face. 'We will find out what happened to your grandma,' he assured her.

Cecilia said nothing. She didn't want to talk about it, nor think about Grandma Snow being reduced to a sketch of dusty bones hidden in a box in someone's shed. Her stomach heaved.

'What's wrong, Cee-Cee?' Then he caught himself. 'That's a silly question. This must be horrible for you.'

She looked at her hands and concentrated on counting the white lines on her mid-finger knuckle. Three or four big ones? Anything to stop the pictures circling her head, like black crows looking for a kill.

Hannah popped her head around the door. 'Can I get you a cup of tea?'

'Would that be nice, Cecilia?' Aldo asked.

She shook her head. She didn't want him in her bedroom when she was feeling so sick.

'I've got a new joke,' said Aldo hopefully. 'It's a New Zealand one.'

'I don't want to be rude,' said Hannah, still at the doorway with Angel standing on tiptoes to look over her shoulder. 'But I think you should leave. Mum needs to rest and to have some space from thinking about awful things. Isn't that right, Mum?'

'Are you saying my jokes are awful?' Aldo teased.

Cecilia slid down the bed and closed her eyes, hoping they would all go away.

Half an hour later, she heard heavy footsteps walk down the passageway. That would be Aldo leaving. Maybe he stayed for a cup of coffee with Angel and Hannah.

Angel? How was she reacting to the news? It must be awful for her, too.

However, Angel seemed to have risen to the occasion and taken over. Towards the end of the afternoon, she popped her head around Cecilia's bedroom door. She told her that Aldo was such a sweetie, and he was concerned about her. He wanted to know she would be well looked after. Of course, Angel would organise the funeral, and Cecilia was not to worry about a thing!

Cecilia wasn't worried. She had stopped thinking, especially about how Grandma Snow had ended up in the Dysons' back shed. The next day, when her kids had gone out, she struggled out of bed, shuffled down the passageway, and took over the sofa in the family room. All she wanted to do was watch mindless TV and not have to be someone: a mother, or an inspector, or a romantic heroine. Enough already. She was shutting down.

With what seemed like an enormous amount of effort, she arranged holiday leave from the council, banned visitors, and made her kids have sleepovers at friends' places. Angel was excluded, too. Reluctantly, her family retreated, saying on the way out that she should have support during this terrible time, and she shouldn't be alone because it wasn't healthy.

But Cecilia was firm. Everything and everyone made her feel anxious.

Although the dachshunds had to stay, they were not so easily accommodated as house guests. She felt it would be unkind to put them in kennels. The weather was fine, and they played outside or snoozed under the orange tree.

A host of renovation shows, cooking shows, and weather channels passed by Cecilia's television as she lay in a blur on the sofa, eating Vegemite sandwiches and tinned pears with custard and jelly. The bowls built up in the kitchen sink, but she didn't care.

She took her medications regularly, only because she didn't want to be told off by Dr Davidson. She needed him because he was the only one who could make sense of what she was going through.

Dry-eyed and twisting the handles of her black handbag, she sat in his office among the mementos from other patients. She wondered what she could give him. A cinnamon tea cake? That seemed like an impossible task, like even getting dressed to see him was a momentous undertaking. She wore Hannah's tracksuit pants because all her leggings were piling up in the laundry, along with her other casual clothes. Driving wasn't an option, either. She had taken an Uber to see Dr Davidson because she was scared to drive—scared of hitting something or, even worse, hitting *someone*.

Dr Davidson sat patiently in silence, waiting for her to open up.

She sighed and trudged on with the conversation. 'I've caved in,' she told him. 'I can't feel anything. Why? It's so weird. I feel like a zombie.'

'Your mind is producing an anaesthetic to dull the pain,' he replied. 'Finding your grandma's body was too much for you.'

'Isn't that feeble?' she asked, thinking of her strong and competent self, who seemed to be lost in the mists of time.

'Everyone has their breaking point, and yours was this.'

'How come Angel hasn't collapsed too?'

'It was you who found the dead cook and then your grandma's body. It's a concept for Angel, and not such a stark reality, as it is for you.'

'I can't seem to snap out of it,' she said dolefully.

'You need a break,' said Dr Davidson. 'I recommend hospital. There's a nice psychiatric hospital in the hills with peaceful, fragrant rose gardens. You'll have plenty of rest, regular meals, meditation, and company.'

'Huh?' Cecilia was shocked. 'What do you mean by company?'

'So you can see you are not the only person who has hit the wall.'

'Jeez Louise,' she muttered. 'I think I would rather have ECT.'

'Electroconvulsive therapy is a possibility, too,' said Dr Davidson smoothly. 'There are facilities at the hospital.'

'Huh?' Cecilia grabbed onto her handbag, clutching it closer to her chest. 'I was only joking. I thought that wasn't done anymore.'

'It's a valid treatment for people who have severe depression.'

Cecilia slumped in her seat.

After that session, Cecilia sat in silence in the back of the Uber, driven by an equally silent young man. The car's mirror had a metal grey Ganesh elephant charm dangling down, attached with a bright red string. Elephants never forget. Nor would Cecilia. At home, she plonked down on the sofa, turned the television on, and searched the channels for the weather in Outer Mongolia.

***

The day before Grandma's Snow's funeral, Aldo appeared at the back door of Cecilia's house, ignoring the ban on visitors. He kept banging until she gave in and stood at the screen door.

'Don't you want to know what happened to your grandma?' he demanded through the door.

Cecilia looked at him. No cautious bedside manners here. 'I sort of know.'

'Well?' he persisted. 'Are you going to let me in?'

When she opened the door for him, the dachshunds pushed their way inside. 'Who said you could break into the house?' she told the dogs.

'Are you talking to me?' Aldo asked.

Cecilia shrugged.

The dachshunds, however, were pleased to have a visitor. It had been boring with only having Cecilia convalescing. They mouthed Aldo's hands until he'd had enough. 'No more,' he told them sternly.

'I'll put them out,' she said and fetched a couple of carrots from the fridge.

Aldo seated himself in Luke's favourite recliner, and Cecilia glanced at the sofa before fetching a dining room chair, where she sat upright, poised and unreachable, with her hands folded primly in her lap, facing him.

'That chair doesn't look comfortable,' he grumbled.

'Nor will be the conversation we are about to have,' she responded tartly.

'Aren't you going to offer me a cup of coffee?' Aldo asked.

She was taken aback. 'Sorry, I didn't mean to be rude. Can I make you one?'

'No, thanks.' He winked at her.

She frowned. He was teasing her, and she was not in the mood for that.

'Have you worked out how Eva Snow ended up in the Dysons' shed?' Aldo took a handkerchief out of his pocket, bent down, and wiped some hair off his trousers. The puppies were moulting in preparation for summer.

'Sort of,' Cecilia replied, startled by his blunt question. He was not tiptoeing around her. He was going full-frontal. Was this one of his interrogation techniques?

She had talked about how Grandma Snow ended up in the Dysons' shed and explored possibilities with her psychiatrist. It was part of her therapy. At first, she couldn't take in the discovery of Grandma Snow's coffin. It seemed too far-fetched. Perhaps it was a mistake. Could it be someone else whom the Dysons' abandoned? A relative whom they couldn't be bothered to pay for a proper burial? But the red polka dot scraps in the cardboard box haunted her and there was a big something unanswered which made her shy away from thinking, whatever it was terrified her and made her feel physically ill.

She spoke in a faraway voice. 'Remember how Phil didn't drive, which is unusual for a bloke? He walked everywhere or took the tram. Garth said Phil refused to drive because he'd been in a bad car accident with his mum when he was little. She must have been a terrible driver. She would have a prang, dump the car, and then get another one. There must be at least six broken-down cars in the front yard.'

Aldo nodded.

'Maybe Mrs Dyson was driving somewhere and knocked Grandma Snow over when she was wandering the streets during one of her forgetful spells. Perhaps Grandma Snow was on her way to the beach with her surfboard when Mrs Dyson ran her over. I guess Mrs Dyson panicked, and thinking she had killed her, she put Grandma Snow and her surfboard in the boot. Then, she drove home and made Mr Dyson dispose of her. He bought the cheapest coffin he could find, a cardboard one, but couldn't be bothered to bury it.' Cecilia clenched her fists. 'Maybe he liked keeping it in the back shed because he liked keeping everything else!'

Aldo nodded, keeping his eyes on her face. 'It must have been a terrible shock to find your grandma like that.'

'There are still things I don't understand, like … didn't anyone smell or notice?' She felt sick saying it. But she had to know. She had to fit the pieces of the puzzle together. Dr Davidson insisted she get the full picture.

'Because the house backed onto a butcher's shop, there were not too many issues with the smell of a decomposing body, although there had been complaints from the neighbours about the weird smell coming from the back of the Dyson's yard. The Dysons said it was a dead possum.'

'Bloody hell!' Cecilia gagged. 'You don't mince your words. How did you know about the complaints?'

'I'm sorry, Cee-Cee.' said Aldo, his brown eyes concerned. 'I don't want to upset you, but I got the information from council records. I checked the year Mrs Snow disappeared, and it was around the same time when complaints of the smell from the Dysons' neighbours were lodged.'

'You found all that?' Cecilia wondered, thinking of the dusty archive room, which housed records of council's meetings since 1855, and was situated next to the men's toilets.

'It's police work, going through old records. I wondered how the Dysons got away with it. A decomposing body smells. The neighbours' complaints and the so-called dead possum explained it.'

Cecilia's mind sheered away from Grandma Snow being a dead body. Her knuckles whitened in her lap.

Aldo shifted his bulk in the chair. He looked uncomfortable. 'I seem to be making things worse for you. I'm making you sad all over again. I just thought if you knew the facts, it might help you. It could give you closure.'

Cecilia's eyes glittered with tears. 'And there's more, isn't there?'

'We found Mrs Snow's DNA, her blood, on the inside of the metal bumper on the old Corolla.'

'Did Mr Dyson confess?'

'He is a wily old bird. He kept saying he knew nothing about it. However, I located the person who sold him the coffin. You know Glenelg Funeral Services?'

'Yes, they are a family business on Brighton Road. They've been around since I was a girl.' Cecilia stood up from her chair and walked over to the window, half turning her back on Aldo while he talked.

'I spoke to old Mr White, and he remembered selling the coffin because it was unusual for someone to buy a coffin and not want a cremation or burial. He said it was like a takeaway coffin, cheap cardboard, and he remembered Mr Dyson as a skinny man who kept complaining about his back. Maybe that's why he didn't bury the coffin—because he had a sore back. It was only when I heaped evidence after evidence on the table did Mr Dyson budge. Even then, he said he did not know what the coffin was for. His wife made him buy it, and she stuffed it into the shed.'

Cecilia scowled at the window. 'I don't think so. Mrs Dyson never lifted a finger; she's far too lazy. She would have made him put Grandma

Snow in the box. He's still an accomplice. But would the courts send an elderly man to jail? Or even a senile old woman?'

'That's for the courts to decide.'

'It was a horrible thing to do!' Cecilia felt her face heat up with emotions. She turned away from Aldo, not wanting him to see her pain. 'He left us in the dark, wondering for more than thirty years, not knowing, imagining her as a prisoner, or being tortured or drowned!'

'No, it wasn't like that.'

'Aldo,' she whispered, giving him a quick glance. 'How did she die? Did she take a long time to die in that coffin?'

He got up quickly, strode over to the window where she stood. He was about to put his arm around her shoulders, but the stiffness of her poise made him drop his hands and stand by her side at the window. 'It was a quick death,' he said. 'According to the autopsy, she was killed on impact when the car rolled over her.'

Cecilia gave a big sigh and faced him. 'Thank god she wasn't left in that coffin to die alone.'

'It must be terrible for you—all that wondering for all those years. Angel told me you have PTSD and you sleepwalk.'

'Did she?' Cecilia felt a spark of resentment that people were talking about her. Then, she thought ruefully that resentment was the primary emotion she had for her friends and family these days. It wasn't their fault Grandma Snow had ended up in the Dysons' shed. She would make it up to her kids, Aldo, and Angel.

'I thought if I told you what happened,' said Aldo, his eyes downcast, 'I hoped it might be helpful and bring closure for you. But now I'm not so sure. Perhaps I should just leave you alone.'

Did she want to be alone? She was standing shoulder to shoulder with him, and it felt comfortable. 'You did the right thing,' she told him. 'Thank you. It will help, eventually. But now I'm still trying to process things.'

There was a sudden outbreak of barking and tinkling of bells. Cecilia's gaze flicked back to the window. A large orange cat sat on the fence, sunning itself and cleaning its paws which sent the puppies into a combustion of outrage. The cat was infringing on their territory.

A flicker of a smile crossed Cecilia's face. 'Life goes on,' she said. 'That cat loves to torment the puppies.'

'You will never forget. You can't,' said Aldo, opening up empty hands. 'I know that. I live with so many bad memories. But at some stage, you have to let go.'

'Maybe after the funeral, after the new medication kicks in, after hospital, after my cruise holiday, after—'

'After you've heard my New Zealand joke?'

'Yes, after that too.'

Cautiously, he wrapped an arm around her shoulder. She turned and buried her face in his chest. He held her and stroked her back. Cecilia's ice poise melted, and she looked up at him questioningly. He cupped his hand on her cheek and kissed her gently—and slowly but surely, she felt good sensations return.

She held onto him, returning his kisses and breathing in his familiar smell.

The End
KJS

Acknowledgements

Thanks to the team at Ocean Reeve Publishing, The Manuscript Assessment Agency, my writing group, my husband Rod J Hearne, my family, and Dr Koopowitz.

Finally, this book is a tribute to Pam and Ham, who taught me all I needed to know about dachshunds and then some more.

Lightning Source UK Ltd.
Milton Keynes UK
UKHW020115241222
414383UK00017B/814